The Song of the Blue Bottle Tree

The Song of the Blue Bottle Tree

India Hayford

John Scognamiglio Books
Kensington Publishing Corp.
kensingtonbooks.com

To Quinn and Aidan
To Carolina and Camila Rose

And most of all
to Roy

ACKNOWLEDGMENTS

Roy Hayford has been my friend even longer than he has been my husband. His love, support, and encouragement have meant everything to me.

Sylvia Hubbard, my aunt and a longtime schoolteacher, started reading my short stories and novels as soon as I started writing them in the fourth grade. She never pulls a punch, always says exactly what she thinks and doesn't sugarcoat literary criticism. When she finished *The Song of the Blue Bottle Tree* and said she loved it, I knew she wasn't just whistling Dixie.

The talented and generous members of Casper Writers made unsociable me feel like a valued member of the group. When I asked for beta readers, four extraordinary people volunteered: Alisa Cochrane, Robin Mundell, Vicki Windle, and Marian Sisneros. Marian left four dozen sticky notes of observations scattered throughout the manuscript, including one that stated the notes weren't color-coordinated.

Carolina Rodriguez, the world's best daughter, took pity on my social media cluelessness and appointed herself my manager and guide through that unfamiliar swamp. Her background in law enforcement and victim services was invaluable when I had questions about certain events depicted in the book. Any mistakes about procedure are mine, not hers.

Despite his reluctance to leave the sagebrush steppes and mountains of Wyoming, my son, Quinn Hayford, accompanied me through the pine forests, bayous, and cemeteries of south-western Arkansas as I pounded out the details of the book. His companionship meant more to me than he can know.

William R. Arnold, my father, told me dozens of stories of his life on Red River, including the one about getting chased by an alligator and the one about Pearlie's witchy wife. If there are better Southern storytellers than he was, I've yet to meet them.

John Talbot, of Talbot Fortune Agency, and John Scognamiglio, of Kensington Publishing Corp., made traveling though the strange land of book publishing much easier than I expected. John T. made one of my favorite comments about the book when he described himself and John S. as "deliciously creeped out" by the recurrence of rattlesnakes throughout the story. For self-confessed snakephobes, they're pretty good guys.

Finally, thanks to the Wyoming Arts Council, which presented me with the Neltje Blanchan Memorial Writing Award in 2023. The award gave me a psychological boost when I needed one the most.

CHAPTER I
OLEANA

❧

Ghosts started whispering to me by name the spring I turned twelve, the same spring the flesh mounded up under my nipples and the dark moon blood began its monthly flow from between my legs. Back in those days, I lived with Meema, my mother's mother, while Papa drove a truck filled with oranges from Florida or onions from Alabama. Meema had a big old house and seventy-five acres on a red clay road outside of Washington, Arkansas. My mother grew up in that house, lived there until my papa swooped in and took her off to live in San Diego, Mobile, Galveston, and half a dozen small towns I can't recall the names of. Their wedding picture sat on a dressing table in Meema's bedroom. I used to perch on the matching chair and hold that picture in my hands, trying to remember what it was like before Mama died and left me and Papa to flounder through life like leaky boats trying to reach land through a thick fog. In the picture, Papa is wearing his Marine uniform and Mama is in a white dress with lace at her throat and a belt that shows off her tiny waist. They're smiling into the camera, and he has his arm wrapped around her like he'll never let go.

Papa came from northeastern Alabama where the last tumble of the Appalachian Mountains play out. Until he joined the Marines a year before the attack on Pearl Harbor, Papa never set foot more than twenty miles from home. He had a hard time in the service on account of the way he talked, and the funny ideas other folks have about Southerners, like "southern" means ignorant and "slow-talking" means slow thinking. Papa put up with them calling him hillbilly and meaner things until they got bored and let him alone. It's still hard for me to understand how he could be so nice about it. I wanted to make those mean mouths bleed even years after most of them died on specks of land in the Pacific Ocean. Some people need to taunt someone the way other folks need someone to love. Papa never said a mean word when I was little, not even about the Japanese he'd fought so hard against. When I asked about them, he said, "Most of 'em was ordinary fellers trying to follow orders and wanting to get back home. Their leaders had brass for brains, but the foot soldiers was just folks like us."

Papa didn't talk much about the war or his part in it, but at times he remembered clearer than he wanted to. More than once he woke up in the middle of the night hollering for someone named Dayton. I never asked who Dayton was or what happened to him, but I knew it was bad. You don't wake up screaming for someone who got shot in the shoulder and went home a hero.

Mama was patient with his nightmares and the times he blocked out the world and sat listening to things in his head that he couldn't or wouldn't share. Her patience extended farther for him than it did for me by a long shot. She loved me, but when she said go, I'd better get, and when she said run, I'd better say *yes, ma'am, how fast and in which direction.*

Thing was, sometimes I could hear what Papa heard, not like reading his mind but like we were both tuned into a radio station no one else could hear. Back then we lived in a little nothing town in central Alabama. He used to sit in his chair on the front porch, rocking and looking at cars go by without really seeing them. I'd creep out and sit in the swing, not to talk to him or bother him in any way, just to be near him. He didn't mind me being there.

Sometimes he didn't even notice me. One summer before Mama died, he and I sat together in the fading light almost every evening, me swinging and him rocking, and all those cars headed south to Mobile or north into Tennessee. I tuned into Papa's mental radio station so gradually that I didn't even notice when voices first came through the static. Pretty soon, though, I could make out a few words or an occasional sentence. Mostly the words made no sense, and those that did weren't very interesting. I was young back then, maybe seven or eight, and the voices were just part of my evenings on the porch with Papa. Sometimes Mama sat with us after she finished the dishes, but she attracted mosquitoes like she was the only red meat around, so she preferred to sit at the kitchen table and read. I asked them once about the sounds I heard in the air. Mama said it was crickets. Well, it wasn't, and Papa knew it wasn't because he looked sideways at me like what I said worried him. I pinned my lips together and concentrated on pulling sandburs out of my white cotton socks. Somehow, I knew better than to ask Papa what he heard.

Some nights the static crackled so bad that it like to drove me crazy, but other times I could hear people hollering and a deep rumble like a faraway thunderstorm. Once while we sat on the porch and watched it rain, a big voice popped into the static and said, "Tarawa," just as loud and clear as you please.

"Tarawa," I repeated. "What's a Tarawa?"

Papa's rocker squeaked to an abrupt stop, and I looked up to see him staring at me like I'd used a word that might get my mouth washed out with soap. I gnawed my lower lip, waiting to see if what I said warranted a chewing out or a rare session with Papa's belt laid across the seat of my shorts.

"Tarawa," he said, and ran his hands over his face like he was trying to tear it off. "It's an island in the Pacific Ocean. A bunch of people had a fight over it in the war. Lot of those people died."

I wanted to ask if he'd been there, but I had better sense than that. I smiled uncertainly at him, wishing I'd kept my mouth shut. He finally shook himself like a wet possum, smiled back, and commenced to rocking again. We never said anything else about Tarawa.

Sometimes on weekends, Papa loaded me and Mama into the old blue Nash and took us traveling. I don't remember a lot about those trips except for the yellow-and-black signs that told us curves were coming up. Papa and Mama convinced me that the curved arrow on the sign was Mickey Mouse's arm waving at me. Papa liked to travel at night. We'd sit up late talking in the front seat while Mama slept in the back and the headlights drilled into the darkness ahead of us. I loved passing through little towns, all quiet and vulnerable in the night like a painted lady who'd washed her face, so her real skin showed through. As we drove down some long tunnel of light, Papa'd tell me stories about our Scotch-Irish ancestors who traced the route in wagons or on foot a hundred or two hundred years earlier.

Most summers, they carried me to stay with Meema on the farm in Arkansas while Mama traveled with Papa. I loved those visits. No one ever raised a voice or hand to me, no matter how dirty my face got or how many times I tore my dress. I played with the barn cat's kittens, rode my secondhand bike down the wash-board road to see my town friends, fed the chickens and ducks, and helped in the great big garden and apple orchard.

Once in a while, Papa'd take us up to a place in the Alabama mountains where he'd grown up to visit an aunt and uncle and a few cousins who were Papa's closest kin. We never stayed long, and I was glad of it. Mama didn't like those folks. She was always polite because she didn't know how to be anything else, but I could tell she hated being there by the way the corners of her mouth twitched when she tried to smile and how she kept picking her feet up off the floor, one after another like she expected something to crawl up her legs if she didn't. I got tired listening to the grown-ups drone on about people I didn't know and things I didn't care about. I whispered to Mama that I wanted to go out and play in the yard, but she made me stay right by her in that boring house with those boring people until it was time for us to leave. I knew better than to argue. Mama was usually gentle, but she had a mean streak that showed up if you crossed her too hard, and when that mean streaked out, she'd as soon blister my bottom as look at me. I wasn't a dummy, and neither was Papa. When the nervous tic of her mouth smoothed out into a hard flat line, he knew it was time to tell his kinfolk, *See y'all later.*

After Mama died of a hardness in her breast, we took her back home to Washington to bury her under a rose bush in the cemetery down the road from Meema's house. I slept in Mama's old room at Meema's house that night after the funeral, just like I always did when I visited in the summer. The next morning, I woke up to find out Papa had left without me. Meema explained that he was taking a job driving a truck to California and that I'd live with her while he was on the road. I cried some, and she gave me the big pink conch shell off the kitchen shelf to play with and take my mind off being motherless and abandoned. I took the shell and hid out beneath the big magnolia tree at the edge of the yard to cry some more. When I put the shell to my ear to listen to the ocean, I heard voices murmuring just below the roar that was supposed to be ocean waves. I couldn't tell what any of them were saying, but they comforted me all the same, especially a low soft voice I thought maybe belonged to Mama.

I lived there with Meema until the spring after the voices started calling me by name. That April, a storm blew up that carried more thunder and lightning than I'd ever seen in my life. When we heard a sound like a train about to drive through the house, Meema grabbed me up and hustled me down into the storm cellar. Lord, I hated that place. It was always damp and looked like a haven for black widow spiders and copperhead snakes. Even seeing the wavering column of the tornado tossing trees in the air on the other side of the pasture, I wanted to take my chances with outrunning the thing. Meema shoved me down the steps ahead of her, though, and closed the door on us thirty seconds before all hell broke loose outside. When we emerged a lifetime later, there was nothing left to see of the house, not even a pile of busted boards like most people had. The magnolia on the lawn was still there. The orchard hadn't been touched, and there were still flowers in the garden borders, but Meema's house was wiped away as clean as the plate of a starving child. Later I found the conch shell on top of the well house, not a chip on it, but that was all that was left of the place that had been her home for sixty years.

Meema didn't outlast the house by too many months. The doctor called it a stroke, but I think it was a broken heart, pure and simple. We buried her in the cemetery next to Mama on a day so hot that the Baptist preacher cut the graveside service short by a good half an hour, an unheard-of concession to weather for the longest-winded preacher this side of Texas.

I expected to live with Papa after Meema died, but he didn't want me. People said there were other reasons, but that's what it came down to. He didn't even come to tell me himself, just arranged for Meema's niece to come get me after the funeral. I went home with her but didn't stay long. She wanted to keep me, but her husband said they had enough of his own children to take care of and didn't need an extra mouth to feed when that mouth had closer blood kin somewhere else. She tried to appeal to his sense of Christian charity, but he didn't have one, so she reluctantly packed me up a bag of clothes, tucked in Meema's shell, and took me down to the car where Papa's Cousin Burgess was waiting to drive me to Alabama to live in hell.

CHAPTER 2
OLEANA

In the shadow of Talladega Mountain, the crossroads of Kingdom Come turned its back on the wicked world and concentrated
grimly on its own salvation. I clutched my little satchel and stared
through the truck window at the dismal houses and trailers that
made up the community. Squeezing my eyes shut, I prayed to
wake up in the garden swing at Meema's house, surrounded by
the smell of cape jessamine and the sound of birds calling to one
another from the top of the big pecan tree.

The truck turned into a driveway, skidding slightly on the loose
pea gravel as it braked to a stop. My eyes snapped open to the
bitter reality of a weathered house slung together from gray wood
and stone, unsoftened by a single rose, unhallowed by a lone sparrow. The yard was hard-packed dirt, swept as clean as a merciless
corn broom allowed. Only the kudzu draped in smothering folds
over the trees beyond the barbed-wire fence defied the relentless
hand of the faithful.

The Right Reverend Burgess Love Darnell seized my upper
arm and dragged me across the front seat. My satchel caught on
the gear shift, pulling it into neutral so that the truck rolled slightly.
With what sounded suspiciously like a bad word, he jerked me
through the driver's door, then reached in to detach my bag and

shove the gear shift back into park. He slammed the satchel into my chest. Automatically, I wrapped my arms around it, not sure if I was protecting it or hoping it would protect me. Grabbing my arm again, he hustled me up the warped plank steps, and across the surface of something that had no business calling itself a porch. I caught my toe on the front door's high threshold. Only his bruising grip kept me from falling face-first into the hall that bisected the house and had doors at each end. Other doors opened off the hall. The Right Reverend Darnell pushed me through the nearest off-plumb rectangle. A reedy old woman enthroned on a straight-backed chair peered critically at me over the top of rimless bifocals. Her dark long-sleeved dress stretched over her knees, revealing ankles clad in heavy cotton hose just above stout lace-up shoes.

"This her, Burgess?"

"Yes'm. This here's Cousin Robert's girl. Oleana, Aunt Nette's waitin' to see your manners." The Right Reverend Darnell shifted his grip to the back of my neck and squeezed. I gulped and murmured some words I hoped sounded mannerly, but I was so damn scared even the long auburn braid down my back quivered. One week earlier, I'd stood next to the rose brush on my mama's grave and numbly watched clods bounce off the plain pine coffin in Meema's grave. Now I trembled in a silent splintered house, trying to understand how I had become the ward of this ugly man with gray hair protruding from his ears.

Papa had merely snorted on his end of the long-distance phone call when I'd begged to stay in Arkansas. "Meema's gone, don't none of her kin have room for you, and I ain't got time to watch you and drive the truck both. Cousin Burgess and Aunt Nette are willin' to have the load of you till you're old enough to marry. No, I don't want to hear no more, Oleana. You go get your bits and pieces together and be ready to head on out when Cousin Burgess gets there."

I had left Arkansas with a few clothes, a ragged fabric dog, and the conch shell from Meema's dresser hidden deep in my satchel.

Now I clung to the bag like it was my last grip on sanity and listened while the Right Reverend Darnell and Aunt Nette wrangled over my future.

"You didn't tell me she was pretty, Burgess." Aunt Nette scowled at me, her eyes narrow and mean as her mouth. "Didn't tell me that."

"Now, Mama, you know the devil's in this girl just by lookin' at her, but I reckon you and me can drive him out and leave behind a good gentle woman. Won't hurt for her to have a shine on her then. Give her a year of the Lord's way and she'll do us proud, ain't that so, girl?" He shook me by the back of my neck and accepted the whiplash of my head as a yes. The space his left incisor once filled showed beneath his upper lip as he grinned at me. I stared at the dark line of snuff that edged his lower lip, trying not to gag. I'd felt safer around junkyard dogs and copperhead snakes.

That night, I cried myself to sleep between sheets that stank of bleach and scratched with starch. My dreams twisted through dark, demon-filled lands with horror at every turn. Sleep held me down and allowed a monster to come close, let it lay its scaly hands on my breasts, let it scratch the tender skin of my thighs. Shrieking in terror, I fought the monster with fists and feet until it swore a human oath and extinguished me with a smothering hand pressed over my nose and mouth.

I awoke alone in a tangle of sheets, scared and sweating in the warm spring night. Light from the setting moon slid through the open window, illuminating Meema's conch shell on the bedside table. At first, I only heard the gentle sounds of ocean waves when I pressed the pink cleft of the shell to my ear, but I waited patiently for the voices to come. They swam to me through the surf, ebbing and flowing beneath the sounds of the sea until the chorus sang loud enough to be understood, sang a single word over and over: *Run.*

The woman waited beneath the crepe myrtle, her flame-orange hair clashing with the deep pink blossoms. When she gestured with a single finger, I looked to see which child she wanted, but the crowd of youngsters flowing out of the doors of the junior high school moved past her without recognition.

"Oleana." I read my name on the woman's lips; the laughter of children drowned out all other sounds. Once more, the woman mouthed, "Oleana," and beckoned again with a long slender finger.

Reluctantly, I slid one foot after the other until I stood in the shade of the crepe myrtle an arm's length away from the woman. A young woman, only a few years older than me, but with a pair of deep lines between her eyebrows that didn't belong with her beautiful face and flowing hair.

"Hail, thou that art highly favored; the Lord is with thee," she whispered. "Once he was with me."

I blinked.

"I was called Anna, but now shall I be called Mara, for the Almighty hath dealt very bitterly with me." Her hand darted out and closed hard around my wrist. "Does he do the laying on of hands with you?"

I looked into the wide, mad eyes and frantically tried to wrestle my arm out of her grip. *Help*, I cried silently to the children streaming past us. *Help me.* I might as well have been invisible.

"His name is Love!" the woman cried. "His name is love and he loved me until you came. Loved me . . ."

I twisted free. She reached out to grab me again, but I shoved her hard enough to send her reeling back into the crepe myrtle. Dropping my armload of books, I darted back into the sunlight and pushed past the children who crowded the schoolyard. When I reached the dirt road that wound south into the forest, I ran like a frightened deer, away from the woman named Bitter, away from the nightmare of hands laid on me, away, away from Kingdom Come. If only I could run clear to the Gulf of Mexico, maybe I could find enough water to wash myself clean. I ran and ran, but in the end, the distance defeated me, and I collapsed into a sandy loam rut, my breath rasping in and out of my raw throat. Turning my face to the sky, I rocked on my knees and bawled like a lost calf, knowing I had nowhere to go but back.

Alabama dervishes spun around the sanctuary, arms outflung, heads thrown back, shouting, singing, praising the name of the Lord in tongues known and unknown. Sister Aileen Dunham clattered her heels across the worn wooden floor, hands uplifted, face twisted into ecstasy that bordered on agony. Skirt swinging in her holy tap dance for the Lord, she traced a slow circle around a pair of woven baskets topped with wooden lids. A grimace snarled her lips back, making way for the harsh syllables forcing their way through her clinched teeth.

"Ah galana la laga hosama nah!"

The congregation of the Kingdom Come Church of the Holy Ghost with Signs Following groaned, swaying in rhythm to her dance around the baskets.

"Praise the Lord!"

"Galana la laga hosama nah!"

The Right Reverend Burgess Love Darnell shuffled toward Sister Dunham, sweat glistening on his red face, his white suit showing signs of collapse along the sternly pressed folds. He squatted down in front of the baskets and beat on their wooden lids with clinched fists, screaming his defiance of Satan and the illusions of sin. Sister Dunham never missed a step. Her unearthly warbling rose and fell over the cries of the congregation.

"Gahana galena ah ah neganah hah!"

"They shall take up serpents!" howled the Right Reverent Darnell. The congregation howled back its approval, hope, and belief. He ripped the lid off the nearest basket and sank both hands deep inside to lift a snarl of tangled bodies. A water moccasin poked its triangular head over the rusty red back of a copperhead to fix the congregation with a cold stare. Moaning and trembling as the spirit came on him, he handed the snakes to worshipers on either side of him. The prize of the collection he reserved for himself: a heavy-bodied eastern diamondback rattlesnake, native to the coastal plains and rarely seen in the northern mountains. Lips sneering back from his prominent teeth, he hoisted the great creature over his head and thrust her toward heaven.

"They shall take up serpents—*and they shall not be harmed*!"

Bedlam. The Right Reverent Darnell stomped across the floor, screaming the name of the Lord. Other people shoved past him to dip into the baskets, pulling out timber rattlers, rusty black moccasins, and the golden red of a thick-bodied copperhead.

"Galana ha laga hosama nah!"

I gripped the pew in front of me, beyond caring whether anyone in the congregation noticed the ward of the Right Reverend Darnell had both feet off the ground and tucked under her bottom. A rope divided the snake handlers from the less faithful among the congregation, but I had no illusion about the snakes' respect for the barrier. Frantically I tried to count the snakes pulled from the basket by the believers, tried to count any that crawled out on their own, tried to keep track of the number of snakes passed from person to person. Every few seconds, my eyes swept the floor beneath me, looking for escaped serpents. My breath came in terrified gasps. As I whipped my head around to check the pew next to me, my own braid snapped against my arm, scaring me halfway into my second childhood.

Ten feet away, Brother Bingham Harkner held his timber rattler within striking distance of his nose. Possessed man and lidless serpent stared at each other with identical unblinking glares.

"Praise the Lord! Stare Satan down, brother!"

"Galana ha laga hosama nah!"

"Ah, Jesus!"

Deciding that the contest was at an end, Brother Harkner bayed like a hound moving in for the kill and shook the snake high over his head to proclaim his triumph over Satan. On the other side of the room, the Right Reverend Darnell joined Sister Dunham in her jittering dance around the baskets, he with his double fistful of conquered Satan, she with her twisted mouth and guttural gift of unknown tongues. A cacophony resounded off the white-washed walls as worshipers on my side of the rope fell into their own frenzies.

"Crima dinahem horganasha dina bah bah BAH!" screamed the white-haired woman on my left. Behind us, a thump proclaimed the collapse of another believer under her own tongue of flame. I turned to see who'd fallen and caught a glimpse of flaming hair as the woman who called herself Mara leapt over a writhing worshiper and ducked under the rope barrier.

"Love me!" she cried. Clenching both hands around the Right Reverend Darnell's arm, she hung on with all her weight, forcing him to lower his deadly burden. She tore the enormous rattler from him and ran her open lips over its head and down its diamond back. The Right Reverend Darnell made a snatch for his snake; Mara swung away from him, pressing the creature to her cheek, crooning and moaning to it. Fangs flashed once, twice, three times, gashing the white skin of her face, the delicate curve of her throat. She embraced the enraged serpent, raining kisses of passion on its body as it rained kisses of death on hers.

"Love me," she begged, and collapsed on the floor with diamond-marked coils wrapped around her wrists.

The steps stopped next to my bed as they did every night. I hugged my arms across my breasts, squeezed my eyes shut, and tried not to breathe as hands traced my hips beneath the thin sheet. A hoarse whisper growled in my ears, growing louder as the hands grew rougher.

". . . death is the sting of sin . . . death is the sting of sin . . ."

Satan stung deep and death flowed out of me in a stream of blood.

I slid off the bed and curled my toes into the braided rug. The Enemy stirred on the mattress, toppled from his side to his back and snored, one arm flung back over my deserted pillow. With a hand that seemed detached from my body, I picked up the shell from the bedside table and held it to my ear. I listened for a moment, put the shell down, and glided my feet over the threshold of the room and out into the long hall. A faint glow from the moon lit the parlor door, guiding my steps past the hall tree, past the table with its load of cheap ceramic knickknacks, past the sentimental picture of an angel hovering protectively over a pair of children crossing a bridge at night. At the doorway of the parlor, I hesitated. A big wicker basket with a black wooden lid sat on the floor, waiting for the next service.

"Don't stop now," a beloved voice whispered in my ear.

I slid on reluctant feet into the room. A cold breath of air stirred the damp curls at the nape of my neck, and I shivered in the humid August night. Dog days, Meema called them, these hot still weeks when the air hung like thick netting over the fields and snakes were blind and more aggressive, more dangerous than usual. Dog days.

Something stirred in the basket.

"I'm afraid," I whispered to the dark.

"I will help you. Go open the lid."

"I can't."

"Oleana, have I ever hurt you?"

"No," I answered and knelt beside the basket. I grasped the lid, but it wouldn't budge.

"The latch."

I undid the hasp and raised the lid. A heavy rope of silk and diamonds flowed over the rim of the basket and pooled on the rug in a gleaming coil. The snake turned its great head toward me. I stared into the black pyramids of its eyes, fascinated despite my fear.

"Lead her down the hall. Do not, for your life, look back until you reach the bedroom door."

Gathering all my courage, I turned my back on the serpent. Behind me, the heavy body slid across the floorboards with a sound like the rustling of taffeta petticoats. I took a deep breath and glided up the hall, fighting the urge to flee, the urge to turn and see how close the snake was to my bare heels.

"I am so afraid."

"It is not your day to die, Oleana. Turn and welcome her into the room."

I turned. Seven feet of serpent slid toward me, stopping within easy striking distance of my ankles. There the snake paused, tasting the air with her forked tongue.

"My grandmother bids you welcome," I whispered to death as it lay waiting. "I welcome you on my own account."

The serpent rippled forward, swinging into the room. Her body flowed across the tops of my feet, cool as satin. I watched the snake gravely, reverently. No longer frightened, I stood until the rattle-tipped tail brushed my ankles in a final caress, then followed it into the room.

Body echoing the circular pattern of the braided rug, the snake raised her great head and sought a way onto the mattress. I knelt beside her and slipped my hands beneath the smooth coils. With an effort, I lifted the snake. The coils slid back on my arms and the tail fell to one side, but as I rose beneath the snake's weight, the creature poured onto the bed. She twined herself in the bloodstained sheets and around the arms and across the neck of the sleeping enemy.

CHAPTER 3
MERCER

❧❧

Voices rose and fell at the far end of his consciousness, Southern voices droning on like cicadas on a hot July night. He wished they'd shut up. Leaning forward in the car seat, he searched the dark pine forest for signs of an elusive enemy, a gleam of metal, a flash of black, a branch bent in a way no normal branch bends. He'd expected to feel safe at home, but Vietnam hung between him and the Arkansas countryside like a movie played on a screen of gray chiffon.

He couldn't grasp the reality of home even when his mother's long, work-gnarled fingers brushed his arm for the twentieth time since his family met him in Texarkana. When he'd limped off the bus, a single tear of happiness and relief slid down Wreath's cheek, and her arms went out to receive her only son. A warning nudge from her husband reminded her of the rigid control he expected of her. She restricted herself to squeezing Mercer's hand for an extra moment when she offered him the handshake John Luther deemed proper for all public greetings. The look in his eyes broke her heart; the damaged leg was obviously the least of his injuries.

John Luther Ives didn't notice any change in his son. Intent as always on the sound of his own voice and the shape of his own thoughts, he pontificated about God, war, and the wages of sin as he piloted the two-tone Buick station wagon down the road toward Columbus. The big car rounded a curve and emerged from pine forest into a broad swath of pasture. Mercer gripped the edge of the seat until his fingers ached, all instincts crying out against driving straight across an open area instead of creeping around the perimeter. He ran an expert eye along the tree line. No snipers; not even Billy Wayne Martin shooting snapping turtles in his catfish pond. He thought he heard the distant rumble of artillery, then recognized the noise as the baritone growl of his father's voice.

"... sinful and violent ways. You refused to heed my counsel to avoid the conflict with the Yellow Man, but God gives me the grace to forgive a repentant and contrite heart. Your wound is the Mark of Cain ..."

The car jolted off the highway onto a narrow dirt lane. At the crossroads, John Luther's church squatted in the middle of an even green lawn edged with azaleas and redbud trees. A carved crown of thorns adorned the front door and at the top of the highest steeple in Hempstead County, a golden hand pointed a stern index finger heavenward. A small church with no known associations to any established branch of Christianity, the Church of the Flock of the Good Shepherd had been established fifty years earlier by John Luther's father after that worthy broke away from a Pentecostal organization that he deemed too lax in its beliefs. Irreverent Baptists and Methodists referred to it as the Church of His Joyful Sheep, but the Flock never dignified the nickname with public acknowledgment. Less inclined to turn the other cheek than most of the congregation, Mercer fought his own private battles behind the school's gymnasium when some schoolmate bawled like a lost sheep once too often. Slight in stature and sternly schooled in pacifism, Mercer swept into each fistfight on a flood of adrenaline that felt like joy. If news of the fight reached the ears of any member of the Flock, Mercer's transgression would be duly reported to his father and the elders of the church, resulting in a Sunday reprimand in front of the congregation and a sound beating from his father when they returned home for the midday meal. More than once, Mercer spent the afternoon service standing up in the back of the church, his posterior being too sore for contact with the unpadded pews. After each fight and subsequent punishment, he resolved to live in peace with his enemies, only to have that resolve dissipate in the face of the next challenge. Sometimes in the heat of pounding a hard-breathing, sweating opponent, Mercer fiercely imagined hitting someone else.

The church disappeared in the cloud of red dust that rose behind the station wagon. Pine trees crowded in on the roadside close enough to brush the vehicle with long green needles. Mercer's three sisters sat in the back seat of the Buick, demur skirts covering their knees, hands folded on their laps in the modest manner approved by their father. From twenty-five-year-old Delilah's prim navy-blue skirt and matching blouse to eleven-year-old Leah's black-and-white saddle oxfords, their clothing was uncompromisingly dull and unbecoming. Jezebel's brown jumper had been handed down to her by Delilah, who had reluctantly worn the scratchy linen after it arrived in a charity barrel years earlier. Jezebel at fourteen was more buxom than Delilah had ever been. The garment strained across the front despite the tight band her father decreed should be daily wrapped around her chest to modestly flatten her breasts. Unless the garment fell apart during its tenure on Jezebel's body, Leah was doomed to finish it out.

". . . intended for you to enter the ministry, but your love of war has left you unfit . . ."

A branch slapped the windshield. Only his mother's gentle touch on his arm kept Mercer from leaping out of the car and running for cover. He closed his eyes against the weird double images of Arkansas and Vietnam, wishing he never had to see another tree as long as he lived.

". . . for no man participates in the Slaughter of War, yet escapes the Wrath of God . . ."

The car rolled to a stop in front of a barred gate. Eager to escape the drone of John Luther's impromptu sermon, Mercer hauled himself out of the car, checked for booby-trap wires, and swung open the gate. As the vehicle slid past him, he caught sight of Leah's face pressed against the window, staring at this brother who'd come home in place of the one who left. He pantomimed a kiss to her and was rewarded with a gap-toothed smile. The little girl kissed back as the vehicle rolled up the hill to park in the shade of the triple cedar trees.

Home. The two-story white house sprawled at the top of a gentle rise where it had stood since before the Civil War. Screened porches edged the house on three sides and were in turn bordered by a riot of spring bulbs in full flower, the only sign of gaiety on the whole place. A vegetable garden stretched west of the driveway in ruler straight rows that would soon be planted with tomatoes, okra, and crowder peas. A double line of pear and apple trees bisected the garden, dividing tall crops from shorter ones. Not a weed dared show the tiniest leaf; even the insects appeared to be intimidated by the strict order. As long as Wreath's vegetable garden supplied most of the family's food requirements each year, John Luther took no notice of it. He didn't disapprove of her flower beds only because Wreath was careful to tend them while he was away and to hide from him the joy the flowers brought her. Her borders and beds bloomed as she and her children could not.

Home.

Mercer dragged air into his lungs, steeling himself to walk up the long tree-lined driveway. In the Vietnam part of his odd double reality, he dived into the shelter of the nearest magnolia, keeping the trunk at his back while he planned his next move. No enemies in sight, but that rarely meant they weren't there. Eyes darting in all directions, he made an imaginary run toward the next tree in line.

At the top of the rise, his parents and sisters spilled out of the car, smoothing creases from their Sunday clothes, worn not to honor a returning hero, but to acknowledge the rarity of a trip to Texarkana. Mercer ignored the ghost images of Vietnam, and paced carefully up the rise toward his family, estimating the number of steps to the safety of the house.

Delilah's husband, Jared Fuller, helloed to Mercer from the shop where he was tinkering with an elderly John Deere tractor. Not even a brother-in-law returning from war could coax Jared away from his beloved equipment. Mercer waved to him without resentment. A fascination with the way things worked was a bond between them, albeit the only bond. Jared was a man forged in the image of the elders of the Church of the Flock of the Good Shepherd. Conservative and lacking in imagination, he devoted himself to the church, the farm equipment, his twin sons, and his wife, usually in that order. Under his husbandry, the farm had expanded from a few acres of vegetables and trees into a smooth operation that included a small herd of excellent cattle, and almost enough income to support eight people. The remainder of the required income came from John Luther's comfortable salary as church pastor, head bookkeeper, and counselor.

"See you at dinner!" Jared hollered across the yard.

Mercer put his foot on the brick path that led from driveway to front porch just as Jared turned the ignition on the tractor. Poppin' John lived up to its name with a staccato of loud bursts that ricocheted off the side of the house.

The bloody light of mortars burst overhead. Tracers walked in on his position, and the last traces of Arkansas sanity shrieked at Mercer to disbelieve what his Vietnam eyes and ears were telling him. He didn't even try. He dove into the nearest bushes and huddled there, arms over his head, silently echoing the voiceless screams of the dying who lay all around him. John Luther and his womenfolk gaped at the sight of their son and brother cowering beneath the camellias, his face the waxy pallor of the white narcissus surrounding him. Wreath released a pent-up breath and went to kneel beside her trembling child.

"Y'all go on in the house," she said in her hoarse, sweet soprano. "Somebody takes a fall like that, he doesn't need everybody standin' around gawkin' at him. Y'all go on inside and get the table set."

Scarlet-faced, John Luther led the exodus to the house. Skillfully avoiding cow patties in the grass, Delilah ran across the pasture toward Jared and a crib that stood in the shade of a sassafras tree. Jared stood next to Poppin' John, listening to its noisy dual cylinders, unaware of their part in the drama.

The war faded. Ashamed and shaking with adrenaline, Mercer pressed his face against the damp, fragrant earth. The pungent smell of crushed narcissus replaced the memory of less pleasant odors. Wreath lay a gentle hand on his shoulder and felt him flinch. Swallowing her own dismay, she stroked his back to comfort him, just as she had comforted him following childhood nightmares. Half afraid that the sound of her voice would startle him into another paroxysm of terror, she whispered, "That old tractor of Jared's is the noisiest thing in this part of Hempstead County." When he didn't respond, she added, "You okay, sugar?" and thought what a stupid question it was.

He nodded and allowed her to help him get to his feet. He even managed a stiff smile, though words of thanks or explanation were beyond him. Clinging to reality with both hands, he followed his mother up the back steps into the kitchen.

Time had apparently stood still in the house over the previous twenty-four months. Even the big green bottle fly beating its wings hopelessly against a windowpane in the front room looked familiar. A breeze from the fan on the high ceiling stirred his hair and wafted the smell of dinner to him. Silverware clattered on the scrubbed trestle table as Jezzie scattered place settings with her usual lack of care, followed by Delilah, who added plates and glasses and straightened the mess left by her younger sister. Leah edged in carrying a basket of buttermilk biscuits, glancing at Mercer as if she expected him to dive under the table at any moment. He tried to smile reassuringly at her. Leah gasped, banged down the biscuits, and ran for the kitchen.

Not reassuring enough, he thought.

The house hadn't changed while he'd been gone, but it didn't feel nearly as homelike as it should have. He walked down the long hall toward the bathroom, pausing a couple of times to look at framed photos on the informal gallery of the walls. Halfway down hung a photo taken the day John Luther had preached at the first tent revival ever held at the Church of the Flock of the Good Shepherd. He stared confidently into the camera, square and lean, but with a puffiness around the determined chin that heralded the weight problem that would plague him in middle age. To one side and slightly behind him huddled Wreath, young and pretty, but with shoulders hunched and face blurred as if she had turned away from her husband just as the shutter snapped. Mercer had carried that blurred image of his mother all the way through boot camp and Vietnam. Taking a closer look at her was liable to show him things too painful to bear and wrongs he couldn't do anything about.

Over the first few years of marriage, Wreath had endured three pregnancies and one live birth before producing the son her husband's dynastic ego demanded. In the next half dozen years, she bore two more girls and a boy who survived his birth by only a few hours. After tucking her youngest child into his grave, Wreath crept around the house on slippered feet, trying not to attract John Luther's attention. She was barely thirty but felt and looked a decade older. Whether in answer to her prayers or in response to her ravaged appearance, his demands on her body ceased. Not long after this, she heard whispers suggesting that John Luther had become friendly with a young matron who arrived in church each Sunday with her husband and small boy in tow. When her second baby was born, the congregation noted with differing degrees of relief and disappointment that the baby's hair was as red as its father's. Wreath recalled John Luther's long dead, red-haired mother, the red hair of two of her own dead babies, and wished she could send the young woman an anonymous bouquet of roses from the garden. Instead, Wreath offered up a prayer for the woman's continued well-being and sent the new baby a blue-and-white crib quilt.

Mercer washed his hands at the bathroom sink and joined his family at the table. All stood behind their chairs and waited for John Luther to complete his silent commune with the Lord before he embarked on an interminable grace that covered the morning's events, plans for the afternoon, warnings to various erring family members, and incidentally thanks for what they were about to receive in the name of Jesus Christ Our Lord, amen. The words flowed over Mercer like so much hot air as he examined the feast spread out on the snowy white tablecloth. John Luther was welcoming the prodigal son home with full oratory and the Southern version of a fatted calf. He believed in dining well and saw no reason why austerity of the soul should extend to matters of the stomach. Mercer counted ham, fried chicken, soda bread, biscuits, okra, hominy, black-eyed peas, collard greens, and cornbread. Three kinds of pie and a triple-layer coconut cake stood on the sideboard along with half a dozen other desserts. Sweat beaded the old carnival glass sweet-tea pitcher and sprigs of mint floated in the glass next to his plate. On the transparent gray screen of his mental movie of Vietnam, his fellow soldiers ate canned peaches out of olive-green boxes and buried tasteless lima beans in holes dug in the ground.

"... in heaven, we thank Thee for Mercer's safe return. Yea, though he walked through the valley of the shadow of death ..."

I feared no evil because I was the meanest son of a bitch in the valley.

"... Thou wert with him ..."

Where the hell wert Thou when Bigger Than You got wasted?

"... power and glory forever. Amen."

"Amen," the women and Jared echoed, and sat down at last to eat.

All of a sudden, Mercer was starving. He ignored the MCIs offered to him by his buddies and eyed the platter of golden chicken that was being passed around the table.

"... Julia Dell McCardle married a boy from Ashdown while you were gone. Nice boy. Baptist, though."

"... see that son of a bitch go up when he stepped on that mine? Man, I never..."

"Cornbread tastes right good, Delilah. You got a fair hand with it."

"... don't bogart that joint, man..."

Mercer closed his ears to all voices on both sides of the screen and concentrated on the basket of fried chicken. Leah passed it to Jezzie, who took a wing for herself and absentmindedly left the chicken sitting between her and Leah.

"Please pass the chicken," Mercer said in her direction. Jezzie didn't hear him. She smeared butter on yellow cornbread and thought how lucky she was to be the only church girl at high school this year with no one to tell on her when she rolled her plain black skirt up at the waistband so that the hem lay a fashionable but still modest two inches above her knees. The day before, a girl in her PE class had given her a tiny Avon sample of Pink Kisses lip gloss. Jezzie bit into her cornbread and wondered if she had the nerve to wear it.

"Please pass the chicken," Mercer said a little louder.

Jezzie picked up her fork and moved peas around on her plate as she considered the lip gloss. Showing her kneecaps was risky but if her father ever heard she was painting like the whore of Babylon, she wouldn't be able to sit down for a week.

"Jezzie," Mercer snapped. "Pass the fucking chicken!"

Conversation around the table crashed to a halt. Wreath's mouth was a perfect circle of shock. John Luther looked like a plugged pressure cooker about to blow. Jezzie held her napkin to her mouth to hide her glee. With Mercer around to say things like *fuck*, no one was likely to notice if she walked to the bus stop with her lips painted red and her hems brushing the elastic of her old-fashioned drawers.

"I don't know how you conducted yourself in the army," John

Luther said sternly, "but the devil's language is not acceptable in my house."

"Navy."

"What?"

"I was a Navy corpsman attached to the Marines." Mercer looked out the window where the redbud trees blossomed into fireballs and pelted the house with shrapnel.

"We are all waiting for an apology."

"I'm sorry I said fuck. I won't say fuck anymore."

Mercer stood up and stalked out of the room, letting the screen door slam behind him. John Luther's face was too terrible to look at. Five pairs of eyes fastened on five plates. In the bedroom, one of the twins began to cry. Delilah jumped to her feet and fled in that direction. John Luther picked up his fork and began to eat without another word. Wreath kept her head down to keep her husband from seeing the tears in her eyes.

Mercer crossed the yard in a crimson haze of fury, the sound of mortar fire half deafening him. At the garage, he shoved open the sliding wooden door and stepped into the musty dimness. The battle noise faded. His motorcycle stood to one side, swathed in an old tractor canvas against dust and bird droppings, and carefully ensconced on a big piece of cardboard to guard the hard-packed dirt floor from leaks. He pulled the cloth off the bike and tossed it on the floor, one more small revolt against house rules made to maintain strict order and cleanliness. The bike gleamed in the semidarkness and Mercer spared a thought of thanks to Jared for maintaining the machine in his absence. He straddled the bike, kicked it into life, and roared out into the afternoon sunlight.

He rode east to the main highway then south toward the Louisiana border, dodging potholes and snarling mongrels that ran out onto the road looking for an ankle to bite. Pine trees and hills gave way to cypress swamps. Mercer had hunted in these swamps, legally and not so legally, all his life. They concealed bugs, mud, alligators, smooth black water moccasins that attacked without provocation, and smooth black and white people who would dig your grave if you looked at them the wrong way or strayed too far down faint trails into clearings planted with some of the best marijuana grown north of Acapulco.

He swung off the highway onto a secondary road that soon narrowed to a bare two lanes, blue-topped and rutted like a washboard. Up ahead, a slim shadow detached itself from darker shadows cast by tree branches, eased its way into a comfortable position in a patch of sun and waited. Once upon a time, Mercer would've paused long enough to kill the cottonmouth, believing the only good snake was a dead snake, but he'd lost any will for killing that he'd ever had. This snake would live another day. He slowed the bike to go around it.

"Hell, that's just a li'l ol' cottonmouth," a voice said in his ear. Bigger Than You leaned over Mercer's shoulder and peered down at the snake as they passed it. Mercer saw the man in his peripheral vision, saw the glisten of blood on his cheek, smelled the green-dust smell of the jungle on his clothes. "You ain't scared of a li'l ol' water moccasin after livin' in Nam with vipers like Mr. One Step and Mr. Two Step, are you?"

"Go away, Bigger," Mercer whispered, twisting the accelerator and damning the potholes to go full speed ahead. The pound of the bike on the washboard blue top rattled his teeth. It must've rattled Bigger, too, because when Mercer got up the nerve to look over his shoulder, no one was there.

He crossed the state line into Louisiana with movies of Vietnam playing on the veil between him and the real world. At dusk, he stopped in a redneck bar somewhere south of Natchitoches and bought a bottle of Jack Daniel's whiskey. The bar's crewcut patrons, hands wrapped around cold cans of Dixie beer, eyed him curiously. He managed to pay his bill and get out of the building before they noticed his mode of transportation.

Backtracking to the last crossroads he'd passed, he turned onto a dirt road and followed it along a bayou to an abandoned church that guarded the gate to a long-forgotten graveyard. He parked the bike in the weeds out back and let himself into the church through a door that hung half off its hinges. His boots thumped hollowly on the wooden floor as he moved up the aisle to the front row of pews where he dropped his butt onto a hard bench. A puff of dust rose around the seat of his jeans. He checked the floor for snakes and saw a mouse skittering away, chirping with alarm. If there were snakes, they weren't doing a very efficient job on the rodent population, but just in case, he swung his feet off the floor and leaned his back against the armrest. He snapped the paper seal with a twist of the cap and raised the bottle to his mouth.

Three columns of darkness separated themselves from the gloom beyond the splintered altar and moved into the weird half-light streaming through the dirty windows from the disappearing sun. Bigger Than You squatted down next to the pew, his eyes level with Mercer's own, as huge in death as he had been in life. Blood glistened on what was left of his ebony cheekbones. Mercer controlled an urge to reach out and press his hand against the streaming wound in the ghost's chest. The second shadow, a full head and shoulders shorter than Bigger, leaned against the wall to support himself on the side where his right leg used to do the job. Mercer locked his eyes on the bottle to avoid seeing what was left of the third ghost, a marine he'd never seen in one piece.

"Why don't y'all leave me alone?"

"We ain't nothing but your imagination, Doc," Bigger pointed out. "You said so your own self. You drink that all Jack by your lonesome, you gonna be one sick pup come tomorrow mornin'."

Mercer offered him the bottle. Bigger's shovel-sized hand passed through the bottle and Mercer gritted his teeth at the ice-and-fire touch that cut to the bone and left his wrist and hand aching. Bigger slapped his bloody leg, laughing at the old joke.

"No spirits for the spirits!"

Mercer tilted the bottle to his mouth and began the grim process of drinking the dead back to death.

CHAPTER 4
GENEVIEVE

I like cemeteries. In the South, they're usually shaded by big trees and filled with flowers left by living folks for their dead friends and relatives. My favorite graves are the ones where someone planted a rose or a camellia and left it to take root in the heart of whoever lies beneath it. That's what I want someone to do for me when I die, plant something on top of me to fill my heart and keep me quiet. Dead people can be good company if you catch them on a day when they aren't too talkative, but some of them get bored, then Lord God, they'll drive you nuts with words.

When they first let me out of the hospital, I didn't know anyone in the world and had nowhere to go except the hell out of Alabama, so I spent a lot of time in cemeteries while I decided what to do with myself. The day I left the halfway house, I took my clothes and started walking west, sleeping most nights in some cemetery or another. I had money I made working at the waitress job the patient welfare people arranged for me, but it wasn't enough to waste on hotels. I'd also left the halfway house without permission and was afraid the authorities might find me if I stayed in a hotel.

It's safer than you might think to sleep in graveyards. Folks don't come in them much at night. One time, a couple of big boys came into a cemetery where I was spending the night, talking real loud to show how brave they were and shoving on tombstones to see if they could knock them over. I was in my sleeping bag up on top of a mausoleum where I'd climbed to keep out of the damp and away from the snakes. They walked right by without noticing me until I raised up on one elbow and asked them what the sam hill they thought they were doing, talking loud enough to raise the dead. They damn near trampled each other on their way to the gate.

One of them left behind a green backpack containing a nice heavy flashlight, extra batteries, a sandwich, and a film can half filled with marijuana. I kept the flashlight, ate the sandwich, and stuffed the pot into my own backpack. Marijuana was the most valuable thing those kids left me; it eventually paid for rides halfway to Vidalia. Louisiana wasn't high on my list of places to go, but it was out of Alabama and that's all I cared about at the time.

I got my name in a cemetery somewhere in Rapides Parish, a real old cemetery half choked with wait-a-minute vines and oxalis but with oaks that must've been two hundred years old, all hung with Spanish moss and resurrection fern. Genevieve Madeleine Antoinette Charbonneau was laid to rest on the bosom of her dead mother on the day I was born, and only a few days after she was born herself. Looked like a clear sign to me, especially when I went to the parish courthouse, put two dollars and fifty cents on the counter, and lo and behold was handed Genevieve's birth certificate with no questions asked. Took me back a bit to see the word "colored" in the space for race, but to tell the truth, that's a better description for a girl with auburn hair and a thousand freckles than plain old "white" is. I embraced my new name and figured if race ever became an issue, I'd just find me another dead baby who didn't need her name anymore.

When I joined the circus, I didn't tell anyone where I got my name or what it said on the birth certificate, and no one cared either. Madame Clara paid us all in cash, and the total of what I made in a year was too far below the poverty line to interest the mighty IRS, even if I'd bothered to file a return. Names changed regularly in the circus. I might be Persephone in my fortune teller robes, Medea when I performed with the thick-bodied boa constrictors wrapped around my arms, The Fabulous LaDonna when I did my solitary flight twenty feet above the ground on a single trapeze, and Demetra or Antoinette or Pasiphae on the nights when I danced on stage in the hoochy-kootch just out of reach of men who threw money at my feet for the privilege of watching me stoop to gather the bills, still warm from hip pockets, into my hands.

No one ever touched me while I danced. I made it clear from the start that I was no hennaed trailer trash to dance on laps and snatch money from the teeth of drunk truckers and off-color bik-ers. The bouncers always backed me up, partly because they liked us dancers and partly because they knew I'd share my tips with them if they had to come to my defense. Men are so perverse. Denying them what they wanted only made them want me more, and they came back night after night, hoping maybe this time I'd give into their blandishments. I'm no plaster saint. I could be had, but the price was high, and not many men had the nerve to spend the night with a woman who kept three boa constrictors in her tent.

The one man who did have the price and the nerve stayed with me for almost six months. One afternoon while I was out, he fell asleep in bed with a lit cigarette, and the resulting fire put an end to him, his caravan, and two of my poor boas. That was right before the circus was sold, and I'd been wandering ever since, dancing here and there when I needed money, but never staying anywhere very long. I had an idea that I might like to go to college and study snakes, but I didn't know how to go about applying for entrance, much less the scholarships I'd need to pay for it.

If I hadn't met Mercer Ives, I'd probably still be out there sleeping on mausoleums. He didn't look like much the morning I first laid eyes on him. He stumbled out of that ruined Antioch Baptist Church looking like something that belonged in the graveyard under a few feet of dirt. I gathered up my backpack and got ready to run, but he didn't see me crouched down in the weeds. He was too intent on getting to the well house out back. I put my stuff behind a tombstone and waited to see what he was going to do.

The broken winch didn't faze him; he pulled that bucket out of the well hand over hand in half the time it would've taken me, strong as I am. He didn't look for a dipper, just stuck his face down in the bucket and drank like he'd been lost in the desert a week. I never saw anyone drink so much water in one breath. It looked good, though, so when he picked up the rest of the bucket and poured it over his head, I made up my mind.

"Hey," I said politely.

He had his face up to the falling water, and I guess I startled him into breathing at the wrong time. While he finished coughing and choking, I slid back a good ten feet in case he got mad and decided to come at me. I wasn't much worried. I can outrun almost anybody. It was the *almost* that made me get a lead on him.

"I didn't mean for you to jump." I talked to him the way I talk to stray cats that don't trust folks much, slow and gentle. "I was just hoping you'd give me a drink of water."

He stared at me like I had green teeth and a hungry look. I edged farther back, but he shook his head to dislodge mental cobwebs, then dropped the bucket back into the well. Coolest thing I heard all day was that bucket hitting the water. He pulled it up, found a dipper on the side of the well house, filled it for me, and held it out. I got close enough to him to take it and figured out what was wrong with him: too much whiskey and no ice. That made me feel easier about my chances of getting away if I had to run. One solid punch in the right place and he'd go down like a mule with a heart attack.

Good, that was the best water I ever tasted. I drank like a greedy little girl. The water ran over the edges of the dipper and down my face to splash on my shirt, which felt as good as the drink. I hung the dipper on its hook, tilted my head back, closed my eyes, and said, "Pour."

He didn't dump the bucket all at once, but emptied it in a slow, luxurious stream, flooding my hair and clothes. I could feel him looking at me as my shirt soaked through. He got an eyeful, but I didn't care. He earned it by saving me the hassle of pulling that bucket up sixty feet of well.

Funny how the worst things can turn out to be positive. The only reason I spent the night in that old cemetery was because I didn't get a ride the day before. I walked all day in a haze of humidity on a highway didn't hardly no one use, and the only person who stopped to offer me a ride was an old boy in a bondo-gray Barracuda who eyed me like I was a Hershey bar and he was a starving chocoholic. I told him no thanks, I was just out for a stroll, but he pushed the issue, and I had to run off into the woods to get away from him. He didn't let up until I hid behind a tree and conked him on the head with a length of wood when he passed by, calling for me and telling me all the things he wanted us to do together. Knocked him for a loop. Before he could come around, I skinned out of there. Idiot left his keys in the car. I drove it down the road a piece, parked it in the middle of a bridge, and dropped the keys in the creek. Night was coming on, so I backtracked and went down a dirt road where a sign said I could find a church. Backwoods churches have saved me more than once, and this one had a fine cemetery with several big, flat tombstones just the right size for me to sleep on.

Anyway, if I hadn't had to run from a redneck Casanova, I'd never have found that graveyard or that nice boy to pour water over my head. I knew he was okay; my voices didn't even murmur while he was wetting me down. The doctors in the hospital did all they could to stop me hearing my dead people. To avoid spending the rest of my life in that place, I had to do some fancy lying to convince the Powers That Be that I was stone-cold deaf to anything but what they could hear themselves. My voices did get kind of quiet for a while, which worried me considerably at the time. It hurt their feelings to be denied three times, but when all was said and the cock done crowed, they forgave me and came back.

Me and my new friend looked each other over, water dripping off our hair and off the tips of our noses. He was a nice-looking man, even considering he was all hungover and real thin. He had the kind of blond hair that bleaches white in the sun, sort of shaggy over his ears, like he couldn't decide whether to grow it long and be fashionable or cut it short and be respectable. Considering he was recovering from a bender in an abandoned church, I suspected the length of his hair was a matter of indifference.

"You get drunk very often?"

"No, ma'am."

"Just as well. Looks like you're pretty bad at it."

He laughed, then stopped like the sound startled him. Probably also hurt his head because he turned a little green around the gills.

"Come over by that oak tree," I said sympathetically. "I got something in my bag that might help."

He followed me willing enough, wincing when he walked out into the bright sunlight. Without turning my back on him, I hauled my bag from behind the tombstone and dug through it for a bottle of aspirin, a bar of soap, a washcloth, and, after some hesitation, what was left of a film can of marijuana. I don't like the stuff myself, but I keep some for the guys who live by the motto Gas, Grass, or Ass: Nobody Rides for Free.

"You hang out in graveyards a lot?" he asked.

"Fair amount."

"Ever see any ghosts?"

I knew he'd laugh or flip out if I told him God's own truth about that, so I shot back, "Do you?"

"Only when I don't drink." He was trying to make a joke, but I could tell there were demons pounding behind his eyeballs and wasn't the least bit surprised when his stomach heaved itself out over Daniel F. Griffin, 1886 to 1951. I went to get a bucket of water while he finished this messy business and came back to find him sprawled a few feet away on the tombstone where I spent the night. Emily Mary Allen, 1914 to 1949.

"Here. Take these and drink this. No, it's just aspirin. Drink slow, but drink. It's ninety degrees out here, and you'll dehydrate all to hell if you don't."

He accepted the aspirin and let a few trickles of water slide over his tongue. For a moment, it looked like it might come right back up, but his stomach finally shrugged and gave up the battle to escape from his body. He gradually drank the rest of the water in the dipper, then dropped off to sleep in the shade. Not having anything else to do or anywhere I needed to be, I pulled a book out of my backpack and settled down to wait for him to wake up again.

CHAPTER 5
MERCER

❧

He awoke, feeling like he might live, but unable to garner much enthusiasm for the idea. He kept his eyes closed and watched the gold light trace patterns on the outside of his lids until a shadow blocked out the gentle glow and startled him into a wide-eyed sitting position. A woman sat back on her heels, gazing at him in amusement. She held up a white washrag and he realized his forehead was damp.

"Just wanted to wet this with some cooler water," she explained. "I've done it twenty times since you fell asleep."

"You did?" He saw the bucket of water by her side and thought about it. "Why?"

"Why not?" She wrung the cloth out with a deft twist of her hands and spread it on a nearby tombstone to dry. "You looked real natural stretched out there on that grave with your hands folded on your chest. All you needed was a sword at your side and a little dog at your feet to make an effigy of a fallen knight." She twisted her head to one side, as if listening to someone speak over her shoulder, then looked at him curiously. "That's not so far from wrong, is it?"

The conversation was going too fast for him. He lay down and closed his eyes again. Wet sounds, then the delicious feel of a cold cloth across his face. *You don't have to do this*, he tried to tell her, but his tongue wouldn't work. He drifted back to sleep.

The sun shone in an orange ball behind the oak trees and the graveyard was wrapped in the stillness of late afternoon when he finally woke for good. Using the woman's soap and towel, he cleaned himself up as well as he could in a bucket of cool water, then accepted the joint she rolled for him. He sucked at it gratefully. When he offered it back to her, she shook her head.

"I don't care about it," she explained. "Makes me feel sleepy and sort of depressed."

"Why do you keep it, then?"

"Standard fare for hitchhikers."

"You hitching?"

She nodded.

"Where to?"

She shrugged.

He took another long drag at the joint, felt the drug creep into his bloodstream, easing the last of his headache and nausea, and relaxing his muscles, including the one in his tongue.

"Where did you come from?" he asked.

"Nowhere."

"That's a mighty big place."

"Which part of it *you* from?"

"Nam."

"I hear that's a good place to be far from."

"You hear right, but I don't know where's a better place to be."
Without meaning to, he found himself telling her about his Arkansas homecoming, about the huge dinner, about his abrupt departure. At this last bit of information, she sat straight up.

"You walked out of the house midday yesterday an hour after you got home? Does your mama know you're okay?"

He admitted that he hadn't called her.

"You . . . come on, get your sorry butt off the ground."

She grabbed him around the wrist and tugged. The strength of her grip as she levered him to his feet astonished him.

"Why?"

"We're going to the nearest phone so you can call your mama."

"The hell we are. I don't—"

"I have money if you drank all yours up."

"I don't want to call—"

"What you want doesn't matter right now."

"Look—"

"No, *you* look." She jabbed her finger into his face; he went cross-eyed to see it wagging at the tip of his nose. "You owe me. I fed you aspirin, watched over your worthless carcass while you slept, gave you stuff to clean up with. You owe me and that's my price: you call your mama and tell her you're okay."

He pushed her hand away. Spun by the unexpected onslaught of words and the effects of the pot, he said, "What do you care about my mother?"

"Someone needs to care about her 'cause you sure the hell don't."

His face got hot. "Well, I can't very well operate that bike while I'm stoned, can I?"

She stuck out her hand for the keys. "I'm not stoned. All you gotta do is hang on."

"You ever ridden a bike that size?"

"One performance a night plus matinees on weekends for three years," she answered. "Hand 'em over."

He slammed the keys into her palm with a hard slap of skin on skin. "Okay, biker bitch, let's see you."

"Thanks. And don't call me 'bitch' like there's something wrong with it."

Even with his beloved machine and his own skin at risk, he hoped she'd dump it before they got to the highway, but she guided the bike down the washboard road without so much as a slight skid. By the time they got to the highway, she'd earned his reluctant approval.

"You're a good rider," he said over her shoulder.

"Told you."

They passed through a couple of small comatose towns before they found a public phone booth outside a weathered service station with rusty red pumps.

"Call," she ordered. When he hesitated, she pulled a nickel out of her cutoff jeans and dropped it into the slot herself. "Number?"

Half expecting her to reach down his throat and drag it out of him if he refused, he chanted the number from memory then watched her dial, riding her finger to the beginning of the cycle each time as if letting the dial turn by itself would take too long. She spoke to the operator, then clattered a few more coins into the slot for long distance. After a moment, she said, "May I speak to your mama, honey? Tell her it's—"

She looked at him inquiringly.

"Mercer."

"About Mercer. Yes, he's fine. Yes, I'll wait, thank you." She tapped her fingernails on the phone while she waited, not meeting Mercer's eyes. "Ma'am? Just a second."

She thrust the phone at him, picked up her backpack, and stalked away, leaving him with the receiver in his hand and the sound of his mother's worried voice floating to him over miles of telephone wire. The lump of shame in his throat nearly choked him, but he spoke to her gently, assuring her that he was fine, and yes, he'd be home soon.

"And Mama," he added, turning to look at the woman who was walking away from him through the heat haze on the highway, "I'm bringing home company."

"Mercer, you sure this is okay?" she asked for the tenth time since crossing the Arkansas line. She'd insisted they stop in the town of Hope long enough for her to change clothes, wash her face, and brush her hair, though she could've just as easily waited until they reached the Ives farm. With her fresh-scrubbed skin, hip-length braids, and freckles, she looked like an anxious fifteen-year-old despite the mature breasts she pressed against his back as they rode north out of Louisiana the next morning. Even with the vibration of the bike, he could feel her heart pounding against him.

"I'm sure," he yelled back over the sound of the wind. "You can have the room Mama keeps for visiting preachers."

"Preacher? I'm not even a Christian."

"As far as my mother is concerned, right now you're a step above angels."

Wreath met them at the front door with lemonade and a plateful of peanut butter cookies, the closest she could get to flinging herself on Mercer's neck and weeping with relief. Despite Genevieve's protests, she relieved the girl of her backpack, staggering a little as she carried it up the stairs and down the long hallway to the room she kept swept and dusted for visitors. In honor of Mercer's friend, a green Roseville vase of daffodils sat on the dresser and a double wedding ring quilt in shades of lilac and blue covered the bed.

"Bathroom's just down the hall," Wreath said. "Fresh towels and washrags in that there chair. You c'mon down for lunch when you get rested." She slipped out the door so quietly that Genevieve, marveling at the room, didn't hear her go.

CHAPTER 6
GENEVIEVE

I loved Wreath from the moment she held out that platter of cookies to me. It was all I could do not to follow her around like a puppy dog, just to hear her voice and watch her beautiful hands pat out biscuits.

The rest of the family arrived at the house in fits and starts. Leah and Jezzie came home from school. Delilah came downstairs from putting the babies to bed. They were all polite enough, but I could tell they didn't know what to think of me. Delilah didn't speak, just gave a stiff nod when we were introduced. She sniffed audibly and straightened the collar of her ugly shin-length dress as she looked over my clean blue jeans and tee shirt. Obviously thought I was no better than I should be, riding up bold as brass on the back of her brother's motorcycle. She was right, of course, about me being a fallen woman, but it irritated me that she had the bad manners to let it show. It's not like I fell with her brother and besides, who was she to pass judgment? When Jared wandered in for a glass of milk before returning to work, she ran to fetch it for him, keeping her eye on me like I might eat him before she got back from the kitchen. He spared neither of us a glance, his mind being concerned with the plowing still to be done before supper. As he went out, letting the screen door slam behind him,

Delilah gave me a hard warning look, then turned her hand to help with the cooking. I almost laughed. Her husband was safe from me. I wouldn't have had Jared Fuller on a tray with an apple in his mouth.

I was sitting in a straight-backed chair in the kitchen helping Wreath chop vegetables for wilted salad when John Luther made his entrance, still steeped in the sanctity of an afternoon spent on church business.

"And who might this be?" he inquired with a lift of his eyebrows and a theatrical bow in my direction. In a theatrical move of my own, I set the knife next to the pile of celery on the cutting board and rose to meet him like a polite child, hiding my eyes by inclining my head and letting my braids fall forward against my cheeks. The voices whispered so furiously in my ears that I nearly hissed at them to quiet down. I didn't need them to tell me this was not a man of any god I'd trust.

"This here is Genevieve Charbonneau from down Louisiana way," Wreath said, proud as if she was offering him a special treat. "She came up with Mercer this afternoon and'll be stayin' with us a few days."

John Luther slid his eyes around the room. "Mercer is back?"

Wreath knotted her hands together and turned back to the stove to stir the soup that bubbled there. "He's out fixin' the barn roof."

John Luther's mouth twisted like he tasted something bad, but he nodded and turned his attention back to me. I stood, head down, waiting for him to speak. When he didn't, I glanced up at him through my eyelashes and bangs and caught him staring at the cleavage that showed in the vee neck of my tee shirt.

You filthy old son of a bitch, I thought, and took a deep breath that sent a harsh red flush creeping up his jaws.

"Charbonneau," he rumbled. "French name. Lots of French names in Louisiana." He pronounced it *Loozyanna*. "How do you happen to know my son?"

"We met at church." Well, sorta.

John Luther raised his eyebrows. "I don't recall you visiting our church."

"He was visiting mine." I dipped my chin slightly to give the impression of blushing without actually doing so. "Seems like a long time ago. I was sure surprised when he turned up yesterday."

"And your parents approve of you coming up here with him?"

"My parents are dead, sir. I'm older than I look."

He opened his mouth to continue the interrogation. I braced myself for a long discomforting harangue, but Wreath crossed the kitchen in two long strides and stood next to me, a blue enamel ladle clutched in her fist like a shillelagh.

"Don't you go upsettin' my guest, John Luther. Genevieve came up to go to school over to Texarkana next fall. She's gonna stay with us a while and help Jezzie pass that algebra class."

"I'm a fair hand in the garden," I added, "and I can help with the chickens and ducks, too. I'm not afraid to get dirty."

John Luther ran his nasty old eyes over my breasts. The tip of his tongue poked out between his thick pink lips. "Surely any garden you grace would be Eden."

I smiled sweetly at the compliment and listened to the voices whisper warnings about Satan in the apple orchard.

That night, I sat in bed with the double wedding-ring quilt over my knees, fingering the curved pieces and the tiny stitches that held the layers together, waiting for the sounds of a household preparing for sleep to die away. I'd slept so long on slabs of granite and hard circus cots that the feather mattress threatened to smother me, even if I propped my head up on an equally soft pillow. When the last stirring of the family faded into silence, I counted to one thousand, then slipped out of bed and crossed to the screenless window. Quiet and graceful as I could, I slipped over the sill and onto the broad, flat roof of the porch. The lopsided moon peeped through the triple cedar trees at the corner of the house as I stretched out on my back and looked up at the familiar stars.

The night before I'd shared a motel room with Mercer who, like a true Southern gentleman, insisted I take the bed. Just as insistently, I resisted, saying with perfect truth that I was more comfortable on the floor in my sleeping bag. I think he thought I thought he might try something, but I could see he was too deviled by his ghosts to be interested in getting laid. I didn't let on that I could hear bits and pieces of what they were trying to say to him. He finally managed to block them out of his own hearing long enough to fall asleep, and he didn't have any interest in inviting them to invade his dreams. I just ignored them.

Most people think hearing voices is the equivalent of being crazy. Despite what the doctors and social workers at the hospital tried to tell me, it isn't true. Some of us just naturally hear what's out there to hear. It can be disconcerting if you aren't used to it, and sometimes even when you are. People who were mean in life are just as mean in death. Some of the things dead people say to the living who have no defense against them is enough to make me wish they were alive so I could kill them again. The best thing for people beset with ghosts like that is to let the doctors muffle their hearing before the mean dead ones convince their victims to kill themselves or someone else.

A woman at the hospital, Sabina, was the exact opposite of Mercer. He drank to kill the voices; Sabina only heard them when she was dead drunk. Since she was an alcoholic, that presented a problem. Watching her go through the DTs the first week she was on my ward was enough to convince me to never take a drink of anything stronger than sweet tea or water. The suffering she endured, oh, my Lord. Shaking and sweating and seeing things the doctors thought weren't there, wishing she could die, or better yet, have a drink and then die. After she dried out and got herself together, they turned her loose. She was back two weeks later to go through it all over again.

Lorcan, the fellow whose caravan I shared for a while before he roasted himself and my poor snakes, liked his whiskey and used to get irritated because I wouldn't sit and have a dram with him. I've danced in front of more drunk men than I can count and never saw anything romantic about having a glass of wine or friendly beer with one of them. I like to keep my wits about me so nothing and no one can sneak up on me. Besides, I got a feeling I'd be a mean drunk or a morose one, and just don't want to find out for sure.

I was halfway asleep when the murmur of voices brought me back to full consciousness, human voices from the window on the far side of my own. Curious, I slid across the roof on my bottom to where I could hear better. Holier-than-thou Delilah would surely have disapproved of eavesdropping, but she'd never lived a life where every bit of information counted toward preparedness and safety. I crouched in the darkness a couple of feet from the window and recognized the rumble of John Luther's voice chastising Wreath.

"You embarrassed me in front of company, woman. You talked to me like you are my master instead of the other way around."

I couldn't make out Wreath's reply.

"Do not make excuses. You submit. Now."

Silence. Thinking the episode was over, I started to crawl back across the roof to my own window. The sound of leather slapping flesh propelled me to my feet. Illuminated by the dim light of a single table lamp, John Luther stood, tall and grim, with a leather belt held over his head. The next second, he brought it down across the naked buttocks of the woman laying facedown across the bed.

I gaped for a moment, too shocked to move, then ran across the porch roof on my toes to my own room. The voices were howling in both ears as I ducked inside the window.

Hush, I silently hissed at them. I'm not running away, so just hush!

I grabbed my backpack off the chair and dug into the front pocket for the fist-sized rock I kept there in case I needed to scare off a dog or crack a would-be rapist over the head. Grasping it hard in my hand, I climbed back out onto the porch roof in time to hear another blow and the low strangled moan of a woman in pain who was trying to not alarm her children. Without another thought, I hurled the rock through the window. It struck John Luther above one eye and sent him reeling backward into the wall, hands clasped across his bleeding face.

I didn't dare wait to see what happened next. I ran across the roof, ducked through my own window, and flung myself into the too-soft bed, heart beating so loud that it almost drowned out the chorus in my head. A split second later, John Luther roared in pained fury, cursing the rock thrower with words I didn't think a preacher ought to know, much less use. The door of the room next door slammed open, and feet ran toward the bathroom. Wreath, no doubt, rushing to get towels and bandages to care for her husband's wounds while her own went unacknowledged. All along the hall, doors opened as alarmed family members called to each other, wanting to know what had happened. I got out of bed, knees trembling, and peeked out my own door, rubbing my eyes as if I'd just woken up.

CHAPTER 7
WREATH

❦

Wreath Hughley had been a pretty teenager with thick brown hair, big hazel eyes, and a nicely curved figure. An only child, she was perfectly cherished. People pointed her out to their own children as a shining example of Southern womanhood. She laughed readily, blushed at compliments, and took religious matters seriously. This might've been enough to make her peers despise her, but Wreath also had the ability to make other people feel comfortable with themselves and with her. She was one of the most popular girls at Columbus High School.

Once in a while, it got to be too much for her. She'd plead a headache, accept aspirin and a cold cloth from her mother, go to bed, and lay in the twilight of her bedroom, wondering why she felt so empty. Sometimes she'd cry a little there in her sweetly decorated room, wishing she had a sibling or two to take on part of the weight of her parents' high expectations for her. Then she'd wonder how she could be so popular and so lonesome at the same time. It was tiresome, always having to be on her best behavior, and showing interest in people when what she really wanted to do was go home and read. Were all teenaged males as hopeless as the crop at Columbus? She could've gone on far more dates than she accepted, and though she'd been offered multiple chances to wear an upperclassman's class ring, she always declined, regarding it as the high school equivalent of laying claim to property, rather than a symbol of mutual affection. She envied her cousin Mirth, who had just married a tall, handsome marine. There was some consternation about the abruptness of the rites, but Wreath found it all very romantic, especially the part where he swept her off to live in Southern California, surely a far more exciting place than Columbus, Arkansas. She stared at the ceiling and wondered if she would ever find a man as fine as Robert Larkin.

Sooner or later, her self-pity became so intense that it entered the realm of the absurd, where her sense of humor kicked into gear and saved her from herself. At that point, she climbed out of bed, combed her hair, and went out to see what had happened in the world while she was hiding from it.

When she saw John Luther Ives preach at a tent revival, she fell hard and fast. He was a good-looking man of about thirty. When he spoke of the hellfire that awaited sinners, she trembled. When he offered salvation, she was among the first on her feet, almost running down the aisle to kneel in front of him. When he laid his hand on her hair in a blessing, she thought she might faint. When he asked permission to sit with her at dinner following the sermon, she thought she'd died and gone to heaven. Under the cover of the table, he touched her hand with his and sent such a hot flood through her body that had he offered her a class ring to wear at that moment, she'd have let him put it on her finger without a second thought.

John Luther's church was one of the small vaguely Pentecostal sects that sprang up throughout the South during the awakening that began in Wales at the beginning of the twentieth century and spread across the western world as the Welsh Revival. Wreath held her breath when John Luther approached her father, asking for permission to court her formally. Both her parents were lifelong Southern Baptists, and she was afraid John Luther's religious affiliation might count against him in their eyes. He had recently returned from missionary work in Appalachia to take over shep-

herding his father's flock after that worthy man succumbed to a
heart attack right in the middle of what people agreed was one of
the finest sermons he ever preached.

To Wreath's delight and relief, her father granted John Luther
the right to court her, first in the presence of her parents in the
front room of their modest home. When they felt they knew him
well enough, they allowed him to escort her to church where she
sat in the front pew and listened to him speak as though her place
in heaven depended on it. At long last, her parents agreed to allow
the couple to meet under secular conditions: dinner at the Main
Street Diner in Hope.

A date, Wreath thought in ecstasy. *A Real Date.*

She started getting ready hours earlier than she usually did before a date, trying on every outfit in her closet before settling on
a dress that brought out the green in her hazel eyes. She washed
her hair and set it in pin curls the night before, then combed it
into rippling waves just a few minutes before John Luther was
scheduled to arrive. She wouldn't have dared to cut her dressing
ritual so close had John Luther not been one of the most punctual
people she'd ever met, never being more than a minute or two
early and never a single second late. She polished her shoes and
smoothed brand-new stockings up her legs, hooking them carefully onto her garter belt. With the war shortages, a new pair of
stockings was a treasure. She had John Luther to thank for these.
She had almost died when she opened the envelope he slipped
her after church. Stockings were a shockingly inappropriate gift
from a man; chocolates and flowers only, she'd been told her whole
life. But she was tired of drawing lines up the back of her legs so
she looked like she was wearing stockings, and he'd slipped her
the package so discretely. She hooked the last garter and thought
the formula for proper gifts surely must be different when the pre-
senter was a Man of God with honorable intentions toward her.

John Luther brought flowers for their first date, a small taste-
ful corsage consisting of a sweetheart rose and a wisp of baby's
breath. Her parents watched approvingly as he pinned it to the

collar of her dress, then draped her wrap over her shoulders. He shook her father's hand, promised to have her back early, and escorted Wreath to his car.

The road between Columbus and Hope was rutted dirt and John Luther had to drive slowly. That was fine with Wreath; any time she spent with him was precious. When they reached Crossroads, he pulled off to the side of the road. She looked at him inquiringly. He took a deep breath.

"Wreath, may I kiss you?"

Oh, my, she thought, trying not to sway in his direction. Distrusting her voice, she nodded. He leaned toward her, so near that she could smell his after shave. She closed her eyes and lifted her face to his. The kiss was as soft as the brush of a bird's wing. He drew back a bit, just a bit, and asked, "May I hold your hands and kiss you again?"

Not so soft this time, but longer and more satisfying. When he pulled away, he smiled at her and returned his hands to the steering wheel. She felt lightheaded. High school boys didn't kiss like that. Even the best of them lacked finesse. Her mother was concerned that John Luther was thirteen years older than she was, but at that moment, Wreath felt the age difference was nothing but an advantage.

At the Main Street Diner, Wreath was too starstruck to be hungry, but she chose a hamburger and cottage cheese dish while John Luther tucked into a rare steak and a pile of French fries that spilled off the edge of the plate. He dipped one into ketchup and held it out to her.

"It's good. Go on, take a bite."

She opened her mouth and let him tuck the long slender piece of potato inside, as if they were enacting some kind of sacrament. After dinner, he ordered a single chocolate malt and two straws. He came around to her side of the table and slid onto the bench seat next to her. They drank the milkshake slowly, their heads almost touching. In between sips, John Luther told her about his plans for his church and for his congregation.

"My father was a good man, but as he grew older, he became lax in attending to the spiritual needs of his congregation. Allow just a small sin to slip in, and it opens the way for larger sins to follow. I have begun counseling sessions for those members of the flock who have slipped away from righteousness in their personal lives: men who have heard the call of the demon Alcohol, women who break their promises to love, honor, and obey." He looked deep into her eyes. "You would never break a promise to me, would you, my little bird?"

"Never," she whispered.

He smiled at her, pushed the empty glass away, and slid off the bench. "I keep my promises, too, and I promised to have you home early."

He held out his hand to her. She took it and let him lead her to the car. He held open her door, then as she slid into the seat, asked, "Did you wear the stockings tonight?"

Wreath blushed. "My mother'd have a fit if she knew, but . . . yes, I'm wearin' 'em."

"Let me see."

She extended one leg and drew her skirt up so that he could admire the curve of her calf and ankle. He smiled down at her and said, "I hope you'll accept more gifts from me."

She laughed and shook her head. "You shouldn't oughta give me presents. I just enjoy your company."

"And I enjoy yours."

He stopped the car at Crossroads again. She made no resistance when he slid across the seat and took her into his arms. When she felt the touch of his tongue, she parted her lips. When he pressed his chest against her, she arched her back and pressed in return. Then his fingers were at her breast, searching for an erect nipple.

"Stop," she breathed. "Please don't do that."

"Has anyone touched you like this before?"

"No. No. Please don't . . . please . . . oh, my dear Lord . . ."

"My innocent little bird. This is but a taste of the joy God gave men and women to share." His lips brushed hers as he spoke, and she ecstatically drew his breath into her own lungs. His big hand engulfed her small breast, kneading and stroking. Her head fell back, and he pressed his mouth to the hollow at the base of her throat. Wreath's senses spun and she closed her eyes against the unexpected vertigo.

This is wrong, she thought wildly. *I know it's wrong, but dear Lord, I will die if he stops.*

She looked down as he kissed the cleft of her bosom. How had those upper buttons come undone? Automatically, she lifted her hand to close her gaping bodice. As her fingertips brushed his cheek, he lifted his face, and his eyes gleamed in the dark like beacons to a world she had barely dared dream of. Her breath came shallow and fast between her parted lips. He kissed her again, and at that moment, she knew she'd do whatever he asked of her.

He pulled mouth and hands away from her and slid out of her reach. Wreath stared at him, shocked by the sudden desertion. He looked at her tumbled hair, her flushed cheeks, her half-exposed breasts, and said roughly, "Old Eve is strong in you, my little bird. Oh, what you almost led me to do."

Confused and embarrassed by his words, Wreath hunched her shoulders and turned aside to do up her bodice with fingers that shook so hard that she couldn't get the small buttons through the holes. His hands cupped her shoulders and turned her back toward him. She brushed away the tears that dampened her cheeks.

"Let me help you," he said gently, and did the buttons up as adroitly as he'd undone them minutes earlier. "Ah, little bird, you are completely innocent, are you not? And yet in your innocence, you led both of us into a situation we are not ready for . . . yet."

He found her brush in her handbag. As she neatened herself, he spoke to her gently. "I must teach you to control your passions, Wreath. If you give into them, no man can fail to follow you down the broad path to hell. There, little bird, don't cry. I forgive you. Come here." He put his arms around her, pressing her head to his shoulder as he whispered words of comfort.

"I'm sorry," she whimpered into the folds of his coat. "I didn't mean to hurt you."

He gave her a last squeeze and slid under the steering wheel. When she started to move across the seat to the window, he hooked a hand under her elbow and pulled her close to his side. He patted her knee reassuringly before starting the car engine. Grateful for this sign of understanding and forgiveness, Wreath told herself that in the future, she would behave like the lady her mama had raised her to be and not the shameless hoyden she'd acted that night. As they drove back to Columbus in silence, she sat close to him on the bench seat, his right arm tight around her, his left hand on the steering wheel.

They settled into a routine. Each Monday night, John Luther settled himself into a living room chair and spent an hour talking with her parents about everything from the Bible to Columbus High School's basketball team. The second hour, he and Wreath retired to the front porch swing, holding hands, talking softly, and watching the neighbors sitting on their own porches. Wednesday nights, she attended prayer meetings at his church. She walked home alone afterward because on Wednesday nights he counseled the erring among his flock. Friday evening, he arrived in his car to take her to dinner, for a drive, or for a walk in the long summer twilight. Sundays found her sitting in the front pew at the Church of the Flock of the Good Shepherd, listening to him preach from the pulpit. That there was an understanding between them became common knowledge. Wreath put aside her pale pink lipstick, gathered her hair into a modest bun worn at the nape of her neck, and began to wear dresses of quiet colors and longer hemlines.

One day at the beginning of summer, he took her on a rare Saturday date. She packed a picnic lunch with the help of her mother, and they drove out to the banks of a picturesque lake overhung with graceful oaks and starred with wildflowers.

"We got it to ourselves," John Luther said, spreading the old quilt from his trunk over the hardpacked dirt. He stretched out on his back and patted the space next to him. She sat down a little way away, feeling discomforted for no reason she could name. He smiled at her and patted the ground at his side firmly. She edged closer. When he held out his arms, she lay down with him, her head on his shoulder.

"Do you take Communion at your church?"

"You know I do, John Luther."

"And does it make you feel close to your Lord and Savior?"

"Yes," she whispered.

"Do you know of the communion between men and women?" His hand crept over one breast. She closed her eyes, trembling at his touch, feeling it was wrong, yet wanting him to go on touching her.

"We are going to take communion together, my princess."

She looked at him then, wide-eyed. "What do you mean?"

"We're going to take communion together. A special holy communion."

He got up and walked to his car, leaving her sitting on the quilt, scared and confused. Her breath came in short gasps, and she wondered if she should slip away while his back was turned.

Where would I go? Why am I so scared?

When he came back, he was carrying a long slim bottle with a cork in it and a crystal glass. He sat back down, filled the glass with a clear liquid from the bottle, and held it out to her.

"Drink this."

"What is it?"

"Communion wine," he said and held it to her lips. She took a sip and made a face. He shook his head. "When we marry, Wreath, you will promise to love, honor, and obey me. Don't you think you should start practicing now?"

"Are you asking me to marry you, John Luther?"

"Drink the wine, Wreath." He tilted the glass against her mouth.

She drank, mostly to keep him from spilling the liquid onto her blouse. It was curiously bitter, unlike the grape juice provided for Communion at the Baptist Church. When the first glass was empty, John Luther poured her another.

"Why aren't you drinking any?" she asked, slurring her words a little. "Don't you want some?"

"I have no need of it," John Luther said, and handed her the brimming glass.

Wreath looked around at the lake and its flowered banks as she obediently swallowed another mouthful of wine. "S'pretty here. How come I never saw s'pretty here? Ooo, everything just went sideways."

John Luther grabbed the glass before she dropped it. Setting it aside, he put an arm around her shoulder and eased her down onto the quilt. She stared up into the leaves overhead, humming to herself tunelessly, watching the noontime sunlight flicker in the gentle breeze. The world slid sideways again. She closed her eyes and slid with it into a very odd dream. She seemed to be losing her panties. Where were they going? She tried to catch them, but her arms lay at her sides, useless as wet ropes. How funny. She giggled, and the silly sound made her giggle again before the dream disintegrated into darkness.

"Wreath. Wake up. It is time to go home."

Disoriented and dizzy, Wreath clung to John Luther's arm as he dragged her from the depths of sleep and hauled her up off the ground. Instead of shining through the tree leaves overhead, the sun hovered above the west end of the lake. She moaned, squeezing her eyes shut against its merciless glare. Her mouth tasted like metal and her muscles had apparently turned to gelatin while she slept. Halfway to her feet, nausea overwhelmed her. She collapsed back onto her hands and knees. He wrapped her hair around his fist and held it away from her face until she finished throwing up.

"Oh, my poor head," she moaned, pressing her fingers against her throbbing temples. John Luther slipped his hand under her arm and patted it with tender reassurance.

"You have been very ill, little bird. Something you ate, perhaps. I let you sleep as long as I could, but now we must go."

He guided her to the car, neatly tucked her onto the front seat, and warned her to not soil the upholstery. Wreath whimpered as the big car bumped down the dirt road, each bump threatening to force her brain out the top of her head. John Luther stopped the car twice to let her throw up. In front of her parents' house, he helped her from the car with conspicuous solicitousness, supporting most of her weight as they mounted the porch steps. Exclaiming in alarm, her mother ran out the front door.

"Food poisoning, I think," John Luther said in a weak voice. "The chicken salad . . . She has been delirious, Mrs. Hughley. I don't . . ." He put a shaking hand to his own head.

"You go on home, John Luther, and take care of yourself. We can manage here. C'mon, sugar."

"Food poisoning," Wreath moaned as her mother helped her up the stairs. "Oh, Mama, I feel so bad."

She sat on the bed and pressed her palms to her eyes while her mother found her nightgown. Who thought food poisoning could come with a terrible dream? *What kind of person am I to have such a terrible dream about John Luther?*

"Go ahead and wash your face off, sugar. I'll run down and get you an ice pack and some Seven-Up and crackers. That'll help."

The mention of food sent Wreath running for the bathroom, but there was nothing left in her stomach. Longing for the cool sheets of her bed, she undressed and saw traces of blood on her legs. As if the horrible headache and nausea weren't enough, now she could look forward to menstrual cramps as well. She cleaned herself off, pulled the nightgown over her head, and rinsed the blood out of her panties so it wouldn't stain. Weeping with misery, she stuffed her discarded clothing into the laundry hamper and staggered off to bed where she stayed all night and for most of the next day.

Monday evening, John Luther arrived promptly at seven

o'clock. He sympathetically noted her pale cheeks, inquired about her health, and informed her that he had fully recovered himself. After a few minutes' conversation with her parents, he led her out to the front porch swing. He held her hand as he always did and spoke of church matters and the value of faith, charity, and chastity. Still humiliated by her illness and by the appalling dream that repeated itself each time she fell asleep, Wreath cast her eyes down and barely said a word. When he left, he gave her a chaste kiss on the cheek and squeezed her hand affectionately. She stood at the top of the steps to watch him drive away, digging her fingers into the flesh where he'd pressed his lips.

He called Wednesday morning to say he'd been called away to preach on the summer revival circuit and wouldn't be able to visit her for a while. She politely wished him a good trip and hung up the phone, relieved that she wouldn't have to watch him lead the Wednesday prayer meeting or keep their Friday night date. When she duly relayed the information to her parents, her mother said, "Well, it doesn't hurt to have some time away from each other."

Once a week, John Luther sent her a letter, proper, respectful, nothing that she couldn't share with her parents who enjoyed hearing about sinners saved and The Word spread far and wide. He apologized for not being able to supply her with a return address since his schedule was apt to change at a moment's notice. Enveloped in the lethargy that had gripped her since her illness, she shrugged it off. What would she write to him, anyway?

Halfway through the summer, she missed a second period and her breasts began to ache. When John Luther had spoken of holy communion between a man and a woman, she'd thought he meant a private prenuptial ceremony to join their hearts and spirits. Now she knew he'd joined his body to hers as well. Panic routed lethargy, and she wondered what on earth would become of her. Every night, huddled on her knees beside her bed, she beseeched God to bring John Luther home so he could make everything right.

This is my fault, she thought miserably. *I shouldn't have worn a dress that day. I should've told him I didn't want the wine. I shouldn't have laid down with him on the quilt. I didn't mean to tempt him. I didn't. I've always been such a good girl. What happened to me?*

The prospect of bearing an illegitimate child terrified her. Sarah, a girl at Columbus High School, had abruptly disappeared from classes during Wreath's freshman year. Her parents said that an ailing aunt in Little Rock needed her niece's help, but everyone knew that Sarah had fallen into sin. When she returned home a year later, whispers followed her wherever she went. No one wanted to be her friend and no good man would ever marry her because she was spoiled goods. Wreath had felt sorry for her, but she'd turned away, too, afraid of soiling her own reputation if she showed the least compassion for the girl. She'd been relieved when Sarah dropped out of school and returned to Little Rock permanently.

I will reap what I sowed, Wreath thought. *This is my punishment for being unkind.*

In all her life, Wreath's parents had never shouted at her, never raised a hand to her. When faced with her childish transgressions, her father's weapon was disappointed silence; her mother employed gentle shaming. What would they do when faced with the humiliation of an unwed and pregnant daughter? When she missed a third period, Wreath wondered what it would be like to walk into Red River and let the current take her.

John Luther came home at summer's end and called her to invite her to the Wednesday night prayer meeting at his church. Weak with relief, she went. Afterward, she stood at his side by the big double doors, smiling politely at departing parishioners while he shook hands with the men and boys, and gave each woman and girl the kiss of peace on her forehead. When the last set of car lights disappeared down the road, he finally turned to her.

"Come with me," he said, tucking her hand into the crook of his elbow. He led her to the small office building behind the sanctuary. The shades were drawn against the warmth of the night; the thick walls and high ceilings held in some small measure of coolness. He lit a kerosene lantern and moved to the door. To her surprise, he closed and locked it. Then, at long last, he took her in his arms.

"I've missed you," he said into her hair.

She stood on tiptoe and whispered into his ear. He smiled down at her and kissed her forehead. " 'If they cannot contain, let them marry, for it is better to marry than to burn.' I will marry you. Wreath."

She flung her arms around him and buried her burning face in his shirtfront. *How could I think he would forsake me? He'll take care of me.*

He tilted her face to his and she opened her lips to his probing tongue. When his fingers moved down the front of her dress, unfastening the long row of pearl buttons, she didn't resist. Her dress slid to the floor followed by her slip. He unhooked her bra, then slid her panties down her legs, trailing his lips along her gently curved stomach, making her shudder. As he rose to his feet, he unbuckled his belt and pulled it from the loops. Lips parted, eyes shining in the lantern light, she waited for him to begin their communion.

"You enticed me to sin the day the child was conceived." At his cold words, Wreath's breath stopped in her lungs. With the belt dangling from his hand, he walked behind her, lifted the mass of her hair, and bit the nape of her neck hard enough to hurt. "Now you entice me to sin again. I will not suffer a wanton wife."

An hour later, he walked her home, kissed her at the door, and disappeared back down the road toward the church. Her parents had already gone to bed, sparing her the effort of pretending everything was all right. She slipped into her nightgown and eased herself into bed, an engagement ring on her left hand and three raw welts disfiguring the soft skin of her bottom.

With no other alternative to the shame of bearing a child out of wedlock, Wreath eloped with John Luther on their next date night. She suffered her first miscarriage three weeks later.

CHAPTER 8
WREATH

❧❦❧

Wreath flung open the medicine cabinet above the sink, grabbing iodine, bandages, and a handful of old, worn washrags. Her hands trembled so that she dropped the iodine; the plastic lid hit the edge of the sink and shattered, sending red-brown liquid all over everything. She moaned, torn between the beating she'd take if he saw the mess and the one she'd get if she didn't get back to tend him immediately. She took a half-hearted swipe at the floor, smearing the mess everywhere.

A gentle hand took the washrags and bandages from her. Mercer helped her to her feet and patted her back. "It's okay, Mama. Just sit down and take a deep breath."

Wreath knew it would be hours before she could sit, though John Luther hadn't had time to get in more than three or four licks before the rock stopped the beating. "I gotta get back to him. He's hurt. Somebody threw a rock through the window. Hit him in the face."

Mercer automatically turned to go to the wounded, but Wreath seized his arm, shaking her head. "No, son. He'd be so mad to have you see him that way."

"I can help," Genevieve said from the door. She smiled reassuringly at the frightened woman. "Won't be the first time I pretend not to see a man shed tears. C'mon, Miss Wreath. You and me'll take care of Mr. Ives. Mercer can clean up the bathroom."

She tucked the extra medical supplies Mercer found in the cabinet under one elbow and slid the opposite hand under Wreath's trembling arm. Out in the hall, the rest of the family was too frightened to move from their respective doorways. Genevieve looked coolly at Delilah and nodded to Jared as she and Wreath passed the couple. Jared jerked his head in return, pulled his wife back into their room, and shut the door. Across the hall, Jezzie protectively wrapped both arms around her little sister.

"It's okay, girls," Wreath said, forcing a steadiness into her voice that she was far from feeling. "Go on back to bed."

"What happened?" Jezzie hissed as she guided Leah back into the room.

"Someone threw a rock through the window and hit your daddy," Wreath said.

"Hit him with a rock?" Jezzie looked from her mother to Genevieve. "He bad hurt?"

"Me and Genevieve'll take care of him. He'll be fine. Y'all go on back to bed now."

Jezzie turned to follow Leah, but not before Genevieve saw, and Wreath pretended not to see, the pleased smile that curved the corners of the girl's mouth.

John Luther was sitting on the edge of the bed holding a bloody pillowcase to his forehead. He made no comment as the two women came into the room. Genevieve carefully pulled the cloth away from the wound. An inch-long cut gaped across his forehead, neatly bisecting his left eyebrow and still bleeding. She took the dampened cloth Wreath handed her and pressed it against the wound to stem the flow of blood. John Luther shot a look at his wife.

"You ought to be tending me, not this child," he said.

"Mr. Ives, she was so upset at you being hurt that I asked her to let me help," Genevieve said. "I have gentle hands, I promise."

He aimed a final glare at Wreath, closed his eyes, and gave himself up to Genevieve's ministrations.

"Looks worse than it is," Genevieve said once she'd managed to get the blood stopped. "Not much padding right there on your eyebrow, so it probably hurts like the dickens. You could use a couple of stitches to keep it from scarring."

"No stitches," John Luther said sharply. "Vanity is not my vice, and I am not concerned about a scar."

Wreath forbore to mention that her husband dreaded the prick of a needle worse than almost anything in his life. The time he'd been forced to have a tetanus shot after stepping on a rusty nail, he'd passed out cold.

"Up to you," Genevieve said, "but it wouldn't be a bad idea to tape the edges of the cut together to keep it clean."

"That will do," John Luther answered with great dignity.

Genevieve left the room to collect the cloth tape from the bathroom. When she returned, she made quick work of the taping and laid a large Band-Aid over her work to keep everything clean and in place. Job finished, she retired to the hall while Wreath helped her husband out of his bloodied clothing and into a pair of clean pajamas. Mercer was leaning against the wall waiting for her. He gestured toward the stairs and Genevieve nodded. She followed him to the first floor and out onto the side porch on the opposite side of the house from his parents' room. They sat down in the metal glider side by side and looked out into the night.

"Mama okay?" Mercer asked in a low voice.

"I think so."

"How's the old bastard?"

"He'll do."

"Any idea what happened?"

"You know as much as me. Someone threw a rock in the window, and he got in the way."

Mercer thought about that. "Somebody has a hell of an arm. Ground to second story is a long way to throw a rock with enough force to bust a man's head."

"Any baseball pitchers you know might be mad at him?"

"Not offhand."

They sat and gazed out into the dark yard until a light went on in the parlor window off the porch. Mercer turned around to look through the window.

"It's Mama. Looks like she's making up a bed on the couch. Guess he wants the bed to himself tonight."

Genevieve peered through the glass. "That couch is too narrow for anyone to rest on. I'll see you tomorrow, Mercer."

She went in the front door and found Wreath spreading a sheet across a small settee.

"What you doing, Miss Wreath?"

The woman tightened the belt of her gray housecoat and smiled wanly at her guest. "John Luther likes to sleep by himself when he doesn't feel good. I'm gonna bed down right here."

"No, ma'am, Miss Wreath," Genevieve said. She scooped up the sheet and pillow Wreath had just put down. "That bed in the room you gave me has a trundle. You come with me."

Wreath acquiesced but insisted that Genevieve take the main bed while she herself took the trundle. Genevieve didn't protest. She was happy to have gotten Wreath into a real bed without an argument. She pulled the trundle out and climbed over the foot of the bed onto her own mattress. The older woman turned out the light before taking off her housecoat and easing herself into bed. They lay in silence for a while, each thinking her own thoughts, then Wreath whispered, "You look just like your mama did when she was your age."

Chapter 9

Wreath

✦✦✦

"How long have you known who I am?" Genevieve turned onto her side and looked down in the darkness at the woman on the trundle bed.

"Moment I laid eyes on you, I knew you were Mirth's daughter, Oleana. Your hair's a different color from hers, and your eyes aren't quite the same as hers were, but when you smile, it's like seeing that sweet girl back here with me."

Wreath shifted into a different position, trying to take pressure off her abused bottom. She was afraid the next morning her nightgown would be stuck to the oozing welts, and she worried how she'd explain it if Genevieve noticed. *Bad fall*, she decided. *Fell on that old gas heater and hurt myself in the shock of seeing him get hit with that rock.*

The moon moved in line with the open window and illuminated Genevieve's face above hers. "Tell me about my mama and you."

"Your mama and me, we were double first cousins. Our mamas married twin brothers. Her and her family lived over to Washington and we lived in Columbus, but we'd all get together of a Sunday at Granny and Granpa's house near Crossroads. Mirth was a little older than me, two years and a bit, but we were like sisters to one another. All the cousins on our daddies' side lived up around Caddo Gap, so we hardly ever saw them. Surely was lonesome after she married your daddy and left home. We didn't see them again until after Robert got hurt."

Genevieve caught her breath. "He got hurt? He never said a thing about it."

Wreath sighed. "No, Robert wasn't one to talk about himself, and if anyone was to ask about the war, he shut up all together. Mirth told me he got wounded in the Battle of Tarawa and was in the hospital for months before they let him come home. Head injury, I think. He had a hard time rememberin' things. Sometimes heard stuff that wasn't there. He got better over the years, but they wouldn't let him fight anymore."

"How'd he meet Mama?"

"He came through here in 1940 on his way from Alabama to a Marine base in California. Just happened to be passin' through Columbus on a Sunday, saw the church was open, and went on in. Mirth was singin' in the choir, and I guess he thought she was an angel." Wreath laughed softly. Genevieve realized it was the first time she'd heard her laugh. Had she even seen her smile? "He wasn't here hardly a week when they up and got married. Her folks about to had a fit, but Mirth said she couldn't live without him. Broke my heart to see her ride off with him an hour after they swapped rings, but he had to get to California and had already stayed longer than he should have done. I never saw two happier people than them."

"She used to say it was love at first sight," Genevieve whispered remembering the soft shine in Mama's eyes every time she looked in Papa's direction. "I didn't know they married so quick, though."

"Whirlwind courtship, folks called it. Seemed so romantic to me, her findin' a good-lookin' marine to fall in love with and sweep her off to see the world. I was about sixteen, and all I wanted was my own big romance." She shook her head ruefully. "Young girls can be so silly. John Luther took Delilah out of school when she finished ninth grade and married her off to one of his friends who was three times her age. She thought she'd died and gone to heaven until the new wore off and the dirty dishes piled up in the sink. Joe died after they'd been married five years, then John Luther married her off to Jared, Joe's younger brother. Been a lot better match. Joe was a plumb sorry husband. You married?"

"No, ma'am. Don't look to be, either. Miss Wreath, how come in all the times I stayed with Meema she never carried me to see y'all?"

"John Luther didn't like Aunt Lela. She didn't remarry after your granddaddy died, even though John Luther offered to find her a husband." The ghost of a laugh crept back into Wreath's voice. "She told him she wouldn't have any man he picked for her were he to stuff the fellow with sage dressin' and serve him up on a silver platter. Lord, Aunt Lela talked back to John Luther every time they got around each other, and he usually came out on the short end of the stick. He called her unwomanly and forbade me to see her and be exposed to her sinful ways. After that, the only people he'd let me visit with were folks from our own church, and them only durin' church occasions."

"How about your parents?"

Wreath shook her head, looking across the dark room, remembering. "When we first got married, he tried to draw them into our church, but they were perfectly happy being Baptists. He saw they weren't gonna change and quit lettin' me go over to see them. Said Daddy was lax, had let me and Mama speak our minds, which was a sin against God. Said he was keepin' me and the children away from my folks to save us from sin. He intended our girls to learn to submit and obey, and not go yammerin' about any stray thoughts that popped into their heads. Mama'd sneak over here sometimes during the day to see me and the babies. No tellin' what would've happened had John Luther caught her here. She kept comin' until Delilah told Mama she was sinnin' against John Luther, and she was gonna tell if Mama didn't quit comin'. Lord, I don't think that girl's got a drop of my blood, though I gave birth to her. She's John Luther's daughter through and through."

Hidden in the darkness, Wreath pressed her fingers against her mouth to keep herself from saying anything else that could be taken for disloyalty to her husband. *Hush*, she told herself. *Hush. This girl doesn't need these troubles laid at her feet.* The fingers weren't enough. More words slipped past them, swept by a wave of long pent-up fear and resentment.

"I worry about Jezzie. She's not like Delilah. She enjoys school and isn't gonna want to quit at the end of this year. John Luther's already huntin' her up a husband; says she'll need someone with a strong hand. A strong hand, oh, my dear Lord." Wreath swallowed so hard that Genevieve heard the gulp. "He says she has a rebellious spirit that has to be broken, but she just wants some pretty clothes and . . . and a bicycle." *Oh, the fight they had over that bicycle*, Wreath thought.

Jezzie'd come home one afternoon from school, drenched in sweat, with the hair around her face kinked into tight curls from the humidity. Wreath was in the backyard boiling clothes in a huge iron kettle set over an open fire. The washing machine quit working a month earlier and John Luther declined to replace it, saying his mother never had such a contraption yet managed to get laundry done just fine.

"March doesn't have any business feeling like the middle of July," Jezzie said, dropping her armload of books onto a wooden lawn chair and pushing back her curls with one hand. "That stupid school district doesn't have any business dropping me off a mile from home because someone's afraid the bus will get dirty if it comes down our road."

"There's cold sweet tea in the ice box," Wreath said sympathetically. "You go get you some of that and cool off."

Jezzie sighed, picked up her books, and walked toward the house just as John Luther's car pulled through the front gate. The sight made her want to scream. At the beginning of school that year, she'd asked for a bicycle to ride between the bus stop and home. Lalie Mueller, the postmistress, said she could park it at the post office during the day. Delilah had a bicycle to run errands. Mercer had bought himself a motorcycle with money he saved up from his job at the local garage. Why shouldn't she, Jezzie, have transportation as well? John Luther had just snorted, made a remark about laziness, and walked away, the subject at an end.

The bus stopped right out in front of the church, and she'd seen her father's car when she alit from the bus. John Luther knew what time her bus arrived, yet he'd allowed her to walk over a mile in the heat when he could've easily called to her to wait for him to drive her home. She jerked open the refrigerator door and stood a moment in the cool air before lifting the tea pitcher off the shelf.

"Fill a glass with ice and pour me some of that," John Luther said as he walked in the door. She silently did as she was ordered and handed the glass to him before turning to pour her own. He downed the tea in a single draught and held the glass out. "More. It's a thirsty day."

"I know," Jessie snapped. "I just walked a mile home."

John Luther raised his eyebrows. "That is not a suitable tone to use with me."

"Daddy, I need a bicycle. I could get home in a quarter of the time, not have to spend so much time walking in the heat. I could run errands—"

"We had this conversation, Jezebel. I said no."

"I'm not asking for a car, just a plain, ordinary, secondhand bike!"

"You are lazy enough as it is, and it would be a needless expenditure of family funds."

Jezzie was hot, tired, and irritated, a bad combination. Upon being called lazy, her temper boiled up and over.

"I'm not the one who drives a car that self-same mile in both directions twice a day," she snapped. "I walk every step of that mile to the bus and every step home in all kinds of weather carrying an armload of books. Who does that make lazy?"

"Go to your room, Jezebel."

"And quit calling me Jezebel! What kind of father names his daughter Jezebel?"

John Luther took a stride forward and grabbed her arm with bruising strength. Jezzie swung at him with her other hand, the one with a glass in it. The next thing she knew, she was on the floor staring at the ceiling, wondering what in the hell just happened. John Luther grabbed her by the hair and hauled her to her feet just as Wreath ran into the room.

"John Luther—"

"Shut up, woman."

He dragged Jezzie up the stairs so fast that she stumbled and fell. He didn't stop long enough to let her get to her feet, just hauled her to the door of her bedroom and dropped her in a heap.

"Get her ready," he growled at Wreath.

"Oh, Jezzie, child, what have you done now?" Wreath moaned, helping the girl to her feet and leading her into the room she shared with Leah. She closed the door and put her arms around her daughter, who began to weep.

"Oh, Mama, don't let him. Please don't let him."

"Oh, child, how am I going to stop him?"

She helped Jezzie out of her school clothes and into a thread-bare dress that fell almost to her ankles.

"I won't!" cried Jezzie. "It's not fair!"

"Don't fight, sugar. You know it's worse when you fight."

Wreath sat down on the bed and held out her arms. Jezzie hesitated a moment, thinking about fleeing out the window and down the cedar tree at the end of the porch roof. She remembered what happened the last time she tried that.

A door slammed down the hall and heavy footsteps came their way.

"Mama?"

Wreath looked at her helplessly.

The footsteps came to a halt outside the door. With a gasp, Jezzie fell to her knees in front of her mother and buried her face in the soft cotton apron, still damp with steam from the washpot. Wreath gripped the child's hands in hers, the closest she could come to an embrace. The door swung open, then closed with a click. Jezzie gripped a fold of the apron between her teeth and squeezed her eyes and mouth shut.

You will not make a sound, she told herself fiercely. *Not a sound.*

Someone lifted the skirt of her dress and draped it over her head and shoulders. A brief pause, an intake of breath, and the belt whistled through the air.

Wreath gasped, remembering. She rubbed her eyes hard. All that punishment over a bicycle. No. No. She couldn't tell this quiet kinswoman that. She took a steadying breath and went on.

"Jezzie's smart. John Luther doesn't like to see her with her nose in a book. Says it'll make her sterile or crazy. She studies up in her bed after we all go to sleep. I gave her a flashlight to read by, buy her batteries with my egg and milk money. She's safe so long as she keeps it under the covers. John Luther doesn't get up once he's gone to bed for the night. I don't know how I'm gonna convince him to let her stay in school instead of marryin' some old man three times her age. You really gonna help her with her studies? John Luther says as long as she's in school she better be a credit to him and get good grades. She doesn't understand algebra, though, and he already whipped her once for failing a big test."

"I'll help her even if I have to climb under the bedcovers with her to do it," Genevieve promised. "He whipped her for failing a test?"

"Yes, ma'am, he did. That girl has had more than her share of whippin's. John Luther only had to paddle Delilah and Leah once to put the fear of God in 'em; they don't mess with him anymore. It's like punishment just makes Jezzie more determined to misbehave. Mercer was that way, too. Last time John Luther whipped Mercer, he had to wrestle him to the ground and tie him up first. He was so mad by the time he got Mercer wrestled down that he striped every part of that boy's body, then left him lyin' facedown on the ground awhile to consider his sins before lettin' him up. Next thing I knew, Mercer was off to Texarkana to enlist in the Navy. He came home to tell me and the younger girls goodbye while John Luther was doin' counselin' sessions at the church, then we never saw him again till he come home a few days ago. Him and John Luther are already buttin' heads, so I don't look for him to stay long."

Wreath's soliloquy continued for some time, low and flat, talking about the abuse of herself and her children the way some women talk about moles in the garden or moths eating good winter clothes. Genevieve listened silently, her heart one big ache in her chest. Wreath's voice gradually weakened and faded away into the soft rhythmic breathing of sleep.

Genevieve turned onto her side to look out at the moonlit night. After considering an array of options, she decided that the very best thing she could do for this beaten-down woman and her children was to kill the son of a bitch she was married to.

CHAPTER 10

GENEVIEVE

❧

I don't remember much about those first few months in the hospital. I think I spent a lot of time in my bed with a pillow pulled over my head, just enough space around the edges to let me keep on breathing. The only reason I didn't spend more time there is the nurses and orderlies would pull me out of bed and slap my face to get me moving in the morning. Then I'd shuffle off down the hall to sit in the grim common area with the other hopeless idiots and crazies until it was time to go back to bed.

Sometimes I wonder what it would've been like if a single person had bothered to lift the pillow off my face, and instead of slapping me had said, "Hello? You in there? Give me your hand and I'll help you out." If a person is in the hospital with a broken back or kidney problems, someone usually thinks to send flowers, maybe make a visit out of curiosity or a sense of duty, if not genuine compassion. No one orders flowers for mental illness. No one sends cards saying, *Don't dwell on thoughts of suicide, hope you'll be back on your feet real soon.* No one cares when dying seems a reasonable alternative to living. No, that's not quite right. Suicide is a real inconvenience for people who work in mental hospitals. The paperwork alone could mean hours of overtime, and someone has to be held responsible for not calling a suicide watch soon enough.

I decided against suicide early on, simply because I wasn't sure what waited for me on the other side of that line. Meema believed that heaven was a place that looked just like her favorite parts of earth, filled with all the people she'd ever loved.

"If there are many mansions in my father's house," she told me after the house blew away, "then I want my old one back. I want to walk up that driveway, hear the gravel crunch under my feet, and smell the crepe myrtle. It'll be real early when I get there, just before dawn when the sky's blackest. There'll be a light in the kitchen window and the scent of good coffee on the air. I'll run up them two steps and through the screen door to the back porch. I'll hear chairs scrape the floor in the kitchen where they'll all be waiting on me, your mama and Papaw especially, but my mama and daddy, too, and all the rest of 'em that's been gone so long. It'll be a great day in the morning when I walk back into my own kitchen and into the arms of my people."

I hadn't liked to hear her talk that way. Knowing Meema was looking forward to going someplace where I couldn't follow for years, if ever, terrified me. If Meema was gone, and Papa wouldn't have me . . . then what? Well, I guess I found that out, all right.

I never knew most of those people Meema used to talk about; they were just names and stories and stones in the graveyard to me. Some of them might've had voices I heard over the years, but if so, they never identified themselves. I reckon the ones I did know—Meema, Mama, and Papa, if he's dead and not just out there driving a truck and ignoring me—well, they'll be glad to see me . . . I think. I can't help but wonder if after so many years we'll know each other, if all the old feelings of love and recognition will come back like a gift from God, or if after the first hellos, we'll all just stand around the kitchen drinking coffee and making conversation about the weather in heaven because we don't know what else to say. Mama wouldn't approve of how I've lived. I know she wouldn't. And if Papa is there waiting on me . . . well, hell, am I supposed to run up and hug his neck just because we're related, when he went off and left me in Kingdom Come and never even bothered to let me know if he was dead or not? Or will it be like when I was little and he was my hero and we'd drive through the night telling stories?

You'd think hearing voices the way I do, I could just ask someone. Well, it doesn't work that way. I don't get to hear just whoever I want to. It's not like a radio. I can't tune into whatever station I want to listen to. To this day, I have no idea why some ghosts come through the static loud and clear, and the ones I want to talk to most of all are never heard from at all. Even Meema disappeared after she helped me with the grandmother rattlesnake.

Anyway, I didn't lift a finger to put an end to my mortal self in the hospital or any other time. At some point, I took the pillow off my face myself, and went out into the halls and social rooms of the hospital on my own. Lord knows, I'd had enough slapping and manhandling to do me.

After I left Alabama, I had some hard decisions to make about who I was and who I wanted to become. I didn't figure it would do me any good to let on that I spent my adolescence in the Alabama State Mental Hospital, or that I came from folks who were called *country* by charitable folks and *poor white* by others. Nothing wrong with being country or poor white, but I saw early on that not having good table manners and saying *he don't* and *I ain't* doesn't get a person very far, even in a hospital where good manners are not emphasized.

I once had a roommate from Mobile, crazy as a pinwheel quilt but elegant, my Lord, she even made nuttiness look cultured. Her name was Diadema, Dema for short. She was a few years older than me, with big wide brown eyes and a nervous tic that bounced the side of her mouth whenever she started to get upset, which was pretty damned often. She had the best table manners I ever saw, though. She unfurled a paper napkin like it was damask and handled plastic spoons with such finesse that I imagined I could see the glint of light off heirloom silver. I copied every movement she made at the table, a risky activity given her level of paranoia and tendency to bust heads when she got mad. I particularly admired the way she let her left hand rest in her lap while she ate, like it was just too much effort to use it for anything except holding a little piece of bread while the other hand spread butter on it. When she fussed at me for buttering my whole slice at once, I didn't fuss back, just broke off a bite like she told me to do and buttered it right before I ate it, even though it seemed like a lot of extra motion for no good reason. I quit gulping my water and learned to take sips like her. I also learned to swallow my food before answering a question and to keep my elbows off the table.

Sometimes she noticed me copying her and she'd have a pure-dee fit, throwing food at me and screaming like she didn't have good sense, which she didn't a fair portion of the time. She'd been in college at the University of Alabama for a couple of years before she wrecked the parlor at her sorority house by upending the grand piano and dumping it on a sideboard filled with crystal. You didn't mess with Dema when the mood to destroy came on her, but when her eyes were clear and the tic on her mouth smoothed out, she behaved like the lady she was. During those times, she went out of her way to help me improve myself. She showed me how to walk and how to sit. She taught me algebra and physics, too. Nothing wrong with the learning part of Dema's brain, and I guess that was part of the problem. Her momma and daddy expected her to go to college and get her MRS degree in rich Southern husbandry. Dema wanted to be an astronaut before most of us even knew what an astronaut was. She could've been, too, except for the moods.

Dema told me stories about her family and their big old antebellum home overlooking Mobile Bay. Her daddy inherited more money than God ever had and made extra when he married Dema's mother. He expected to go through life buying whatever he wanted until Dema got sick and he couldn't buy her well. Her fancy-ass family was so ashamed after the piano-throwing incident that they hustled her right out of college and right into a place where nobody they knew was likely to find her. You'd think with all that money they could manage something better for her than the state insane asylum, but Dema said her daddy didn't believe in throwing good money after bad investments. Sure as hell, none of their society friends were going to be drying out in the Alabama State Mental Hospital.

Dema left the hospital a few months before I did. I never did see her again, but she sent me a book she said was written by the world's foremost authority on Southern manners, Miss Leola Battle Cunningham of Savannah, Georgia. I studied that book like it had the answer to all life's questions, and by the time I convinced the doctors I wasn't a threat to myself or others, couldn't anyone fault me on which fork to pick up or how to write a thank-you note for a gift I despised, even though there wasn't anyone to give me gifts, despised or otherwise. To this day I can tell you how to serve a meal à la russe, not that any red-blooded Southerner would serve any meal in the style of Russia.

Learning to talk was harder. I tend to lapse back into country dialect when I get tired, drunk, or angry. That's half the reason I don't drink. It's not just a matter of grammar, of when to say "who" and when to say "whom." It's more like learning to sing the alto part of a song when you've sung soprano all your life.

I never understood why the doctors decided I was sane enough to return to the world. One day I was on the ward with the loonies, the next in the halfway house at the gate of the grounds. Looking back, I suspect it had something to do with me reaching my eighteenth birthday and the directors' desire to save the hospital some money by discharging a charity patient. Whatever the reason, they declared me "much improved," thanks to the medication they thought I was taking and the hard work I pretended to do in talk therapy to free myself from psychosis, which is what they called my ghosts. Honesty is not the best policy in a mental hospital. I learned to tell the doctors and staff what they wanted to hear and taught myself to palm my meds so deftly that I never got caught.

When they shifted me out of the hospital into the halfway house, they also found me a job as a waitress in the dimmest little hole-in-the-wall café in that little hole-in-the-wall Alabama town.

There were better places to work, but most places weren't willing to take a chance on transitioning mental patients. For two long weeks, I worked from six thirty in the morning until two in the afternoon, then again from five in the evening until closing at ten o'clock at night, day after endless day. My tips, when I got them, had to be divided with the cook and the busboy, and my salary was barely enough to buy the stockings they insisted I wear. They supplied a uniform made of ugly gray polyester with a pinched waist and knee-length skirt that I had to share with the girl who worked on my day off. I hated coming in on Wednesday morning to my uniform smelling of her stale perfume and cheap talcum powder. The day I came in to discover she'd spilled beef hash on the bodice and hadn't even bothered to sponge it off was the last straw. I went into the bathroom, practiced deep breathing until I hyperventilated, then walked into the restaurant, held my breath, and keeled over like a poleaxed mule, dropping a whole tray of silverware in the process. I wasn't stupid enough to drop glasses. I might've cut myself when I passed out and they'd have charged every broken glass against my pitiful salary. As it was, they picked me up, fussed a bit, hinted about the possibility of "a delicate condition," and sent me back to the halfway house for the day. I went back to that miserable room long enough to pick up my bag, my tip money, and a plastic bag of dried leaves that my roommate kept to sell to her friends. There were several and I figured she wouldn't miss one. Then I marched out the door, turned left instead of right toward town, and headed down the road on my way the hell out of Etowah County, Alabama.

I didn't hitch that day because I didn't know how. I just walked down the road like I was going somewhere special, and before long, I heard air brakes and a shiny red tractor-trailer rig pulled up next to me. I looked to see if the driver was my father, and when it wasn't, I accepted the ride. I got lucky. The driver was a nice fellow who took me seventy miles down the road with hardly a word beyond asking if I was hungry and did I mind gospel quartet music on the radio. I showed him the bag of weed, asked what it was, and he kindly explained. Even more kindly, he bought it from me, handing me a bigger pile of bills than I'd ever seen in my life. He made a few suggestions as to what I might need to buy for my travels, then dropped me off in front of a farm supply store at the end of his route. Never saw him again, but to this day, I remember him.

I walked a good distance the next couple of days, catching short rides here and there, and sleeping in the woods. Finally got a long ride with a college boy in a fancy blue car who offered to show me things I'd never seen before. I was hungry by then, having spent most of my drug money on a few toiletry items, clothes to replace my hospital hand-me-downs, and a pair of shoes that didn't chafe my feet. He bought me dinner in return for what he called a hand job and a good long look at my breasts. Then he let me sleep clear into Natchez where I got away from him in the dark while he was renting a motel room. I spent that night in a cemetery on a Confederate soldier's grave, and he was sure better company than that rich-ass college boy would've been. The soldier let me sleep on the nice cool marble slab covering his resting place and didn't ask a thing of me except news of the outside world.

I didn't have much luck getting rides west out of Natchez, probably because I looked like I'd slept in my clothes (I had). The bridge across the Mississippi River had no walkway, and I sure as hell couldn't swim a mile-wide river even if I knew how to swim. I was feeling pathetic by the time a lady in a tired-looking Ford pickup truck stopped and let me ride with her and her dog into Vidalia. When she asked where I was going, I told her the honest to God truth: that I had no idea. She asked if I needed money, and I allowed that I did. She offered me a job bagging the big yellow onions that grew on her truck farm. Before long, I was walking up and down furrows gathering up the curing onions that lay thick in the fields. It was hot, thirsty, backbreaking work. To this day, I can't eat an onion, but she fed and housed me for two weeks and paid me enough money to last a while if I was careful. When I hit the road again, I felt closer to human than I had since I was thirteen years old.

Louisiana was a funny place. Though people were generous enough with rides, they weren't real friendly and didn't try to carry on conversations. That suited me fine. I'd found a map somewhere and chose Baton Rouge as a destination for no more reason than I liked the name and it was a capital city. I decided I was going to collect capital cities, stringing them like mental beads on an imaginary necklace for myself. I'd seen Little Rock and Oklahoma City on trips with my parents when I was little; they counted, though I didn't remember much about them.

My last ride promised to take me clear into Baton Rouge with no strings attached, but a few miles north of town, I saw something that made me holler, "Stop!"

The middle-aged businessman pulled the Oldsmobile to the side of the road and looked past me. "Huh. Circus. You figure on seeing the show?"

"Sure. I can see Baton Rouge another time." I was actually figuring on asking for a job.

He was a nice man, a gentleman. He didn't argue with me about what I was doing, just reached in the glove compartment, pulled a few bills off a roll he had in there, and held them out to me. It surprised me. I had him pegged as looking me over like meat he might buy if it didn't spoil before he got it to town, then he went and did something like that. I was ashamed of myself and didn't want to take his money, but he grinned and slapped the bills into my hand.

"Honey, I come a long way in this life, and it's a pleasure to treat a sister traveler to a circus matinee and a hot dog or two. Have a good time."

He was down the road and out of sight before I realized I was looking at pictures of Andrew Jackson and not George Washington or even old Abe Lincoln. In 1962, eighty dollars was a fortune. If I'd been a sentimental kind of person, I'd have sat down on that blacktop and cried. If I'd been a religious person, I'd have said a prayer for that good man. Instead, I shoved a week's salary in each of my front pockets, blew a kiss toward Baton Rouge, and headed across the fields to the Havilland Dixieland Travelling Circus.

Circus people aren't hostile, but they can be reserved with strangers. When I walked onto the site, most of them glanced my way, then went on about their business setting up tents, booths, and stringing electrical wire. A girl carrying an armload of ropes and wooden bars smiled when I caught her eye, so I screwed up the nerve to ask her who I'd see about getting a job. She looked me over doubtful-like, but kept her opinion to herself, for which I was grateful. One negative word at that point and I'd have turned tail and run. She smiled again and pointed toward a caravan sitting in the shade of a big live oak.

"Ask for Madame Clara," she said in a soft, sweet voice. "She owns the circus."

"Oh. Do I just go up and knock on the door?"

"Yep." She hesitated a moment, then took pity on me. "How about a drink of water first, and maybe a place to comb your hair?"

She delivered her armload of equipment to a pile near the largest tent, then led me to a wall tent in the middle of a row of similar tents. I ducked inside the canvas door and realized she'd brought me to her home. A neat cot covered with a pink satin comforter sat against one wall. A folding table occupied the middle of the room. A big brass-bound trunk sat against the back wall. She gave me a glass of water from the pitcher sitting on the trunk. While I tried to sip and not gulp the water down, she fetched a hand mirror and dampened a washcloth for me.

"You're nice to help me like this."

"It's not completely altruistic," she answered.

I froze, wondering what the hell she was talking about, and not wanting to admit she'd used a word I didn't have stored in my head.

"It's not just because I'm a helpful person," she amended, seeing my confusion, but having the good grace not to mention it. "So happens we've got a couple of folks who are going to need help soon and you . . . can you dance?"

I thought of Nutty Nina the Belly Dance Queena, resident of the Alabama State Mental Hospital, late of the bars on Bourbon Street in New Orleans, and the dance lessons she loved to give on Ward B when she wasn't recovering from electric shock therapy. "Sort of."

"Scared of snakes?"

Weirder and weirder. "Not particularly."

"Well, then we might all be in luck." She grinned at me, smoothed an errant curl off my face, and handed me a deep coral lipstick. I looked at it in dismay, never having held one, much less used one. She took it from me, made a face to demonstrate what she required of my own, then smoothed the color onto my mouth. It felt odd, waxy, and somehow constraining, but I didn't protest. I looked at myself in the mirror and almost laughed. Yeah, I was on my way to being the whore of Babylon now, but wasn't I pretty?

I followed her to the caravan in the shade. Up close, it proved to be a slightly beat-up Airstream trailer with blue curtains hanging in the windows. She knocked twice.

"It's Livia," she said. "Got a girl here looking for a job."

"Tell her she may enter." The voice beyond the door was deep and rich.

Livia winked at me. "Don't let her scare you."

With that reassuring piece of advice, she pulled the door open, thrust me inside, and closed off my escape.

An odd but not unpleasant smell filled the caravan: a smell of cinnamon, green plants, and—I blinked in the dim light and saw a pile of glistening coils on the bed—snakes. Big ones. I studied the creatures on the bed for a moment, then looked deeper into the trailer to see two women sitting at a small table set with a teapot and two cups. The taller of the two was young, with blond hair, a lovely face, and a belly just beginning to strain the front of her sundress. The other was short and soft, dressed in a billowing caftan and crowned with hair of such an astonishing shade of orange that it must've come straight from a bottle.

"Who are you?" the older woman drawled and reached for, of all things, a hookah.

"Alice," I said before I thought good about it.

The woman choked on her lungful of smoke, then to my everlasting relief, burst into gales of deep-throated laughter. The blond fanned smoke away from her face and motioned toward the third chair at the table.

"Rest yourself," she said over the sounds of the older woman's coughs and guffaws.

I edged around the table and saw a second pile of coils, green as envy, already occupying the chair. Aware of four human eyes watching me, I laid a gentle hand on the snake. Sensing no hostility, I scooped it into my two hands and sat down, settling the creature into my lap. The serpent moved lazily, fit its coils to my curves, and settled back down.

Over to you, I thought.

Madame Clara looked like a dumpy little housewife and spoke like the French countess she claimed to be when she wasn't Grand Duchess Marie, the last of the Romanovs, or the seventh daughter of a seventh daughter born into a New Orleans Creole family. She made all these claims with such solemn sincerity that I wondered if she wasn't a refugee from a mental hospital herself. I accidentally glimpsed the truth one day when I came upon her washing her hair in a basin outside her caravan, sleeves rolled to her elbows. The blue number on her left forearm told me all I needed to know. I slipped away without her ever knowing I was there, and never mentioned what I'd seen to anyone.

French countess or survivor of Auschwitz, she was a hardheaded businesswoman, and the Havilland Dixieland Travelling Circus was as big a financial success as a small circus could be in the mid-twentieth-century South.

Her blond friend was Mireille—just Mireille. I never heard her use another name or refer to the person who planted the baby seed in her womb. I politely assumed it was an immaculate conception. In any case, Mireille was faced with giving up both the hoochy-kootch and the snake show since the jobs involved costumes that weren't best filled by a pregnant lady. She could still hide behind the fortune teller's robes, but Mireille had had enough of the traveling life and wanted to move to Galveston to await the virgin birth of her child.

"Picking up Esmeralda won you the job before you even opened your mouth," Mireille told me later when she was introducing me to the rest of the snakes. "I know my darlings will be safe with you."

Mireille was taller than me, but the costumes fit without much alteration: a hem shortened here, a bust dart let out there. She introduced me to the other two girls in the hoochy-kootch, a bottle blond named Tina Fae and a voluptuous young woman called T'shara, Queen of the Night. Mireille was a stern teacher, but a good one. She showed me how to move my hips so that the beaded fringe swung enticingly, how to sway my upper body like I was one of the snakes, how to smile and flirt with the audience even if I hated the way the guy in the second row rubbed himself while he watched me.

"It's a job," Mireille told me when I expressed my discomfort to her. "The hoochy-kootch brings in more money than any of the other sideshows, and we're paid accordingly."

"You'll get used to it," T'shara added. "Once you are, there's outside work that pays even better than the kootch."

Mireille tugged the top of my costume into place over my breasts. "Tish, hand me one of those pads. She needs more cleavage. Yeah. That's better. You want this line to cut right down to the top of the areola. Little bit of tape'll keep it from slipping. Some of these little ol' towns'll bust you for showing the least bit of color." She snorted at the well-worn joke. "Damn Baptists."

"What outside work?"

"Circus goes into winter quarters down around Gulfport from

November until early spring," T'shara said. "Mireille and me head for New Orleans or Houston for a couple of months, find jobs dancing in the bars and clubs. Usually make enough money to see us thorough most of the next year."

Mireille patted her tummy, smiling down at its smooth curve. "Guess you'll have to talk Tina Fae or Gennie into going with you this year, Tish. I got other plans for March."

"You can make more money if you're willing to turn tricks," T'shara continued, "but us Havilland dancers ain't likin' that none."

"Tricks? You mean tumbling and such like the Rubber People?"

T'shara's rich laugh rolled out. Mireille just rolled her eyes. "No, baby, not acrobatic tricks. I mean being with guys for money."

"Prostitution," Mireille put in.

"You shocked, baby?" T'shara asked, her voice sympathetic though her eyes still danced with suppressed mirth.

I thought about the dinner a hand job bought me and what the recipient had promised for the full act. "No, I'm not shocked, but I reckon I'd rather not do it if I don't have to."

"You're better off not," T'shara said. "Them gals can go down fast."

"But don't you get to thinking you're better than girls that make that choice," Mireille added sternly. "Sometimes they're just doing the best they can with what God gave 'em, and we don't have any business criticizing them."

"I won't," I promised, and shook off the memories.

They told me how to deal with the stage door Johnnies, the guys who waited around after the shows to talk to us and offer to buy us drinks or dinner or whatever our little hearts desired. Most of them were just regular fellows trying to live in a fantasy for an hour or an evening, but some were downright scary.

"Don't you never go off by yourself after a show, not until the crowd's been cleared out for the night by our security boys," T'shara warned. "You ever get into trouble or see someone threatening a circus person, you holler out, 'Hey, Rube!' at the top of your lungs. Everyone who hears you will come running to help. Don't you never holler it to be funny, though. That's worse than that ol' boy Aesop hollering wolf."

"I won't holler wolf," I promised.

So, I worked and learned and gradually became part of the circus; "with it," the circus people called it. I was Demetra in the hoochy-kootch, Medea in the snake show, Persephone the fortune teller on days when Mireille's ankles swelled and she had to stay in bed with her feet up, and just plain Genevieve or Gennie when I helped bed the horses down.

The palming skills I developed to avoid taking my medicine in the hospital came in handy when the Magic Man started teaching me easy tricks to satisfy my curiosity about his trade. When his regular assistant came down with pneumonia, I substituted for her, showing my teeth in a fake smile and half my ass in a sequined leotard, gesticulating to the crowd with a big, *Ain't he grand, folks* sweep of my arms. Until I developed a few skills of my own, I spent a lot of time wearing costumes cut down to the tops of my nipples, gesturing at magicians, animal tamers, and guys who swallowed flaming swords. When the Amazing O'Ryan Circle of Fire lost a member to a broken back, I learned to operate a motorcycle well enough to ride in circles around the ring while the skilled riders performed stomach-dropping stunts. After a year of practice, I wasn't too bad on the single trapeze, but I was too old and too tall to learn to work on the double trapeze like the Flying DuBuissons. I pounded my share of tent pegs, shoveled my ration of horse and lion shit, and mended costumes for the fumble-fingered in return for lessons in juggling, tumbling, or a little cash.

What I liked best about the circus were the animals. At first, I was shy around self-assured, focused circus people. Most of them paid me no attention, either because they weren't interested in a newcomer to their insular world or because they recognized I was more comfortable when they treated me as if I were a tent peg. The performers were so many professional rungs above me that I slid out of their way every time it looked like my path might cross with one of them. Some of the performers were vain and looked down on the sideshow workers and carnies, but a precious few went out of their way to be kind to me.

Mireille taught me to care for the great boas: how to feed them, clean their cages, how to care for them when they took on a dull matte grayness that even covered their eyes. The first time I saw Esmeralda after she shed her skin, I understood how she had come by her jewel name. As I sank into the life of the circus, I shed my own skin, leaving behind the gray creature of B Ward with her perpetually dirty hair, leaving behind, too, the clumsy-pawed waitress in her soiled polyester uniform, and becoming someone with a future ahead of her: a tall, capable, attractive snake charmer called Genevieve.

Back then, I was starved for affection, yet suspicious of the most innocent physical touch. A person gets manhandled in an insane asylum. If you aren't pinned down by nurses for an unwanted injection, you're being wrapped in cold wet sheets to calm you down. Hands everywhere, everywhere, and none of them gentle or loving. I got awfully lonesome at times.

"Don't fall for it," Mircille warned me after she noticed me smiling at a good-looking and persistent young man who came to every performance and sent me roses twice during a four-day stop in southwestern Louisiana. "It's easy to think all the attention means he loves you. When I was learning to jump my horse, my daddy told me to throw my heart over the jump and all else would follow. I see you thinking about doing the same thing with this boy. Well, most men will balk at the first hazard, toss you plumb over their heads, and leave you there to pick yourself up out of the dirt."

She looked down at the bulge of the child under her dress, and I knew she was speaking from experience. I believed her and kept away from the men who came to watch the show. What I didn't do was extend that caution to Lorcan, one of the circus riggers.

A rigger's job is to keep people from falling out of the sky. He's the one who strings up the trapeze, the tightrope, the nets that

catch the artists when they fly earthward at the end of a performance. Riggers make the world safe so artists can concentrate
on their performance and not on whether the rope from which
they dangle is going to come untied. Everyone in our circus spoke
highly of Lorcan's dependability, so when he came around showing an interest in shy little me, I thought I'd be as safe in his arms
as I was on my single trapeze. I'd have done well to remember all
those times I fell into the dirt before I got the hang of what I was
doing.

Not many men have the nerve to make love to a woman who
keeps three big boa constrictors in her tent. That Lorcan had the
nerve was impressive enough. He not only thought I was pretty,
he thought I was smart, and that was, in the long run, what mat-
tered most to me. He talked to me like I had good sense and like
he really wanted to know what I thought about things. After a few
sweet evenings together, I left my small tent for his caravan, and
we set up housekeeping with the boas for company. Life was good
for a few weeks, but then he got to acting like he was a landowner,
and I was private property. He didn't like me too far out of his
sight, and if anything male spoke to me, Lorcan's eyes narrowed
and he got a bruised look that heralded fights with them and hard
slaps for me.

After Lorcan, I decided to forego romantic entanglements until
I understood better what I was letting myself in for. It wasn't like
I was alone. I had folks to talk to in the circus, but even without
them, I was never completely by myself. When my own familiar voices weren't whispering to me, I could hear the low hum of
other people's ghosts like distant voices on a phone line. Sometimes I wonder what part of my own voices twitter in the ears of
other listeners, but I wouldn't dare ask. That sort of curiosity gets
you locked in places like the Alabama State Mental Hospital.

I never took to being a fortune teller, though I was good at it.
Too good. I heard things I knew the folks who crossed my palm
with silver (or at least the higher-value folding version of silver)
didn't want to hear. Once a mother came to me hoping for a word

of comfort about a child who had just drowned. I saw the little girl plain as soda bread standing at her mother's side, trying to tell her the important thing that held her to earth. I heard every word the girl said but for the life of me, I couldn't repeat them to that grieving mother, even to release the child to her reward. I stammered out a bunch of chicken feed about beautiful light and flowers and love, and the poor lady went away comforted in her heart. It was me who carried the burden of knowledge about how the child drowned and who her murderer was. I carry it with me to this day along with the guilt of seeing that bastard go free because no one was going to believe that a child's ghost told a circus sideshow fortune teller who murdered her. I dreaded the weekends the circus set up in that little bitty Louisiana bayou town. Maisie was always there waiting for me with her waterlogged curls and blue lips.

But fortune telling was my job, and day after day I put on my purple robes, bound my hair back with a green silk scarf, hung heavy gold rings from my earlobes, and went to sit in the hot dimness of the tent before the useless crystal ball. I never saw anything in the crystal ball except the distorted image of my own face, and once the upside-down image of the devil walking toward me dressed in jeans, a leather vest, and with a braid longer than my own hanging down his back. Turned out to be Lorcan. Maybe I'd have had better luck had the ball been genuine crystal instead of glass.

Folks expected a crystal in a fortune teller's tent just like they expected a tarot deck and a woman dressed in a gadji's idea of Gypsy clothing. I gazed into the crystal and handled the tarot with every sign of seeing something mysterious there, but the ghosts preferred to stand next to me or behind me. I especially hated the séances I was forced to hold for the folks rich enough to demand one. The dead that joined us at those gatherings weren't the wonderful friends and family their loved ones created in their memories. Daughter wanted to hear that Daddy had found sobriety in heaven, not that the old bastard was as mean and hateful as ever, maybe more hateful since his state of ex-being prevented him from drinking or grabbing the daughter (and it was always a daughter) by the hair and smashing her face into the table to punish her for outliving him. No one wanted to hear that, so I ignored the shrieks of the vengeful dead while I murmured that Daddy had a message for Baby, a message of everlasting life and angel song that had turned his soul to Jesus. And if you don't think it's a challenge to croon such boondoggle while a furious ghost cusses you out, just try it some time.

Another time I was telling fortunes during a summer twilight somewhere in Claiborne Parish. I stared into the crystal with my hands cupped around it, trying to decide what to tell a sorority girl from LSU about her future husband while she and a couple of friends giggled behind their manicured hands. It was hard to concentrate with the white luminescence of her skin shining in my eyes and her dead family plucking at her life glow with their fingers. The cancer that got most of them was going to get her, too, and at an awfully young age. I murmured about a tall young man with—

"Blond hair?" she asked eagerly. "Blue eyes and a dimple in his left cheek?"

I nodded. She settled back in her chair with a happy shiver, her two friends hugging and congratulating her on her good luck. P. T. Barnum was right about suckers, but I bet he never saw Death walking among them like I did, or he might've been kinder.

All in all, I preferred my snakes and the hoochy-kootch, preferably in tandem. Even men with chronically roving fingers are reluctant to cop a feel on a woman who has a six-foot boa constrictor draped across her breasts and wound down one arm. T'shara and Tina Fae were energetic dancers, shaking and shimmying the gracious good plenty the Lord had given them. All that jittering around upset my snakes, so I specialized in slow, undulating performances that I'd learned from Nina at the hospital. Lots of people laughed at Nutty Nina the Belly Dance Queena, but I never did. As a result, I could mesmerize all but the rowdiest audiences. Even then I had a good sense of when things were about to get out of hand and could get off stage before some snaggle-toothed yahoo with corn liquor on his breath took into his head to jump up on stage and propose an evening alone with me. Lord, there's nothing worse than a liquored-up farm boy from a dry county. Some of them were so stupid they didn't even know they were clichés.

We weren't a first-class circus, and were even kind of a borderline second-class one, but we gave good value in return for the price of a ticket, and people in the towns we visited across Louisiana and East Texas turned out in droves to see the performances and visit the sideshows. Fortune telling paid good, dancing even better, and before long I had me enough money to buy a tent and camping gear. Some of the performers made enough money to afford a truck and overhead camper or even a caravan like Madame Clara's. I could only aspire to such luxury in my dreams.

Each time we stopped at a new venue, we set up our circus community the same way it had been set up at the last stop. We had the same neighbors, the same locations, just as if we lived in a stationary town. Occasionally the space allotted to us forced us to modify our arrangements. That never bothered me, but it unsettled some of the circus people. Circus folks can be mighty superstitious. Had any of them known I spoke with spirits, they'd have not let me stay among them. I kept such matters to myself, not only because I was happy with the circus, but because I had nowhere else to go.

Circuses have hierarchy. Even in an outfit like ours that prided itself on Liberté, Égalité, Fraternité, some animals were more equal than others. As a newcomer, I was at the bottom of the heap socially and professionally, but my skill with the big snakes won me respect years earlier than I could otherwise have expected. The high-wire acts commanded the top layer of privilege and respect. We were barely large enough for a swinging trapeze act and lost the one we had when LaDina DuBuisson slipped during practice, hit the net wrong, and continued a hard plummet to the ground that broke her back and her spirit. She came back to us with her partner long enough to gather her things and leave. By then she'd taught me enough that I could do a simple act on the single trapeze, so I filled the gap in a modest way, though nothing I did brought me to the level of greater equalness that LaDina and Shadrack enjoyed.

Despite the popularity of the Flying DuBuissons, the horse-back acrobats were the cream of our circus. It was a miracle to see this brother, sister, and cousin diving back and forth between charging horses, over and under each other, doing what the tumblers did on the ground, only doing it between the backs of galloping horses. When Christiana stood up on Frieda's broad back and made a wild run around the ring, arms flung out, head back, spotlight shining in her silver hair, the audience did everything but throw babies in the air.

Since I didn't have a car, I rode with Jean-Narcisse Aristile, the lion tamer who drove the truck that transported some of the circus's animals. The Havilland Dixieland Travelling Circus was short on animal acts, but we had liberty horses, the snakes, a dog act, and Henri and Henriette, an old, mostly toothless lion couple. Henri was pretty henpecked, but he and The Boss put on an exciting show, roaring ferociously, and pawing the air on cue from their best buddy, Jean-Narcisse. That dear man treated those big old lions like housecats; it was a sight to see 250-pound Henriette trying to crawl into his lap. Once Madame Clare got too sick to continue the circus, she sold the lions to some redneck boy who owned a bar on stilts out in the middle of some godforsaken bayou in Plaquemines Parish. When Jean-Narcisse heard about the sale, he took off into the woods with both old cats and a hunting rifle. The sheriff and the dogs found them a couple of days later, all crumpled up together under a live oak with matching bullets in their heads. The circus folks buried cats and man right where they lay and left them there without so much as a headstone to mark their passing. I felt awful bad about it. When I went to say goodbye, Jean-Narcisse tried to dry my tears with fingers like a cool wind and told me the burial suited him and the cats perfectly. At first, I didn't believe that lonesome, unmarked resting place was what they wanted, but they seemed cheerful as could be. Death didn't stop Henriette from curling up half on, half off Jean-Narcisse's lap, and I reckoned I'd eventually get over missing them. I never have, though.

I didn't know what to do with myself once the circus changed hands and so many of the old people moved on to new jobs, either with different circuses or in the real world. I wandered down to New Orleans and spent the rest of the year dancing for tourists and dissolute locals in French Quarter bars. Lord, some of those tourist men were worse than farm boys when they got drunk, but the tips were good, and I didn't have to do it forever. From New Orleans, I went to Houston, then down to San Antonio for a while, and back up to Austin where I was crossing the college campus on my way to a job interview just in time to get shot at by a lunatic in the bell tower. I spent the longest afternoon of my life hiding behind a big old statue with a bunch of poor folks who didn't realize they were dead. After that, I got myself the hell out of Texas.

I took a waitress job on the coast of Louisiana for no better reason than to live on the beach while I decided what I wanted to do next. Somewhat to my surprise, what I wanted to do next was stick my thumb in the wind and head back to a place I hadn't seen since I was thirteen years old. I didn't realize that I'd end up running into Mercer on the way or planning a murder that was long, long overdue.

CHAPTER II
GENEVIEVE

The big magnolia has stood on its lot in Washington since 1839. It's such a huge tree that a family could live under its canopy and never lack for room. On a childhood trip back to Arkansas, Papa stopped and picked a flower from one of its branches for me. I was about five or six and didn't know anything about ghosts or dying mothers or deserting fathers back then. Life was good. Unlike too many childhood memories, the tree hadn't shrunk an inch in size or a bit in grandeur. If anything, it was more beautiful than I remembered. What would the woman who planted it think if she could know it outlived her, her children, her grandchildren, and her great-grandchildren? How many lovers have sheltered under it, how many children defied parental orders to not climb it, how many flowers have bloomed and graced homes and the bosoms of party dresses? How many generations of my own family have stood right in this spot and stared at the wonder of it?

So many of those generations are buried within a few miles of here in graveyards graced with sweetgum, pine, and other magnolias, though none as magnificent as this one. There are some oaks nearby, their branches covered in resurrection ferns. In dry months, the ferns crumple into brown debris, dead and gone as my family lying beneath their timeworn tombstones. When rain graces the land, the ferns rise from their own dust and ashes, unfurling green fronds and turning the brown limbs of oaks into a garden in the sky. Sometimes I feel like one of those ferns and I wonder if I came back here to see if I can green up in the land where generations of my mother's family were born.

Follow the dirt road past the magnolia and down the hill to come to a cemetery so old that it doesn't even have ghosts. The souls buried here have long since faded into eternity, leaving only a gentle melancholy echo of what they used to be. There are fewer stones here now than when I was a child. Dozens of graves are nothing more than a slight swell or swale in the mossy ground. The oldest stones date back to when Arkansas was just a splotch in the Louisiana Territory and Washington was the jumping off place into the wilderness of Texas. David Crockett passed through here on his way to die at the Alamo, though I reckon if he'd known what he was heading to, he might've thought twice about making the trip. Maybe not, though. Maybe thirteen decades of people knowing his name was worth an early death to him. Blacksmith James Black invented the Bowie knife here, following instructions from Jim Bowie himself.

The same year the magnolia was planted, my great-great-great grandmother arrived to live under an assumed name among the pine forests of Hempstead County where her two little girls would be able to grow up free and white as they'd never have been able to do in their former home. She's buried somewhere in this graveyard, her stone long gone, probably buried beneath several inches of soil and pine needles like so many of these old stones, her name lost in the mists of the nineteenth century. Meema told me her story late one night as we lay together on the bed on the screen porch, warning me I wasn't to repeat it. She might not've told me at all except I was always hungry for stories when I was little, always wanting "just one more."

"Lord a mercy, child, you wear me out telling stories," she'd exclaim before launching into what she swore was the very last story she'd ever tell me. It never was the last story until the day I saw the white light shining in her.

Easter Sunday that year was blessed with clear blue skies, warmth, and jonquils wherever I looked. Washington was famous even then for its jonquils. For years whenever people dug up their flower beds and divided jonquils in their own yards, they'd stop along some road and drop their extra bulbs into holes they scratched into the bank of a ditch or a forest clearing. For two or three weeks in March, gold and yellow flowers filled gardens, blanketed graves, marked the sites of long-gone homesteads, and billowed into ditches along the roads from one end of town to the other. Even the meanest shack, and there were some real dumps around Washington, had their share of spring's floral bounty.

Long beds filled to overflowing with jonquils and sweet narcissus edged all four sides of the lawn at the Washington Baptist Church that Easter. The pastel dresses of the women further brightened the green swath of grass. Back in those days, hats and gloves were expected at church each Sunday, and on Easter Sunday, people wore their best and newest finery to honor spring and the rising of Jesus from the crypt. I used to imagine the stone rolling away thanks to thousands of jonquils pushing their way to the surface beneath it, and thousands more yellow flowers lining the path Jesus took to leave the tomb. I also got in my head that jonquils were my flowers since they were almost always in bloom on my birthday. The year I turned eight, I got jonquils and an Easter birthday. Lord, I thought that was fine.

The ladies of the church spread a feast across a dozen tables standing under the arch of branches sweet with spring's new green: Easter hams, fried chicken, cornbread and biscuits, deviled eggs, okra, hominy, black-eyed peas, and turnip greens. One table held nothing but sweets, everything from black bottom pie to Meema's famous spice cake with caramel icing. Most of the time at church dinners, women waited for the men to fill their plates before serving themselves, and we children hung back politely, holding onto good manners while our tummies grumbled in protest. But on Easter Sunday, the daddies and granddaddies urged us to the front of the line, standing back themselves as their wives and mothers heaped our plates for us, filled our glasses with sweet tea or lemonade, then sent us off to eat in the shade.

I sat at one end of a long trestle table, picking the golden crust off my fried chicken leg, waiting for Meema to join me before I lit into my meal. She eased in beside me, the bench giving under the comfortable width of her hips so that I leaned slightly toward her. She smiled at me and picked up her fork, motioning me to do the same.

As she took her first bite of Cora Johnson's bread pudding, a white glow appeared deep inside her, coming from a place I can't describe to this day. I watched, fascinated, as it spread and lit up her skin and hair with a luminescence so lovely that it made my heart ache. I had never seen the like of it, smoothing out the wrinkles on her cheeks and sparkling in her deep-set eyes.

I opened my mouth to ask her about it, and a voice whispered in my ear, "Don't."

"Why?" I whispered back low enough that no loving ear would hear me.

"Because she doesn't want to know."

"Know what?"

Meema turned her head to look at me. "You say something, dumplin'?"

"No, ma'am," I answered. Then, inspired to please her with what was only a tiny white lie, "Just a special prayer before I eat."

She put her hand on mine and gave it a loving squeeze. I looked at her fingers wrapped around mine, lit up like lanterns with the soft glow that cast a faint reflection on my own skin.

Though my great-great-great grandmother's stone was gone, her husband's stone was still straight and readable. Jacques Quatrepomme, 1815 to 1846, lay far back in the woods beyond the split-rail fence that bordered the pioneer cemetery. Here rested slaves, free blacks, and a handful of white people who either disdained or were denied the company of those buried in the main cemetery. Meema showed me his grave once, deep in December when frost sparkled on the dead grass, snakes were far underground, and the understory of the pine forest shed its leaves and revealed its secrets for a few bare weeks.

"He come to town about a year before she moved here with the girls," Meema told me, scraping at the lichen that half obscured his name. "She was fair, but he was a shade too dark to pass for white. They never spoke to one another so no one might guess their secret, but every Sunday, she'd hook up the buggy and ride by his place real slow on the way to church so he could see his girls."

I've always wondered what it would be like to belong to a place as completely as these generations of my family did. My grandfather and Meema were buried just down the road in Old Washington Cemetery, less than a mile from where they were born. Neither had ever lived any further away than Ozan except for the long year Papaw spent in the French trenches of World War I. Their parents were there, and their aunts and uncles and cousins, all people of the same bone and blood as me. My mama was there, too, planted beneath a rose that Meema called Glory of the World.

Most of those folks were just memories of stories told to me by Meema in the long Southern twilights. Despite the summers I spent here as a child and the couple of years I lived with Meema after Mama died, this land and place that should've been mine didn't embrace me the way I hoped they would. Guess it takes people to do that, and mine were long gone. It was my holy land, the home of my heart, but a lifetime of wandering cut me off and divided my memories among towns scattered from Alabama to the Gulf Coast of South Texas.

Still, no matter where my father's wanderlust took us, sooner or later we came back to Arkansas to visit, to rest, and then go on to the next town, the next job, the next set of friends I wouldn't be able to keep. I always cried when I had to say goodbye to Meema and my Arkansas friends. My crying made my mother so mad that she didn't speak a kind word to me for hours. She didn't like me making a fuss. I was supposed to be seen, and if I had to be heard, to be polite and quiet about it. Meema understood. She always cried, too.

What I wanted back then was to live in Meema's house and go to school with the same friends year after year. Every time Mama and Papa packed the car with our things, eager to be on to the next adventure, I wandered through the old house, touching the keys on the piano no one could play, patting a quilt, running my hand along the stair banister, feeling the smooth wooden floor beneath my bare feet, trying to store up all the feelings of home to take with me into exile. I used to wish that something would happen to force my parents to leave me in the old house with Meema, that I would be stricken with an illness so grave that I could never travel more than a few miles ever again. I imagined myself, pale and brave, bidding my parents goodbye with dry eyes while my mother, for once, was the one who wept at leaving.

I remembered these childish fantasies when we came home to bury Mama beneath the oaks and resurrection ferns the spring I turned eleven. I awoke the day after the funeral to discover Papa was gone. He left without telling me he was going and so nobody cried at the parting. I reckon I should've been more careful about what I wished for.

I lived with Meema for two years, far off the main road on a red-dirt lane that was impassable when it rained. She had an Arkansas State Teacher's Certificate, earned at the age of sixteen in those long-ago days before Prohibition, and she taught me in the kitchen of the old house just as she had once taught my mother. The first time she gave me lessons, I was a very little girl, staying with her for most of one summer when Papa was between jobs but had enough money for him and Mama to take an extended vacation. While they pursued their marriage alone in honeymoon cottages in the Ozarks or travel courts in the Texas hill country, Meema taught me my letters and numbers. When I started first grade in Kingsville, Texas, the teacher asked who knew how to write to ten. I raised my hand. She invited me to the front of the room, handed me a piece of yellow chalk, the first I'd ever seen. I turned it over, feeling the cool smoothness, noting the powdery fineness that transferred from it to my fingers. At the teacher's invitation, I began to write the numbers on the board, one after another in a straggling line.

"Oh, Oleana, that's not . . ." Teacher's voice faded away as I doggedly continued to write all the way up to ten. Only then did I stop, not because I couldn't go further, but because the effort of writing on the board made my uplifted arm ache. I looked at her and found her staring at the uneven line of numerals.

"Where did you learn this?" she asked softly.

"My Meema taught me."

"Did she teach you another way, too?"

"Yes, ma'am, but those are harder to make." At her request, I wrote numbers the hard way, getting the three backward as I usually did. I told her, "I like the Roman ones best, 'cause they always turn out right."

Teacher gave me two gold stars that morning: one for me and one for Meema. I saved the extra star and gave it to her next time we went to Arkansas.

"Why did she teach you Roman numerals?" Mercer asked when I told him this story.

"Why does anyone teach anyone anything?" I retorted, quick to sense criticism. Mercer wasn't being critical, though. He was just curious. Ashamed of my prickly defensiveness, I made it up to him by writing the date of his birth in Roman numerals: MCMXLVI. Then I wrote mine: MCMXLIV.

I got Mercer to carry me over to the pioneer cemetery on his motorcycle one afternoon and we spent an hour or so wandering around the old graves and reading the names of those long-dead folks. His own ghosts didn't come any closer than the top of the hill, fading away as we rode down the narrow lane to the graveyard. I don't know why. They didn't speak to me, so I didn't speak to them, though we could hear each other clear as a bell. None of us let Mercer know that we were aware of each other, at least not then.

We drifted along on parallel courses, reading headstones, stooping to make out dates and verses that had been almost erased by summer sun and winter ice storms. He was real taken with the monuments that marked the graves of three Revolutionary War veterans.

"I didn't know these guys were here," he said.

"Haven't you ever been here before?"

He shook his head.

"There's a bunch of Confederate soldiers buried a piece up the road," I said. "Want to go see?"

He looked at me curiously. "How come you know so much about the cemeteries around here?"

I hesitated, then decided to tell a partial truth. "I came here on a visit when I was a little girl. My papa liked history and Washington was the capital of Arkansas during part of the Civil War. We were in the neighborhood, and he wanted to look around."

"Not much to see. Handful of old run-down buildings."

I shrugged. "I guess. You want to go look for Confederate graves or not?"

At Old Washington Cemetery, we left the bike in the shade and slipped through the gate. This one was newer than the pioneer cemetery, as well as a little more orderly and a lot more crowded. The gentle rumble of voices filled my ears. I listened close but didn't hear anyone I knew. I was half afraid of hearing Mama and half afraid of not hearing her. Meema's voice had faded away long ago. I missed her, but knew she'd gone on to where she needed to be. Under the pretense of looking for the Rebel soldiers, I gradually made my way to the far corner of the graveyard until I stood at the foot of the two graves I really wanted to see. Glory of the World grew from my mama's heart; in a few weeks, small roses as red as blood would cluster among the green leaves. Meema's grave was bare except for grass. I'd been taken away to Alabama before I could plant anything for her, and apparently no one else had thought to do it. No voices that belonged to me here. I sorta wished I could cry but didn't know how to start. I couldn't remember the last time I cried more than a tear or two, but figured it was sometime before the child welfare people left me off at the hospital. I think that's part of the reason they took me there: I couldn't cry, couldn't talk, couldn't hear anything except what was in my own head. Catatonic, they called it. Said it was the shock of finding that man dead. Said it was terror at being in the room with that big old diamondback rattlesnake. Said a lot of things, most of them wrong. I was real glad that she got away before someone came with a gun or something to blow her to bits, but I reckon she wasn't in much danger. I've always wondered what she was in addition to being a rattlesnake.

CHAPTER 12
MERCER

"Hey, man, that li'l gal you with is lookin' kindly peculiar," said Bigger Than You. "I'd see 'bout her my own self 'cept we ignorin' each other."

Mercer wound his way through the rows of tombstones over to Genevieve. She glanced up as he approached. "You find those soldiers?"

"Not yet." He read the inscriptions on the headstones that seemed to be holding her attention. Mirth Hughley Larkin. Lela Caroline Hughley. He thought about that a minute. "Kind of familiar names."

She nodded. "Yeah. I guess maybe they are." She nodded at Mirth. "That's my mama. Lela was my grandmother."

"Lela was my great-aunt."

"I know."

"How long?"

"Swear to God, I had no idea until we rode up in front of the house that first day. You didn't tell me your last name. I just thought I was lucky to come across someone headed in the direction I wanted to go." She looked over at him, meeting his eyes squarely. "You mad about this?"

He shook his head. "No. I'm not even all that surprised. You've always felt . . . familiar."

"I don't know how. Wasn't like we ever saw much of each other. I didn't even realize Mama had a cousin Wreath until someone dropped me off at y'all's house after Meema's funeral. I wasn't there long enough to get to know anyone even if I'd been in a sociable mood." She looked at him skeptically. "You're not going to tell me you remember me. You were just a little kid."

"I don't remember you, but I remember the fight my folks had over you being at the house. Mama wanted you to stay in the worst way. One of the only times I ever heard her try and stand up to John Luther."

Genevieve laughed like nothing was funny. "Bet she paid for that."

"Where'd you go after you left our house?"

"Alabama," she said shortly, turning from the graves and starting back toward the gate.

That sounds like a no-trespassing sign, Mercer thought. "Hey, Genevieve."

She kept moving. "What?"

"I'm glad you came home."

She halted abruptly, one fist flying to the center of her chest as though something hurt her. He caught up with her, hesitated, then said, "I got cousins on John Luther's side, but I reckon you're it on Mama's. Anyone else know?"

"Miss Wreath knew right away. Said I look like Mama."

"She won't tell anybody if you don't want her to. Me, neither. You going to stay around for a spell?"

Genevieve nodded. "Thought I'd look and see if I can find a job and some place cheap to rent. I was telling the truth when I said I want to go to college. Don't have a high school diploma, though. Not sure what to do about that."

"Easiest thing in the world," Mercer said. "GED. I got one after I joined the Navy. John Luther didn't want any of us going to school after we turned fifteen. He'll probably pull Jezzie out later this year and make her marry someone. She's a handful, Jezzie, but she's smart and deserves better than being married off to one of John Luther's friends."

"How come you call him John Luther?"

Mercer snorted. "You get to know him better, then tell me if you could call that old son of a bitch 'Daddy.'"

Genevieve thought of the woman lying naked across a bed and the wide leather belt leaving its mark on her. "I reckon I'll stick to 'sir.' Tell me about this GED thing."

"Tell you later. Too nice a day to talk about school. Where you want to go from here?"

"Is there a swamp or bayou nearby? I seem to remember one with a long walkway going out over the water."

"Bois d'Arc Bayou's not too far from here." He pronounced it *bo-dahr*.

"Can we go there?"

"This cousin of yours is plumb crazy, Doc," said Bigger, looming up between him and the motorcycle. "What's a pretty girl want with a swamp?"

Mercer gritted his teeth and kept walking straight at the ghost. To his great relief, and somewhat to his surprise, Bigger evaporated just before he'd have been forced to either stop or walk right through the marine's shade.

"That was fun," Genevieve said under her breath.

"What?"

She smiled at him. "So, what are we to each other if our mamas were cousins?"

"Hell, I don't know. That's the kind of thing you'd need to ask Mama."

Bois d'Arc was exactly as Genevieve remembered. She walked out onto the pier and looked down into the clear water of the bayou, watching for fish. A pair of mallards coasted into a landing on the water and an egret perched on a stump not too far away. Watching his companion's rapt expression, Mercer laughed out loud.

"You got the most peculiar notion of how to spend a spring afternoon. Graveyards and swamps."

She turned from her contemplation of the water and cypress to size him up with narrowed eyes and a defensive scowl. "You laughing at me?"

"Nah. I'm laughing because . . ." He stopped and thought about it. She waited, looking ready to pounce if he dared to make fun of her. He thought some more, then, as if it surprised him, said, "I'm laughing because I feel happy."

She relaxed a little, one corner of her mouth turning up in a tentative smile. "Really?"

"Yeah. Yeah."

He looked across the slow-moving water of the bayou at the green of a cypress tree against the blue sky. A flat boat bumped gently against the pier, its oars stowed on the floor beneath the seats. "C'mon."

He dropped into the boat and steadied it while she clambered over the top rail of the pier and joined him. The boat was old, with peeling red paint revealing an even older layer of green paint over bare boards. It smelled of fish and heat, and mud. Mercer slid the oars into their locks while Genevieve undid the line and shoved the boat away from the dock.

"Kinda lost my touch," Mercer commented as the boat swung in a wide arc out into the bayou. "Hell of a thing for a sailor."

"It'll come back," she answered, and it did, quicker than he thought it might.

It had been a long time since he took a rowboat out on a lake. The last time had been with Barbara Lynn Gunderson, the girl from Hope that he intended to marry when he got out of the service. He'd reluctantly complied with her request to keep their engagement a secret until he got home. She said she didn't want anyone making a fuss about them until he was there to enjoy the fuss with her. She sent him a wedding announcement two months after he got to Vietnam. No explanation, just a creamy white engraved card announcing that she and Bryan Grayson had been married in the First Methodist Church of Hope on the Saturday after Labor Day. Six months later, he got a letter from a mutual friend in which the friend mentioned that Barbara Lynn had given birth to a premature eight-pound baby girl in the hospital at Texarkana.

He'd read the birth announcement with monsoon rain dripping from the hood of his poncho and onto the paper. The words blurred and ran off the page into the ankle-deep mud of Southeast Asia. He thought of his last night with Barbara Lynn just before he left for Vietnam and wondered who Baby Girl Grayson would look like. He crumpled the letter into a hard ball, dropped it on the ground, mashed the ball into the mud with his boot as he set off with his unit on yet another recon mission.

Nope. Don't go thinking about things like that today, he told himself.

"I like your mama," Genevieve said. "She's one of the sweetest people I ever met. She doesn't laugh or smile much, though. Reckon she's bashful."

"Mama's always had a good sense of humor when John Luther isn't around to shame her out of it. She used to catch word plays and puns; never was one for big horse laughs, but they always made her smile. Now they go right past her. I throw jokes out like we used to share, thinking she'll get it and grin, but she never does."

"Why, do you think?"

He shrugged. "Don't know. Maybe because of me. My joining the Navy made John Luther so mad that I'm afraid he took it out on the rest of them after I left."

"I'd have thought he'd be proud of you going off to save lives."

Mercer snorted. "All he cared about was that I made a decision on my own, and it didn't include studying up under him to be assistant preacher in his damn church. Saying church, John Luther's gonna want you to attend services with the family come Sunday."

"Church?" Genevieve laughed out loud. "Mercer, closest to church I've been since I was a kid is a series of graveyards. I don't have anything to wear that wouldn't raise every eyebrow in the house, and I don't think much of churches or preachers, if you want to know the truth."

"I'm not telling you to go. Just wanted you to have fair warning."

"Well, I appreciate it. I don't want to be the cause of unpleasantness in your mama's house, so don't be surprised if I go to bed sick on Saturday night and don't recover until Sunday afternoon."

"Then you can go to the evening service," Mercer teased.

"You're kidding."

"I'm not. Morning service eight to ten. Sunday school ten to eleven thirty. Lunch. Afternoon service one to three. Afternoon break and early dinner, then back at the church from six until eight with prayer meeting following to nine."

"Holy hell," Genevieve said, appalled. "How many preachers y'all got?"

"Just John Luther, though Jared or one of the elder deacons take over occasionally to give him a break."

"Holy hell," she repeated. Mercer laughed at her horrified face.

"Long as you're shook up, I'm going to shake you up some more. This is just a suggestion, and if the answer is no, just say no without hitting me, okay?"

"All right," she said cautiously.

"I can't stay at Mama's house much longer without butting heads with John Luther. Man I used to work for at the garage in Hope is willing to take me back on, so I'll have an income here next week. He also gave me the keys to a two-bedroom apartment over an old carriage house in Washington. It ain't much, but one of the bedrooms is yours if you want it. No obligations and no strings attached."

Stunned didn't begin to sum up her thoughts. Under her breath she said, "I don't have money for rent, Mercer."

"Won't matter for a month or two. You can start paying your half when you find a job. Until then . . ." He grinned at the look that passed over her face. "Until then, you can do all the cooking."

"Two bedrooms."

"Yep. I'll even put a lock on the inside of one of 'em if you want me to."

"And I cook in return for rent until I can pay my half in cash."

"You cook. We share washing the dishes and cleaning the place. I'm not fixing for you to be the maid."

She thought it over a minute, then, "Deal."

They shook hands over the oars.

"Well, ain't that jus' the sweetest thing I ever did see," said a familiar voice. Bigger strolled alongside the boat, walking on the water like it was solid as land. "You got yourself a lady friend. Cousin, but I reckon you an Arkansas boy, all right."

"Aw, Christ," Mercer muttered, turning his head away.

"Now that's plumb blasphemous, Doc. I ain't nowhere near like Jesus, but this walkin'-on-water stuff is a pretty good trick, don't you think?"

"Go away, Bigger."

"Okay, but I be back."

Mercer looked sideways to make sure he was gone, then turned back to Genevieve, thinking, *fuuuuck, now what do I say?*

"At least Bigger leaves when you ask him to go," Genevieve said. "Some ghosts aren't that considerate."

CHAPTER 13
MERCER

Bullfinch's Mythology and a tale-bearing, ambitious older sister were responsible for Mercer's abrupt entrance into the United States Navy. He'd been secretly reading through the senior English book list to keep up with the high school classes he'd been forbidden to attend after his sophomore year. Each day after school, Jim Allen brought a list of assignments to the garage where Mercer was changing oil and installing mufflers. Unless there was a rush job to be done, Gil Herndon always coordinated afternoon breaks with Jim's arrival so Mercer could take advantage of a few valuable minutes of instruction from his friend.

The Bible was the only truly acceptable book in the Ives household, though John Luther allowed Wreath a small collection of gardening manuals and cookbooks. Novels were strictly forbidden, and books involving foreign gods and goddesses were considered the work of the devil himself. Delilah had always been both sanctimonious and conniving, but upon her marriage to Jared, she redoubled her efforts to maneuver herself into the position of favored child. She regularly slipped into Mercer's room to dig through his possessions in hopes of discovering illicit drugs or compromising letters from that trashy Barbara Lynn Gunderson he was so sweet on. She laughed aloud when from his backpack she pulled a book decorated with a scandalously clad goddess on the pale-blue-and-mauve cover. She slipped it under her apron, spirited it down the hall to the room that she shared with Jared, and waited for John Luther to come down for breakfast the next morning.

Five minutes after Delilah tearfully presented the book to her father, murmuring about her duty to alert him to this evidence of sin under their roof, John Luther roared into Mercer's room, bellowing like an enraged bull. Mercer was sound asleep, having been up until almost dawn taking care of a snakebit calf. He awoke to the solid crack of *Bullfinch's Mythology* against his skull and the thunder of his father's condemnations in his ears.

". . . tearing this family apart . . . bringing Satan's own book into this house . . ." John Luther seized the half-stunned Mercer by the collar of his pajama shirt, pulled him out of bed, and dumped him hard on the bare floor. Unbuckling his belt, he growled an order.

"No," said Mercer. He sat up, glared at the big red-faced man towering over him, and realized he'd just declared war.

The leather made a swishing sound as John Luther jerked it through his belt loops. He raised the weapon over his head. "You will submit—now."

"Hell, no," said Mercer. The belt caught him on the cheekbone just below his left eye.

Blinded by tears of pain and rage, Mercer lunged to his feet and caught John Luther's arm in mid-swing. For a long moment, he held off the next blow by sheer will and adrenaline, but John Luther was five inches taller than he was and outweighed him by eighty pounds. He shoved Mercer into the bedside table, toppling the lamp and a glass of water.

All of a sudden, every fight he'd ever fought behind the gym or in an alley made perfect sense. Mercer hurled himself at John Luther, fists doubled, with a relief that felt like ecstasy. John Luther took two hard blows to the head before he absorbed the enormity of what was happening. With a roar, he tackled his furious son around the waist and rammed him into the wall. The glass in the picture of Jesus smashed under the impact of Mercer's head and clattered to the floor.

"What on earth?"

John Luther looked up through his rapidly swelling eye to see Delilah gaping at the scene from the doorway. He heard feet running up the stairs and voices crying in alarm. "Get me a rope, some clothesline, something!"

Delilah disappeared, her face bright with malice and excitement. John Luther swung a half-stunned Mercer away from the wall, kicked his feet out from underneath him, then landed on him with one knee in the small of the younger man's back. He pinned Mercer's arms with difficulty since Mercer kept fighting despite his bloody head and aching back. Small hands wrapped themselves around John Luther's wrists and tugged with surprising strength.

"Stop! Stop!" Wreath demanded, digging her nails into his flesh.

John Luther grabbed both of Mercer's wrists in one big hand and pressed them hard against his back. As thoughtlessly as he'd have swatted a fly, he backhanded Wreath. She tumbled halfway across the room. Her head thudded against the chest of drawers as Delilah ran back into the room with a coil of white clothesline. The girl hopped over her mother's legs and held out the rope to John Luther. He jerked it from her grasp.

"Put your knees on his shoulders."

Intoxicated with the violence and hot copper smell of blood, Delilah landed so hard with both knees on Mercer's shoulders that he let out an involuntary cry of pain. John Luther got the line wrapped around Mercer's wrists before Wreath cannonballed into him again. He swung at her, but this time she clung like a pit bull to his arm, deflecting the blow.

"See to your mother!" he ordered Delilah. She launched herself upward and hauled Wreath away. Wreath struggled but couldn't bring herself to hit her child to free herself. Finally, she sagged in Delilah's grip, covered her face, and began to sob. John Luther tied Mercer's ankles, clambered to his feet, and retrieved his belt. Mercer pressed his face hard against the floor and silently wept as the blows fell. He was so still that for a moment after John Luther stepped away, Wreath feared her son was dead. John Luther allowed her to use Mercer's own pocketknife to cut the bonds around his wrists and ankles but forbade her to so much as wipe away the blood from the cuts on the back of his head. Once Mercer was free of the ropes, John Luther grasped Wreath's upper arm and forced her out of the room, nodding to Delilah to precede them.

Mercer lay unmoving for a long time before he managed to pry his aching body off the floor and ease it into the bathroom. Standing under a hot shower with his hands braced against the wall, he watched pink water swirl into the drain. When the water ran clear, he shut off the tap and dried himself on an old towel. He used the same towel to clean up the hardwood floor and walls of his room, then swept up the glass, crumpled the damaged print of Jesus into a ball, and tossed it into the trash can in the corner of the room. There wasn't much he could do about the bedclothes except bundle them into a pile to be boiled in the big iron kettle outside. He wouldn't have done anything had he not known the work would otherwise fall to his already traumatized mother.

Riding the motorcycle was beyond him. One eye was swelled shut and the other was reduced to a mere slit. He dialed Gil's number and without explaining the circumstances, requested a ride. Gil asked not a single question but turned up forty-five minutes later and drove Mercer straight home to his wife, a registered nurse he'd met in a MASH unit in Korea. Kathleen's eyes narrowed as she tended his wounds and put him to bed with a cold compress for his head. It wasn't the first time Mercer had arrived with a black eye or other injury, but this exceeded anything she'd ever seen.

Someone, she thought fiercely, should kill that son of a bitch preacher.

Mercer spent ten days with the Herndons, biding his time until the worst of his bruises faded to pale violet and the cuts on his head healed over. As soon as Kathleen declared him fit, he borrowed a car from Gil, drove himself into Texarkana, and enlisted in the United States Navy. He'd never seen the ocean, never been on a vessel larger than a pontoon boat on Lake Catherine. Since he could swim well enough to keep himself from drowning, row a boat, and operate a trolling motor, he figured the Navy would be as good an escape as any. When he told the recruiter that he had one part-time job at a garage and a second part-time job at a veterinary clinic, the recruiter decided he'd make a dandy corpsman.

Compared to life at home, the weeks he spent at Naval Station Great Lakes were a vacation despite the physical and mental abuse inflicted by boot camp drill instructors. The first time a drill instructor slapped him across the face for some minor infraction, Mercer almost laughed aloud.

You hit like my baby sister, he thought, then straightened to attention and stared serenely back at the man who was screaming curses at him six inches from his nose. A scant month later, the same drill instructor shook his hand, grumbled, "You'll probably do," and sent him off to the Hospital Corps School.

He was immersed in medical training courses when he was summoned into the main office one clear, bright afternoon where he and three other young men encountered a tall, erect, hard-faced man in an immaculate Marine uniform. Without preamble, the officer stated, "You have the honor of being assigned to the Fleet Marine Force where you will learn to take care of marines on the field of combat. See that you are worthy of their trust." Without another word, the officer turned and walked away.

Out of the hospital and into the mud. Mercer adjusted his expectations and devoted his energy to keeping up with the Marine recruits, most of whom seemed to think they had something to prove about their ability to take mental and physical abuse. Medical training focused on triage and wounds common in combat situations. In between medical classes, the corpsmen-in-training studied basic combat skills and strove to complete increasingly difficult field exercises alongside the marines who accepted them into the group with good-natured razzing and lent an occasional hand to drag them through the grueling experience.

Early in the program, Mercer incurred the wrath of the small-arms instructor by refusing to entertain the notion of carrying the presented M-14 rifle into combat.

"If I'm busy taking care of marines, I won't have time to shoot people," he explained politely but firmly.

The instructor glared at him. "Carry a weapon or not, you *will* learn to shoot, Corpsman."

Mercer took the rifle thrust at him, looked it over, and said, "What do you want me to hit, Sarge?"

The instructor marched him to the firing range and indicated a target at some distance. The other recruits paused in their own practice to watch the fun of a conscientious objector making a fool of himself with a rifle. Unperturbed by their grins and sneers, Mercer stepped up to the firing line, sighted down the rifle barrel, and fired half a dozen rounds. He lowered the weapon, squinted at the target, and shrugged.

"I'm out of practice." The others stared at a grouping of holes in a space about the size of a fifty-cent piece. The instructor turned a narrow gaze on him.

"You belong in sniper school."

"With respect, Sarge, I'm already in the right place."

"Where'd you learn to shoot?"

"Hunting squirrels."

"Southern boys," the instructor muttered and turned away. It was the last thing he said about Mercer and firearms.

Eight thousand miles from Camp Lejeune, Third Battalion, First Marines landed on the beach of Quang Ngai Province in South Vietnam. In far less time than Mercer imagined possible, he found himself on board ship and headed across the Pacific Ocean to an Asian country he'd never heard of before joining the Navy. He had time for a short leave home to say goodbye to his mother and spend a few passionate hours with Barbara Lynn Gunderson, but that was all. He met his mother secretly and made damn sure John Luther didn't know he was anywhere in the county.

Immediately upon reaching the verdant shores of Vietnam, Mercer climbed into a Sea Knight helicopter for transport to his new unit in the First Reconnaissance Battalion. Most of his fellow passengers rode in silence, staring into the distance. One marine immersed himself in a paperback copy of Louis L'Amour's *Hanging Woman Creek*. Mercer edged as close to the open door as possible and watched the helicopter's shadow flicker over fields, hills, and rivers.

It's like riding a magic carpet, he thought, lifting his eyes to a horizon foreshortened by steep jungle-cloaked mountains. *Probably noisier than a magic carpet, but even so . . .*

The helicopter dropped its load of passengers atop a flat hill, hovering a few feet above the ground while troops leapt through the door. Mercer stumbled as he hit the dirt and reached out to stop himself from tumbling ignominiously onto his nose. A huge black hand grabbed his elbow and hauled him back onto his feet. Mercer looked up and up into the smiling face of one of the biggest men he'd ever seen.

"Welcome to Nam," the giant said in an accent Mercer had heard all his life. "I'm Bigger'n You."

"So are a lot of other people." Mercer straightened his pack and looked around as the man broke into a deep, rolling chuckle.

"Naw, man, that's my nic. My name. What they call me here in this place. I'm Bigger. That fella with the radio, he called Wire. That one over there with the fancy bolt rifle, he called Tak, short for Otaktay. Indian from Wyoming. Name means 'kills many' in English. Good name for a sniper."

"Mercer Ives."

Bigger beamed at him. "We related, you think?" He pointed to the stenciled name over his shirt pocket. Ives.

Mercer grinned back. "What part of Arkansas you from?"

"Ozan. You?"

"Columbus."

"Damn, we really might be related." Bigger cocked an eyebrow at him. "You got a problem with that, Doc?"

"Not if you don't. Me, I got three sisters and a bunch of female cousins. Wouldn't object to an extra male or two in the family."

"Okay, then. Now you got a brother and I'm not an only child anymore. C'mon. I show you where to go and what to do." He scooped a handful of red dirt from the ground. "First thing we better do is take the shine off that pretty uniform of yours. You look like you just crawled off the boat."

"I did," said Mercer and submitted himself to the ensuing dirt bath.

Two hours later, they headed off with ten other men to search for Viet Cong and North Vietnamese Army troops. The sergeant in charge of the patrol explained to the newbies in the group that the Viet Cong weren't just ignorant Asian rednecks with antique weapons; they were a serious threat. "What's more, the North Vietnamese Army has infiltrated this province. The NVA kicked French ass at Dien Bien Phu a dozen years ago and they're doing their best to kick American ass now. Do not—I repeat—do not underestimate the enemy."

He looked over his new recruits and paused his eyes on Mercer. "Where's your weapon, Doc?"

"Don't have one, Sarge. Don't want one."

"What in the hell are you gonna do if you need to shoot somebody?" A redheaded marine called Alice demanded. A couple of other men scowled agreement.

Mercer smiled. "That's what I got y'all for. Y'all got to keep me alive to take care of your sorry asses."

He adjusted his medical pack and followed the others into the jungle, wishing he felt a quarter as carefree and cocky as he sounded. He'd never been so scared in his life. It wasn't just the prospect of taking enemy fire, though that surely concerned him. As he took his first step into the thick vegetation, all he could think of was the class he'd had on Vietnam flora and fauna.

One hundred and forty species of snakes, he thought as he gingerly put his boot on the ground. *Thirty-five of them capable of killing me deader than a doornail in five minutes flat. I hate snakes.* He shuddered, took another step, and put his snake-spotting reflexes on automatic pilot. That freed up his mind for worrying about how he'd react when the shooting started.

They came under fire before they'd walked a mile. Despite his misgivings, Mercer neither ran nor curled up into a whimpering ball of cowardice. Weeks of training snapped him into medical mode as soon as he heard the first howl of pain, and he was crouched beside a wounded marine without realizing he'd run through bullets to get to the man's side. The attack lasted only seconds but cost the patrol two men. Both were more or less mobile, but in no condition to continue a seven-day patrol. They staggered back toward the landing zone after Wire radioed for a helicopter to pick them up.

"You done good, li'l brother." Bigger slapped him so heartily on the back that Mercer 's knees threatened to buckle.

"Sure you don't want a weapon?" Sarge offered Mercer an M1911 Colt pistol, butt first.

Mercer shook his head. "Nah, y'all were just about adequate. Thanks, though."

Sarge shook his head and holstered the weapon. "You're crazy as fuck, Doc, you know that?"

Other recons followed the first one, each so much like the other that before long, they all blended together into one long trek across Vietnam. They went out, they took fire, Mercer patched the wounded up as well as he could, and they returned to the relative safety of the base. Snipers, mortars, booby traps, mines, and small-arms fire took their toll as did the climate and sheer exhaustion. They never saw the enemy.

Ghosts, Mercer thought, watching a Sea Knight helicopter lift off with its load of two wounded and one dead marine. *Ghosts are killing my marines.*

CHAPTER 14
DELILAH

❦

Despite Mercer's misgivings and her own, Genevieve accepted the invitation to accompany the family to church on Sunday. She didn't want to go, but short of making good on her threat to take to a dark room with a spurious headache for twenty-four hours, she didn't see any polite way out of it. She'd tried pleading a lack of appropriate clothing, but Delilah dug into the back of her closet and found a threadbare olive-green dress that she hadn't gotten around to cutting up for rags. Genevieve accepted it with courteous thanks and a curious gleam in her eye that made Delilah uncomfortable.

"Why didn't you let her use your second-best dress?" Jezzie asked, watching Genevieve carry the dress downstairs to the ironing board.

"Because it's purple, and wouldn't that have been a disaster with her red hair and freckles?" Delilah snapped, irritated at being caught out in a lack of Christian charity by her younger sister.

The dowdy dress should've dowsed Genevieve's beauty to ashes, but she pulled the loose garment in at the waist with the belt that usually held up her jeans, knotted a scarf over her shoulders, and turned up on Sunday morning looking like she could step into the pages of a fashion magazine. Boiling with resentment that the woman had done so much with so little, Delilah zeroed in on the battered state of Genevieve's shoes. The Ives women all had small feet, so no one expected Delilah to loan Big Foot a pair of church-worthy shoes. Genevieve didn't seem to feel the shame of having to wear her dilapidated sneakers to church, though. When Delilah sweetly sympathized over their tattered state, Genevieve had the gall to throw back her head and laugh out loud.

"'These our garments and our shoes are become old by reason of the very long journey,'" she quoted, sticking one foot out to examine it. When Delilah looked startled, Genevieve added, "Joshua 9:13."

"I know my Bible," Delilah snapped, "and I know better than to quote it for frivolous reasons."

Uncrushed by the chilling rebuke, Genevieve just laughed again and said she'd meet the family at the church since she felt like a walk would do her good. Jezzie and Leah volunteered to accompany her, and the three set off down the dirt road to Columbus in higher spirits than either Ives girl generally showed on Sundays. They were almost to the church when the Ives' family car passed them, bearing John Luther, Wreath, Delilah, and the twins. Jared and Mercer would come as soon as they finished dealing with a cow that had struggled through a difficult birth early that morning and was hesitant about accepting her calf.

Delilah greeted friends and other church members with the sweet smile expected from the daughter of the preacher and the wife of the associate preacher. She shifted one baby boy into the arms of Gayla Conger, the teenager in charge of the nursery, and handed over the other child and the bag containing diapers to Doreen Conger, who assisted her older sister. Delilah spent a few minutes repeating the same instructions she gave the girls each Sunday, then turned to her own duties as alpha female of the preacher's family. Over the preceding two years, Wreath gracefully and gratefully faded into the background as her efficient daughter took over everything from leading the women's prayer group to planning the Wednesday night potluck suppers each week. Had she had a choice in the matter, Wreath would've returned to the Baptist Church of her childhood

where the love of Christ was emphasized over the vengeance of an
ever-angry God. She never had gotten used to John Luther's habit
of speaking directly to sinners by name from the pulpit, harangu-
ing them to confess and repent of their evil ways, demanding that
they approach the altar and fall on their knees before it to publicly
beg the God of Anger's forgiveness. Too often, she herself was the
subject of John Luther's thundering criticism. As she eased herself
onto the hard pew, she could tell by his burning gaze on her that
this was going to be one of those sermons.

Delilah sat bolt upright in the front pew, her hat set squarely on
her unadorned hair and her gloved hands folded in the lap of her
navy-blue church suit. Jezzie and Leah sat on either side of their
quiet, downcast mother. Genevieve, sitting next to Leah, smiled
as the child moved closer, pressing her small shoulder against Genevieve's arm. Mercer slid into the pew next to her just as Brother
Franklin Ross started the call to prayer. At the other end of the
bench, Jared seated himself next to Delilah.

"Calf and cow okay?" Genevieve whispered from the side of
her mouth.

"Yeah," Mercer said under his breath, then in a different tone,
"Aw, God." It didn't sound like an answer to Brother Ross's call.
Genevieve slid her eyes sideways to see Bigger Than You leaning
against the end of the pew. The big black marine winked at her
with one damaged eyelid and shifted his attention to the front of
the church as John Luther took his place at the pulpit.

"From Proverbs, Chapter Twelve, Verse Four," John Luther intoned. " 'A virtuous woman is a crown to her husband: but she that
maketh ashamed is as rottenness in his bones.' "

Wreath, feeling the burn of the unhealed welts across her buttocks, didn't move a muscle. Beside her, Jezzie took a shuddering
breath and reached for her mother's hand. She'd heard variations
on the upcoming sermon a dozen times and the public humiliation of her mother always upset her.

"Jezebel," Delilah hissed. Jezzie pulled her hand back into her
own lap. Much as she wanted to comfort her mother, she dreaded

having her tight-assed, tattletale bitch of a sister bring down their father's wrath on her own shoulders. She didn't concern herself about using bad language in her head during church despite regular sermons on impure thoughts and the road to hell. If God were going to strike her dead for impure thoughts in church, He'd have done it years earlier. Probably knew that silent cussing was the only thing that kept her from screaming out loud at times.

"Old Eve lives in the hearts of women, driving them in the direction of the serpent, driving them into sin," John Luther rumbled. "My own wife, sitting there among you, the woman who vowed to love, honor, and obey me, has gathered opinions unto herself without counsel of he who stands unto her as God stands unto men. Not only has she gathered these sinful thoughts, but she has expressed them in my presence. She had defied me and in doing so has defied God as well."

Genevieve didn't expect to like any sermon John Luther chose to give, much less be uplifted or enlightened by it, but she listened with growing horror as the man excoriated his own wife, aiming his finger at her like a pistol, firing verbal bullet after bullet at her bowed head.

"She has contradicted me. She has disdained my wishes. She held her own thoughts and did not submit willingly to my instructions." He pointed dramatically to the big bruise and cut over his own eye, and declared, "God has punished me for not bringing this woman to heel sooner, for being lax in controlling her willfulness. He caused me to be struck with a missile out of the darkness, making me understand what must be done here today, however hurtful it is to me to make our private life public."

Eyes flickered from John Luther's face to the front pew where Wreath sat, head down. Her two youngest daughters looked ready to burst into tears. Delilah sat straight and tall, her bright eyes fastened on her father, head bobbing in rhythm to his vilification of her mother. Mercer stiffened as soon as he realized where the sermon was headed. Standing beside him in the aisle, Bigger muttered about what he'd do to any son of a bitch who talked about his mother that way. Genevieve was too stunned to move. She sat with her mouth open, hearing echoes of other sermons and other times, hardly able to breathe.

"Corporal punishment has taken place at my hands, but now must she face He who is greater than I. Wreath Hughley Ives, are you prepared to beg forgiveness for your trespasses on bended knees at the altar of God?"

Before the poor woman could move, Genevieve stood up. She stepped past Mercer into the aisle and walked past Bigger toward the door at the back of the church, fists clinched, hoping she could get outside before she lunged at the sanctimonious bastard at the pulpit and tore off his face. She saw Bigger's huge black hand attempt to open the door for her, placed her own hand where his lay, and pushed into the outdoors.

In the front of the church, John Luther forgot for a moment his wife's wickedness in the face of even greater wickedness. No one had ever walked out of his church while he was speaking. He brought both fists down on the pulpit so hard that those in the front pews heard the wood crack. Before he could speak, Mercer stood up.

"She's sick," he said, feeling ill himself. "I'll go see about her."

A young woman across the aisle started to rise and offer her help, but her husband jerked her back into their pew. A murmur swept the church as Mercer strode up the aisle and out the door. John Luther took a deep breath and opened his mouth.

"I repent," Wreath said, getting to her feet. "I stand righteously accused, and I repent of my sins to God and to my husband." She slid out of the pew and knelt in the aisle facing the altar. For a moment, she stayed there while the congregation grew silent around her. Then she fell forward onto her hands and started the long slow crawl to the altar, whispering with each movement, "I repent. I repent."

A tiny sob escaped Leah as she watched her mother's humiliation. Jezzie slid over next to her. Ignoring Delilah's furious hissing, she put her arm around the child's shoulders and held her until the horror was at an end.

CHAPTER 15
GENEVIEVE

The carriage house stood at the end of a narrow lane about half a mile outside of Washington. I loved it at first sight, run-down and sad as it was. The original plantation house was long gone, the blocks of its raised foundation hidden in a tangle of wisteria and grass. It hadn't been a plantation house like Tara or Oak Alley in Louisiana, just a good-sized frame house that burned one night twenty years before I was born. The owners had abandoned it decades earlier when the railroad went through the town of Hope, and most of Washington's businesses and population relocated to the new county seat. Pitiful old carriage house, with nobody to love it and just a succession of no-good poor whites making use of the place until the present owner ran them off for failure to pay rent. Well, Mercer and I were about as poor as any whites who ever lived here, but I wouldn't call either of us no-good.

When Mercer offered to put a lock on the inside of my bedroom door, I declined with thanks, not being the least bit concerned that he might not behave like a gentleman. However, I put a brand-new lock on our front door myself since there was no telling how many people had keys to the place. Neither of us had much anyone would want to steal, but I didn't like the idea of someone unlocking the door and walking in without warning while we were sleeping or at work.

Wreath made it clear that the visiting preacher's room was mine for as long as I wanted it, but I moved into the carriage house before Mercer's family got home from church that horrible Sunday. Mercer would've been happy to move in right on my heels, but I told him he needed to give his mama a few more days of his company. Late Monday morning, I set out to fix up what would be the first home of my own that wasn't a tent. Wreath insisted on loading up some cleaning supplies and coming over to mop floors and clean what may have been the dirtiest oven I ever saw. I was happy to have her company and her help. Away from the constraints of her husband and critical oldest daughter, Wreath relaxed. Though I wouldn't call her a chatterbox, she made conversation and I saw the sense of humor Mercer mentioned shine through her reserve.

"I figured it out," she said, giving the stove a last wipe and dropping her sponge back into the bucket. "You and me are first cousins once removed."

I looked up at her from my place on the kitchen floor where I was scrubbing up some mysterious substance I didn't want to examine too closely. "Well, Miss Wreath, I couldn't ask for a finer first cousin once removed."

"That makes you and my children second cousins," she added. "Second cousins aren't too close for marriage."

At the sight of my stunned face, that dear lady laughed out loud, a full, rolling chuckle that caught me by surprise.

"Miss Wreath, Mercer and I—"

"Oh, honey," she interrupted, "I know y'all aren't plannin' a weddin', and I know he's figurin' on movin' in here with you soon as he decides how to tell me he's leavin' home."

"There's two bedrooms. We're just going to be roommates."

"I know, honey," she said, reaching down to pat me on the shoulder. "But a mama can hope, can't she?" She sat down on the floor next to me, folding up with a grace and ease that made me realize what a young woman she was. "Reckon I ought to be shocked to the marrow of my bones at the idea of y'all settin' up a household together, but I'm not. One you're liable to have some trouble with is John Luther once he finds out. I'm not gonna tell him, but someone will, and then he'll be over here breathin' fire and brimstone on y'all."

"I'm not scared of John Luther," I said firmly.

She nodded. "Wish I wasn't. But I am."

I hesitated, then asked, "You ever think of leaving him?"

She was quiet a long moment, pulling at a loose thread on her apron. Finally, she said, "I've thought about it almost every day since we married. Huh. Never said that out loud to another person and I'm hopin' you won't repeat it."

"I wouldn't ever, ma'am."

"Problem was, I never had anywhere else to go. Even when my folks were alive, they'd not have let me come home if I'd left him. Believed marriage was something you couldn't go back on, no matter what. Don't know that I believe that myself anymore. Still, I got nowhere else to go, and there's the younger girls and my grandbabies to be thought of. Was I to leave, he and Delilah'd make sure I never saw any of them again, and I surely could not stand that."

I couldn't think of a thing to say. I reached over and took her hand, feeling the calluses that hard work had embroidered on her palms. She looked over at me. "It's gonna be bad enough him not lettin' us see you anymore once he finds out Mercer is moving in here. Jezzie, 'specially. She's thrivin' on them extra lessons you're givin' her."

"Don't you worry about that," I said. "I'll find a way to keep right on giving her those lessons and seeing you and Leah, too. I didn't just get a family back to give y'all up that easy."

"I hope so, honey." Wreath patted my hand, then got to her feet as gracefully as she'd descended to the floor and slapped the seat of her house dress. "Well, sittin' here visitin', pleasant as it is, isn't gettin' that bathroom clean." She smiled and disappeared into the back of the apartment, carrying her bucket and mop.

When the place sparkled, I called Gil from the phone booth in front of Washington's little grocery store and asked if it was okay for me to paint the walls. After work that day, Mercer arrived at the house with drop cloths, paint brushes and rollers, and several gallons of white paint.

"Gil sent the stuff," he said, setting it down on the kitchen floor. "He said he'll trade us a month's rent in return for the labor you're putting into fixing the place up."

"Well, that's nice of him." I smiled impishly at Mercer. "Guess that pays my half of the rent and you'll be cooking some."

"Only until you find out what terrible things I do to eggs and meat," he answered good-naturedly. He rolled up his sleeves and peeked into the clean living room. "Where you want me to start painting?"

He moved his gear into the second bedroom a couple of days later. We didn't have any furniture. Both of us slept on the floors of our respective rooms and we ate our meals sitting on the floor of the kitchen.

I found a job as a groundskeeper of some of the country cemeteries. Since the job involved a fair amount of driving, it came with the use of a truck older than I was. For the first time in my life, I needed a driver's license. I'd driven plenty in the circus, but never legally. Mercer helped me study for the written test, Gil loaned me a car for the driving part, and before I knew it, I had me an official Arkansas driver's license in the name of Genevieve Madeleine Antoinette Charbonneau. With that, I buried Oleana Larkin forever. I cannot tell you the satisfaction that gave me. I liked my job, I liked my truck, I liked my new home, and I liked my roommate. I put money away in the bank every paycheck to pay for college, and I started studying for my GED.

Mercer struggled, though. Some days were worse than others. He'd do pretty good for a while, showing up at the garage every day and putting in a solid eight hours. Then something would shift in his mind and Bigger'd come to visit, sometimes bringing other ghosts whose names I never heard. Mercer'd have trouble concentrating on what was real and before long, all he could do was sit in the yard, staring at the shades of old ambushes and dying men. I couldn't always hear or see them, but I knew they were there. When it got really bad, he gave up, crawled into a bottle, and drank himself comatose. Afterward, he'd sober up and go back to living his life. Between drunks, he didn't touch a drop of liquor. I never knew how long Mercer was going to stay drunk. Usually, it was just a day or two. Once he went a week without taking a sober breath. He wasn't a mean drunk, but he was a silent one. I don't think he ever liked it. Just every once in a while, he'd sit down and get the business over with one glassful at a time.

The first time, he passed out on the kitchen floor with his head on his arms and the last of the whiskey spilling from the bottle. The next time, I tried getting him into his own room before he was completely obliterated, but that was a disaster. Moving disturbed his descent into oblivion, and after that, he couldn't let go. He tossed and moaned and cried out like a child with night terrors, held back from complete unconsciousness by the ghosts that whispered to him and whatever horrible memories that came with them. I was afraid to leave him alone, so I stayed there beside him, sitting cross-legged on the floor, hands pressed over my ears to block out the voices. I watched over him for hours, not even dozing for fear he'd hurt himself or me. After that terrible night, I let him drink himself insensible and fall wherever he happened to be. As if he understood the problem without discussion, he started making sure he was in his room when the inevitable happened.

Gil Herndon owned the garage where Mercer worked, as well as the place we lived, being a descendent of the original owners. Gil thought the world of Mercer, and by association, me. He was patient and understanding above and beyond the call of friendship, maybe because he had his own ghosts and bad memories of Korea. Whenever I called him up to say that Mercer was sick and couldn't work until the chills and ague from his nonexistent malaria went away, Gil'd just say, "You tell him to come on back in when he feels better. Y'all need anything?"

"No, sir, we're fine," I'd say, even when we weren't. He'd wish us well and hang up.

I don't know exactly why I stayed. I didn't have to once I had money and transportation of my own. Partially it was a bond of family; Mercer, Wreath, Jezzie and Leah were the first family I'd had since Meema died so many years ago. I don't include John Luther in family, or Delilah and Jared, who were just extensions of that abusive fool. They did their best to keep me from seeing Wreath and the younger girls, but somehow that dear lady contrived to visit Mercer and me regularly and bring the girls with her. Mercer was as sick as anyone I ever met in the Alabama State Mental Hospital, and maybe that's why I stayed, too. Lord knows, being around him on a bender made me certain that I was as sane as a glass of sweet tea, and he needed me. For the first time in my life, somebody needed me, and I needed to be needed. It was enough, at least for a while. Sometimes, it even felt like being loved.

Of course, when he was sober, Mercer was the one who thought he was living with a crazy person. Voices and ghosts were bad enough, but the day he found me moving a small den of rattlesnakes out of the well house and back into the woods, I thought he was going to cut and run screaming down the road.

Now, Mercer was a sucker for stray dogs and cats. At any given time, we had a good half a dozen living around the place. The worse shape they were in when he found them, the more he cared about them. He cleaned their wounds, pulled off their ticks, fed them better than he ate himself, then found them homes somewhere. Except for a half-grown blue tick hound who was blind in one eye and lame in one leg, he never kept any of them. I think he was afraid of loving them too much, so he always sent them on their ways. The only reason we kept Boomerang is because he kept coming back no matter where Mercer sent him. When he limped home from Blevins, ten miles away, Mercer gave up and Boomerang slept with one or the other of us ever after.

Despite his break with his father and his father's religion, Mercer still had not only a Southerner's ingrained hatred of a snake, but a Christian's philosophical loathing of a serpent as well. Seeing me standing there with a couple of timber rattlers draped peacefully across my hands sent him into a pure-dee conniption. Then when I wouldn't let him kill the one still in the well house, he really pitched a fit and fell in it. Finally, he shut up, gritted his teeth, and followed me at a safe distance as I carried the three snakes back into the woods where they wouldn't do any harm or come to any harm themselves. I knew he expected to have to perform first aid on me at any second, but the snakes stayed as calm as he was not.

"Why do they bother you so much?" I asked over my shoulder as we followed a twisting path to the creek that ran along the bottom of the property.

"Because they're snakes! Fucking poisonous snakes, and you're carrying them around like they were kittens."

"They have their place in the world."

"One had its place in Eden, too," he grumped.

I stopped and turned to him, the snakes dangling limp and content across the palms of my hands. "Seems I did read that a serpent gave people the gift of knowledge of good and evil, and freed them from living like tame animals in a luxurious zoo."

That shook him, shook him up so bad that he turned white. "That's blasphemy."

"Well, I don't know about that, Mercer. I always figured someone put that serpent in Eden for that exact reason. Or do you think it just sneaked in past God on its own?"

His eyes locked on the snakes in my hands, waiting, no doubt, for lightning bolts, or at least the snakes, to strike me dead. Poor Mercer, try as he might to escape his upbringing, he still believed in the God of Wrath, ever ready to smite anyone who steps out of line with church doctrine, feeding children to bears and faithful men to big fish in a never-ending attempt to force at least part of the human race into proclaiming him the most important god in the universe. I believe in this wrathful god of the Christians and Hebrews, too. I just don't believe he's as all powerful as he'd like to be, and that some greater spirit somewhere keeps the God of Wrath from destroying the world.

But Mercer sure didn't want to hear this bit of personal philosophy. Not now. Maybe not ever. None of my business. I turned and continued on my way to the rattlesnakes' new home. He followed silently, thinking so hard that he didn't even notice the shadows flickering down the path on either side of him, whispering his name. They finally gave up and drifted away like so much smoke. Good riddance. I felt sorry for those poor souls, but Mercer was my first concern, and I didn't like them messing with him.

We came to the creek and followed it a way downstream to a nice thick patch of underbrush near an opening in the pines that would allow the snakes to bask in the sun if they so desired. Lots of mice and other meals, so maybe the snakes would be content to stay put. Kneeling down, I lowered my hands so that their bodies touched the ground.

"Y'all get on out of here now, and don't go back to the well house," I warned. The wedge-headed serpents slid through my fingers and into the shade beneath the brush.

"How did you learn to do that?" Mercer whispered.

"My grandmother taught me." I stood up and dusted my hands on the seat of my jeans. "I don't think you ought to try it, though. Not yet."

"Not ever." He shook his head as he watched the snakes disappear, then glanced around at his feet the way people do when they've seen one snake and expect to see more. "I know you're not a Christian, but . . . a buddy in the Marines was from East Tennessee. He said he went to a Jesus Only service one time where some folks handled snakes as a test and proof of faith. Said he'd a thought the snakes were defanged or had their mouths sewn shut, but not one of 'em showed any sign of wanting to strike or bite."

I thought a while about what I wanted to say. The worst time of my life had been spent within a snake-handling church, but that was no fault of anyone but the evil man into whose hands I was given. Most of those folks were good people, but their philosophy of life is so different from mine that I hope never to see any of them again, this side of the grave or the next. When Nette, who was one mean-hearted old lady, found me in that room with her dead pedophile nephew and the grandmother rattlesnake on the bed, she screamed and ran to get someone to kill the snake. By the time Nette got back with neighbors, I'd gotten the snake out of the house. They caught us in the yard as I rushed the grandmother rattlesnake toward the safety of the woods. Since they couldn't take vengeance on her, some of them tried to kill me instead. Mean old Nette started shouting about not suffering witches to live. When the first rock hit me, it was just like I went somewhere else and didn't take my body with me. Next thing I knew, I was in a mental hospital, wondering just who in the hell decided I was the crazy one.

Mercer watched me while I tried to decide what to say and how to say it. Finally, I just opened my mouth and let the words fall out.

"After Meema died, I had to go live with an aunt and cousin up in the tail end of the Appalachian Mountains in Alabama. The cousin was the preacher for a group of snake-handling Holiness people that called themselves the Kingdom Come Church of the Holy Ghost with Signs Following. They're true believers, Mercer. When what they call The Holy Ghost comes on them, they speak in tongues, pick up snakes, drink poison, stuff no sane person would consider. I don't know what other snake-handling churches think, but in this church, every single person believed that Satan was in every single snake. By picking those snakes up, they were proving their faith and defeating Satan.

"But I'll tell you something: if Satan exists on earth, he takes a human form." My voice rose with old anger augmented by new anger ignited by what I'd seen in Mercer's own parents' house. I clamped my witless tongue between my teeth to shut it up, but it broke free as if I had no control over it at all.

"He dishonored the snakes and he dishonored women and girl children, and he used Eve and the serpent as an excuse for doing it. Well, damn him and damn his—"

A gentle touch on my shoulder stopped me.

"I think," Mercer whispered, "that he dishonored you. I'm sorry, Genevieve."

I put my hand over my mouth, but it was his sympathy as much as my hand that finally stopped the spate of words. To my horror, tears welled up in my eyes. That was bad. Crying let people know they'd gotten to you, and then they could get to you even more.

"Do you want to tell me about it?"

I pushed my hand hard against my mouth and thought of a story Meema read to me when I was a child, about a boy poking his finger in a dike to keep it from breaking. After she was done reading, she snorted just like a horse. It was the rudest sound I ever heard her make and I'd laughed out loud.

"What a load of turnips," she'd said. "I saw a levee on Red River break back in '27, and I don't reckon anybody could've stopped it with a bulldozer, much less a finger."

I pulled in a ragged breath, half laughing, remembering it. Then . . .

"Let it go, sugar. You've carried it long enough."

I never in my life expected to hear her voice again. I flung out both hands, crying out her name. Mercer caught my hands in his, and the levee inside me broke.

I have no idea how long I cried or exactly what I said while I cried, but I told him everything, about Burgess Love Darnell, about Mara, about the grandmother rattlesnake, and about the mental hospital. When the flood began to abate, all I wanted to do was lie down and sleep for a very long time. Mercer got me back to the house, up into bed, and was putting a cold wet cloth on my head when I fell asleep.

The next day was Sunday. I got up when the sky was barely light and went out to make coffee only to discover Mercer already spooning grounds into the electric percolator. I pulled eggs and milk out of the ice box and set about making pancakes. We worked and ate together in companionable silence as the day brightened.

"Got anything planned for today?" I asked.

"Thought I'd take a ride somewhere. You want to come?"

"Sure. I wonder, though, could we stop by Meema's old place?"

The old home place was a couple of miles off the dirt road that ran northeast out of Washington. This was the old Southwest Trail that once linked Mexican Texas with the United States. A good number of men who died at the Alamo traveled down this road, some of them with their families in tow. In the early 1830s, my grandfather's people arrived from Alabama and Tennessee to settle in Hempstead County. Right behind them came a long, sad parade of exiled people as the Choctaw tribe made its way down the road toward Oklahoma, having given way to the power of Andrew Jackson's administration. If any road deserves to be haunted, this one does, but I never heard more than a distant murmur on it.

We rode through the dark shade of pine forests, across old wooden bridges with no railings and barely room enough for a single vehicle. Places that had been homes when I was a little girl had become weathered houses with empty windows that breathed wisps of haunts into the still, humid air. We passed new pickup trucks parked in front of neat homes on green pastures and houses that were occupied by people who had long ceased to keep up appearances. I almost missed Meema's place, did miss it at first, and only a sharp bend in the road told me we'd gone too far. We doubled back, riding slow, until we came to the rusted gate that marked the entrance to what used to be the driveway.

I climbed off the bike and stood at the gate, too stunned to do more than whisper over and over, "Oh, my sweet stars. Where's the driveway? Where is the orchard?" The house was long gone; this I knew and expected, though the image of it still rose in my mind, two stories with tall, broad windows and a front porch on which two swings hung facing each other. What I wasn't expecting was the desolation of the land itself, the return to a tangle of pine and vines.

"It's been logged," Mercer said softly. "This looks like second growth."

"Not logged. Tornado."

"Oh. You want to go in?"

I didn't know whether I did or not. What I could see from the road was bad enough. Gradually, though, my eyes picked out things I recognized: the big crepe myrtle to the north of the gate, now grown to monstrous proportions, the magnolia tree that stood where the foot of the lawn once ran, a random scattering of jonquils, long past bloom, beneath the magnolia.

"There used to be a bench under that magnolia," I said, gesturing. "Big old wooden thing my grandfather built when my mama was a little girl. I wasn't supposed to climb trees, which made me determined to climb every single one in the yard. Meema used to make me sit on that bench for a quarter hour every time she caught me."

"Guess you probably sat there a lot."

I laughed softly and nodded. "Yep. My bottom and that bench were well acquainted. I wonder what happened to it."

Through a tangle of low branches, I spotted a low-roofed rect-angular shape that was the old well house at the top of the drive-way. It sat closer to the road than I remembered and the hill to it seemed lower.

The fence posts and trees along the road were painted orchid, the familiar color that denotes "no hunting" in Arkansas, but I didn't see any no trespassing signs. I climbed the gate and for the first time in ten years stood on what had been my family's land for generations. Without waiting to see if Mercer was following me, I twisted and turned my way to the well house to get my bearings.

It sat about thirty yards from the road, but I had to walk almost twice that to get around bramble patches and fallen branches. From there, I found my way to the foundation stones that once supported the house and the pile of bricks that was what was left of the chimney. My great-grandfather made those bricks out of clay he dug and fired a mile or two from the house.

Watching carefully for snakes, I managed to pry a couple of whole bricks out of the pile. I had no idea what I was going to do with them. I just knew I wanted to take them with me. Mercer had caught up with me by that time, though he maintained a polite distance in case I wanted or needed it.

"Let me carry those," he said, and I handed them over without a word.

A pile of wood scraps and rusted chicken wire marked the yard where Meema's chickens and ducks used to scratch in the dirt, but I couldn't even make an educated guess as to where the old horses and a single milk cow used to graze. What had been pasture was now nothing but pine woods. A few more steps, and I came to the raised concrete rim of the storm cellar. The door was long gone, but someone had overlaid the opening with corrugated metal held in place by pieces of the old house foundation.

I never knew a storm could have a ghost, but I heard the roar of the approaching tornado as if ten years hadn't passed. Only the perfectly still air kept me from looking over the trees for the funnel cloud. I closed my eyes and listened to Meema screaming at me to get in the cellar, her voice almost lost in the roar.

"Genevieve?" Mercer's grip on my elbow pulled me out of the storm and back to the broken remains of the best part of my childhood.

"What?"

He heaved a sigh and shook my arm gently before releasing it. "You hadn't moved in ten minutes. It was beginning to freak me out."

Ten minutes? I'd have argued that he was exaggerating until I saw his face. Freaked out described the expression on it. His eyes darted around the trees and brush like he was watching for hungry Mercer-eating wolves. When I heard a distant murmur of shouts and gunfire, I realized what was happening.

"I'm moving now," I said gently. "C'mon, let's get out of here. I've seen all there is to see."

It took us a quarter hour to make our way through the pine jungle back to the gate. Once I caught a glimpse of Bigger trying to pull a low hanging limb out of Mercer's way, but his big hand right passed through the wood. Mercer muttered something to him and kept moving. The dead marine looked back at me, all the mockery gone from his expression.

"He couldn't save me," Bigger said. "Couldn't save a bunch of us. And now he cain't let us go."

"I know," I answered. He nodded to me and evaporated.

CHAPTER 16
MERCER

The ambush was planned for a trail known to be in regular use by NVA soldiers. Mercer trudged along toward the chosen site, watching for trip lines, pongee pits, enemy troops, enemy serpents, and all the other normal dangers of the Vietnamese landscape. The subtle sounds of skilled men in cautious transit echoed in his ears as loud as the cathedral bell he'd heard ring in San Diego as the transport ship set sail for Asia. He wondered what the surrounding countryside looked like before years of fighting reduced it to red clay, burned trees, and sword-edged grass. He wondered if he was carrying enough medical supplies. He wondered who he'd have to paste together this time and who he'd help haul back to the helicopter for the trip to graves registration. He wondered how in the hell he got himself into Vietnam instead of a nice clean hospital ship somewhere off the coast of Okinawa.

He glanced over at Bigger, who was making his own way across the broken ground. As if the glance was a tangible touch, Bigger turned his head to look at Mercer. He lifted his chin in acknowledgment just as the ruined jungle exploded around them. Mercer's right leg gave way, and he crumpled into a stunned heap. Two seconds later, Bigger landed on top of him and commenced firing at the shadows of NVA soldiers hidden by the broken trees and cratered ground. From beneath the shelter of Bigger's body, Mercer watched little geysers of dirt spit up as bullets bit into the earth a few inches from his face.

The percussion from Bigger's M14 split Mercer's eardrums as he tried to figure out what in the hell had just happened. *Ambush*, he thought. *They beat us to it. God, how many of them are there?* Amidst the noise of war, voices of the wounded galvanized him to action. He shoved Bigger off him and rolled sideways to scan the area for victims. Redheaded Alice lay on his side a few yards away, face set in a grimace, still firing his rifle despite what oozed from his abdomen. Mercer tried to crawl toward him only to collapse with a yelp of pain. He rolled over and looked down at a welter of torn cloth and streaming blood above his knee. Swearing like the sailor he'd aspired to be, he dug in his pack for a bandage and without pausing to see how bad he'd been hit, tied it over the wound. He flipped onto his stomach to pull himself across the ground, grimly driving his elbows one after another into the red soil.

"Hang on, Alice," he said as he took the rifle from the man's shaking hands. Alice tipped onto his back, looked up at the hot blue sky, and died. For a moment, utter despair washed over Mercer. Too late. Too late. If only he hadn't stopped to bind his own wound. He rested his head briefly against Alice's shoulder, then raised himself up on his elbows to look for the next wounded marine.

For an hour or a day or a year, Mercer pulled himself from man to man, patching head wounds, slapping plastic over sucking chest wounds, tightening tourniquets around shredded and missing limbs. As the battle wore on, he gathered ammunition from the dead and transported it inch by hard-won inch to those still fighting. When he ran out of bandages, he tore strips of cloth from uniforms. He ran out of morphine, gauze, antibiotics, alcohol, iodine, and bandages. All around echoed cries of "Corpsman up!" He couldn't drag himself fast enough to reach them all.

A grenade went off, splattering hot metal and dirt like a rock thrown into a pond splashes water. Mercer yelped, fell on his face for the twentieth time that afternoon, and looked down at himself to see if the damage was bad enough to prevent his crawling progress among his marines. Flesh wounds, he thought, and almost laughed at the unbidden memory of some World War II movie he'd seen where a character growled, "It's just a flesh wound. I can still fight, Sarge."

"John fuckin' Wayne," he muttered aloud, and pulled himself toward the man who had caught the worst of the blast, laughter forgotten.

One tall marine was on his hands and knees, shaking his bloody head as if trying to clear the noise and confusion of battle from it. When Mercer reached out to touch him, the man leapt to his feet, glared wild-eyed from side to side, and started to run. Mercer wrapped his forearms around the man's boots, bringing him crashing to the ground. The marine lay stunned for just a second, then kicked out at his rescuer.

"Rudy, stop! Goddamn it, it's me." Mercer ducked the kicks, but he couldn't escape when Rudy grabbed a chunk of wood and swung it at him like a golf club. The blow connected with Mercer's left ear, knocking him sideways. He rolled down a slight incline and came to rest on his back in a shallow muddy stream. Rudy scrambled away from the ditch and died in the next mortar blast. Barely aware of the blast, Mercer drifted out of consciousness with small wavelets brushing his cheeks.

Later he learned that a platoon of reinforcements arrived and fought off the attack. By that time, only a third of the original unit was still standing. He eased back into something resembling cognizance to find himself lying in a helicopter with a muddy but unwounded Bigger sitting by his side. The man's face split into a grin when Mercer opened his eyes and grimaced in recognition.

"Good to see you, Doc. Had me worried there for a sec."

"What in the fuck just happened?"

Bigger shrugged. "Charlie knew 'bout the ambush. Got there fustest with the mostest men."

Despite the pain and confusion that beset him, Mercer squinted up at his friend and said incredulously, "Why in hell . . . would a black man . . . quote Bedford fuckin' Forrest?"

" 'Cause Bedford fuckin' Forrest was a fuckin' military genius."

Mercer let out a grunt that might've been a laugh, then closed his eyes. "How many?"

Bigger didn't pretend to misunderstand. "Most of us. Tak still on his feet. That son of a bitch got a charm on his life. Holes all over his shirt and pants but not a one in him. Sarge still up and movin'. Handful of guys come out with nary a scratch. Handful more you saved. You done good, Doc."

"Handful," Mercer muttered, and drifted out of the conversation and awareness again.

> *June 21, 1966*
> *Dear Mama,*
>
> *I'm sorry I haven't written in so long. Been busy here and I'm not much hand at writing anyway. Thank you for your letters. They tend to arrive in batches, but I save them to read, never more than one new one a day.*
>
> *Don't be worried, but I had a little accident that put me on crutches for a while. You know how clumsy I can be. Few more days and I'll be good as new.*
>
> *Hug Jezzie and Leah for me and tell them I wish I was there to help with the chores.*
>
> *Your son,*
> *Mercer*

Mercer Ives received a Purple Heart and a recommendation for a Bronze Star. The paperwork for the latter got lost somewhere between his commanding officer's desk and Washington, D.C. The Marines shipped him to Japan for major surgery on his leg and lesser surgeries on other wounds he wasn't even aware he'd incurred. He spent weeks in rehab, working determinedly to move from crutches to cane to unassisted, albeit painful, walking. One doctor told him the leg wound was bad enough to buy him a ticket home. Mercer snorted and said, "My marines are dying in Nam while I'm sitting on my ass in Yokosuka. Patch me up and get me back to my unit. Uh, sir."

Six weeks after the botched ambush, he watched the earth flicker by beneath the chopper, as fascinated by flight now as he'd been on his first helicopter ride into the bush. When the helicopter reached the landing zone, it hovered, as always, a few feet above the muddy ground, too high to safely hop down and too low to use a parachute. Mercer regarded the drop with disgust, shrugged, and jumped out. The impact of landing sent a jolt of pain rocketing through his bad leg. Swearing, he stumbled and would've gone sprawling had not a huge black hand grabbed him by the arm and jerked him back on his feet.

"Li'l brother, you a special kind of stupid," said Bigger. He dropped Mercer's arm as soon as the smaller man caught his balance and led the way off the dirt landing pad. "What the fuck are you doin' back in this hellhole when you coulda gone home?"

"Garden season in Arkansas," Mercer said. "I hate hoeing weeds. I hate picking okra. I hate hand-watering shit during dry spells. I hate—"

Bigger started to laugh. "Could be worse. Ever pick cotton?"

"No. You?"

"Naw, but my daddy's stories about it give me nightmares." Bigger pointedly looked over Mercer's gear and added, "You still not carryin' a gun."

"Nope."

"What if you need to shoot somebody?"

"That's what I got you for," Mercer answered, and grinned.

Nothing had changed in his absence except the monsoon rains had begun in earnest and what had been choking dust turned to cloying mud. Patrols went out. Patrols came back with more or less the number of men they started out with. New guys filled the spaces left behind by Alice, Rudy, and too many others to contemplate. Mercer examined their faces and wondered if he'd ever been that young and scared.

"How old are you?" he asked one baby-faced marine as he swabbed a suspicious rash on the boy's back with calamine lotion. The kid looked about fifteen. Mercer had heard tales of underage boys altering dates on their birth certificates so they could sign up for service.

"I turned twenty-one a couple of weeks ago." The boy dug in a pocket and pulled out a fistful of black-and-white snapshots. He sorted through the stack, chose one, and handed it to Mercer. "This is the cake my grandmother baked for me." A beaming woman with a soft, wrinkled face tilted a large sheet cake toward the camera to show off an inscription that read, *Happy 21st Birthday, Willy. Wish you were here.*

Mercer blinked. His own twentieth birthday wasn't until October. He told Willy to put his shirt on, try to keep his back dry for a while, and sent him on his way. Two days later, Willy's rash was obscured by wounds left by the small-arms fire that killed him. Mercer never asked anyone's age or personal information again.

In addition to battling unseen foes, the Marines established the Medical Civic Action Program to serve the medical needs of civilian Vietnamese. Periodically, Mercer followed the battalion's chief medical officers into the small villages that dotted the Vietnamese countryside, carrying whatever medical supplies and diagnostic equipment they could beg, borrow, or liberate for the good of people who otherwise lacked even basic medical care. For an afternoon or a couple of days at a time, they did what they could to improve lives ravaged by war and the diseases endemic to Southeast Asia. Mercer treated endless cases of glaucoma, infected insect bites, and chikungunya. He talked timid mothers into letting him examine their babies, set broken limbs, dispensed antibiotics, and wondered how many of these smiling people would emerge after dark in the ranks of the Viet Cong.

When he wasn't working with MEDCAP or going out on patrols, Mercer fought an ongoing battle with the marines in his company over taking malaria pills.

"What the hell is wrong with y'all?" he demanded. "You know how many men go down with malaria every day just because they won't take a pill? It's not just one short bout with the damn stuff and then you're done. It'll keep kicking your ass for the rest of your life."

A few swallowed the pills. Bigger was among the resisters.

"I don't like pills, Doc. They stick in my throat," he explained. "Don't matter how much water I suck down after 'em, they stick and then they burn. I ain't gonna take 'em so quit askin' if I want 'em."

When the monsoons set in, conditions went from merely miserable to damn near unbearable. Recon patrols traveled light: no tents, no sleeping bags, "just some toilet paper and a couple boxes of inedible food," Mercer grumbled. Much of the time, men rolled up in their ponchos and slept on the ground with the rain beating on their shoulders.

One night, Mercer and Bigger huddled together in the relative luxury of a fighting hole. Despite carefully mounded berms and an extra poncho for a roof, water seeped in through the walls, turning the dirt to slick mud. The trench in the floor, meant as a drain, was woefully inadequate in the face of the flood that fell from the sky.

"Hey," said a voice above them. "Got room to squeeze in one more?"

"If you don't mind bein' extra cozy," answered Bigger.

He nudged Mercer over to make room. Tak, the sniper, slid between the poncho roof and the side of the hole, releasing a couple of gallons of water onto the heads of his companions who amiably swore at the liberal addition to the pool they were sitting in. Tak apologized, tucked himself into a corner of the pit, and checked his bolt rifle for the hundredth time that day to make sure it was safe but immediately accessible in its waterproof wraps.

"Thanks. Our hole sloughed its sides all at once. I swear, more rain falls in this damn country in an hour than falls in a year back home in Wyoming."

"Where's Taggert?" Mercer asked, referring to Tak's spotter.

"Stretch had room in his hole." Tak shook his head morosely. "Holes in the ground."

He emulated Mercer and Bigger who had rolled their pants legs to the knees so they could pull off the leeches that had adhered themselves to calves and ankles. The three de-leeched themselves in silence for a while, each man thinking his own glum thoughts. Tak's arrival made for close quarters, but no one complained; he'd have done the same for them.

"I ever tell you 'bout my uncle Perlie?" Bigger asked, expertly tossing a leech through a small gap between poncho and hole rim.

"Don't think so," said Mercer.

"My daddy's brother. Good-lookin' fella but had the damndest trouble getting himself a bride. Asked two or three girls to marry him but they all said nuh-uh. Don' know why. Had himself a nice little house on the bayou, nice little business fixin' shoes and harnesses and such. Made some hooch on the side but not 'nough to attract unfav'able attention.

"Well, Perlie got to feelin' pert near hopeless about the whole thing when one day what should come right up the bayou to his front door but a woman with quilts to sell. Pretty woman. Big hazel eyes, cinnamon skin, and long, smooth hair plumb to her butt. Fell for her like he'd been poleaxed.

"Well, to make a long story short—not that you boys got much to do but listen to me tell stories—Perlie and this gal stepped out regular, and when he asked her to marry him, she said she would. He was all ready to stand up in front of the preacher with her, but she said she didn't want no church weddin', jus' a visit to the courthouse in Hope. Perlie was so het up to finally have one on his line that they went down and got married jus' like she wanted."

"Why do I get the feeling there was something wrong with this girl?" Tak asked from the shadows.

"'Cause there was, and if you just tread water for a minute, I tell you about it."

"Treading, sir," Tak answered.

"Well, first night, she fed him a good supper then sat workin' on a quilt, her fingers slidin' that shiny needle in and out of them little squares. Lo and behold if he didn't fall plumb asleep watchin' her. Same thing happen the next night. You can imagine 'bout how frustrated he was gettin'." Bigger tossed two more leeches through the gap. One plopped back into the water in the bottom of the hole.

"Well, on the third night, he fell asleep again, but some noise she made woke him up in time to see her head upstairs. She didn't look right, so he followed her quiet as could be right up to where he could peek into the bedroom without her seeing him. She opened a window, put both hands on top of her head, and stroked downward. Perlie like to fainted when her dress, skin, and hair all fell in a heap at her feet. What was left of her wasn't nothin' like anything he ever saw, just naked muscles and a pair of black wings. When she flew out the window, Perlie knew he'd done gone and married himself to a witchy woman.

"Well, boys, it near broke his heart, her bein' so pretty and sweet when she was human, but he knew it wouldn't do to keep her 'round. He found him a bag of salt, poured it into that empty skin of hers, then went back downstairs to wait. Sky was just turnin' light when he heard her come in the window. Couple seconds later, she commenced to screamin', then everything got deathly silent. He crept back upstairs, scared white—which is sayin' somethin', 'cause Perlie was a real dark man. Anyway, he got up there and wasn't nothing left but a pile of ash and a hank of long black hair."

Mercer's skin prickled, and Tak moved uneasily on his side of the lightless hole.

"Well, old Perlie, he got him a broom and a bucket and swept up them ashes and that hair. Carried 'em down to the bayou and tossed 'em in 'cause he wanted her gone, hide and hair. Soon as they hit the water, the ashes hissed and smoked, and every strand of that hair turn into a rusty-backed water moccasin that tried to get at him."

"Aw, fuck, you had to mention snakes," Mercer muttered irritably. Bigger chuckled.

"Give you somethin' other than your wet feet to think about. What we got to eat?"

Tak shook himself like a dog waking up and dug into his pack for a couple of small boxes. He flicked up the flame on his Zippo lighter and peered into the light it cast on the labels. *"Meatballs with Beans in Tomato Sauce* or *Ham and Lima Beans.* Which sounds less terrible?"

The leeches, the rain, the hole in the ground, the unseen enemies planning their imminent deaths, and the sudden descent from supernatural creepiness to the contents of the despised MCIs combined to smack Mercer right in the middle of his funny bone. His involuntary snicker quickly escalated into full-on guffaws. Without a clue as to why their companion had erupted into hilarity, Tak and Bigger began to laugh, too. They pressed muddy hands against their mouths to stifle the noise and laughed until tears mingled with the rain on their faces. By the time they got themselves under control, Mercer's stomach ached and Bigger's breath came in moaning gasps. Tak laboriously smoothed his features back into their habitual inscrutability and checked to make sure his bolt rifle was dry.

"Fucking marines," Mercer muttered. Exhausted, he wrapped his poncho closer around his shoulders and curled himself into an upright ball against one muddy wall. "Take your goddamn malaria pills and shut up." His companions snorted and he fell asleep to the sounds of their renewed laughter.

CHAPTER 17
GENEVIEVE

I liked my new job. Even in the unseasonal spring heat, the physical labor wasn't too onerous, and as long as I drank plenty of water and kept my hat on, I felt just fine. By leaving the house every morning by six, I could work in the cool of the day and head home by midafternoon. Whoever had the job before me either had been gone a while or was bone lazy because some of the cemeteries looked like they hadn't been touched by a caring hand for years. I dug weeds, mowed grass, trimmed bushes, and gradually restored order to even the most neglected graves. One afternoon, I slipped over to the graveyard where Mama and Meema lay and took a few cuttings off the Glory to the World rosebush that adorned Mama's grave, hoping I could get at least one to root so I could plant it on Meema's grave. No matter how long I stood next to those gravestones and no matter how carefully I listened, I never heard a thing except the dim rumble of voices I didn't care about. The cuttings never rooted, either.

My bosses, an older couple named Fred and Nan Beaty, cautioned me to avoid cemetery visitors unless they approached me with a question. That suited me just fine. I've always been content with my own company and had no desire to talk to either the bereaved or their dear departed. Of course, I couldn't hardly avoid the folks who'd died recently. Most quietly accepted their new reality and moved on, but some hung back, talking to me because they were still more comfortable with the living than the dead and couldn't get the loved ones who visited their graves to pay attention.

"I cannot believe this," said Randa Sue Jenkins, 1917–1967, as I filled in a hollow in the surface of her fresh grave and tamped the soil down. "No one in my family ever had heart trouble. I certainly hadn't, then one day—wham! I found myself floating in the air watching my brand-new car roll off into the swamp on Sixty-Seven between Hope and Fulton—know where I mean, sugar? I tried to get myself out before the dang thing sank, but my hand passed plumb through the door handle. I knew right then I was dead as General Lee's horse."

Floyd McElroy, 1950–1967, kept me company while I cleaned lichen off his grandmother's headstone. "Now I look back on it, it was pure-dee stupid to put that gun to my head. I never could hit the broad side of a barn if I was standing in a dadgum stall, and sure enough, I shot my damn face off. Hurt, Lord, it was a relief to choke to death on my own blood and leave it all behind. What I shoulda done was shoot the son of a bitch who stole my girl. I wouldn't 'a cared if I shot *his* face off."

A new resident of Old Washington Cemetery, Nina Frances Colter, 1883–1967, delighted in giving me advice on how to trim back the overgrown yellow rose at one corner of her family plot. When I asked, she also told me how to slip the roses on Mama's grave. Miss Nina Frances had met her end while tending her own roses, which were the pride of her life. "Why, honey, I never dreamed a person could die from a little bitty ol' bee sting. My stars, I been stung a hundred times out working in the yard, but this time my face and neck blew up like a bladder and before I knew it, I'm standing here talking to you. Tsk. I kept meaning to get over here and cut that rose back. How come you can hear me, anyway?"

Nina Frances was still following me, and my ear was about half talked off by the time I loaded up my truck at the end of the day and headed to Hope to pick up a bunch of tools I'd taken in to be sharpened. I can put a nice edge on my own tools, but not a blessed piece of equipment left by my predecessor would cut soft butter. It saved time to have someone else do it. I drove into town, parked in front of Delaney Hardware Store, and was half-way through the front door when I heard someone say, "Excuse me? Ma'am?"

I glanced over my shoulder to see a young, pregnant woman standing a few feet away from me on the sidewalk, looking like a puppy who'd wag her tail if only she had a tail to wag. She twisted a worn leather handbag in hands clasped beneath the swell of her unborn child, ready to turn her nonexistent tail and run at the least harsh word.

"Do you remember me?" she said hopefully. "I heard you were staying around here, so when I saw you, I thought I'd say hey and see if you needed anything, like where to find good stores or something, I don't know what, but I thought I'd ask since it's prob-ably hard to be new in town, even though I guess you're related to the Ives family, aren't you?"

Oh, dear Lord, who was this? I wanted to duck my head and run. Ever since I'd started going out and about, I lived in fear of being recognized, and had no idea what I might do if that time came. Wreath had asked some casual questions on my behalf to discover that my two closest girlhood friends had married and moved, one to East Texas and the other somewhere up around Fayetteville. While I valued those old friendships, neither was worth the risk of resurrecting Oleana. Was the woman staring at me from the curb a younger sister of one of those girls who saw in me the pale, plain ghost of Oleana Larkin? Surely not. I had changed a lot.

I eyed the young woman's face, seeking any resemblance to either of my former girlfriends. I noted the ugly calf-length dress, the awkward bun from which fine strands of hair escaped to float around her face, the lack of makeup and jewelry. As I stared, the young woman's smile slipped. She glanced down the street, lowered her head, and began to move away.

"I'm sorry," she muttered. "I shouldn't . . . my husband says I'm nosy and I talk too much, but there aren't a lot of people my age around that I can visit with, and I thought maybe since you know the Ives family . . ."

My conscience hauled off and clobbered me. I put out a hand to stop her.

"Please wait; I'm the one who should be sorry, standing here with my mouth hanging open. I didn't mean to be rude. I'm trying to place where we met, and I'm afraid I'm drawing a blank." I smiled at her. She stopped her retreat and cautiously smiled back.

"I'm Maylene MacCallan," she said, offering me her hand. I shook it and gave it back to her. "We met at church. Well, sort of. I surely hope you're feeling better than the last time I saw you. Sunday. Well, a bunch of Sundays ago. At church. Church of the Flock of the Good Shepherd. Reverend Ives's church? When you left during the sermon. Mercer said you were sick and went to help you. I got up to help, too, but my husband said it wasn't our concern and made me sit down and mind my own business." The burbling flow of her words stopped, and she covered her mouth as if she'd said something embarrassing.

"Well, I'm proud you stopped to say hello, Mrs. . . ." Oh, Lord, what had she just told me her name was?

"MacCallan. But you should just call me Maylene. I thought you looked so nice that day in church and made up my mind that maybe I'd say hey next time we ran into each other, if we ever did, because Henry—Henry's my husband—because Henry might think it was okay if I had a friend who was a friend of Reverend Ives's family. Henry's real strict about who I talk to because I wasn't raised in the church and he's real stern about me associating with people I used to know before I got saved and became his wife and part of the Flock, but surely it'll be okay if I just stop and see how you're feeling now?"

Whoa. I needed a deep breath almost as bad as she did at the end of that headlong speech. Before she could catch enough wind to start up again, I said, "Well, thank you, Maylene. I'm fine now. My name is Genevieve Charbonneau."

"Well, I'm proud to meet you, Genevieve. That's the most romantic name. Some folks might think it's showy, being French and all, but I do admire pretty names. I want to name the baby something real pretty if it turns out to be a girl, but Henry thinks all my suggestions are silly and says we'll call her Wilma Jean after his mother." Maylene shook her head. "All the pretty names like Celeste—Celeste Rose, don't you like that?—and he wants to call her Wilma, like an old lady."

"Maybe he'll come around," I suggested, doubting it if Daddy-to-be belonged to John Luther's humorless congregation.

"You haven't come back to church," Maylene said, without censorship but with a gleam of curiosity.

"Um, no, I'm not a churchgoer."

"That is such a shame, because Reverend Ives does preach a lovely sermon," Maylene said. "You missed such an inspiring moment when Mrs. Ives made her way back to God on her hands and knees. When she prostrated herself at the altar and Reverend Ives forgave her in front of the whole congregation, I cried." Sure enough, tears welled up in her big round eyes at the memory. "Of course, I felt so bad for her, with her sins on public display like that, and I know just how it feels because Henry reported my bad behavior once and I had to go to the altar to beg forgiveness, but I didn't have to crawl and I'm so glad I didn't because I don't have Mrs. Ives's fine Christian soul and would've died right there on the floor, with my arms spread out like our Dear Savior on the cross, except I shouldn't say that because it makes me sound like I'm comparing myself to Him, and of course, I'm not." She put her hand over her mouth again and blinked. "I'm sorry," she said, her voice muffled by her fingers. "I do talk too much, don't I?"

There was no arguing with that, so I made a noncommittal sound, wondering how anyone could find Wreath's shaming inspirational and what this child had done to deserve a similar, if less severe, public shaming. Child. She wasn't a child, not with that tummy on her, but neither was she an emotionally mature adult. Maylene took her hand away from her face and I braced myself for the next onslaught of words.

"Reverend Ives is strict, but he has such a big heart; there's nothing he can't forgive, just like God. Nothing is so trivial that he can't give it his full attention and compassion."

"Not a sparrow falls," I murmured, but Maylene didn't notice the irony and nodded her head in vigorous agreement.

"He has been such a help and comfort to me personally," she said with a blush and an upward twist of her lips that caught my attention as her spate of words had not.

"Oh?" I said encouragingly.

"Oh, yes. I am not always a good wife to my husband, and it causes . . . problems. I go to the Reverend to confess my sins against Henry, and he helps me understand how to behave. The preacher, not Henry. Reverend Ives chastises when he must, but then he soothes all the wounds with his own hands. He has the power of the Lord in his hands. I've felt it myself." Maylene's cheeks flamed red, and the color drained into her throat, leaving it mottled and ugly.

Huh, I thought. The girl was obviously dying to expound on the experience of being chastised and healed by the miraculous hands of the godlike Reverend Ives. Aloud I said, "Are you in a hurry to get somewhere, Maylene, or do you have time to visit a while longer?"

This time her flush was one of pleasure. I was a wee bit ashamed of myself for planning to pump her for more information about John Luther. Knowledge is power, but this girl was so patently eager for companionship that it hardly seemed fair to use her as a means to an end.

"No, ma'am. I mean, yes ma'am, I have time to visit. I came to town to pick up some things for Henry, and my appointment with Reverend Ives isn't until early evening after he finishes his daily work. He's teaching me how to be a good wife to Henry so that I don't drive him out of my arms and into the arms of Demon Alcohol or make him so mad that he—" Maylene clapped both hands over her mouth this time and looked terrified at what she'd almost said. I pretended nothing improper had been suggested, but I could feel heat in my own face, put there by anger instead of chagrin.

"Well, listen. I have to run in here and pick up some tools, but then let's you and me head down the block to the Dairy Queen and get us a malt or coke or something. My treat. I just got my first paycheck and it's burning a hole in my pocket."

"Oh, I couldn't," Maylene said sincerely, though everything in her face said, *Please, please, talk me into it.*

"Of course, you could," I answered firmly. "I insist. How 'bout you go on over and get us a table while I grab my tools?"

Five minutes later, I walked into a scene from childhood. Whenever Meema and me went on grocery trips to Hope, she always carried me to the Dairy Queen for lunch or a treat. I'm still half convinced that a hamburger, fries, and chocolate malt from the DQ are the pinnacle of fine dining. I could've sworn the same red vinyl upholstery protected the seats of the booths as when we made our regular visits so long ago, and if the menu had changed, I couldn't tell. Even the high school kids behind the counter looked familiar in their white hats and aprons.

"Miss Genevieve? Over here!" Maylene waved vigorously from a booth at the very back of the eating area. *Miss* Genevieve? Holy hell, I was about twenty years too young for that. I could almost feel gray spreading through my hair and wrinkles etching my skin. As I approached the booth, she slid out of the seat facing the door and into the opposite one where, I assumed, she could hide from inquisitive eyes that might report her presence in an establishment not approved of by His Joyful Sheep.

"I haven't been here since I was in high school," Maylene said as I sat down across from her. Her eyes shone with delight so simple that she looked ten years old. "They still have orange slushes.

I loved orange slushes. My daddy used to bring me here so much that the folks who worked here had my slush ready before we even walked in the door. It was just me, no brothers and sisters, so I guess I was kinda spoilt, but it was wonderful. Used to come here after football games, too. I was always starving back in those days, and I put away a lot of chili dogs and fries, always with an orange slush. My friends liked cokes and they all used to laugh at me about orange slushes, but it was nice laughing. I haven't seen any of those kids in a year," she added wistfully.

"Orange slush, then?"

"Oh, yes, ma'am, please."

"Maylene?"

"Yes, Miss Genevieve?"

"I'm only about five or six years older than you. No more 'ma'am,' okay? And no 'Miss Genevieve,' either. My friends call me Gen."

Maylene blushed. Lord, that girl spent so much time turning red that it was a wonder she had enough blood leftover to run the rest of her body. "I'm sorry. You just seem so . . . I don't know, sophisticated and smart that I feel like I ought to show you some big respect."

The laugh that burst out of my mouth sounded a lot like a hoot. "Oh, I'm real sophisticated, sitting here in my blue jeans and work shirt with dirt still under my fingernails. The e-pit-o-me of elegance. So, you want an orange slush or something else?"

"Orange slush would be like heaven. Thank you . . . Gen." She folded her hands on the table like a polite child to wait while I went to put in our order.

When I got back, her eyes widened at the sight of the tray. I sat down an orange slush in front of her along with a paper boat holding a chili dog and a pile of French fries. My own dinner represented the haute cuisine of my childhood.

"I'm gonna have heartburn tonight, sure as the world," Maylene said. "And sure as the world, it's gonna be worth it."

She chattered like a whole row of birds on a telephone wire in between bites of Dairy Queen's best and sighs of rapture. Content to listen to her, I ate my own meal and realized that I was enjoying myself. The girl wasn't overloaded with brains, but she didn't have a mean bone in her body and radiated a sort of innocence so pure that it hurt my heart to see it. She took another bite of ketchup-drenched French fry, followed it with a sip of orange slush, and closed her eyes in gastronomic ecstasy.

"You been married long?" I swirled the melting ice cream in my malt and spooned a bite into my mouth.

"No, not hardly a year yet. It's . . . not what I expected." Maylene looked at the French fry in her hand and laid it back in the pools of ketchup. "My mama and daddy did their best to talk me out of it, but Henry . . . well, he needed me."

The story came out in another breathless swirl of words. At first, she believed they'd live happily ever after, but things hadn't worked out that way and instead of Henry getting happier, Maylene just got sadder. He made her get rid of her pretty clothes and dress like she was fifty instead of eighteen. That bothered her a lot at first, but it was just vanity. What hurt most was the lack of sweet talking and romance after the wedding. Discovering that Henry drank in secret caused her considerable anguish. Henry turned out to be a mean drunk.

"He . . . says terrible things that he forgets all about later," Maylene said, fiddling with her food. "I thought about leaving him and going home, maybe even finishing high school. I was partway through my senior year when we got married and I thought he'd let me graduate, but he said to not be silly. I'd about made up my mind to call Mama to see if they'd let me come home when I found out the baby was on the way. Reverend Ives said it was God's way of telling me to stay right where I was and not go backsliding my way into hell. Reverend Ives preaches that it is a grievous sin against God and Man for a wife to divorce her husband. When I told Henry about the baby, he got hopping mad because he doesn't like children."

Maylene looked around to make sure we were still alone in the restaurant, then leaned across the table toward me and lowered her voice to a tremulous whisper. "He . . . he carried me to see some old woman near Foulkes that he said knew how to bring on a missed period. I didn't want to go, but he made me. When we got there, she said I was too far along for herbs to work and that a proper . . . bloodletting would be expensive. Henry asked how much, and I like to have lost my mind. I ran out of that evil house, just wanting to find a phone and beg my mama and daddy to come get me. Henry caught up with me, dragged me into the car, drove us home, and . . . The baby is still coming, but Henry's been drinking ever since that day. I can't get him to quit."

Maylene wiped her eyes with the corner of her napkin, sighed, and finished the last bite of her chili dog. When she was done chewing, she said, "I'm going to talk some more to Reverend Ives about it; have me an appointment with him this very day. Surely a man with four children and two grandchildren will tell Henry, man to man, about his obligations to me and the baby."

She glanced at her watch and gasped. "Oh, my stars, look at the time, and my errands aren't anywhere near done. I do thank you for dinner. I'd love to return the favor someday and for us to be friends, but it's so hard right now with Henry being difficult and the baby coming. I know God sent you to me, though, because you're so easy to talk to and I feel so much better now, and I'm so glad that I worked up the nerve to say hello to you this afternoon."

She piled the remains of her meal on the tray, profusely thanked me for dinner, and slid out of the booth. Before she headed back to her abandoned errands, she put her hand on mine and said, "This has been a pure pleasure, Gen. I'm sorry to run off, but I need to be home by seven to fix Henry's dinner. That's late, I know, but he has to work late tonight, which gives me just enough time to stop and see Reverend Ives. Most nights I couldn't do it, but God has planned it all and laid the opportunity right in my lap. Thank you again for dinner. I haven't had an orange slush in over a year and forgot how good they are. I'll be seeing you. Think about coming to church, okay? Bye!"

She tossed the last few sentences over her shoulder as she trotted toward the door. She was gone before I could wave. I sat there a moment, hand half raised, feeling like my hair had been blasted back by a strong gust of wind. Lowering my hand to the last of my hamburger, I finished dinner and thought about the Church of the Flock of the Good Shepherd, the Kingdom Come Church of the Holy Ghost with Signs Following, and the absolute power of the tyrants who ruled them for the greater glory of themselves and, only incidentally, of God.

"Knowledge is power," I said to myself, wadding up the paper trash from dinner into a big ball. I lobbed it into the garbage can at the end of the eating area. *Two points*, I thought, and got up to leave.

CHAPTER 18
JOHN LUTHER

❦

Maylene MacCallan hung her head and wept as she confessed her guilt over her husband's backslide into alcoholism, accusing herself of not being good enough or pretty enough to keep him sober and at home. She was just a little bit of a thing with small bones and the face of a child but the early second trimester curve of her belly bespoke her claim to full womanhood. John Luther wrapped comforting arms around her, smoothing her hair with his big hands while he murmured comforting words, some of which were actually in The Good Book. He shifted his pelvis away from the erotic press of her stomach to hide his arousal. Maylene, oblivious to anything but her own emotions, didn't notice.

The moment Maylene was old enough to marry without parental consent, she had eloped with Henry MacCallan, a taciturn, brooding man whose silence she mistook for depth of character conferred by a tragic past. From the moment that they met, she strove to make him glad to be alive. Henry, tired of being celibate, took a good look at Maylene's figure, and decided it was better to marry than to burn. The marriage had been a disaster from the beginning.

As pastor of the Church of the Flock of the Good Shepherd, John Luther offered spiritual counseling to members of the congregation as needed. He'd spoken with the MacCallans a couple of times, but neither of those previous sessions had been as satisfying as this one promised to be in Henry's absence. Maylene perfectly suited John Luther's taste: vulnerable, unhappily married, pregnant, and still in her teens.

He guided the sobbing woman over to the large, overstuffed chair in the corner of the office. Gently but firmly, he pulled her down into his lap. He pressed her head against his shoulder with one big hand and rested the other on her hip. "Tell me exactly what happened this past week. No, do not blush, child. I am a Man of God and will not judge you unless you lie to me."

She hid her face in his shirtfront, then in a whisper enumerated her husband's drunken acts. Encouraged by the preacher's deep-voiced urging, she went on to tell him about the trip to the house in Foulkes. He stroked her hip and upper leg as she spoke, calling her a brave little woman and an abused princess of the Lord.

"Has he struck you since we last met?" whispered John Luther, caressing her hair with his lips.

"Oh, yes, sir."

"With what?"

"His hands or a belt, mostly. Once he grabbed a spatula and whacked me with that."

"Where did he strike you, my princess?"

She gestured feebly with one hand.

"Don't be afraid. Use the words God gave you. Tell me."

"I'm too ashamed."

"Did he strike you . . . here?" Maylene shuddered as his index finger grazed the tip of one breast, but she nodded. His other hand cupped her buttock. "And here?" Another nod. "Are there bruises or other marks?"

"Yes, sir."

"Show me," he commanded. "Don't worry, child, this is part of the work I do for the Lord, soothing sorrow, laying hands on the aching and ill, and teaching wives to please their husbands so those men are not driven to violence. Yes, that's right. That's right. Just slide down this strap and . . . ah, poor lamb of God, what has he done? The bruises here . . . and here. Close your eyes and let His healing flow through my hands to your wounds, imagine my hands are His, soothing you. Imagine this is His healing kiss . . ."

Maylene's breathing changed as he brought a breast to his mouth with one hand and used the other to lift her leg across the arm of the big chair. Her modest skirt slid up her thighs, revealing slender legs below the ugly, old-fashioned drawers that the church required women to wear for modesty. "Where else, my angel? Show me. Guide my hand. Ahh . . ."

Forty minutes later, the taillights of Maylene's old green Chevrolet faded down the highway toward Hope. John Luther emerged from the quiet church and locked the door behind him. The southern twilight had come and gone, leaving the world swathed in darkness lit only by a few stars. The light that usually brightened the parking lot hung cold and dead from its pole, a scattering of glass suggesting it had once again been used for target practice. He made a mental note to send someone out the next day with a replacement bulb and a ladder.

Sticking his hands in his pockets, he strolled toward his car, whistling tunelessly to himself. The car sat in its usual place near the graveyard gate where it was hidden from easy view of the road by the deep shadows of several ancient sweetgum trees. His eyes flickered across his religious kingdom as he complacently contemplated life's possibilities. Maylene's farewell contained an element of warmth that her greeting had not, and he looked forward to the session he'd scheduled for the following week. He'd send her husband to Little Rock on church business that day and grant him the rare treat of remaining in the city overnight. A smile flickered on John Luther's mouth. Lord, there was nothing more satisfying to handle than a pregnant woman before she was too distorted for pleasure. He couldn't do much with her tonight, but come next week . . . Well, poor, stupid Henry would be mighty pleased when he returned home to a sweet little wife who had learned to submit to his embrace with a smile. He didn't need to know it was because she had new things to imagine while he tumbled her.

Shadows shifted in the trees beyond the car. John Luther stopped whistling and peered into the dimness. "Someone there?"

A rustle answered him, and something arched through the air, glinting in the last shreds of twilight. The rock hit the ground a yard from his feet and gently rolled to a stop against his left shoe. For a long moment, he stared down, transitioning from lingering eroticism to shock. His hand rose of its own accord to the gash in his eyebrow. He took a shaky step backward. A second rock thudded six inches closer than the first.

John Luther ran for his car, digging in his front pocket for keys that immediately dropped from his nerveless fingers and disappeared against the mottled camouflage of the pea gravel. He squatted down, feeling around with both hands, gasping in his anxiety. Another thud, this time from somewhere behind him. He fell to his knees and scrabbled in the gravel, snapping a fingernail to the quick before he found the splayed ring of keys. Lumbering to his feet, he snatched open the unlocked door and dropped his butt into the driver's seat. It took him two tries to get the proper key into the ignition. The engine coughed to life. He jammed the stick into reverse and spun backward out of the parking spot. One more shove of the gear shift and the car shot down the road, leaving church and graveyard faintly illuminated in red light.

CHAPTER 19
GENEVIEVE

❧❦❧

One day followed another, and upstairs in the carriage house started to feel like home. Blessed with the cemetery truck for transportation, I set out to explore the roads in southwestern Arkansas, stopping at every little out of the way junk store and antique shop that I came to. Before long, my possessions expanded from what could fit in my backpack to a skillet, a saucepan, a set of mixing bowls, a couple of knives, some mismatched spoons and forks, and a full set of slightly chipped Pfaltzgraff dishes with a blue design centered in each plate. I'd never had a place to cook, and despite my agreement with Mercer to do the cooking, I had no idea how to do more than boil an egg or mix up a batch of pancakes using Bisquick. I found a *Betty Crocker Cookbook* at a junk store and read it like some folks read the Bible, looking for the answers to all life's cooking questions. I started out making soup and bread and moved on to scarier stuff, like fried catfish and breaded okra. To my surprise and relief, things generally turned out to be edible, if not always very pretty. My first attempt at a cake was a disaster in terms of symmetry and elegant swirls of frosting, but it tasted fine and gave us both a good laugh.

Mercer came home with a couple of armchairs for the living room and a round wooden table and upright chairs for the kitchen, courtesy of Gil. Neither of us put any effort into locating beds or mattresses. I bought a cot at the Texarkana Army Surplus that suited me fine, and Mercer just slept on the floor of his bedroom without so much as a sheet between his skin and the cool, bare boards of the floor. He worried about Boomerang's comfort, though, and brought home a couch that had seen better days for the big pup to sleep on.

Once I started paying rent, Mercer offered to take over part of the cooking. New as I was to the job, I was still a better cook than he was, and the agreement shifted to me cooking and him doing dishes afterward. I'm neat in the kitchen, washing pans as soon as I'm done with them, so cleanup wasn't a huge chore, and I didn't feel guilty about him being stuck with it day after day. We worked out the rest of the chores to our mutual satisfaction. I left way earlier in the morning than he did to do most of my caretaker duties before the sun got too hot, so our paths rarely crossed until he got home in the evening. We generally had dinner together, then went about our own interests afterward. The situation suited us both.

During one of my rambles around the countryside, I stopped in a shop in DeAnn that specialized in quilts, weaving, and related crafts. The lady who ran the place, Luenell Campbell, was more than willing to talk me through the basics of making a quilt. She sold me a big stack of old flour sacks and feedbags in pretty patterns, some thread, needles, and scissors and I was on my way to making an Improved Nine Patch quilt before I knew quite what hit me. She invited me to join her and some friends every other Saturday for an informal quilting group, and so I made my first acquaintances in the area.

I enjoyed the company, but at the same time, I felt like I was walking a tightrope over a pit of hungry ducks who were ready to nibble me to pieces should I make a slip. If Southerners aren't the most family-conscious people on the face of the earth, I want to know who is so I can stay away from them. I swear, no matter where I went, no matter who I talked to, one of the first things they said after hello was some version of "Who are your people?"

I didn't dare invent a background for myself out of whole cloth because relationships in the South are so complicated that I was liable to find myself accidentally related to someone just by virtue of the name I was using. I'd have been proud to claim kinship with Wreath, Mercer, Jezzie, and Leah, but I was afraid if I did, Oleana Larkin would slip back into my life. For all I knew, the hospital was still looking for a runaway crazy person by that name, though it had been five years since I left the place.

"Charbonneau," mused an elderly lady with lavender hair, the sharp eyes of a bird dog, and the unlikely name of Cassandra. "Don't believe I know anyone by that name in this area. You have family around here?"

"My branch of the family originally came from around East Feliciana Parish in Louisiana," I answered, then added firmly, "There were never many of them, and they're all gone now. I grew up a long way from there and didn't know any of them."

"Where'd you grow up, honey?"

"South Texas." Lord, surely she wouldn't know anyone seven hundred miles from her own stomping grounds.

"And you have family in Arkansas?" Cassandra persisted gently but inexorably.

"I'm distantly related to some folks named Hughley," I admitted, hoping Meema had been gone long enough that the name wouldn't ring an immediate bell. "I don't think there's any of them left, though."

"There's a few over toward Nashville," said Careen Fuller, who at about thirty-five was the youngest member of the quartet gathered around the quilting frame that hung from the ceiling of Luenell's living room. She pushed a strand of blond hair back from her face and concentrated on threading a tiny needle with white thread. "You any relation to them?"

"Not that I know of," I said, and deliberately jabbed myself in the index finger with the needle I was wielding. Conversation shifted to rueful commiseration for the wound common among quilters and the best ways to get blood out of cotton fabric. After that interrogation, I practiced my people skills by directing all conversation back to Cassandra's grandchildren or by asking for cooking and quilting advice.

I had just gotten home from the quilting group one afternoon when the door of a car slammed out front. I didn't pay much attention, figuring it was Jim Allen bringing Mercer home from their fishing trip to Bois d'Arc Bayou. Despite Mercer's reluctance to socialize, Jim doggedly persisted in dropping by for a glass of sweet tea or to talk Mercer into going fishing. I liked Jim a lot, would've liked him even if he wasn't so good to Mercer. He was a long, tall drink of water with crewcut brown hair and a dry wit who understood Mercer in a way none of the rest of us could. Not only were they lifelong friends, but Jim had completed a tour of duty at the 95th Evacuation Hospital in Vietnam not long after Mercer came home from the Navy. Jim couldn't see or hear the ghosts, but he knew Vietnam haunted Mercer every waking moment.

Anyway, I was sitting cross-legged in one of the armchairs in the living room, concentrating on putting straight stitches into the curved seam of a quilt block. Hearing the screen door swing open and footsteps echo on the bare boards of the kitchen floor, I called, "Fresh pitcher of tea in the icebox and one of the quilting ladies sent me home with a plate of cookies. Help yourselves."

No one answered and I looked up to see what was keeping those boys so quiet. To my horror, John Luther stood in the doorway between the kitchen and living room. From my position hunkered down in my chair, he looked a lot bigger than usual. I put aside my quilt block and unfolded my legs. As I stood up, I reached into the chair next to me and wrapped my fingers around the handles of my scissors. The blades were only a few inches long, but I felt better with them in my hand than I would've without. He glanced contemptuously at my poor excuse for a weapon and took a step toward me.

"Far enough," I said and held the scissors at hip level in front of me, the blades pointing up out of my fist just like Alibaba the sword swallower had taught me to hold a knife. Before he started swallowing swords while pretty girls gestured to him with wide arms, Alibaba had been Joe Davies, one hell of a mean street fighter from a bad part of Houston.

"You do not have the nerve to attack me," John Luther said, but he didn't offer to come any closer. He looked around the room, scowling. "Where is Mercer?"

"You need to leave now." As he moved to peer down the hall that led to the bedrooms and bathroom, I edged toward the kitchen door and the sole route out of the apartment. He turned to look at me and his face changed into something truly scary. It was hotter than any day had a right to be, and after getting home from quilting club, I'd changed into a pair of cut-off blue jeans and an old bikini bra. Not what I'd have worn for company, particularly this bit of unsavory company.

I won't dignify the things he said to me by repeating them. The nicest thing he called me was "harlot," which I'd have found quaint except for the venom behind it. He told me what The Good Book said about women like me and how a good beating was the least of what I deserved. Well, I can quote scripture for my own purposes as well as John Luther or the devil.

"Have you read the part of that book that says, 'Thou shalt not commit adultery'?"

The shock of that statement snapped his head back like I'd hit him in the jaw. I ran for the kitchen door and made it halfway across the room before he caught me. He twisted my arm behind my back so hard that I dropped the scissors. I whipped around and sank my teeth into his bicep until I tasted blood. He howled and loosened his fingers enough for me to twist out of his grip. By this time, I was so mad that I could barely see, so mad that I forgot all about running for safety, screaming my head off as I went. Stupid, yeah. Even with my collection of dirty fighting tricks learned from Joe Davies, I didn't stand a chance of taking down this rank chunk of Christian formidableness that was fouling my home. I was too furious to think straight, though. I grabbed the rolling pin off its holder above the kitchen counter and charged him, screaming like a banshee, rolling pin hoisted with both hands into attack position. He reached out with his right hand to grab my wrists. I spun around and cracked the pin down on his unprotected left collarbone.

The image of a medium-sized woman attacking a large man with a rolling pin and bringing him to his knees is funny, worthy of space on the cartoon page of a Sunday newspaper. There's nothing funny about that particular weapon when used right, though. How in the hell I didn't shatter his collarbone, I do not know; the son of a bitch must have had bones of iron. Shattered or not, he went down howling like a pack of wolves were eating him. When he got his hollering under control, he threatened me with the police and attempted murder charges.

"I don't think so," I said coldly, retreating to the outside door and a clear path of escape in case he came at me again. "If you did that, I'd have to bring out the photos of you and that little pregnant girl you 'counsel' on lonesome evenings. What's her name? Maylene?"

His face turned so purple that I thought he was about to have a stroke. He was welcome to stroke out, but not in my house.

"Liar!" he spat. "It is an innocent relationship."

I have to admit, I was lying. I didn't have a single photo, but I also didn't think he could take the risk. "Oh, my, is that what you call it? I'm not familiar with your church but laying on of hands in the churches I've attended didn't include grabbing a girl's boob. There's a particularly good photo where you've got your fingers—"

He rose up with a roar that was checked by a hard jab from his badly bruised collarbone. I brandished the rolling pin and backed toward the door.

"You've got fifteen seconds to get down these stairs and out of my house," I said. "One word out of you about any of this, and the pictures go to your church board, or whatever the hell you call that pious bunch of wife beaters."

"You will stay away from my church and my family!"

"I wouldn't set foot in your church again for love nor money.

But Jezzie's study sessions will take place once a week like always at the library in Columbus; Miss Wreath and Leah can come with her. And if I see a single sign that that you've hurt any one of them, some fine Sunday morning, those pictures are going to turn up tacked to the front door of the church."

"Let's see these famous pictures," he snarled.

I laughed out loud. "You don't think I keep them here, do you?"

"There's no way you could've taken pictures. I always draw the blinds—" He bit off his words, realizing what he had just tacitly admitted.

"There's a gap between the blind and the edge of the window. Not much, but enough, and the lamp makes such a lovely spotlight."

He blundered to his feet, right hand supporting his aching shoulder. "You peeping bitch."

"Now, is that any way for a preacher man to talk?" I asked, pushing the screen door open without turning my back on him,

He took a step toward me. I took two steps backward onto the porch, readying my rolling pin for further action. Since physical intimidation hadn't subdued me, he decided to try a different tactic. He lowered his voice and narrowed his eyes, looking me up and down. The conceited bastard even licked his fat pink lips, like that suggestive gesture would drop me in my tracks. "Seductress . . ."

"Wow," I said. "I didn't figure you knew a word that big. Get out of here, John Luther, and don't come back, or I swear I'll spread copies of those photos from one end of this county to the other."

I turned and ran down the wooden steps to the ground and around the side of the carriage house. There I waited until I heard him slam his car door and drive off down the lane. Once he was gone, I went back upstairs to sit in my chair and catch my breath. I put my elbows on my knees, rested my chin in my cupped hands, and thought about so many things.

I don't know how, or if, John Luther explained the damage to his collarbone, but it was the last I heard of it. I never told anyone about it, either, except to tell Mercer that John Luther had come and gone, and that I didn't think he'd be back. Mercer just looked grim and nodded.

On Tuesday afternoon, I drove to the tiny building that housed Columbus's branch of the county library and waited to see if Jezzie would leave the bus stop and come over, or head straight down the road to the Ives farm. The bus drove up, put on its flashing lights, and children began to pour out the folding door. When I saw Jezzie, I held my breath. She paused a moment at the foot of the steps, talking to someone inside the bus. Then she turned and walked toward me, smiling and waving as she came.

CHAPTER 20
GENEVIEVE

As spring rolled toward summer, I realized I wasn't going to have enough money for tuition and books and still manage to pay my rent and eat unless I could earn a nice chunk of decent money before September. I made a couple of phone calls, arranged for a few days off, and asked Mercer for the loan of his motorcycle in return for him using my truck. He wondered why, of course, and I told him the truth: I needed extra funds for school and had lined up a weeklong job just north of Houston to make the money.

"The tires on the truck are bald, and I got my doubts about the transmission, too," I explained. "I hate to ask, but I don't dare set out on a trip clear to Houston in it. I'd take the bus except I couldn't get there in time to work tomorrow night."

"What're you going to do down there you can't do up here?"

"Bartend during the day, dance half a dozen nights."

He shook his head. "Genevieve, you don't need to go stripping anymore. I can give you the money for school."

"That's good of you to offer, Mercer, but I'm not going to borrow money. I don't like debt."

We argued a little, or rather he argued and I just let him do it. My mind was made up, and no misguided notions of propriety on his part were going to change my mind. To do him credit, he was less concerned with the respectability of my dancing than he was about the safety of me walking home by myself from a men's club at three in the morning.

"The management has rooms for temporary workers just around the corner, and one of the bouncers will walk me to the hotel." I didn't tell him that dancers had to pay for not only the room, but the right to use the stage on the nights when they danced. It had taken me some firm talking, but I'd managed to get the owner to agree to a lower room rent than he charged the other girls and a waiver of the stage fee. I was a name draw, a moneymaker for the place, and Wiley B knew he was damn lucky to get me back there.

In the long run, Mercer borrowed a car from Gil and drove me to Houston on Friday morning so I could make my early performance on time. He suggested that he might stay and watch me dance, but I told him I got self-conscious working in front of people I knew. He said, okay, he'd drop me off at Wiley B's, go to visit a friend who lived in Galveston, and head home on Sunday in time to go to work Monday morning. I'd work eight days and come home on the bus. We checked the bus schedule to see when he should pick me up at the Texarkana bus station, then he headed down the road, leaving me to my job.

I wouldn't have asked Mercer for his motorcycle or accepted his offer to take me to Houston had there been any chance of getting myself there in time by bus, or if I'd had anyone else to ask. Though he knew I'd danced in the kootch and at roadhouses and gentlemen's clubs in the past, I didn't want him to watch me take my clothes off or see what I pretended to be on the runway at Wiley B's. I'm not ashamed of being an exotic dancer, but I was afraid that if Mercer ever once looked at me the way my audiences did, all that was sweet and innocent between us would be spoiled.

I've always had a love-hate relationship with dancing. On one hand, I'd never have been able to do it if I wasn't able to slip out of my own personality and into one that I called Eugenie at Wiley B's, Antoinette at La Place in New Orleans, or Bahira at Arabian Nights in Dallas. I had a dozen names, a dozen personas, and drove them all with imaginary levers located in an imaginary compartment behind my eyes. From that vantage point, I watched men staring at my body, examining each part I so deliberately exposed. They never saw or cared about the real woman beneath the makeup and filmy costumes, just the illusion of spotlighted gilt on warm skin.

On the other hand, dancing gave me a feeling of power, the only power I'd ever had over anyone. Men looked at me with their eyes wide and their jaws slack, and I knew any one of them, from roughneck biker to millionaire businessman, would give me whatever I wanted in return for an hour of my time or even for permission to touch me for a moment. I never, ever gave that permission because it was in withholding myself that the real power lay. One weak moment when I gave myself over to Lorcan proved that to me forever.

Lorcan had been a big man, more than twenty years my senior, with muscles out to there, thick brown hair worn down his back in a braid longer than my own, hazel eyes, and a Scots accent that just plain did me in the very first time I heard him talk. When he joined the Havilland Dixieland Travelling Circus a couple of years before it dissolved, I admired him from a distance. He was so beautiful in a dramatic masculine way that I barely regarded him as human. It sure as hell never occurred to me to approach him; in fact, if it looked like our paths might cross, I scurried myself off down the nearest escape route. I nursed a crush on him, envying the women he honored with a smile or touch of his broad hand without ever expecting to find myself among them.

He never said a word to me or so much as looked in my direction until one morning he slid onto the bench opposite me at the table where I was eating breakfast. He made a few pleasant remarks before finishing his own meal and going on with his day. The whole time I sat with my head down, blushing in that way that redheads are so cursed with. After that encounter, he occasionally paused to watch while I practiced with T'shara and Tina Fae or worked with the big boas in the cool of the evening. Even in the circus, lots of folks were scared of snakes and viewed me with suspicion because I liked and respected the boas. Mireille warned me about this, but it took me a while to notice people's reactions because I was so wrapped up in learning about and caring for the snakes.

Lorcan wasn't afraid of the snakes, and he didn't dislike them, either. He got in the habit of stopping in the evening to talk with me. While he talked, he ran his hand down Esmeralda's long back like she was a kitten. When I mentioned this to Tish, she raised an eyebrow at me and said, "It's not Esmeralda he wants to touch. Watch your step, honey, 'cause you're coming into a danger zone."

I knew she was right, but I just couldn't help myself. No one had ever talked to me or looked at me the way Lorcan did. It wasn't the sort of lustful ogling that I'd seen in some other men, though there was an erotic element in his approach to me that set my senses tingling. He'd led the kind of life most of us can only dream of, and I soaked up every word of every story he told me. Generations of his family had been circus aerialists, and he himself had been born in a circus caravan somewhere in the middle of Europe. He, his parents, a brother, and two sisters had traveled pre-WWII Europe with a circus that crossed borders and strips of no-man's-land as if they didn't exist. He trained as a catcher but had to retire from the family business at a young age due to a shoulder that popped out of socket at awkward moments. Grounded from flying, he became one of the best riggers in the business, combining technical ability with an inborn understanding of the people who depended on his expertise. When he was barely out of his teens, he escaped France with his Scots father and Hungarian Jewish mother as Hitler's forces closed in on Paris. He joined the Scottish infantry and returned to fight in mainland Europe until Germany and its allies were defeated. After the war, he crossed the ocean to America, looking for better opportunities in a land not so scarred by war.

Somehow, he got the impression that I was the black sheep of an old, cultured Louisiana family, and I never disabused him of the notion. I told him that my parents died when I was little, which was more or less true, and that my grandmother raised me, which was also more or less true. If he took my description of Meema's big old white house surrounded by roses and confederate jasmine to be that of a plantation house, and the slow cadences of the accent I learned from Dema to point to my own elegant pedigree, who was I to argue? I told him the truth as far as possible since I knew I couldn't keep track of too many lies. His interpretation of that truth was his own lookout.

Lorcan was the first man who ever made love to me. Though someone else had ripped my virginity from me years earlier, I was innocent of the tender aspects of intercourse, and Lorcan led me into our relationship gently and with great skill. For the first few weeks, I felt like the heroine at the end of a romance novel, wrapped in love and sure to live happily ever after. When he asked me, I folded up my tent and moved into his caravan along with my snakes.

I didn't tell him the truth about me, so I shouldn't have been surprised to learn the truth about him. We'd been living together for a couple of months when things began to unravel. I was terrified of getting pregnant, and at first Lorcan took careful steps to prevent this. Eventually, he began to complain about the inconvenience and discomfort of what he called French letters. He pressured me to discard them. I resisted the pressure. One night, he flatly refused to use one of the things, and I flatly refused to continue the evening's activities without one. To my horror, he shoved me onto my back on the bed and held me there with his left hand against my chest. With the other hand and one knee, he pried my legs apart and moved between them, watching the rising terror on my face with a half-smile on his lips. My head spun, and for the first time since the mob stoned me in Kingdom Come, I reeled into oblivion, my pulse pounding against the pressure of his hand on my heart. When I returned from wherever I'd been, dawn had softened the sky. Lorcan was holding me in his arms and kissing the top of my head. My face rested against his chest. Nothing in his manner indicated something bad had happened between us. In fact, he was so normal and affectionate that I convinced myself I had dreamed the whole thing.

Jealousy came next, with Lorcan trying to control my interactions with other people. He reacted with equal suspicion whether I paused to talk to old Jean-Narcisse about his lions or fourteen-year-old Timmy Allen, the youngest member of the family that owned the performing dogs. He didn't expect to be held himself to the same standards he erected for me, however. The day I came across him with his hands in the front of the tightrope walker's practice leotard and his tongue halfway down her throat, I admitted to myself that our perfect romance was a perfect sham. I also discovered that I was capable of sheer cold rage. I didn't blame Ariella for her part in the event; I knew how hard it was to resist Lorcan at his best. I told myself I wanted to save both of us from Lorcan at his worst, but I knew in my heart that all I wanted to do was make him rue the day he betrayed me.

We were nearing the end of the season, and Lorcan didn't want me to go to New Orleans or Houston with T'shara to pursue the off-season jobs that enabled me to build up a savings account for the future. In the first flush of passion, I'd made the mistake of joining my income with Lorcan's only to have him gradually take over all finances for both of us. Whether through forgetfulness or some sense of self-preservation I didn't know I possessed, I never mentioned the savings account in Baton Rouge that I added to each offseason.

For the last venue that year, the circus set up outside a small town a mile or two from one of the many bayous that meander through Louisiana. Bayous are a great place to find snakes, and on my first afternoon off, I walked down to see what I could find to damage my philandering soon-to-be ex-lover. The voices that had been whispering soft warnings to me ever since I took up with Lorcan yowled in protest when their ghostly owners realized what I intended to do. I tried to ignore them, but they had a point: I was too furious to think the plan through, and murder planned in haste was likely to go wrong. I didn't really want to kill him anyway. Well, I *did* want to kill him, but in such a way that he remained alive to regret every trespass he'd made against me. Okay. I'd give him a fighting chance. Instead of dumping a couple of pissed-off rattlers on his useless carcass while he slept, I'd put an edgy nonvenomous water snake under the bedclothes, insuring he'd get a nasty bite or two on a lower leg when he slid under the covers. That would hurt without killing him. The voices continued to grumble. I finally but reluctantly agreed that I'd be better off spending my energy on setting up my old wall tent and vacating Lorcan's caravan that very afternoon.

I was on my way back to the circus when I saw the smoke. Smoke in a community of tents is never a good thing. I ran the last half mile and arrived in time to see Lorcan's caravan collapse in a pile of burning debris. Esmeralda had managed to escape with slight injuries, but my other two boas had not been so lucky. I stood with her in my arms, watching the firefighters spray water on the inferno. My heart broke for my lost snakes. A couple of the circus people who weren't afraid of Esmeralda came to stand with me, arms around my shoulders, whispering comfort and expressions of sorrow for my great loss. It was only later that I realized they thought my distress was for Lorcan, who had died along with the boas.

CHAPTER 21

MERCER

After she stowed her gear in the room allotted to her, Genevieve walked Mercer to the car. She hesitated a moment, then asked once more, "Mercer, this isn't going to change the way you think about me, is it?"

"Not a chance," he said, and wondered if he was lying.

He didn't go to Galveston that evening. At nine o'clock, he sat in the dimmest corner of the roadhouse and tried to keep his chin from hitting the table when Genevieve/Eugenie strolled onto the runway and proceeded to gracefully divest herself of a high-necked, long-sleeved, floor-length black dress to the slow sway of New Orleans jazz. He barely recognized the elegant woman who imbued disrobing with a sparkle of humor and a touch of shyness that made the process all the more erotic. She turned her back to the audience, peeked over her shoulder, and peeled the gown down one arm. Mercer took a deep breath and tried not to notice what the guy at the next table was doing to himself.

Not a bump, not a grind in the whole performance. Nothing, in fact, that Mercer had been dreading. She never approached the crowd jostling along the runway, not even to accept the tips they waved at her. At the end of the dance, she draped a filmy robe over her bare shoulders, managing to reveal more than she concealed, and stood on the runway, kissing her hands to her audience and laughing at them and with them until they threw their offerings at her feet to be gathered into a basket by those same kissed hands. As she bent down to retrieve her tips, she caught modestly at the gaping neck of her robe but didn't quite manage to hold it closed. The tips piled higher on the boards in front of her.

Mercer wondered how in the hell he'd managed to sit across the table from this woman almost every evening for weeks without really seeing her.

Her next set came an hour later. She spun onto stage wearing a glittering bra, a narrow hip band heavy with sequins and beads, and a skirt that was nothing more than two strips of filmy chiffon, one in front and one in back, with her legs and hips revealed on either side of the strips. Nutty Nina the Belly Dance Queena had taught this student well: her intricate muscular gymnastics to the beat of a wild drum solo brought the crowd to its feet with a roar of approval. She started the dance in spike heels, then kicked them aside to dance in bare feet that were somehow more sensual than her naked stomach and barely concealed nipples. Mercer forgot the girl he met in a cemetery, forgot the girl who growled the first twenty minutes she was awake each morning, forgot his freckled cousin running a lawn mower across the grass once a week, and lost himself in contemplation of the dancer who held an entire room of drinkers, brawlers, and hecklers in thrall.

He left at the end of her third set just after midnight while she was still gathering her tips and kissing her fingertips to the crowd. He drove back to Arkansas that night, thinking about her and trying to reconcile his testosterone-fueled reaction to the dancer's exuberant eroticism with his platonic affection for his redheaded cousin. He wondered if Genevieve knew he'd broken his promise to return home without watching the show, if she'd seen past the glare of the spotlight into the shadows at the back of the bar. He hoped not, though he couldn't regret having stayed.

He drove until he caught himself nodding off, then pulled into a roadside park to sleep for a while. He arrived home just after dawn and climbed the steps to the apartment with no bigger goal in mind than a very large, very hot cup of coffee. When he went to put his key in the lock, the door swung open under his touch. A closer look showed the lock had been forced. He went back down the stairs, picked up a length of wood from next to the firepit, and eased his way inside the building.

Pots and pans barred his path into the kitchen. Genevieve's carefully collected plates and glasses appeared to have been hurled against the wall; pieces were scattered everywhere. In the living room, furniture was upended, pictures and books lay in drifts on the floor. Nothing much in his own bedroom was disturbed, but Genevieve's room looked like a tornado had hit it. Her clothes had not just been pulled from the closet and drawers, they'd been stepped on and torn apart. The glass in her window was smashed and when he looked through it, he saw her conch shell laying on the grass. Beads from her few bits of jewelry crunched underfoot.

"Look like somebody don't like you girlfriend, Doc," Bigger said at his shoulder. "If I was you, I'd find out who and beat the shit out of him."

For the first time since he'd left Vietnam, Mercer turned to look at Bigger without flinching. "How about you find out for me, and I'll see what I can do about kicking his ass."

Bigger shrugged and a shattered bone poked out beneath the ripped-off sleeve of his bush uniform. "Wish I could, but I pretty well stuck to hangin' around you."

"Well, don't let me keep you if you got other things to do.'

"I ain't busy."

Mercer sat the cot back on its legs and scooped an armload of clothing onto it. Methodically, he started folding tee shirts and jeans, then decided he didn't want Genevieve to have to touch them until they'd been washed. He piled them into the wicker basket she kept for laundry and retrieved a stack of panties from the corner where they'd been thrown. For a moment he stared, stunned, at the substance that stained the lingerie, then a wave of sheer fury washed over him.

"I am going to kill the son of a bitch that did this." He slammed the bits of fabric into the garbage can.

"Now you talkin', Doc," Bigger said. "All we gotta do is find him."

CHAPTER 22
GENEVIEVE

I'd been away from the stage at Wiley B's for months, but it's true that absence makes the heart grow fonder and the libido grow stronger. Wiley B's Place stood on a highway crossroads in a rural area just northeast of Houston, nicer than most roadhouses, with a restaurant attached to the gentlemen's club. Wiley B met me with shouts of joy and showed me the ad he'd run in half a dozen Houston-area papers announcing Eugenie's triumphant return to town for a command performance. Unless I'd completely lost my touch, I'd make enough to pay for a semester of school and my books, with change left over. Wiley B wanted me to agree to several more gigs over the summer, but I put him off without telling him that once I could pay for school, I was done with strip clubs. I intended to be a lady, an educated one, and educated ladies support themselves without having to dance on stage in front of construction workers, bikers, and slumming corporate attorneys.

Like Mireille told me all those years ago, stripping's a job, and all the things that go with it are just part of the job. I was a seasoned performer whose advantages included a pretty face, good hair, a killer figure with boobs that hadn't begun to sag, and something most of the others were missing altogether: the ability to dance and not just shake my butt. The first night back on stage, I did just fine, going through the motions, enticing, revealing, teasing, then taking myself away when my audience thought I was right in their grasp. Even as I peeled my dress down over my breasts or raised one leg to coyly smooth a thigh-high stocking into place, the yelling, bantering crowds aroused in me no more emotion than a bunch of bawling calves would've done. I made a ton of tips that night, probably twice what any other girl made.

Then the second night came. I woke up with a sense of dread that increased throughout the day. By the time I joined half a dozen other girls in the stuffy, dimply lit, poor excuse for a dressing room, I knew I'd made a huge mistake in coming back. I got on my makeup and backcombed my hair into a bouffant, but to my shock and dismay, it took every bit of resolve I could scrape together to put on my costume. When the music cued up for the first of my three dances, panic kicked me in the stomach and brought me to a dead halt in the wings. I cupped both hands over my mouth, breathing slowly and shallowly to keep from hyperventilating.

"You okay, honey?" asked a big-eyed brunette dressed in a short nurse's costume. I looked at her over the tops of my hands and nodded, even though the real answer was a resounding no. The girl—Chili, I think she called herself—patted my shoulder and shoved a glass of water into my hands. "Take a sip and get out there, or Wiley B'll be on you like white on rice."

I gulped the water, gave Chili a quick nod of thanks, raised my face out of my hands, and sashayed my ass onto the stage like there was nothing in life I'd rather be doing than exhibiting my all-but-naked body for a bunch of testosterone-poisoned males. At long last, Genevieve moved to the back of my mind, allowing me to concentrate on being Eugenie, God's gift to mankind. Every single night that followed was a slightly different version of the same nightmare.

Despite the panic attacks, I finished out the week and made a nice pile of money, but when Wiley B pressed me to set another performance date, I told him I'd have to let him know what my schedule looked like. I let him kiss me goodbye on the cheek, suffered him to lay his hand on the curve of my butt like he always did while he kissed me, then I fled down the road to catch the bus to Texarkana, swearing I'd never again set foot in Wiley B's or any place like it.

I'd walked about half the mile toward the bus stop when a car pulled up behind me. Oh, Lord, what now? With my luck, it was some old boy who'd seen me dance and had been hanging around the place hoping for a chance to ask me for a date. Wouldn't be the first time. The driver beeped the horn lightly to catch my attention. I put my head down and kept walking. The voice of the car's engine changed as the driver put it into park. I hurried my steps when I heard the door open. I was not in the mood for this.

"Hey, Genevieve, wait up."

"Oh, dear Lord," I said, spun on the ball of my foot, and ran back to the car to fling myself into Mercer's arms.

"Oof," he gasped, staggering a little before catching balance for both of us.

For the second time in my adult life, I burst into tears on his shoulder. After a moment, I managed to tell him that I was fine, not hurt, not molested, just so very, very glad to see him. He bundled me into the car, handed me a clean handkerchief from his pocket, and drove us north toward home. After I calmed myself down and dried my eyes, I told him about the week, about the panic attack, about it not just being a job anymore.

"I felt like I was losing bits and pieces of myself, Mercer. Nobody ever lay a hand on me, but I swear I could feel them pulling me apart like cinnamon bread, everyone wanting to taste a piece." I stared out the window, watching the pine forests of East Texas blur as we sped down the two-lane road. "I'm done. I'm not going back. If I have to wait an extra semester to start school, I will, but I'm not going back."

We stopped at a café in downtown Nacogdoches for lunch. I didn't think I was hungry until we walked inside, and the smell of frying potatoes broadsided me. I ordered fried catfish with okra and black-eyed peas, ate every bite, plus one piece of Mercer's catfish as well before ordering a chunk of coconut cake with icing an inch deep. The waitress quit trying to keep my glass filled and just left the pitcher of sweet tea sitting on the table.

"When's the last time you ate?" Mercer asked, bemused and amused by my appetite. I made it halfway through the cake, then sighed contentedly and shoved the rest over to Mercer. He picked up my fork and tried a bite. "Mmm. Almost as good as yours."

Remembering my poor lopsided first effort at a cake, I burst into laughter that was only slightly tinged with hysteria. Oh, Lord, I needed to laugh.

"I don't rightly recall," I said. "I nibbled some here and there. Can't eat before I dance. Other times, we were shorthanded at the bar. If Wiley B could've had us on stage and serving drinks at the same time, he'd have done it. No time for lunch or dinner as long as customers were spending money." Impulsively, I stretched out my hand toward him. "Mercer, thanks for coming to get me. I surely did not expect it."

"I know you didn't." He patted my hand and went back to eating cake.

Half an hour from home, he pulled into a roadside park, switched the car off, and turned to face me. Without preamble, he said, "Someone broke into the apartment. I don't think they stole anything, but they smashed the dishes and messed your bedroom up. I got it put back together as good as I could, but . . ." He shrugged. "I think they were looking for something. Drugs, maybe."

Pictures, I thought. He was looking for the damn pictures.

CHAPTER 23
DELILAH

Wreath hung up the phone and stood for a moment, staring at the wall.

"Who was it, Mama?" Delilah asked. She walked to the back door, stuck her arm out into the open air, and shook the dust cloth vigorously. The action was for show; nothing in the Ives household ever sat untouched long enough to gather dust. She turned back into the house, eyed the kitchen, and thought of the improvements she'd make when the place was hers to fix up. First thing, she'd make Jared replace the washing machine. John Luther was too tightfisted to replace the old washer and Mama too mealy-mouthed and beaten down to insist, but there was no way Delilah was going to broil her skin and hair in the sun standing over an open fire to boil clothes in a filthy iron kettle. She'd get herself a dryer, too, or know the reason why. If Jared resisted, she wouldn't say a word, not a single blessed word. Delilah could speak louder without words than most women could holler at the top of their lungs. She'd have her dryer in a week.

Wreath was still looking at the wall. Irritated, Delilah sharpened her tone and repeated the question. "Well, who was it?"

"Genevieve. Someone went into her house and broke the mixin' bowls I gave her along with most of the rest of her dishes."

"'Someone'?" Mimicked Delilah. "She broke them herself and won't admit it. Why'd you go and give her those, anyway? They were my grandmother's and white trash like her doesn't appreciate nice things."

"Hush, Delilah," Wreath said with surprising firmness. "You got no call to go talkin' about her or anyone else that way. It's not like we're sittin' at the top of the social register."

Delilah's mouth tightened. She sulkily swiped the cloth over the china hutch, then burst out, "Why do you defend her? She's living over a garage with Mercer, bold as brass, without a thought in her head about decency and sin. How can you treat her like . . . like *family* when the two of them are dragging our good name down in the dirt? And Jezzie—you let her sit with Jezzie right out in public every week."

"Jezzie learns more about algebra in two afternoons with Genevieve than she learned all year in school."

"Algebra!" Delilah tossed her head. "What's she need with algebra? She'd do better to learn to bake decent bread. Huh. No telling what the child is really learning from that trashy witch. I don't know why Daddy doesn't put a stop to it and make her come straight home from school."

Wreath looked at her red-faced daughter, her own feelings chilling as Delilah's heated up. Where in the Lord's name had she gone wrong with this one? Sanctimonious, uncharitable, tale-bearing . . .

"Well," Wreath said evenly, "I reckon Jezzie would be better off sittin' home listening to you if I wanted her to grow up to praise Jesus with one side of her face and mean-mouth folks with the other. But I don't, so I reckon those algebra lessons will just keep on going."

Wreath walked straight past her stunned, infuriated daughter without another word, letting the screen door slam behind her. Delilah hurled the dust rag after her, wishing good Christian women could occasionally say a few bad words when the situation called for them.

"I cannot take this much longer," she said to the empty room. She was twenty-five, married, with two children, and no kitchen of her own while that white trash Genevieve swanned herself in a two-bedroom apartment with a man she had no right to and was leading down the road to hell just as fast as the two of them could go. And there was Mama, giving her mixing bowls, teaching her to cook, spending time with her as if she were a favored daughter instead of a little piece of skirt Mercer picked up on that motorcycle of his. Delilah had protested to her father, sure that the most righteous man she knew outside her own husband would come down on her side. To her surprise, John Luther had muttered something about throwing the first stone, and changed the subject. Delilah didn't believe he had a bit of liking or patience for Genevieve, but he refused to prevent Wreath, Jezzie, or Leah from seeing her even after Delilah pointed out the harm such an association was doing. In fact, he refused to talk about Genevieve at all. Had any other woman done what she was doing, John Luther would verbally flay the skin off her in church, not that Genevieve ever set foot in church after that first Sunday she stayed with them.

Of course, there had been other repercussions for that scene. Delilah smiled, remembering the occasion of Genevieve's only appearance at church and Mercer's last appearance. Genevieve had packed her bag and was gone before they returned from church, leaving a warm thank-you note for Wreath and telling Jezzie they could meet for tutoring at the Columbus Public Library after school on Thursdays. Mercer disappeared, too, though he eventually returned to the house for a few days before packing up and leaving himself. That night after evening prayer meeting, John Luther called Jared into the dining room. They remained closeted there together for some time. When Jared emerged, he drew Delilah into their bedroom and told her that John Luther had disowned Mercer and drafted a will leaving all his property to Jared.

"We'll take care of your mother and the girls, of course," Jared said. His eyes shone. He thought it was hard luck for Mercer, but

Mercer didn't care two peas about the place. Jared, on the other hand, had put his back and his time into the Ives farm ever since he inherited Delilah from his dead brother. The will was just.

Delilah looked around the kitchen, imagining it with crisp white curtains to replace the faded blue gingham, a new stove, and pretty dishes without a single chip. Wreath wouldn't like it, but Delilah intended to move her out of the kitchen just as surely as she'd moved her out of church work. So far, though, it had been hard going. Wreath accepted help with the cooking and cleaning, but she ignored Delilah's attempts to get her name added to the special bank account that John Luther had set up for household bills and expenses. Just thinking about that hurdle made Delilah mad enough to chew ten-penny nails and spit out thumbtacks.

I just want what's good for Mama, she assured herself righteously. *She needs to retire and let someone else be in charge. Lord knows, she is forty-five if she is a day and can't work like she used to. Why, Friday afternoon, I caught her sitting in a chair reading some book about roses that Jezzie brought her home from the library. I do believe she spends as much time on those flowers as she does in the vegetable garden. Huh, like there isn't plenty of important work to be done around this place. I'm surprised Daddy hasn't put a stop to it, though the yard does look real nice when people see it from the road. Well, it is just time for her to get out of my way. Of course, it'll take a while for me to convince Daddy and Jared to replace that washer, so I'll need her to help with the laundry, but . . .*

Still musing, she filled a bucket with clear water and vinegar, and found the soft cotton rags used for cleaning windows. Wreath had neatly hemmed each square on the old treadle sewing machine to keep them from leaving frayed threads on the windows. Delilah examined one square, wondering if it had gotten too threadbare to be of use. Threadbare. John Luther was beginning to act a little threadbare himself. Maybe it was time for him to retire and let Jared step behind the pulpit full-time.

I wouldn't dream of telling him that, Delilah thought, tossing the rag into the trashcan under the sink, *but maybe I could just sorta ease*

*him into considering the idea. He and Mama could use their savings
to buy a place in Hope or Saratoga, close enough for Mama to babysit
when I need a break, but not living right on top of us like we are now.*

She wrung out the rag, raised it to the first window, and ex-
claimed in exasperation at the sight of her mother standing next
to a small dogwood tree, face close to one of the blossoms, looking
for all the world as if she were kissing its petals. Delilah approved
of the vegetable and herb gardens but her mother's dedication to
flowers riled her. The church had flowers on the altar every week,
thanks to Wreath or one of the other gardening ladies in the congregation. It was a heathenish practice that Delilah intended to
stomp out as soon as she had perfect control of the women's circle.

*Mama just better be careful kissing flowers like a heathen. Some of
those things are poisonous.*

Lips tight and white with disapproval, Delilah attacked the
windows with her rags and vinegar water, thinking about poisonous flowers and people who kissed them. So intent was she on
her job and dark thoughts that the sound of the screen door slam-
ming made her jump. Irritated beyond reason, Delilah whirled
and threw a wet cloth at her younger sister, who was piling her
books on the kitchen table. Jezzie snagged it out of the air and
hurled it back. It smacked the bosom of Delilah's dress, leaving a
wet splotch.

"Which side of the bed did you get out of this morning?" Jezzie demanded as Delilah slammed the cloth back into the bucket.

"You . . . you . . ." Delilah clinched her hands into fists and
ground her teeth. The sight of Jezzie, hair curling around her
pretty face, nothing in the world to worry about but her homework, made her want to scream loud enough for Jared to hear her
down at the church. How dare Jezzie look so innocent and carefree and happy? A boy, Delilah decided. She must've taken up
with some nasty teen-aged boy at school. Well. That would have
to be nipped in the bud.

Controlling her voice with difficulty, Delilah said, "Sit down.
We need to have a serious conversation."

"You sit down," Jezzie shot back. "When you're around, I feel safer on my feet."

The desire to wound someone flooded Delilah. She leaned back against the kitchen counter and regarded Jezzie with a smile that wouldn't have been out of place on a hyena about to pounce on its evening meal. When she spoke, her voice dripped false sweetness and concern.

"We need to have a serious conversation about your future and the facts of life."

"My future's not up to you, and if I want to know anything about life, I'll ask Mama or Genevieve."

Delilah's temper slipped another notch. "Well, I guess a woman living in sin would know more than is seemly about the facts of life, but your upbringing isn't up to Genevieve."

"Last time I checked, it was up to Mama and not you."

"Mama—" Delilah cut herself off, took a deep breath, and plastered the fake smile back on her face. She sat down in a kitchen chair and folded her hands primly in her lap. "Mama didn't tell me what I needed to know at your age, and she's not gonna tell you either, so I will. Now, Jezzie. One day soon, Jared and me will take Mama, the twins, and Leah off for a weekend, maybe to Little Rock to visit his grandmother. While we're gone, it'll be up to you to take care of the house and Daddy."

"Mama's not going to want to go see that old woman," Jezzie said flatly. "Last time Miss Hazel came here, all she did was talk about her sore feet and criticize the way Mama planted her sweet potatoes. Even Jared doesn't like her, and she's his kin."

"Mama will do as she's told," snapped Delilah. "So will you. It's time you learned to take care of a house and please a husband without her telling you every blessed step to take."

"I'm fourteen, Delilah. Got a few more years before I need me a husband, if I ever do."

"Well, Daddy and I think you need one a lot sooner than that— someone to get you under control before you ruin yourself with some trashy boy and disgrace this family as bad as Mercer's doing."

Jezzie's mouth dropped open at this stunning injustice. Delilah barreled on, blocking the girl's protest with a raised voice.

"Come your fifteenth birthday, you're gonna find yourself standing in front of the congregation hand in hand with John Evert, telling him you'll obey his every wish and command from then until Doomsday."

"Delilah, you are the biggest liar this side of hell!"

"Am I?" Delilah smirked. "You were too little to remember, but Daddy married me off on my fifteenth birthday. First, he taught me everything I needed to know about how to serve a man, then he stood me up in church like a princess of the Lord and married me to old Joe Fuller. Read the marriage lines himself." She sat back in her chair and grinned nastily at her aghast sister. "What makes you think you're gonna get out of it if I couldn't?"

"John Evert is a hundred years old and has three of the brattiest kids it was ever my misfortune to babysit! People say his wife drowned herself in Red River because he hit her once too often."

"John Evert isn't even forty yet, and he's rich as cream cake. Soon as he gets hold of you, you won't be able to walk for all the husbanding he's gonna do to you."

Jezzie clapped both hands over her ears and ran from the room. Delilah yelled after her, "Think you're better than me with your algebra tutoring and your scribbles in the school newspaper. Huh. Wait'll Daddy gives you your wife lessons. We'll see how high and mighty you feel then."

She chortled to herself as she set about dumping the bucket of vinegar water down the drain and putting the cleaning cloths over the clothesline. Wreath had moved into the vegetable garden and was bent over with a hoe, clearing new weeds from between the rows of baby okra and tomatoes. Delilah watched her for a few moments, feeling the old resentment building up in her heart. That should be her vegetable garden. This should be her house. Wreath was keeping her from living her own life, something she'd been anticipating for ten years.

After a lifetime of relative indifference, John Luther had started to take an interest in Delilah the spring of her freshman year in high school: a nod of acknowledgment when she served him a perfectly fried egg, a small compliment about her complexion, a word of praise for her womanly modesty. Delilah basked in the attention and searched for ways to get more. She learned to keep her eyes demurely cast down when in his presence and never argued with him. Even when the provocation was strong, she bit her tongue and murmured, "I'm sorry. I was wrong. Thank you for correcting me." This submissive attitude also kept her from the whippings the others endured on a regular basis. Daddy's girl knew how to behave.

Delilah moved into her very own room when her first period started, a singular mark of favor as well as tacit acknowledgment of her new womanhood. The room was no more than a walled-off section of the old back porch, but it held a bed, a dresser, and best of all, privacy. She was exquisitely self-conscious about the changes in her body and dreaded being seen unclothed even by her mother or five-year-old sister. Wreath showed her how to deal with the monthly flow of dark blood without explaining what was happening beyond a mumbled phrase about Coming Sick each month being part of A Woman's Curse. Though her breasts swelled, they remained small enough to spare her having to bind them in cloth bands as many church women did for modesty. Other signs of puberty shamed her deeply, especially the coarse black hair that sprouted in the most private parts of her body. She wondered uneasily if this, too, was normal, or if the dreadful growth had resulted from some unrecalled sin. She dealt with the shame by focusing her eyes on the wall while she bathed, then dressing her body in clothing as plain and dowdy as her mother's.

One weekend Wreath took the younger children to visit an elderly aunt on John Luther's side. They'd all intended to travel to Shreveport, but at the last minute, John Luther had declared himself too busy to take time off. Wreath assumed the trip was cancelled and started to unpack, but John Luther insisted she and the youngest children make the trip via train. Delilah could stay home

and do for him, he said. Delilah swelled with importance and relief at his words. Aunt VeraAnn had called her a mean-mouthed
sneak last time they were together, and Delilah hoped never to
see her again.

After seeing Wreath, Mercer, and Jezzie onto the train at Hope,
John Luther dropped Delilah at the farm and drove back to the
church to take care of business. She fed Wreath's chickens and
ducks, picked a basket of fresh tomatoes, then fixed dinner. She
breaded and fried veal cutlets, warmed a few of Wreath's hand-
kneaded rolls, and opened home-canned jars of green beans and
corn. In a burst of enthusiasm, she consulted a big red cookbook
and managed to bake a pie. The crust was a little sorry, nothing
like her mother's flaky creations, but Delilah believed the apple
filling was every bit as tasty as anything her mother ever produced.

She and John Luther ate dinner that night at the dining room
table instead of the homely wooden rectangle in the kitchen. She
obediently and repeatedly rose to fill her father's glass with sweet
tea, to serve him another cutlet from the china platter, or a spoon-
ful of green beans from the swan-shaped tureen. As the meal pro-
gressed, John Luther spoke about a woman's duty to men, first to
her father, and later to her husband.

"You have been schooled in modesty and obedience from birth
and I am well pleased with you," John Luther said. He looked du-
biously at the pie on his plate, took a bite, and nodded acceptance,
if not complete approbation. Delilah sat on the edge of her chair,
barely nibbling her own dessert, so enrapt was she by his praise.
John Luther put down his fork, finished chewing, swallowed, then
looked her straight in the eyes. She froze, half frightened by the
intensity of his gaze.

"You will finish the ninth grade this summer, will you not?"

"Yes, sir."

"Do you enjoy school?"

"No, sir." She didn't tell him she hated every minute of every
boring lecture about every boring subject. Home Economics
might've been okay except for the Baptist and Methodist girls

who snickered about her clothes and referred to her as a Joyful Sheep. Delilah had not a single friend at school. Not. One.

"Well," her father said, "then what I have to say will be welcome to you."

She held her breath.

"Once you walk out of that school in May, you will never have to walk back in until you take your own children there."

Delilah's mouth fell agape as she considered this. At last, she said, "What will I do instead?"

"Help your mother in the kitchen, continue to practice the domestic arts, and learn to be a good wife. Then, on your fifteenth birthday, I will seal you to your husband in holy matrimony."

Delilah's head whirled. No more school? A husband? Her own house? She asked the obvious question, but John Luther refused to tell her who he'd chosen for her groom. Well, she'd find out soon enough. For now, it was enough to know she was free of algebra and the Missouri Compromise and parsing sentences. It was icing on the cake to think that she was going to have a wedding while Ideen Miller and Tansy Sue McWilliams had to go on to geometry and biology, where she heard students used razor blades to cut up earthworms.

John Luther pushed himself away from the table and stood up. "Clear the table, wash the dishes, and then you may have the rest of the evening to yourself. I suggest a good long prayer session, then early bedtime. You've worked hard today and deserve a rest."

She did the evening chores in a sort of daze, contemplating the new future spread before her, and wondering who would share it with her. The list of young men in the church wasn't long, but there were a couple she thought might do well enough. John David Anderson had blue eyes and dimples. Raymond James was dark and brooding. Both were older than she by some years, early twenties perhaps, but a girl—no, a woman, she corrected herself—a woman wanted a mature man to guide her through life.

Stars lit the outside sky before she finished the kitchen chores. She closed herself into her room, folded her clothes, and dropped her voluminous white cotton gown over her head. She sat down on the room's single chair and took up a sock she was knitting to work a little before turning out the light. She had just gotten to the tricky part of turning the heel when the door to her room opened and John Luther walked in. She leapt up from the chair, clutching the knitting to her heart. John Luther had not walked unannounced into her room since she talked back to him at the age of eight and got the whipping of her life.

"Sit down, Delilah." He indicated the bed and she eased herself down onto the edge of the mattress. He drew the straight-backed chair away from the wall so he could sit facing her, his knees almost touching hers.

"Your mother has taught you household skills and arts, but there are other lessons you must learn to be a good wife—lessons in obedience, submission, and how to please a husband. A comely face and figure are desirable traits in a woman, but without certain other skills, they are naught but vanity. It is up to me to teach you those skills. Stand up."

Delilah obeyed awkwardly, hemmed in between John Luther's knees and the bed.

"Unbutton your nightgown and drop it to the ground."

Delilah froze, suddenly sick to her stomach. He'd see the marks of shame on her body. He'd see— She opened her mouth to protest. His right hand went to his belt buckle. She gasped and subsided. She knew what that gesture meant.

"Do you need a lesson in obedience before we even begin your wife lessons?" he asked softly, dangerously.

She shook her head and raised trembling fingers to the buttons down the front of her gown.

"Faster."

She bit back a sob, half tore the buttons from their holes, and let the gown slip to the floor. Unable to help herself, she hid her face in her hands as he drew his eyes over her without expression. Hot, frightened tears spilled through her fingers.

"Turn around so I can look at you." As she revolved before him, he muttered in a harsh voice, " 'Thy desire shall be to thy husband and he shall rule over thee . . . for the man is not of the woman, but the woman of the man. Neither was the man created for the woman, but the woman for the man.' Do you understand?"

She gulped and nodded, though she did not understand anything that was happening.

He gave her one more order. She obeyed.

The things that followed felt wrong, but she did them all, anxious to avoid a beating, hoping that her perfect submission and obedience would earn approval and maybe even love. Some of the things felt good. A couple were indescribably disgusting. Afterward, he drew the covers over her and tucked her into bed like she was Jezzie's age.

"You did well," he said, brushing her cheek with a finger. "By your birthday, you will be everything a man wants in a wife. Good night," he added and shut the door behind him.

The lessons continued irregularly over the next few months, sometimes in her room when the rest of the household was asleep, sometimes in the office behind the church, once in the church itself. On the morning of her fifteenth birthday, she dressed in a plain white gown and John Luther escorted her down the center aisle of the church to meet her husband. Not John David, not Raymond, but a church elder well into middle age who owned a general store with an apartment on the second floor of the building, and who had donated generously toward reroofing the church.

Mr. Fuller, she thought in dismay. *Joe Fuller.*

Ten years later, the memory of her first day and first night as a married woman was still enough to make her shudder. At first, the sheer novelty of keeping her own kitchen sustained her, but within a month, she felt lonely and neglected, and by her first anniversary, she hated Joe Fuller worse than any person she'd ever known. He treated her more like a maid than a companion, and she never needed a single one of the wife lessons she'd been taught except obedience and submission. Three minutes beneath his soft white body and it was over until the next time the mood moved him to her side of the bed. He was so miserly that he wouldn't even let her choose vegetables from the store but took her out and showed her how to identify poke salad, raspberries, and other wild foods to supplement their meager table. He was fond of a mushroom that grew prolifically in the pine forests, and painstakingly taught her to tell the difference between it and a related but highly toxic variety. She hated the taste of the things and refused to put a single slimy piece in her mouth.

One dark day in the fourth year of their marriage, Delilah put dinner in the oven and sat down to rest a moment before making biscuits. She'd been working hard all day despite menstrual cramps that were far worse than usual and had kept her up most of the night. Without even noticing it, Delilah drifted off to sleep.

A hard slap to the face woke her to a roomful of smoke. Disoriented, she leapt up and almost fell over her own feet. Joe had already thrown the charred remains of a small, expensive roast down the back steps and stood ready to discipline her in the way prescribed by the church for wayward children and roast-burning wives. He beat her until she screamed for forgiveness, for mercy, then dropped her hard on the floor and shoved her knees apart to finish the punishment. For the next week, she kept her eyes downcast in his presence and ate her meals standing up. Two weeks after her last bruise faded to a dull yellow, she secretly added a couple of special mushrooms to those her husband had gathered in the woods the day before. She cooked them as usual and served them alongside fried chicken, potatoes, and gravy. Joe Fuller died in agony a few days later. People had long shaken their heads over his dangerous devotion to mushrooms and were smugly satisfied when their dire predictions came true.

Widowed, Delilah moved back into her room on the back porch of her parents' house. Joe's brother, Jared, was working on the farm by that time and living in a room over the garage. He was hardworking, reasonably good-looking, and much kinder than his older brother. By right of survivorship, he'd inherited the store he co-owned with his brother. He promptly sold it for a good price, having no desire to become a shopkeeper himself. Delilah looked him over with a calculating eye, decided she could make something of him, and set about convincing him that he couldn't live without her.

Upon their marriage, Jared moved into the house, bought a few cattle, and eventually had himself a nice herd established on the farm's pastureland. When John Luther asked Jared to take the pulpit for prayer meeting one Wednesday, Delilah saw new possibilities. Jared was a natural preacher, calm and soothing where John Luther was emotional and demanding. Delilah had slapped Jezzie's face when the girl referred to the two men as bad cop, good cop, but it was true that they balanced each other. Jared wasn't, however, imaginative or a gifted writer of sermons. Delilah came up with the subjects, found the pertinent Bible verses to support each, and stood over Jared's shoulder making suggestions as he labored with pen and paper.

Five years later, Delilah was still ghostwriting sermons and living in her parents' house, albeit in the second largest bedroom, which had once been Wreath's sewing room. She turned away from the sight of her mother's labors in the garden, thinking back to that deadly dish of mushrooms. She walked to the shelves where Wreath kept her small collection of books and pulled out a volume on medicinal plants. Sitting down at the kitchen table, she opened the book and began to scan the pages without a single idea of what she was looking for but determined to find it anyway.

Chapter 24
Genevieve

Though there wasn't much left to see at Meema's old place, I kept going back to sneak over the rusty gate in the disintegrating fence that encircled the property. The great sassafras tree that once shaded the backyard lay splintered on the ground, and a mass of fifteen-foot pine seedlings drowned the pasture, but the pond was still there, spring-fed, quiet, and so clear that I could watch turtles making their way across the rust-red mud at the bottom. I caught my first fish from the raised banks of this pond, a sunfish. I was so proud, but thirty seconds after I pulled it from the water, I realized it was dying and tumultuous grief and guilt replaced the pride. Meema freed it from the hook, but it was too late. The little fish had smothered in the thick Arkansas air that only felt humid enough to drink. We buried it with full ceremony beneath Meema's prized Glory of the World rosebush. Back then, the pond banks were kept clear of trees, and you could swing a cane pole without catching your line in the branches. Trees had encroached on the pond in the last few years, tucking their roots securely into the berm. After so much time, I didn't expect the pond to have fish, but something was keeping the turtles alive.

One afternoon I carried a fishing pole over the fence with me, having long ago overcome my scruples about catching and eating fish. I didn't give a rip about trespassing, had no idea who owned the place now, and no interest in finding out. Long as I could sneak across the locked gate once in a while without getting caught, I could pretend the place was mine, left to me by Meema. With each trip across the fence, I uncovered another memory: a clump of crepe myrtle that had marked the corner of the front porch, a tangle of wire that was all that was left of the duck and chicken pen, a pile of collapsed wood that once housed Papaw's prized tractor. The fence along the road was in decent shape, but back in the woods, the damp acid earth had eaten away the bases of most of the wooden posts. One day I traced the fence line around the place by following a rusty, broken thread of barbed wire, almost indistinguishable from the wait-a-minute vines. It was hard work to climb over deadfall and detour around impenetrable bramble patches. The journey took three times as long as I thought it would. By the time I got clear back around to the gate, I looked and felt like the last tattered rose of summer.

The neighbor to the north of Meema's farm had timbered his land, probably selling the wood to one of the papermills or saw-mills. He burned the pathetic broken remnants in slash piles, leaving behind an open meadow where a couple dozen white-faced cattle now grazed. My great-grandfather had settled that piece of land when he moved to Arkansas from South Carolina following The Late Unpleasantness of the 1860s. He married Meema's mother and sold his land during the Depression to keep from losing her family's place. Somewhere out there in the cow pasture is the old pit where Great-grandpa dug clay to make a big stack of bricks. He used a bunch to build the chimney of Meema's old house and sold the leftovers to folks around the county. Bricks were heavy things to haul, though, and he only made the one big pile before he turned his hand to farming and selling produce across the county.

I listened for voices while I wandered the old farm but heard no one until one day someone I wasn't expecting spoke up behind me while I was fishing.

"Next time you come, you need to bring you something to cut

back them vines," said Bigger. "May as well make you a good path to the pond long as you fixin' to keep hangin' around here."

I automatically looked around for Mercer.

"He ain't here."

"Then how . . . ?"

Bigger shrugged uneasily. "Don't know. Just all of a sudden, I got here. Kindly lonesome to look around and be somewhere he ain't. Not," he added graciously, "that you ain't fine company, 'cause you are."

"Thanks. I like you, too, even if you are kind of a mess."

"Yeah, reckon I could put most folks right off they food." He smoothed his big hand across his destroyed face. For a moment, the bones solidified, the skin smoothed itself into a solid sheet of black satin, and I saw what a good-looking man he'd been before the grenade caught him. For a moment, we smiled at each other, then the skin split, and his face sagged back into the familiar ruin.

"Can't keep it up long," he said by way of apology. "Takes a lotta energy. You might try casting you line over by that big log. Bet they somethin' nice lurking there."

I pulled my line out of the water, moved a couple dozen feet east, and tossed my line where he indicated. "You like to fish?"

"Yes'm. Watchin' you ain't quite as good, but it's better than nothin'." He squatted down to peer into the water. "Used to fish over at Cypress Lake by McNab. Hunted ducks, too. Man, I loved me some duck huntin'."

That surprised me so much that the pole jerked in my hands, probably scaring away any fish that had been nosing around my bait. "You from around here?"

He nodded. "Just this side of Ozan. My great-great-aunt lived down this very road, maybe five, six miles from here. Mama used to carry her an' me to church ever' Sunday. Aunt Simma'd sit in the backseat, hold me in her lap, and tell me stories. She died out tendin' her garden when she was one hundred and five."

I lowered myself to the ground next to him, holding my cane pole so the line didn't drop clear into the water. "A hundred and five?"

"Yes'm. Hundred years older than me. Born before freedom came."

We sat silently, looking at the pond and contemplating all the things Aunt Simma must have seen, a lot of them not good for a black woman.

"Thought maybe I might come across her, being back home and on this side of the wall," he said wistfully. "But I ain't seen her. Ain't seen nobody to talk to 'cept Doc and now you. Even them marines that hung around Doc at first is gone."

"Lonesome."

"Yes'm. Real lonesome." He reached down for a small rock, but his fingers passed through it. Knowing what he wanted to do, I picked up the rock and tossed it into the pond for him, scaring fish be damned. We watched the concentric circles spread out around the splash.

"I keep thinkin' I wanna go home," he said at last. "Jus' not sure what that means anymore. My mama and daddy's place . . . I can't seem to get there to see how they doin'. Think maybe I'm scared they might see me like this." He flicked a finger toward his face and shattered chest. "I surely would not want that. Maybe sometime Mercer'll go and see 'em for me. I don't like to ask him, though." He reached for another pebble. I picked it up. He pointed at a spot, and I lobbed his rock in that direction.

"Sometimes I wonder if I done gone to hell and don't know it. Hang out with live white folks 'stead of all the black folks I thought'd be here waitin' on me. Ain't nobody over here. Just me.

Voices murmured in the air around us, but Bigger didn't hear them. I used to wonder why I can hear the dead and other people can't, but I don't wonder anymore. I just can and they just can't and that's all there is to it. Listening to Bigger talk, though, I wondered what will happen when I die. Will anyone be waiting for me, or were the doctors right and the ghosts are all my imagination? I looked over at Bigger, head and shoulders taller than me. Had to admit he looked pretty damn real, even being translucent as he was. Mercer could see him, too. Lord, life is complicated, and it looked like death might not be any simpler. The thought depressed me, so I shook it off and picked up the rock Bigger was staring at. He pointed. I threw. The rock splashed. Concentric circles blossomed across the water's surface.

"Any idea what's holding you here?" I asked cautiously, keeping my eyes glued to the ripples. Some dead folks are almighty sensitive about that question because they aren't convinced that they're dead. Bigger seemed to have a good handle on the reality of his own death, though, so I ventured to ask. Can't tell if you can help someone along until you ask or they tell you, one.

"No, ma'am, I don't. Like I said, maybe I'm just scared, death bein' a new experience and all. Mercer is familiar to me. Closest thing to a brother I ever had. Closer'n a brother, to tell the truth." He turned his battered face to look straight at me for the first time in the conversation. "Mercer's bad off, Genevieve. I can't leave him like he is, but at the same time, I think I make things worse."

He'd never called me by name before. Hearing it in his voice gave me a shock. I've met a lot of ghosts in my life, but I never made friends with one who was dead when I met him. I wasn't sure how I felt about it.

"You got something on you line." Bigger pointed at the pond.

I swiveled my head just in time to see my bobber sink. With a wordless exclamation, I scrambled to my feet and eased and teased and drew in the line until I could see dinner attached to the hook. Just as I reached out to grab him, that damn fish gave one more ferocious tug against the line, tore the hook from its mouth, and disappeared from sight. I straightened, growling with irritation.

"Dang, I was so sure I had him." I turned to grimace at Bigger, but he was gone. I looked forlornly at the spot where he'd crouched and, to my surprise and irritation, felt the prickle of tears behind my eyes. Well, there was no accounting for ghosts. I blinked sternly, pulled in my line, and hightailed it out of there for the day. Lord, I knew it, I knew it—once I started crying, I wasn't ever going to be done with it.

CHAPTER 25

JEZZIE

Terror. There was no word except terror for the feeling Jezzie lived with following Delilah's terrible pronouncement about her future. Fearful of crossing John Luther's path, she waited in her room until the last possible minute in the morning before rushing down the stairs and heading for the bus stop. Her mother protested that she needed to eat something, but Jezzie cried, "No time! I'm late!" as she flew down the stairs and out the door. She shunned her usual bus stop across from John Luther's church in favor of walking an extra half mile in the opposite direction to the bus stop in front of the CME church. At home she became as quiet and furtive as Wreath, moving around the house with her eyes darting in every direction, her ears sharp for the sound of John Luther's footstep or the growl of his voice.

Between the end of classes and the arrival of the school bus to Columbus, she escaped into a stall in the girls' restroom, pressed her fingers to her eyes, and wept from sheer dread of going home. She didn't have the vaguest idea of what wife lessons might involve, but she knew she wasn't ready for them and knew sure as hell John Luther was not a proper person to teach them to her. Dear Lord, what if he turned her into the same kind of self-righteous bitch as Delilah? And marry John Evert? Take care of his nasty snaggle-toothed children? Let him touch her? Kiss her? Jezzie gagged. Delilah's spiteful words came back to her: "Soon as he gets hold of you, you won't be able to walk for all the husband-ing he's gonna do to you."

What could that mean? That husbands must beat wives worse than fathers beat daughters? She clutched at her stomach with both hands and wondered what she was going to do. She wanted desperately to go to her mother, but what could Mama do? She'd never protected Jezzie. Best she could manage was to sit and weep into her hands while John Luther laid his belt hard across Jezzie's bottom and thighs. Fat lot of good crying like a baby did anyone.

Sheer fury at her mother's helplessness boiled up in Jezzie's throat, spilling out in something between a moan and a muffled howl. Sometimes she hated Mama as much as she did John Luther. More, maybe. John Luther was an abusive bully, but Mama was . . .

"Coward. Wimp. Stupid . . . whiner." Jezzie wanted to beat her head against the stall door. No. Mama wasn't going to save her. She had to find another way to escape the future that John Luther had lined out for her.

She wiped her eyes, flushed the toilet, and let herself out of the stall just in time to board the bus. Watching the green countryside roll by, she tried to think her way to a solution. Run away from home? Too bad she was too young to join the Navy like Mercer had done. She might make a good nurse. Probably make a better warrior. She sure as hell felt like going to war against John Luther, Mama, and that mean-ass Delilah. Jezzie imagined herself stand-ing in the kitchen, sword drawn and dripping with blood, the bod-ies of those who'd wronged her sprawled on the floor at her feet. For a moment, fierce satisfaction blazed in her heart. Then, still in her imagination, Leah's face peeked around the doorjamb.

Leah. Oh, dear God. Leah. She was next if Jezzie didn't man-age to save herself and in the process save her baby sister.

She chewed on her thumbnail, her mind swinging from one wild plan to the next until the bus rolled to a stop in front of the

CME Church. She gathered up her books and followed the other children off the bus.

"Well, hey, Jezzie," said one child. "Whatcha gettin' off here for?"

"Need the extra exercise," she said shortly, and walked toward the dirt road leading home. She hadn't gone more than a few steps when it occurred to her what day it was. Genevieve would be waiting for her at the library. Jezzie gasped, spun on her heel, and ran down the highway toward Columbus.

Genevieve was standing at the side of the road, hands on her hips, looking after the bus when Jezzie rounded the curve coming into town. By the time she got close enough to holler at her, Genevieve had one foot up in her truck, getting ready to swing the rest of herself onto the seat.

"I'm here! I'm here!" cried Jezzie, waving one arm desperately as she ran. "Genevieve, don't leave me."

Genevieve smiled and climbed back down to the ground. Jezzie ran up to her, dropped her books in a heap on the ground, flung both arms around her startled cousin, and burst into sobs.

"Hey, now, sugar," Genevieve said, hugging the weeping girl close. "What's going on?" She let her cry for a few moments, then set Jezzie on her feet, pulled a red bandana from the hip pocket of her own jeans, and handed it over.

"Gennie, oh, Gennie," Jezzie said, pressing the bandana to her wet face. "Please, can we go somewhere? Somewhere private to talk?"

"Don't know why not. Too nice an afternoon to sit in the library. I'll call your mama from the store and tell her we're going over to Bois d'Arc to study on the pier today. Get on in the truck and I'll be right back."

Jezzie climbed into the passenger side of Genevieve's truck, moving a set of pruning shears, a short-handled hoe, and a heavy pair of gloves to make room for herself. She took a couple of deep breaths and felt calmer. She should've thought of Genevieve sooner. Nothing scared Genevieve. She'd somehow forced John Luther to let Jezzie's algebra lessons continue, even forced him to allow Mama, Leah, and Jezzie to visit her and Mercer at their place in Washington. Nothing short of a miracle. Delilah griped about it to John Luther every chance she got, but he just ignored her and walked away.

Genevieve must be magic, Jezzie thought, then with an adult burst of insight added, *I wonder what she knows about him the rest of us don't.*

The magic algebra tutor climbed into the truck, dropping a small paper bag on the seat between them. "Got us a couple of cokes and some fruit. There's a peanut patty in there for you, too."

Jezzie smiled and riffled through the bag to find the sweet. "How'd you know I like these things?"

"Mercer told me during a silly conversation we had about favorite food."

"How's he doing?" Jezzie peeled away the cellophane and took a nibble of the pink confection. Amazing how much better the right kind of sugar could make a girl feel, especially when combined with the right kind of company.

Genevieve didn't believe in treating teenagers like idiots who needed to be protected from life. She made her answer straight and to the point. "Had a couple of real bad days, but he sobered up yesterday. Seemed to be doing okay this morning. Went back to work, anyway."

"Do you think he'll ever get back to being like he used to be?"

"I don't know, but I don't think so."

"Me, neither," Jezzie said. She looked at the pink circle of sugar and peanuts in her hand, sighed, and took another bite. Around a mouthful, she added, "Thank you for taking care of him. Mama says she doesn't know what we'd have done if you hadn't come home with him that day."

Genevieve was silent for half a mile. Then, very softly, she said, "I don't know what I would've done if he hadn't brought me."

"Y'all gonna get married?"

Genevieve smiled sideways at Jezzie's eager face and shook her head. "It's not that kind of relationship, sugar. Mercer and I, we're—"

"Best friends?" Jezzie suggested when Genevieve hesitated.

"Maybe. Very good friends, anyway." Genevieve turned her attention back to the road.

They rode the rest of the way to the bayou in companionable silence that was easier to maintain than conversation, given the wind blowing in through the open windows. Genevieve stopped the truck in the parking area and reached into the back to pull out a couple of fishing poles and a can of bait. Jezzie grinned.

"That doesn't look like algebra."

"No reason we can't talk about algebra while we're fishing."

They strolled out onto the pier and climbed into the boat that always sat there, rain or shine. No one seemed to own it. Certainly, no one bothered to paint it. Genevieve slid the oars into the locks and pulled away deep into the bayou. Beneath a blue sky accented with a few white clouds, they took up the fishing poles, threaded worms onto hooks, and dropped their lines into the water.

Jezzie watched the red bobber move up and down in the gentle ripples. It was the wrong time of day to be fishing, and the wrong kind of bait to use even if it was the right time of day, but she didn't care. For the first time since the fight with Delilah, she felt safe and sane. A quarter of an hour peacefully drifted by before Genevieve's bobber sank beneath the water.

"Ha! Got one," she said, and worked the line to bring in a small bream. She pulled it out of the water, removed the hook, and slid the fish back over the side of the boat. "We'll let that one get a little bigger before we take it home."

"Genevieve?"

"Hmm?"

"What do you know about wife lessons?"

"Wife lessons?"

Jezzie took a deep breath, fastened her eyes on an egret gliding toward a roost in a cypress tree, and told her what had happened in the kitchen with Delilah. Genevieve said not a word as the story spilled out of Jezzie's mouth. She grew as still as one of the cypress knees sticking up through the clear water of the bayou.

"I don't want to get married, Gennie. I don't want wife lessons. I don't want to have to ever look at John Evert again, much less live in his house and take care of his nasty brats." Jezzie knuckled away the tear that crept down one cheek. "I'm not like Delilah. I want to finish school and go to college and be a . . . a . . . I don't know, an algebra teacher. I'd rather clean out chicken houses for a living than live in John Evert's stupid house."

Genevieve reached out and grabbed Jezzie's hand. Firmly she said, "You are not getting married until and unless you want to get married. You are not going to have wife lessons. You are going to finish school if it takes every ounce of my blood to get you through it."

Jezzie clutched her hand. "Really?"

"Really. Jezzie, has anyone ever touched you in a way that you didn't like? Anyone?"

"I don't like being whipped."

"I bet not."

"It's not just that it hurts so bad, but he . . . he . . ." Jezzie gulped. "He sees . . . sees parts of me . . ."

Fury flashed into Genevieve's face. Even though she knew the anger wasn't aimed at her, it rattled Jezzie. She hadn't seen Genevieve look angry since she walked out of church in the middle of John Luther's sermon. Her expression then had been alarming, but now, for the first time, Jezzie understood the expression, "If looks could kill."

She hates him, Jezzie thought, elated. *She hates his fucking guts, and she isn't scared of him. Oh, Gennie.*

In a perfectly level voice that didn't match the color flaming beneath her skin, Genevieve asked, "Anything other than the whippings? Does he put his hands on you, on any of those parts you don't want him to see?"

Jezzie shook her head. A new idea rose in her mind, a horrible idea. "Not . . . yet. Is that what wife lessons are, Gennie?"

"I think so."

"He did them to Delilah."

"Sounds like. Do you remember anything about when Delilah got married the first time? I know you were real little."

Jezzie squinted her eyes, thinking back. "All I remember is she got her own room before she left home. We shared a room until then and Delilah just hated it. Said I messed with her things. Probably I did. Mama was expecting Leah, so she put a crib in the room with me and Delilah moved into the room off the porch."

"Anything else?"

Jezzie shrugged and shook her head. "No."

"Anybody said anything about giving you your own room?"

"No. Mama has the room off the porch now. Leah still shares with me."

"Jezzie, we need to tell your mama what Delilah said."

Jessie waved her hands, warding off the very idea. "Mama's scared to death of him. She couldn't stop him, wouldn't even have the nerve to say anything to him. We'd just upset her for no reason."

"She didn't have anyone to back her up before," Genevieve said. "She's got me now, and I'm not scared of the old bastard."

Jezzie shook her head vigorously. "You don't understand. Mama tried stopping him when he beat up Mercer the last time. Before he joined the Navy, you know? She grabbed his arm and yelled at him. He knocked her across the room like she wasn't any bigger than Leah. She hit her head and made it bleed, but she got up and went after him again. He just hit her harder and yelled for stupid Delilah to hold her back while he beat on Mercer. Then after Mercer ran off, he did something so bad to her that she had to go to the hospital and have her spleen taken out."

Remembering her mother's furious and futile assault on John Luther, a wave of mingled shame, envy, and admiration swept Jezzie. Her mother hadn't been a coward that day.

Oh, Mama, she thought despairingly, *why can't you fight for me the way you did for Mercer?* On the tail of that thought came another one, utterly terrifying.

"Gennie, I was wrong. If we tell her about the wife lessons, she'll try to stop him. I know she will, and he will be so angry. He might . . . kill her." She barely got the words out, but she believed every one of them. Wreath would fight. Wreath would lose. Wreath would die. "We can't tell her."

Genevieve closed her eyes, opened them again. "Okay. I'll think of something, sugar. Looky, Mercer and I just got a phone put in the house. I'll give you the number. If there is any trouble at all, if he tries to move you into your own room, if he makes a single weird gesture at you, run like hell, find a phone, call us, and either Mercer or I will come get you. Okay?"

" 'Kay." Jezzie sniffed and dabbed her nose with the red bandana. With a final sigh, she picked up her fishing pole, attached another worm to the hook, and tossed the line back into the water.

Genevieve tilted her head back to watch an egret flapping its way across the bayou to land in a cypress tree. Five minutes later, the egret spread its wings and flew away. Though she was still staring directly at the spot where the bird had perched, Genevieve didn't register its departure.

CHAPTER 26

GENEVIEVE

I didn't know who I was madder at: John Luther for being a pervert, Delilah for aiding and abetting him, Wreath for not seeing what was going on, Mercer for being lost somewhere between reality and Vietnam, or myself for not having a damn clue about what I was supposed to do about any of it. I was even mad at poor innocent Jezzie for dragging me into the middle of the Ives family mess, though I told myself I was glad she trusted me enough to ask me for help. Dragging me, hell. I jumped right in the middle of it on my own, so greedy for family connections that I never stopped to think that those connections might come with some heavy obligations. Lord, the sole person in the family with good sense was Bigger, but he was related only by name, and was dead to boot.

I could go to the police, but would they believe Jezzie's story, much less act on it? Nah, John Luther would open his big, stern preacher mouth and convince the cops, men all, that Jezzie was just a lying teenager trying to cause her honorable daddy problems because he wouldn't get her a bicycle. I thought about asking Mercer for advice (she was his sister, damn it, not mine) but shied away from that idea immediately. Mercer had all the trauma and strife he could handle right in his own head. Now, a truly good woman would have found some compassion for that venom-tongued bitch Delilah since she was a victim of John Luther herself, but for the life of me, I couldn't see how a person would go over to the enemy as completely as she had done. Compassion, hell. I wished I could dropkick her butt from Columbus straight into Red River with a big helping of Daddy to follow her into the drink.

For a few minutes, I considered doing a midnight flit, leaving one letter outlining the situation for Wreath and one for the sheriff. Just pack what was left of my stuff after John Luther busted up my home and hightail it . . . somewhere. I rowed the boat into the shade of a cypress tree and pulled the cokes out of the sack that I'd tucked under the seat. Digging the opener out of my back pocket, I popped the cap on one bottle for Jezzie and acknowledged to myself that I wasn't going anywhere. For better or for worse, Wreath, Mercer, Jezzie, and Leah were my people, and I wasn't running off on them the way my father had done me. Resigned to my fate, I sipped my coke, thought of the pistol hidden at the back of my closet under a floorboard and the dirty clothes basket, and wondered what my chances were of getting away with murder.

Jezzie and I stayed out on the boat fishing and talking of inconsequential things until the shadows of the cypress trees lengthened across the smooth surface of the bayou. Having turned the problem of wife lessons over to me, Jezzie recovered most of her good spirits and seemed to enjoy the afternoon on the water. Her complete faith in my ability to handle the situation touched and terrified me. In all my life, I had never been responsible for anyone except myself and a trio of boa constrictors, and look what happened to two of those poor snakes. I spared a wistful thought for Esmeralda as I rowed back toward the dock. Madame Clara had sold my good girl in a single lot along with the few other animals she owned personally, including Henri and Henriette. Jean-Narcisse took care of his cats, and I took care of Esmeralda. Before I left the circus for good, I poked a big nail in the screen covering the side of Esmeralda's cage, then used my gloved hand to make a snake-sized hole on through so it'd look like she'd escaped on her own. I left some strips of her recently shed skin on the ragged wire and artfully sprinkled a few drops of blood around the hole as well. The blood was mine. I got to poking the hole too enthusiastically and the ragged edges of that screen ripped open both my glove and the top of my index finger. The buyer probably pitched a fit when he discovered both lions and a snake were missing from the inventory, but before he took possession, Madame Clara died in the hospital at Gulfport so he couldn't hassle her for reparation. As soon as that dear lady took leave of her poor ravaged body, I took leave of the hospital, folded Esmeralda into my duffel bag, and caught the bus to New Orleans less than an hour later. I didn't wait for the funeral. No need. Madame Clara stood next to me, shoulders shaking with her deep, rich chuckle, as I turned Esmeralda over to the herpetologist at the Audubon Zoo in New Orleans and told him a long, tall tale about how I came to own her and why I was forced to give her up.

"Knew the moment I laid eyes on you that you were going to be the best snake handler I ever hired," Madame Clare said, "but I had no idea what a good liar you'd be."

I laughed softly, remembering, and Jezzie lifted her head from contemplating our small string of catfish to smile at me.

"What's funny?"

"Just remembering something that happened when I was with the circus," I said.

Jezzie's eyes and mouth became perfect circles. "You were in the circus? No. You're teasing me. Really?"

I nodded.

"Wow!" She said, drawing the word out like it had half a dozen syllables. I could see my stock had just risen more points than I deserved. "What did you do in the circus?"

"Little bit of a whole lot of stuff," I said, taking one more dig at the oars. The boat glided over the last stretch of water to bump gently against the dock.

"No, really, Gennie," begged Jezzie, clasping her hands beseechingly beneath her chin. "Tell me."

I cocked an eyebrow at her as I wrapped the line securely around the boat hook. "Umm, a lot of those stories aren't what your mama might consider appropriate for a young lady to hear."

"Those are exactly the ones this young lady has been waiting her whole dang life to listen to," the wretched child said firmly, a mischievous spark lighting her eyes. Lord, but she looked like Miss Wreath. Not an eyelash worth of John Luther in this one's makeup and thank the Lord for that. I must've scowled at the very thought of him because Jezzie's expression changed from pleasantly excited to apprehensive in just a blink. I turned up the corners of my mouth to reassure her.

"Okay. Give me a while to think about it and I'll come up with a story somewhere between scandalous and boring. I suppose I could tell you about all the lion sh— poop I shoveled."

Jezzie giggled. "You can say 'shit,' Gennie. I've heard the word before. Were you a lion tamer?"

" 'Fraid not. I worked with big snakes, though."

"What kind of snakes?"

"Boa constrictors."

"They poisonous?"

"Snakes aren't poisonous. Snakes are venomous," I said, automatically starting what I thought of as Standard Rube Lecture Number One. "So are things like dirt daubers and those big old bumblebees that hang out in your mama's garden. Venomous critters poke holes in you with fangs or stingers and pump toxin directly into you. Poison is something that you have to breathe in or eat or soak up through your skin."

Jezzie pulled her single braid over one shoulder and chewed the end of it, thinking over this new idea. I unloaded the fishing gear and empty coke bottles onto the pier, then climbed onto it myself. She abandoned the braid to accept a helping hand up from the boat.

"Okay. Venomous, not poisonous. Were the boa constrictors venomous?"

"Nope. They squeeze their prey to death, like—*this*!" I grabbed her around the shoulders with both arms and demonstrated proper boa constrictor technique until we both laughed so hard that we nearly toppled into the water. We gathered up the abandoned fishing gear along with our pathetic string of fish and headed for the car, Jezzie still giggling and me sinking back into dread despite the smile on my face.

CHAPTER 27

LEAH

Leah put her books on the kitchen table and followed her nose to the platter of chocolate chip cookies on the countertop. Fifth-grade lunch took place at the stupid hour of 10:45 A.M. and by the end of the half hour afternoon bus ride from Hope, Leah was always starving. She lifted the clean towel covering the cookies, happily contemplated them for a moment, and reached out to take a nice fat one. Her fingertips no sooner touched the sweet than a sharp voice punctured the quiet.

"You little thief. Leave those cookies alone until somebody offers you one."

Delilah. Leah's heart plummeted. She'd perfected the art of avoiding her stern rumbling thundercloud of a father, aided by his heavy-footed inability to sneak up on anyone. As long as she didn't do anything to bring attention to herself, he barely noticed her. Delilah, on the other hand, seemed to lie in wait for her. At church and around company, the eldest Ives girl shone with dimpled smiles and soft murmurs of Praise Sweet Jesus. In private, she was a venom-tongued demon who pinched, slapped, criticized, and took pleasure in describing the special hell that awaited younger sisters who displeased her. No one would believe what a threat Delilah presented to Leah's self-confidence and peace of mind.

Unfortunately for Leah, Delilah had had a bad day and a worse night, with both colicky twins squalling until all hours and precious little help from anyone calming them down. Jared had gone out to sleep on the hammock in the yard. Wreath, isolated in her room off the back porch, didn't hear the uproar. Jezzie and Leah put pillows over their ears, and John Luther would probably sleep through the trumpets of Judgment Day. By midafternoon, Delilah was so worn, bad-tempered, and mean-mouthed that Jared bundled the boys into the car and drove off to spend a couple of days with his parents in Mena. Wreath headed for the garden to get away from her. With no one left to yell at, Delilah was spoiling for a fight by the time Leah came in from school.

"What gives you the right to come in my kitchen taking things? You keep those dirty paws to yourself." Delilah snatched up the platter of cookies and banged it down on a shelf out of Leah's reach.

"Mama told me this morning she was making cookies for me and Jezzie to have after school," Leah said tearfully. "You got no call to boss me around and call me names."

"Don't sass me, you heathen, or I'll get Daddy's belt and blister your bottom for you."

"You let me alone or I'll tell Mama!"

Delilah lunged forward and fingernail-pinched the skin between the child's shoulder and collarbone. Even in her fury, she attacked where the marks wouldn't show. "You miserable little tattletale. You say one blessed word to *anyone* about me and I'll tell Daddy that Mama is talking against him. He'll take her *apart*. Not only will you go straight to hell for tattling, it'll be *your fault* if Mama dies in the hospital this time."

"Mama! Mama!" screamed Leah. She twisted out of Delilah's grip and made a run for the back door.

Delilah lost what control she still had after an hour of broken sleep. She caught Leah's elbow and slung the child around, smashing her backward into the china hutch. Half a dozen glasses tumbled off the shelf and smashed on the scrubbed pine floor.

"Clumsy brat!" Delilah dragged the terrified child away from the hutch and shook her like a dust cloth. "Those glasses were part of a set. Ruined! Ruined!"

"What on earth?" Wreath ran through the screen door, garden clippers still in her hand. She dropped them on the table and pried Delilah's fingers away from Leah's arm. "What are you doin', Delilah? Turn her loose."

With a wail, Leah collapsed against her mother, pressing her face into Wreath's apron front. Wreath put both arms around the child and looked to Delilah for an explanation.

"She was running through the house like a wild Indian. Look at this mess!"

"It's just old glasses," Wreath whispered into Leah's hair. "Don't mean a thing to any of us."

"They do to me!" Delilah shrieked. "That's my grandmother's crystal."

Wreath looked at her in astonishment. "Crystal? Those glasses came in boxes of laundry soap."

Delilah snapped her attention to Leah. "Stop bawling like a sick calf and go get me the broom and dustpan so I can clean up this mess." The child peeked over her shoulder. Delilah pinned her in place with a basilisk stare: one word, just one blessed word about what just happened . . .

"Your legs aren't broken, and you know where the broom stays, Delilah," Wreath said, narrowing her own eyes at the sight of her older daughter's expression. "What's gotten into you?" To Leah, she added, "C'mon, sugar. Let's get you something cool to drink. Look, I made cookies for you. We'll take them and a big glass of sweet tea up to your room, put the fan in your window, and you can do your homework up there today instead of on the kitchen table."

They headed upstairs with Leah clutching a small plate of

cookies in one hand. Delilah snatched up the base of a broken glass and flung it against the wall. The sound was so satisfying that she seized another but caught herself before she threw it. Very deliberately, she placed it on the table. No sense battering the wall and ruining the paint. She examined the mark made by the thrown glass, tightening her lips at the depth of the gash in the crisp white paint. She shook her head and went to find the broom.

Little heifer, upsetting me like that. Now I'll have to repaint when I take over the kitchen from Mama.

Upstairs, Wreath placed the tea on a table between the twin beds. She brushed Leah's forehead with a gentle hand. "Stretch out on your bed, sugar, and rest a minute."

She left the room long enough to get a cold washcloth from the bathroom. Leah closed her eyes as her mother sat next to her and patted the cloth against her flushed cheeks.

"You weren't running through the house, were you, honey?"

"No, ma'am," Leah whispered. Comforted by her mother's presence, she sighed and slid into sleep.

The sun hung lower in the sky when she woke from her nap. She drank the still cool tea, ate her cookies, did the assigned math and reading homework, and changed into playclothes. Then, like a kitten whose tail has been pulled once too often, she crept down the hall, peeking around doorjambs into other rooms before slipping by. At the top of the stairs, she crouched next to the newel post to scope out the living room below. No one in sight.

Leah sucked in a deep breath and descended the steps on tiptoe, eyes darting toward the kitchen to make sure no one was about to attack from that direction. Dinner smells wafted through the door, making her tummy rumble despite the cookies she'd eaten. Unconsciously, she rubbed the pinched spot on her shoulder as she paused at the foot of the stairs to check for danger. Out in the kitchen, Mama's gentle voice murmured something about watering the roses while the cornbread browned. The screened back door clattered shut behind her, leaving Leah alone in the house with the demon. Over the sound of rattling silverware, Delilah's voice, clear and sweet, rose in an old hymn.

> *"Spirit, oh melt and move all of our hearts with love . . .*
> *We will glory in Thy power; We will sing of wondrous grace.*
> *In our midst as Thou has promised, Come, O, come and take*
>   *Thy Place."*

What a hypocrite, Leah thought as she scurried across the living room, her bare feet soundless on the braided rug. *God's a hypocrite, too, giving Delilah the singing voice of an angel.*

Jezzie was the one who taught Leah the word *hypocrite*. Jezzie taught Leah lots of things; she'd even taught her to swear when she reached her eleventh birthday, explaining that thinking bad words would help keep Leah sane during John Luther's endless sermons.

"Won't God be angry at us for cussing in church?" Leah asked, tentatively trying out a naughty word in the privacy of her own brain.

"God knows what we're dealing with here," Jezzie promised. "He won't hold it against us."

Though Mama loved her, it was Jezzie who Leah depended upon for support and guidance in practical matters. Lately, though, there was something wrong with Jezzie. It worried Leah to see her beloved sister slipping around the house, head down, shoulders hunched, avoiding eye contact with everyone.

She acts more like me than she does her, Leah thought. *Like all the starch got boiled out of her.*

Reflecting on a sad, frightened Jezzie, Leah felt alone and more scared than ever. She slipped through the front door and eased it shut behind her, wincing at the small click made by the latch. She sought solace behind the chicken coop where eight or ten downy chicks and half a dozen hens pecked enthusiastically in the dirt. She sat down on her special three-legged stool and her favorite white and red hen trotted over to sit in her lap. Leah loved animals as much as Mercer did, and the chickens were the closest thing to a pet that she was allowed. She cherished the afternoons when Mama took her and Jezzie over to Mercer and Gennie's house. Mercer had a small animal infirmary set up in the old carriage area beneath the apartment, and he let her help doctor and feed the animals. The most important job, he said, was giving them lots of love, and she gave it with all her heart, stroking rabbits, cuddling cats, and brushing dogs as long as there was one that needed her attention. Occasionally it occurred to her that it was plain weird that John Luther didn't forbid their visits since he plainly disapproved of both Mercer and Genevieve. He hadn't spoken Mercer's name since he moved in with Gennie. John Luther didn't mention Genevieve either, but it was a different kind of silence, almost as if he was afraid to name her. Leah wondered if Gennie could make magic, like a witch. Well, if she was a witch, she was the good kind, and Delilah, despite her angel voice, was the worst of the bad, the kind Jezzie said was spelled with a *B*.

Truck tires crunched up the gravel driveway to the house. It was too early for John Luther to come home. Jared wasn't expected back before tomorrow evening, though if he had any sense, he'd stay in Mena and pretend he never met Delilah. Cuddling the hen in her arms, Leah got up to peek around the corner of the coop. An old blue pickup truck rolled to a stop under the big sassafras tree and Jezzie climbed out of the passenger side, looking happier than Leah had seen her look in a week. She set the hen down among the chicks and ran to say hello.

"Don't you leave yet, Genevieve!" Wreath called from the rose garden on the far side of the house. "I got something for you to take home with you."

Genevieve turned off the ignition as Wreath hurried across the yard and into the house. "Well, hey, Leah. Been playing with the chickens?"

Leah gasped. "How'd you know?"

Jezzie giggled and pulled a feather from Leah's tousled hair. "You smell kinda chickeny, too."

Leah pretended to pout. "I thought you'd done some sort of magic, Gennie."

"Would one of you girls come up and help me a minute?" Wreath's voice floated down from an upper window.

"I'll do it," Leah said.

Inside the kitchen, Delilah was just setting a plate with a big piece of raisin pecan pie into a napkin-lined basket. The slam of the screen door startled her, so she almost dropped the plate. The pie slid sideways against the plastic wrap that protected it from falling out. Her perfect creation marred by a flat side now, Delilah slapped the plate onto the countertop and grabbed Leah's upper arm.

"Let me go!"

"I spent all afternoon fixing dinner for Daddy, and you had to go and spoil it," Delilah hissed.

"Mama cooked dinner," Leah said tearfully. "All you did was put it in that basket."

"I made the pie special for him, and now look at it!"

Leah twisted out of Delilah's iron grip and ran for the stairs, leaving Delilah to toss the squashed piece of pie into the garbage and carefully cut another perfect wedge, grumbling all the time.

Leah found her mother upstairs in what the family had always called the junk room, an area that held everything from an ancient pie safe with a chipped enamel countertop to out-of-season bedding and clothing. Wreath knelt on the floor, tying together several long narrow boards that made up an old-fashioned quilt frame. A small wooden box of hardware sat nearby.

"What you doin', Mama?" Leah asked.

"Genevieve finished piecin' her quilt top, and now we're gonna quilt it. Figured as long as she has the truck here, it'd save havin' to drive the frame to Washington with the boards stickin' out the car windows. Pick up that end, sugar, and I'll get this one and the box."

The frame wasn't heavy, but its awkward length required a bit of fiddling to get it through the junk room door and around the sharp angle at the top of the stairs. Delilah had just hoisted John Luther's dinner basket onto her arm when they passed through the kitchen.

"Where y'all going with that thing?" she asked suspiciously.

"Loanin' it to Genevieve," Wreath answered. "She's ready to put her quilt together."

Delilah bristled. "You got no call to go loaning her anything. That frame was my grandmother's!"

"No, it was *my* grandmother's," Wreath said. "My mama didn't quilt, and neither do you, Delilah."

Leah smothered a giggle at the sight of Delilah's affronted expression, but not before Delilah noticed and snapped, "And just what are you looking at, young lady?"

The screen door slammed behind them, saving Leah the trouble of answering.

Simmering like a teakettle about to set up a howl, Delilah huffed herself out the back door and over to her bicycle. With exquisite care, she fastened the dinner basket to the handlebars, then pinned up one side of her calf-length skirt to keep it from getting caught in the chain. With every vertebra in perfect alignment, nose in the air, and a sour set to her mouth, she sailed down the driveway, ostentatiously ignoring the happy group that was stowing the quilting frame in the back of Genevieve's ancient truck. Her majestic departure was marred by the uneven surface of the gravel driveway: she skidded turning onto the dirt road and had to put down one foot to keep herself from toppling over. Regaining her balance, she pedaled away, still erect, but with cheeks flushed a dull red.

Genevieve burst into laughter. Wreath put her hand over her mouth to hide a broad smile, but the two girls were mystified by their elders' reactions. "What's so funny?"

"Almira Gulch," Genevieve said. To the girls' astonishment, their mother whistled a few bars of music and giggled. Giggled!

"Y'all done lost y'all's minds," Jezzie said wonderingly.

"The mean old lady who carried Toto off on her bicycle in

Wizard of Oz," Genevieve explained. She got two blank looks in
return.

"They never saw the movie," Wreath said. "John Luther . . ."
Her voice trailed off, but Genevieve understood. Wreath hesitated, then gestured everyone over to the wooden table in the
shade of the cedar trees. "Y'all sit down, and I'll bring us out some
turnip greens and cornbread."

"I'll help," said Leah. Jezzie and Genevieve likewise followed
Wreath into the kitchen to dip the fragrant steaming greens into
bowls and lavish butter on the crisp cornbread.

When they were settled back at the picnic table, Wreath
launched into the story of Dorothy Gale, her little dog Toto,
Almira Gulch, and the tornado trip over the rainbow to the Land
of Oz. Jezzie and Leah listened, eyes wide, poking barely tasted
food into their mouths. Even Genevieve, who had seen the movie,
got caught up in the tale as Wreath narrated, gestured, and re-
cited lines in the voices of the characters. The sun slid behind the
pine forest as the story reached a crescendo and the Wicked Witch
melted away. At last Wreath proclaimed, "There's no place like
home!" She bowed her head and spread out her arms to acknowledge the spontaneous applause of her audience.

"Oh, Mama!" Leah gasped, pounding her hands together until
her palms stung. "You never told us a story like that before."

"Did you see the movie?" Jezzie asked enviously.

Wreath nodded. "It came to the theater in Hope when I was
in high school. My daddy drove me and my cousin Mirth to see
it." She cast a glance at Genevieve and smiled. "It was the most
amazin' thing we ever saw in our lives. Started out in plain old
black and white like all movies back then, but when Dorothy
opened her door in Oz, everything turned to color. My favorite
was the Horse of a Different Color that pulled Dorothy's cart. He
changed colors every time you looked at him."

"It used to come on television once a year," Genevieve added.
"Nothing in my life was as long as the afternoon before that movie

started. The flying monkeys scared me to death. I had nightmares for a week every time I saw the movie, but I never told a soul for fear they wouldn't let me watch it the next time it came on."

Wreath reached across the table to pat her hand. "Well, sugar, your secret is safe with us."

Watching her mother, sister, and Genevieve laughing together, Leah said, "Why, y'all look just alike when you laugh."

The laughter gargled to a halt. Everyone stared at Leah, who wondered what on earth she'd done wrong this time. Fear snaked its fingers around her stomach and squeezed. Jezzie looked from her wide-eyed sister to the two women and grew wide-eyed herself.

"You're right," she said. "You're right, Leah, and you and Gennie have got that same little bit of a droopy eyelid. I didn't see it before now."

Wreath shrugged at Genevieve. "Cats got a way of crawlin' out of bags, don't they?"

"Leah, you are going to make a hell of an artist or police officer or something someday." Genevieve sighed and took Leah's hand in hers. "I'm . . . a kind of cousin, but I didn't know it when I first got here."

"What kind of cousin?" Leah whispered. Jezzie leaned closer, eyes alight with curiosity.

"Miss Wreath and my mama were cousins. That makes us all cousins a limb or two up the family tree."

"Is that true?" Jezzie appealed to her mother, who nodded. "Does Mercer know?"

"He guessed, too," Genevieve said. "No one else knows."

"Why didn't you tell Jezzie and me?" Leah asked. "Are you ashamed of us?"

"No, not all! I'm just . . . scared, I guess."

"Scared of what? Of who?"

"It's . . . it's a long story. I promise I'll tell you the whole thing someday, just not tonight."

"She needs to know she can trust us absolutely," Jezzie told Leah. "We can prove that to her by not saying a single solitary word to anyone about it until she says we can."

"Not a soul," Leah intoned after her. Facing Genevieve, she solemnly drew a cross over her heart. "We promise, Gennie."

Genevieve pressed a hand to her chest to ease the ache in her own heart. *There's no place like home . . .*

"After all," Leah added, "I can see how you might not like to claim kin to . . . some people in this family." *Wish I didn't have to,* she thought wistfully.

They talked of other things as afternoon melted into twilight: Jezzie's progress in algebra, Leah's chickens, Wreath's garden, the mild case of poison ivy that Genevieve had gotten pulling weeds at one of the cemeteries. Upon hearing about this last, Wreath went inside and came back with a small tin of salve.

"Smear some of this on the rash," she said.

"What is it?" Genevieve opened the lid and sniffed. "Smells good."

"Jewelweed, lavender, and beeswax," Wreath said. "New batch. You're the first one to try it, so let me know how it does for you."

Genevieve dipped up a bit on one fingertip and gingerly spread it across the rash that ringed her left wrist like a blistery bracelet. "Oh, my. That feels good."

"Mama's salves are better than anything you can get in a store," Jezzie boasted. "She makes teas and tonics and all sorts of stuff to keep us healthy."

Wreath waved the words aside, but her cheeks pinkened with pleasure at the praise. Her skill in herbalism grew from being a gardener, and from being married to a man who refused to spend money on doctors or medicine for anything less than a heart attack or spurting arterial blood. "Jezzie and Leah both help. Leah found the jewelweed down by the branch not long ago and carried it to me. Even Delilah's got a fair hand with cooking herbs."

"Long as she doesn't have to grow them," Jezzie said. "She says she hates digging in the dirt and sweating like a hillbilly."

Genevieve glanced at the sky and reluctantly climbed to her feet. "If I don't get myself home and to bed, I'm not going to want to wake up for work tomorrow." She stacked the plates, piled them with silverware, told the others to stay put, and carried the dishes toward the kitchen.

"Note my skill," she said airily. "I was a professional waitress once upon a time." She pulled the screen door open and disappeared inside. A second later, the sound of metal crashing to the floor rang out. "Plates are fine! It was just forks. I never said I was a *good* waitress."

When they quit laughing, Jezzie and Leah took advantage of the fading light and warm mood to move close to their mother. Wreath put an arm around each of them. She even pressed her lips to each child's hair, something so rare that Leah held her breath for a second to savor the wonder of it.

"Oh, fiddlesticks," Jezzie said, nodding toward the road. "Here comes Miss Gulch just in time to spoil the fun. Too bad someone doesn't drop a house on her."

"Jezzie," Wreath chided.

Leah put both hands over her face to smother her giggles. Drop a house on the wicked bitch and put Genevieve in her place. Wouldn't that be fine?

Delilah rattled up the drive, leaned her bike against the corner of the house, and swept a disapproving glance toward the table. Grabbing her basket off the handlebars, she stomped up the three steps into the house and let the door slam behind her to show how little she cared that her mother and sisters were having such a good time without her. She banged the basket down on the kitchen table, tied an apron around her waist, and turned to find Genevieve running water into a sink full of dirty dishes. In one hand she held a dishrag. In the other she held an open packet of morning glory seeds that had been in a bowl on the countertop and was idly reading the planting instructions as she waited for the sink to fill.

"Just what do you call yourself doing in my kitchen?"

Genevieve arched one eyebrow halfway to her hairline. That always irritated people who couldn't keep from raising both eyebrows at the same time. Genevieve was in a mood to irritate Delilah until the Wicked Bitch was ready to call in the winged monkeys. She tossed the seeds back into the bowl. "I'm about to wash dishes."

Delilah took two long strides, grabbed the morning glory seeds, and stuffed them into her apron pocket. Stamping her foot like a kid throwing a temper tantrum, she snatched the dishrag out of Genevieve's fingers and shook the cloth in the auburn-haired woman's face, splattering soapy water everywhere. "Who told you could come in here washing dishes like you're family? You're nothing but a nasty piece of white trash that Mercer picked up in some . . . some . . ."

"Den of iniquity?" Genevieve suggested in a deceptively gentle voice, so damn mad that she could hardly hold still. She picked up a kitchen towel and dried her hands to keep from using one of them to punch Delilah in the nose.

"We don't need your help, and we surely do not need your company. Why don't you just get in that rattle-trap old truck of yours and take yourself on out of here?" Delilah threw the dishrag back into the sink and reached out to shove Genevieve toward the door.

Genevieve's eyes widened, her jaw dropped, and her breath came out in an inarticulate hiss. She looked at Delilah's throat, then slid her glance to something beyond Delilah. "Wow. I did not expect that."

Delilah spun around to peer behind her. Seeing nothing, she transferred her glower to Genevieve, who still stood apparently staring at nothing. "What are you looking at?"

"A ghost," Genevieve said. "He keeps trying to strangle you, but his fingers just slide through your throat. Frustrated, Lord, listen to him howl."

"A ghost! You are such a liar."

"Sometimes I am," Genevieve acknowledged, "but not right now. A man, maybe in his late forties. Sharp chin and cheekbones.

Real hatchet of a nose. Mousy hair, pudgy body, but long, thin arms and legs. Mole under his left nostril."

Color evaporated from Delilah's face. She reeled backward, grabbing the countertop for support.

"He surely doesn't like you," Genevieve continued in an interested voice. "Seems to think you had something to do with him dying before the Lord was ready to call him home. His words, not mine. I doubt the Lord wants this one."

Terrified, Delilah thrust her hand forward in an ancient sign. "Witch! Witch! Thou shalt not suffer—"

"Oh, shut up, Delilah, and do not start that nonsense with me," snapped Genevieve. "You quit picking on Jezzie, too, with your stupid talk about wife lessons."

"She told you!" Delilah gasped. "That little heifer!"

"She told me, and you tell that daddy of yours to keep his ham hands off her or he will find himself in a world of hurt."

"You're threatening him with black magic!"

"Black magic, hell. I'm promising to castrate him with a spoon if he so much as looks at her crooked." Genevieve watched what Delilah couldn't see and shook her head. "Missed again. That is one frustrated dead man." She wheeled on her heel, shoved open the screen door, and stalked out into the fading twilight.

Three sets of eyes stared across the yard at her. Wondering how much they'd heard, Genevieve strolled to the picnic table as if not a single harsh word had been exchanged. "Miss Wreath, thank you for one of the nicest dinners I can ever remember having. I hate to run, but Mercer and Jim are camping at the lake tonight and I have critters to feed."

Wreath rose to kiss Genevieve on the cheek. Jezzie and Leah gasped. Three kisses in one evening. The earth was tilting on its axis. "You're welcome, honey. Drive careful. Me and the girls'll look forward to the next time. Jezzie tells us you have circus stories to share."

"I do," Genevieve promised. She hugged each girl, climbed into her truck, and backed down the long drive to the road. Leah followed to shut the gate behind her. She stood and waved at the dwindling taillights until they disappeared around the curve.

With her adversary gone, Delilah stormed out the backdoor to confront her mother and sisters. "Y'all just wait till I tell my daddy what's been going on here tonight!"

Leah ran up just in time to hear the threat. Furious, still emboldened by the evening's spirit, she snatched up a forgotten napkin and hurled it at her eldest sister. "Delilah, you are a big, fat tattletale, and tattletales go straight to hell! You told me so your own stupid self!"

Jezzie threw her head back and shouted with laughter, "Preach it, sister!"

Delilah turned a fierce scowl on them both, then transferred it to Wreath. "Are you gonna sit there and let that sassy-mouthed imp talk to me like that?"

"Well," Wreath answered mildly, "I reckon she was rude, but we can't hardly call her a liar now, can we?"

One more shock in an evening of harsh surprises was too much for Delilah. She stood stock-still, mouth open, stunned to the depths of her shallow soul. Hoarse with disbelief, she whispered, "How dare you?"

"Y'all go on up and get ready for bed," Wreath told her younger daughters. To their delight, she delivered an additional hug and kiss to each child. "I'll come up and say good night in a little bit."

Hand in hand, they scurried past a still stupefied Delilah and into the house. Once inside, Leah pressed her finger to her lips and dragged Jezzie into the seldom used dining room and over to the open window.

"What?" Jezzie whispered.

"We can hear without them seeing us," Leah whispered back. "I want to know more about the ghost that's after Delilah."

"Why, Leah Salome Ives, are you an eavesdropper?"

"Yes, ma'am, I surely am. Now hush up."

Jezzie hushed as a voice drifted through the window from the darkness of the backyard.

"What," Wreath said distinctly, "are 'wife lessons'?"

"Oh, you don't need to hear this," Jezzie said, and herded Leah out of the room and toward the stairs.

"But—"

"No buts, baby girl." Jezzie hugged her fiercely. "You were a tiger out there tonight, and I'm so proud of you I could bust, but we're done with Miss Gulch for the night. Time for a cool bath and . . . tell you what: I sneaked home a book from the school library. A storybook." She dragged the last words out enticingly.

Leah's mouth formed a perfect *O*. Five hours earlier she'd have asked what would happen if John Luther or Delilah found out. Now she said, "What's it about?"

"A secret garden," Jezzie said. "Once we're in bed, I'll get out the flashlight and read to you under the covers."

"Okay." A wave of exhaustion swept over Leah. For a moment, she wondered if she could climb the twenty-one steps to the second floor, but Jezzie linked arms with her and drew her upstairs. Leah went along meekly. The world had shifted around her that evening, but she was only eleven. Someone else could sort things out.

CHAPTER 28
DELILAH

"What are 'wife lessons'?"

Still stunned by the rebellion of her previously cowed sisters and mother, Delilah gaped for a long moment before pulling up her jaw and focusing a glare on Wreath. "That is something private between Daddy and me."

"I asked you a question, Delilah, and I want an answer," Wreath said. "You can keep your own secrets, but anything involving Jezzie is my business. I'm going to ask you one more time: what are wife lessons?"

Delilah tossed her head and started back into the house without answering.

"Stop right there."

"Just who do you think is going to make me?"

She barely finished the sentence before she found herself drawn up short by a hard grip on her arm. Wreath leaned in close to her ear and whispered, "I don't like laying hands on anyone, daughter. I've had too many rough hands laid on me and seen too many rough hands laid on my children. But you *will* answer me."

Wreath stepped back. Delilah turned to face her and was astonished to realize that she and her mother were the same height. She'd always thought of Wreath as inches shorter. For the first time in her life, she felt a qualm of uncertainty about her mother's position in her world. She hid her discomfort by straightening up and brushing off her skirt.

"No need to get nasty about it," she said.

"Talk, Delilah."

"Well, with Jezzie getting married this summer—"

"First I've heard about that. Who does he plan on givin' her to?"

"John Evert. Better'n she deserves. He's got a big old house and a big ol' pile of money."

Wreath stared stonily at her. "Wife lessons."

"Well, with Jezzie getting married, she needs to know more than *algebra*." Delilah sneered the last word. "She needs to know how to cook and clean and serve her husband without questioning his wishes. Daddy is going to teach her everything she needs to know about serving John Evert, just like he taught me to serve my husbands. The Lord knows," Delilah burst out passionately, "*you* never taught me anything about what to expect."

Wreath looked like she might faint. "What did he . . . teach you?"

"Everything," Delilah said. "Every little old thing, Mama."

The stricken look on Wreath's face told Delilah she was back in control. She turned on her heel and walked back into the house, certain that from now on, Wreath would give her anything she wanted just to make up those wife lessons to her. Delilah paused inside the door to look at her kitchen, her dining room, and her whole life finally laid out in front of her. A few extra whacks on the nails in Wreath's cross of guilt, a few more special treats for John Luther, a husband to crush the arrogance out of that know-it-all Jezzie, and they'd all be out of her way.

CHAPTER 29
GENEVIEVE

～※～

What in the holy hell made me open my big mouth about the dang ghost trying to strangle Delilah? Heaven knows I wanted to strangle her myself, but admitting I saw him—describing him to her, for crying in the beer—was the stupidest thing I'd done in years, and I'd done some godawful stupid things. Even with her dramatic recoil and warding-off gesture, I didn't believe for a minute that Delilah thought I was a witch. Surely no one outside a handful of maniacs in the backwater of Kingdom Come, Alabama, was that superstitious.

Mad clean to the tips of my fingernails with myself, I headed for home down County Road 13. I knew I was driving way too fast, but I didn't give a rip. Should have, because as I reached the Columbus Cemetery, a white-tailed deer jumped out in front of me, so close to my front bumper that I thought I'd hit him. I wrenched the steering wheel hard to the right, sending the truck into a heart-bumping skid toward the cemetery fence. The front bumper narrowly missed the big old sweetgum that guarded the driveway entrance as the truck spun 180 degrees and fetched up in the ditch between road and fence. The force of the stop slammed my chest into the steering wheel, knocking every bit of breath from my lungs.

Gasping and disoriented, I shoved open the door and threw myself outside, tugging with both hands at the neckline of my tee shirt, which suddenly felt like a noose around my throat. A tree root snagged the toe of my sneaker before I'd taken two steps, sending me into an awkward lurch up the hill toward the gate. Panic churned my stomach, far more panic than a close encounter with a deer should've caused. My chest ached and I could hardly focus my eyes as I fumbled with the latch on the gate to let myself into the graveyard. Once inside, I stumbled along the irregular lines of tombstones, ignoring the astonished comments and small bursts of laughter that followed my erratic progress until I collapsed on my knees atop Ellen Josephine Delaney, born June 11, 1853, death date obscured by gray lichen. I wrapped both arms around her modest stone to keep from toppling over. The light faded before my eyes, then rose again on a hot summer morning in Alabama.

"Hurry, oh, hurry. They're coming. Can't you hear them?"

The grandmother rattlesnake slithered down the steps of the house and across the packed dirt of the yard at a stately pace that belied the precariousness of her situation. It had taken me far too long to untangle the sheets and free her lower body from the weight of the dead man. Kingdom Come was tiny, with no house more than a few minutes' walk from another. I could hear Nette screaming at the top of her mean old-lady lungs and the answering shouts of folks who came running down the road to see what was the matter.

Desperately, I knelt and gathered the diamond-embellished snake into my arms. She was a big snake, much longer than I was tall, and heavy-bodied, even for her species. She made a mighty awkward bundle. As I straightened up, she slid her great wedge head onto my shoulder and tucked it into the curve of my neck where it bounced with each step of my dash across the yard toward the forest beyond. We were two-thirds of the way there when the first stone hit me in the middle of the back. I stumbled, almost went down, but kept my hold on the snake and my eye on the tree line.

Hurry. Hurry.

All my life I'd been able to run faster than almost anyone I knew, but that day I ran like Atalanta herself. Other stones bounced around us, one or two struck my body, but none with the force of the first. In seconds, we reached the barbed-wire fence that divided the yard from the forest and its protective undergrowth. I dropped to my knees and stretched out my arms toward the ground. She slid down them to land in a shimmering heap before winding her way off into the underbrush.

"Hurry!" I cried. "Hurry!" A fist-sized rock bounced right next to her rattle-tipped tail. My breath sobbed in my lungs as I watched her slide from sight. Safe. Safe. I stood up and looked over my shoulder to see half a dozen familiar faces rendered almost unrecognizable by fear and hatred.

A big rock slammed into the left side of my rib cage, spinning me around. I threw my arms across my face just in time to keep from catching the next stone in my teeth. The crack of my arm bone breaking sounded like a rifle shot in my ears and I shrieked with pain. A volley of stones followed, accompanied by incoherent screams. I wheeled away from the mob, intending to dive through the strands of barbed wire into the trees, but a solid hit on the back of my skull sent me sprawling onto my stomach. For a moment, I lay with outstretched arms, staring at the line of trees, too stunned to even think of protecting myself as missiles rained down on me.

Just like a candle flame guttering out, the flashback ended, and I found myself on my knees clinging to Ellen Delaney's tombstone. I have no idea how long I knelt there before kinder murmurs drowned out the echo of the mob in my mind. A few new voices belonging to folks in the Columbus Cemetery joined the chorus of my familiar ghosts, urging me to get up and get moving before night closed in. Sucking a huge draught of air into my half-paralyzed lungs, I struggled to my feet and stood there for a moment, swaying back and forth. With one more deep breath and some special encouragement from Ellen's granddaughter, I managed to flounder through the deepening shadows to my truck. The truck tilted into the ditch with the driver's side door hanging open. I slid onto the seat and closed the door with exaggerated care. My hands trembled as I reached for the keys dangling from the ignition. They were still turned to the on position. I must've killed the engine in the crash. I hoped I hadn't drained the battery as well. It was old and needed to be replaced. Fingers mentally crossed, I turned the key off, then on again. Nothing. Tried again. *Click. Click.* I closed my eyes and pressed my left cheek against the cool window glass. Lord, what an afternoon.

To this day, I don't have a single blessed recollection of what happened after I blacked out in the middle of getting stoned by the good people of Kingdom Come. One of the doctors at the mental hospital told me about it after I regained some semblance of awareness weeks later. The doctor was young and excited as hell to be shrinking the head of an alleged witch who communed with the dead, had traffic with satanic snakes, and who'd been stoned by a ravaging mob. Someone told me later that he'd written a paper about me that was printed in some fancy journal for psychiatrists, but if he did, I never read it.

The woman who lived across the road from the Right Reverend Burgess Love Darnell and his evil old aunt heard the commotion and peeked out her front door to see what was going on. I surely do regret not remembering her name; I think it was Iris. God bless her, she ducked back inside her house long enough to grab her granddaddy's double-barreled shotgun, then ran across the road, shouting at the top of her lungs, threatening to shoot the next person who raised a hand against me. I reckon they must've believed her, because there I was a decade later, sitting in a truck in a ditch next to a rural Arkansas graveyard. That dear lady coerced or shamed a couple of males (I won't call them men) into loading me into the backseat of her car. She saved my life, then drove me straight to the hospital. I never saw her again, but if I ever get brave enough or stupid enough to go back to Alabama, I will surely look her up to say thank you.

I had not had a flashback like that one in a long, long time, and hoped to never have another one. I sat up and stared into the twilight as I considered my state of mind and wondered which scared me worse: the prospect of more hallucinations or the threat of Delilah whipping up a mob of Joyful Sheep to come after me with John Luther leading the charge? The former, I decided. Delilah would have some explaining to do about the ghost of her murdered husband if she tried to rally folks against me.

I slid out of the truck and walked down the road toward Columbus where Sam and Charity Woolsey lived just off the highway. They were a nice older couple who'd taken in a couple of Mercer's cats. When I dropped the kitties off, Miss Charity had insisted on feeding me sweet tea, pecan pie, and bits of information about the folks who lived in the area. The funniest stories were the ones she told on herself and her husband of sixty years. He sat silently at the table with his long, gnarled fingers wrapped around his glass, smiling at her as she chattered away. I knew Mr. Sam would be happy to give my dead battery a jump.

It took a while to get back to the truck. Miss Charity insisted on checking me out for damage, then had me wait a minute longer while she wrapped me up some cold fried chicken and cornbread for tomorrow's lunch. By the time Mr. Sam and I got out to my truck, we had to hook up the jumper cables by the headlights of his own truck. I'd never jumped a vehicle before, so he took the time to explain the process to me. As he slammed the hood of my truck, I noticed a light burning somewhere deep in the trees past the ruins of the old Columbus High School that stood not far from the cemetery. He looked where I was pointing and told me it was the light in the parking lot outside the Church of the Flock of the Good Shepherd. Mr. Sam was a nice old gentleman and possibly the only non-church member in the county who didn't call it the Church of His Joyful Sheep.

"It's a lot closer than I thought it'd be," I said.

He nodded. "Farther by the road. Only about a hundred yards through the trees. When our children went to the high school, they used to cut through the forest and save themselves a good ten minutes of walking."

He waited for me to pull out of the ditch and get back on the road before heading home himself. I sat for a moment, looking through the windshield at the light, pondering the problem of John Luther Ives, and getting madder by the minute. By the time I slid the gearstick into second, my cheeks were hot, and my pulse pounded in my ears. Wife lessons. Sending little orphan girls to live with pedophiles. Beating his family. Nearly killing Mercer. Publicly humiliating his wife and molesting teenaged girls who were stupid enough to marry into his stupid church. Breaking every last one of my dishes and throwing my conch shell out the window.

It took me fifteen minutes to drive home. I left the truck running while I dashed inside and pried up the floorboard in the closet where I hid the pistol. I pulled on a dark shirt, covered my hair with one black scarf, and wrapped the pistol in another. In three minutes flat, I jumped in the truck and headed back to Columbus, my mind made up. I could park out by the Columbus Cemetery, duck down the path to John Luther's church, shoot the son of a bitch, then hightail it to the nearest bridge over Red River to toss the gun into the river's roiling depths. Someday the sheriff might catch up with me, but no court in the heaven of a righteous god would ever condemn me to hell for taking that bastard out of the world.

I glanced sideways at the scarf-shrouded pistol laying on the seat next to me. Truth be told, I hated touching that gun. I got it from an old boy out behind Wiley B's Place in return for something I hadn't done for a very long time. I gritted my teeth through every moment of that hand job and wanted to scream my head off when he slid his fingers up under my shirt, but that was his price, and I didn't know where else I could get an untraceable gun. After he finished manhandling my breasts and unloading himself, he showed me how to load the pistol, and let me go after one last, lingering, disgusting French kiss. I went back to my motel room and damn near scrubbed the skin off my hands, mouth, and breasts. Didn't help—I still felt filthy when I was done.

As I drove through the night back to Columbus, I realized that my cheeks were damp. Lord, I was crying again. Irritated, I brushed the back of my hand over my face and concentrated on ignoring the usual swell of voices that beset me when the owners disapproved of something I intended to do.

"Shut up," I said through clenched teeth. "Just shut up and leave me alone. Somebody has got to kill him, and it may as well be me."

"You won't like it," Bigger warned. He sat in the passenger seat, hand over the pistol as if the thin veil of his fingers could prevent me from snatching up the weapon any time I took a notion to do so.

"Do you know what he is?" I demanded. "What he's done? What he's going to do?"

Bigger shook his head. "You don't want a death marked on your soul."

"My soul is already marked, thank you," I snapped. Lord, it was bad enough I had to deal with the usual ghost chorus bitching at me without taking on someone else's ghost as well. "One more dead pedophile on my conscience is not going to keep me up nights, Bigger."

"You didn't kill the last one, so he ain't ridin' your conscience. This one will."

"What the hell do you know about the last one?"

"I was standin' right there when you told Mercer about that grandmother rattlesnake."

"Go away, Bigger," I growled, wishing I had something other than the pistol handy to throw at him.

"I know you think you gotta do this, li'l sister," he said gently, "but you don't. This here is a bad idea."

The small endearment almost broke me. I blinked hard, pressed my lips together, and concentrated on driving down the long dark tunnel of trees, determined not to argue with him or anyone else about killing John Luther Ives. Bigger didn't say anything else, and when I glanced his way, he was gone. I wished he'd taken along the chill of uncertainty that his words left on my heart. Chill or not, I drove on.

Instead of turning off the highway onto County 13 at Columbus, I turned onto County 48 and made my way to the cemetery by a long back route, bumping along dark dirt roads that I'd only driven a time or two in the daylight, hoping I wasn't going to get myself plumb lost. When I reached the intersection with County 13, I breathed a sigh of relief, turned off my headlights, and crept down the dirt track to avoid another near miss with a deer. The back porch light and an upstairs light were on at Wreath's house. I held my breath as the truck rattled past the place, hoping no one was sitting on the front porch enjoying the night, and if they were that they couldn't recognize my truck in the dark. By the time I turned into the cemetery parking lot and hid my truck behind the ruins of the high school, moonless night obscured the world. I pride myself on not being jumpy, but my teeth chattered like castanets as I climbed out of the vehicle and into the shadows. My voices had long hushed. For one weak moment, I wished Bigger would come talk me into going home.

Took me a couple of minutes to find the opening to the path through the woods. It was overgrown some, so I tucked the pistol into the back waistband of my jeans to free both hands for pushing aside branches and boughs that barred my way. Even once my eyes adjusted to the dark, I couldn't see much of anything that lay in my path. More than once, I caught my foot on something and barely kept from falling. I locked my eyes on the parking lot light outside John Luther's church and soldiered on until I came to the end of the path and emerged onto the back lawn.

The parking lot light lit up the area like Wiley B's roadhouse on Saturday night. I slipped around the perimeter of the lot, keeping close to the cemetery fence, until I found half a dozen good-sized rocks. It took me two throws to smash the bulb. I slunk back into the shelter of a magnolia tree to see if anyone came out of the church or office to check on the noise, but no one did. Looked like Mohammed needed to go to the mountain.

A light shone behind the curtains of the office building. Taking a deep breath, I dashed across parking lot and lawn on tiptoe. I lacked five feet reaching the nandina bushes clustered below the side window when the high beams of a car swept across the parking lot. I slid headfirst into the shelter of the bushes like I was coming into home base and the catcher was holding out the ball. A split second later, the headlights swept over my head. They reflected off the wall for a moment before going out. Talk about a near miss. I checked to make sure the pistol was still tucked into the back of my jeans, then peered through the nandina branches to see who was walking from the car to the office. The glow from the window illuminated her face as she passed within six feet my hiding place. Maylene MacCallan. I sat my bottom down on the ground with a thump.

Well, hell's gate, I thought. *Now what?*

She stepped up onto the concrete square that was too small to be called a porch, hesitated like she wasn't sure of her reception, then tapped on the door. A moment of silence, a chair scraped across the floor, and the fall of heavy footsteps reverberated through the thin wall I had my back against. Maylene stepped off the stoop and stood several feet away, wringing her hands in front of her pregnant tummy. A click of the door handle. Light poured out of the office, illuminating Maylene's anxious face and silhouetting John Luther in the doorway.

I didn't recall pulling the pistol out of my waistband, but it was in my hand. I aimed carefully, placing the iron sight in the dead center of John Luther's bulk as he stood there, scowling at poor Maylene. She was clean out of the way; I doubted even the blood splatter would hit her. I wrapped my finger around the trigger. Fifteen feet. I wouldn't miss.

CHAPTER 30
JOHN LUTHER

❧

Maylene's appearance infuriated John Luther. Ever since Mercer's redheaded whore had threatened to nail compromising photographs to the church doors, he'd sought to distance himself from Maylene. He explained that his heavy schedule of church activities prevented him from continuing her wife lessons for the present and expected that to be an end to the matter. Unfortunately, the girl hadn't been schooled to obedience by a lifetime in his church. She was an only child of indulgent parents, used to having her own way, and sure that John Luther would give into her pleas if she presented them properly. In short, she had become a problem, calling him at church, at home, even writing him letters begging to know why he had forsaken her when he'd promised to teach her to be a good Christian wife and she had been making so much progress under his tutelage. Now she appeared at his office door after dark with her car parked right out where anyone passing by could see it.

"I told you that I cannot meet with you," John Luther said tightly. "Go home to your husband and practice what you have already learned before you seek further instruction."

"But, sir, that's why I came," Maylene said. "He isn't home. He . . . he hurt me and then he left. He's on his way to Miller County and the bars. Look—look what he did to me." She quickly unbuttoned the bodice of her dress and pulled it open to reveal the tops of two small, bruised breasts. She came farther into the light, and he could see fingermarks on her throat as well. "He started drinking early this afternoon and I tried to stop him, tried to lead him into prayer, but it just made him mad, and he started hitting me and hitting me and then he choked me and threw me in a heap and walked out the door and now I don't know what to do, please help me, please help!" She held out pleading hands to him, her breasts trembling with each beat of her heart.

Aroused despite himself, John Luther barely managed to keep his voice cold and his face stern. "You have failed your husband, woman. Worse, in failing to turn him from demon alcohol, you have failed God."

Maylene burst into tears. "I tried! I tried! I told him God didn't want him to drink, told him if he'd pray with me—"

"You talk too much," John Luther snapped. "Be silent—now!"

Maylene choked off her stream of words with both hands and stared at him through streaming eyes.

"You interrupted my evening meal," he said irritably. "I intend to finish it before I give you tonight's lesson. First, move your car under the trees by the graveyard fence. Then go into the church, get down on your knees, pray for salvation from your sins, and wait for me. Don't turn on the lights; the nightlight behind the altar will be sufficient."

She nodded. Clutching the gaping neckline of her dress, she ran across the lawn to move her car into the shadows where no casual passersby could see it. That accomplished, she hurried past him, head bowed, toward the front of the church, and disappeared around the corner of the building. John Luther looked after her a moment, then turned back into the office.

He cursed to himself as he sat back down at the desk to savor the last two or three bites of his pie. It was very good pie; Delilah was a fine cook with a knack for special seasonings. He put a bite into his mouth and chewed mechanically, contemplating the possibilities and the complications of the upcoming counseling session.

The evening had started well. He'd made excellent progress writing Sunday's sermon before Delilah arrived with his dinner basket. He moved to his armchair and made small corrections to his notes while she warmed the turnip greens and cornbread in the church's kitchen. She set his desk with the plate, linen napkin, and silverware she'd brought from home, then filled a glass with ice and tea from the church's refrigerator. Lastly, she uncovered the perfect wedge of raisin pecan pie she'd made just for him and placed it on the table next to a small bowl of sweetened whipped cream.

He relished every scrap of the meal, then left the dirty dishes on his desk for Delilah to deal with in the morning. That he could take them home himself never occurred to him; the chore was beneath his dignity. For a moment, he regarded his notes, then decided against working on the sermon anymore that evening. It was nearly done, and he wanted to resolve the problem of Maylene once and for all. He left the lights burning when he left the office to give the illusion that he was still hard at work; people knew not to disturb him when he was writing his Sunday sermons. Well, most people knew, he thought grumpily.

Outside in the warm evening air, he paused to frown at the broken light over the parking lot. He'd just had that fixed, and now it had to be done again. Irritated, he rubbed a dull ache in his temples. His stomach rumbled, then subsided. The front of the church seemed much farther away than usual, and the outside wall looked oddly bowed and out of focus. He wondered if he was coming down with the flu and shuddered. He hated being sick.

He pulled open one of the double doors into the church and stepped inside. The interior was plain, with unpadded wooden pews and tall narrow windows of frosted glass that let in light without allowing glimpses of the outdoors that might distract the congregation from his sermons. Maylene knelt humbly in front of the lectern in a dim halo of light, hands clasped beneath breasts now covered decorously by a buttoned bodice. Upon his entry, she lowered her eyes as he had taught her at their last meeting. He paced toward her, his shoes thumping hollowly against the pine boards of the floor until he stood in front of her. Maylene gnawed her lower lip, scared half to death by his regard. After he loomed silently for several minutes, she ventured to ask a timid question.

"Are you mad at me?" When he didn't answer, she blurted, "I'm sorry, I know you're busy, I know you told me not to come, but when Henry hit me so many times and took off to go to the bars, I didn't know what to do, all I could think of was to find you and ask for help and—" She bit down on her tongue at a gesture from the preacher.

"Tonight, you are going to learn the value of silence," John Luther intoned. "First Timothy, Chapter Two, Verse Eleven: 'Let the woman learn in silence with all subjection.' Tonight, you will remain silent. Any word, any sound will result in a lesson in submission. Do you understand?"

She nodded. Her dress stretched taut over her burgeoning belly, and she was forced to spread her knees to shoulder width and lean slightly backward to keep her balance. Her vulnerability aroused in him a desire so reckless that caution evaporated in its wake. He slapped his hand down on top of her head with such force that she toppled backward with a frightened cry. Irritated by the plaintive sound, he grabbed a fistful of her hair and hauled her back onto her knees.

"Father," he thundered into the dark church, "grant me the power to cure this woman's malign influence on her husband. Give me the strength to drive from her body and soul the devil that tempts Henry MacCallan to follow the path of alcohol instead of the path to You. Grant me a sign that I might know Your Will and—"

Angels appeared all around him, urging him on with wordless song and graphic gestures. Speechless, he stared at them. He never expected angels to be naked, much less so handsomely endowed with masculine parts. Hand still tangled in her hair, he jerked Maylene to her feet, brought his face down to hers, and sank his teeth into the softness of her lower lip. Her shriek echoed through the empty church.

The frosted window to the left of the double entrance doors imploded. A split second later, the window on the right shattered in a sparkling cascade of glass. John Luther ducked, shielding his head with his arms as every window on the south side of the church burst inward, one after another. Mouth dripping blood, Maylene dove to the floor and crawled under the front pew. She huddled there, arms wrapped protectively across her unborn child, adding her screams to the cacophony. Blows thundered across the wall, as if unseen hammers pounded the outside of the building from one side to the other and back again. Two furious blows landed on the front doors, rattling them on their hinges. Then, as abruptly as it had begun, the attack ceased. Beneath the front pew that the Ives family occupied every Sunday, Maylene curled around her child and sobbed.

Crouched low with his arms over his head, John Luther stared at the glittering shards of glass carpeting the wooden floor. Light rose from the glass like vapor, making him queasy. He extended a hand to let the light filter between his fingers. He thought maybe it was the essence of the angels who'd urged him to bring to heel his wayward ewe a few moments before.

He watched the shifting colors play across his hand for a minute longer, then duckwalked across the floor to flip the nightlight switch to the off position. Shielded by darkness, he stood and peered through the broken window. He thought he saw a human-sized shadow on the far side of the lawn, but it merged with the trees before he could be sure. Fury swept over him, burning away most of his fear, as well as the hallucination of angel mist.

He looked around the room for something to use as a weapon and saw nothing heavier than a hymnal. His eyes lit on Maylene, who had gotten to her feet and was edging toward him, still crying, holding out her hand in a mute request for comfort. He seized her by the wrist. She started to say something, but he hissed, "The lesson is silence. Not a word."

He plucked her handbag off a pew, thrust it at her, then looked around for anything else that might show she had been there. Satisfied the place was clean, he dragged her up the aisle. "Get in your car and leave."

"But—"

He slapped her hard across the face, hissing, "That was a word." He opened the door. Hand clasped around her upper arm, he hustled her down the steps and across the yard, keeping her body between him and the woods. He pulled her along so fast that she stumbled as they entered the parking lot. He let her sprawl into the rough gravel before dragging her to her feet by the collar of her dress. Transferring his grip to the back of her neck, he shoved her onward.

"You're hurting me!" she cried, trying to wrest free from his grasp. "Stop it! Stop it!"

He shook her so hard that drops of blood flew from her torn mouth. Maylene quit fighting and drooped hopelessly, head down, shoulders hunched. Thinking he had subdued her, he loosened his grip. That was all she needed. She pulled free, took a long step backward, and swung her handbag at him with every bit of strength she could muster. Muscles hardened by her days of pitching for the girls' softball team served her well. The purse caught him square in the face. Blood spurted. He reeled sideways with his hands clasped across his nose. Maylene sprinted for her car and leapt inside. Headlights blazed as the sedan lurched out of hiding and onto the road. Tires squealed on the pavement, and she was gone.

"Fuck," John Luther said to the night.

Back in the office, he flipped on the restroom light and glumly regarded his bloody, swelling nose. After he washed his face, he soaked a cloth in cold water and sat down at his desk. He draped it over his nose, then tilted his head back when even that gentle touch caused a small trickle of blood from one nostril. He cursed Maylene, wondering if she'd broken his nose, wondering how he'd explain his appearance to people. He couldn't very well tell the truth about what happened. Uneasily, he considered the possibility of Maylene spreading the tale. Well, if she did, he'd just shake his head gravely, mention the instability he'd observed in her during her pregnancy, express hope that it wouldn't pursue her after the birth of her child, and then forgive her for the unprovoked attack she made on him when he tried to lead her in private prayer.

Gravel crunched in the parking lot. John Luther growled, not being in the mood for further company that night. He peeked out the office window and almost choked when he saw a pickup emblazoned with the shield of the county sheriff's office. A split second later, he realized the vehicle belonged to Sheriff Wes Ferguson, Maylene's father. He didn't know whether to send up a fervent prayer of thanks that she was gone or an equally fervent prayer that the sheriff had not arrived in response to her accusation.

Laying the cold cloth aside, John Luther took a few deep breaths, then forced himself to walk calmly across the office to turn on the outside light and open the door. He stood in the doorway as a broad-shouldered man climbed out of the pickup and adjusted a Stetson hat on his head. Light glowed on the polished toes of his western boots and off the badge on his shirt.

Two-bit John Wayne wannabe, John Luther thought contemptuously, trying to hide his trepidation from himself.

Wes took two steps toward the building, then stopped. For a moment, the two regarded each other silently. Wes's broad-brimmed hat threw his face into shadow. John Luther wished he hadn't turned on the porch light, knowing it illuminated his swollen face and bloody shirtfront.

"What brings you out here, Sheriff?" As soon as the words passed his lips, John Luther cursed himself for being the first to speak. Might make him look weak, nervous, or both.

"Got a call from Sam Woolsey. Said he heard screams and breaking glass over here." Wes looked toward the broken windows in the church, then let his gaze drift back to the preacher's face. "You look kinda rough, John Luther. Want to tell me what happened?"

"I am flattered that my little problem was deemed worthy of sending the sheriff himself to investigate," John Luther said, avoiding the question.

Wes moved to a position just outside the spill of light from the office door. "Don't be. I'm only here because I lost the coin toss after dispatch called and said somebody broke a window in your church."

John Luther snorted through his nose, then brought his hand up to see if the bleeding had begun again. "The damage is considerably more extensive than a broken window." He moved off the brightly lit porch, imperiously motioning for the sheriff to follow him to the church. Inside, he flipped on the overhead lights and stood back to let the other man enter. Seeing the place in full light for the first time, John Luther ground his teeth. The window damage was worse than he'd thought; even some of the wooden crosspieces between panes lay broken on the floor. Wes looked around the room at the piles of glass shards.

"Lot of broken windows," he observed. "What happened to your face?"

"The attack startled me. I stumbled into the door when I jumped up to chase the miscreant," John Luther said firmly.

"A door?"

"A door."

Wes walked up the center aisle, an occasional errant piece of glass crackling beneath his boots. At the front of the room, he pulled a powerful flashlight out of his utility belt and swept the beam back and forth across the floor. John Luther blinked a couple of times as the glow of angel mist rose around Wes, then disappeared.

"Some blood here." He swung the light up the aisle. "Nice trail of drops to the door, too."

John Luther cursed Maylene and her bleeding lip. Clenching his teeth to keep his jaw from trembling, he dabbed at his nose with the back of his hand. "I was at prayer when the attack began. I may have hit my face on the altar railing as I rose. I do not recall. I was too intent on catching the vandal to worry about small injuries to myself."

"Don't see any rocks," Wes commented. He glanced up at John

Luther with a slight upward quirk to his mouth. "Heard you had some trouble with folks throwing rocks at you a while back. Anyone else here this evening?"

John Luther forced himself to look dignified and benevolent and hoped Sam Woolsey hadn't reported Maylene's car burning rubber out of the parking lot. "Earlier I provided counseling services for a member of my congregation."

"Who?"

"A young wife was here for a marriage counseling session."

Wes's thick brown eyebrows rose in twin arcs. "Just her? Don't couples usually come in together for marriage counseling?"

A hot-red flush ran up John Luther's neck to his jawline. "Her husband is unwell. He did not wish for his wife to miss a session, though."

"I see."

John Luther wondered just what Wes Ferguson thought he saw.

"She leave before or after the windows broke?"

"Before." The lie came smoothly to his mouth.

"Who is she?"

John Luther drew himself up. "She saw nothing. She knows nothing. The sacred bond between shepherd and his flock, counselor and counselee, demands that I keep the names of troubled members of my congregation between myself and my Holy Father."

Wes didn't blink an eyelash. "Well, tell me what happened after she left."

The next fifteen minutes were acutely uncomfortable, with John Luther trying to provide a bare bones scenario and Wes Ferguson apparently bent on torturing him into revealing every detail of the event. The preacher wished that Sam Woolsey had minded his own business.

Wes made some notes in a small spiral ringed notebook, then tucked it and a pencil stub back into his shirt pocket. Without a word, he walked out the door to turn the flashlight beam on the outside wall. He paid special attention to a series of half-moon-shaped dents that ran the length of the wall and cumulated in a deep gouge in one of the front doors. He shifted his gaze from the wall to the ground and noticed a shovel lying in the grass a few feet from the building. He picked the tool up, fitted the curve of its head into several of the dents, then walked back into the church where John Luther sat in a pew, fuming, mentally urging the sheriff to leave so he could put the cold cloth over his nose again.

"Recognize this?" Wes hoisted the shovel in his right hand.

John Luther shrugged. "It is a shovel. Handle is red, showing it belongs to the church. The men who take care of the grounds mark our tools that way so they do not accidentally go home with anyone. Why?"

"Somebody used it to break out your windows and tear up your outside walls." Wes set the head of the shovel on the rug and leaned on the handle, like an irrigator waiting for the water to reach the end of a field. "Who dislikes you enough to do something like this, John Luther?"

"No one! I am well-respected in the community."

Wes's eyes flicked upward to John Luther's bisected eyebrow, then returned to his battered nose. "You can't think of anyone who might make a personal attack on you?"

"No, sir." John Luther snapped his teeth down on the last word. Wes scribbled a few more words down in his notebook, then snapped it shut like an echo of the other man's teeth.

"Kids," he said, heading toward the door. "Give us a call if there's any more problems."

John Luther forced himself to close the door gently, though he longed to slam it hard enough to knock the remaining shards of glass from their frames. He waited until he heard the sheriff's car pull back onto the pavement, then turned out the lights and left the building himself. He considered finding a broom and dustpan to sweep up the glass but had no idea where to look for such alien items. Delilah, he decided, could clean it up when she came to fetch the dishes tomorrow morning. Even if the chore was not beneath his dignity, he might cut himself trying to pick up glass off the floor.

He kept a careful eye on the tree line as he crossed the parking lot to his car, but nothing moved out there, heavenly angel or human vandal. The dome light brightened the car's interior with the opening of the door. John Luther raised a foot to climb into the driver's side and saw something move on the seat.

He walked every step of the mile home that night, arriving after midnight, out of temper, and footsore. He thought about wakening Wreath, sleeping in the little room off the porch that had once housed Delilah, then decided he could not put up with her anxious eyes and fumbling attempts to soothe him. He opened the refrigerator and saw the raisin-and-pecan pie. He cut a thick wedge, poured himself a glass of milk, and sat down at the kitchen table to unwind from the stressful evening. He barely paid attention to what he was eating, though he knew Delilah made the pie especially for him. He swallowed the piece in a few bites, drank down the milk, took a couple of spoonfuls of bicarbonate of soda for his burning stomach, and made his way up the weirdly glowing stairs toward bed.

Even though he'd been assured by the county animal control officer and mechanic Gil Herndon that there were no snakes in the car, John Luther was done driving it. One snake on the driver's seat was one too many, and he'd seen several. What if they'd been on the floor? They could've bitten him when he sat down. He could not even bring himself to drive the big Buick into town the following Monday. Jared guided it down the road to the car dealership in Texarkana while John Luther followed in Jared's old car. After an afternoon of wheeling, dealing, and stalling for effect, John Luther drove home a brand-new, two-tone blue Ford Country Squire Station Wagon. He never left a car door unlocked again.

CHAPTER 31
MAYLENE

Maylene cried all the way back to the small one-story brick house she shared with Henry. Her bruises and abrasions ached, but the latest blow dealt to her spirit by The Reverend John Luther Ives threatened to overwhelm her with despair and loneliness. She parked in the narrow driveway and shuffled up the sidewalk into the house, too dispirited to lift her feet. Inside, she ran the tap until the water was cold, filled a chipped Flintstones jelly jar glass, and sat down on the ugly green couch to stare at the picture of Jesus raising his face to a light that apparently came from somewhere beyond the picture frame. The protective plastic slipcover crinkled unpleasantly beneath her bottom. She hated living with plastic on every blessed piece of upholstered furniture, but Henry said plastic covers would keep things looking new, especially once It arrived.

It, thought Maylene, wrapping her arms around the child within her. *What kind of a life is Celeste Rose or Ashton Wesley going to have with a father who calls her or him It? Wilma Jean or Henry Chester, Junior are bad enough.*

She looked around the dismal house that contained Henry's plastic-covered furniture, Henry's mismatched dishes, and Henry's empty liquor bottles. Even the clothes she wore were Henry's, re-flecting what he thought suitable. She hadn't had anything pretty in so long she wanted to cry thinking about it. Her wedding ring was a thin, battered band he'd gotten from a cousin who owned a junk store up in Hot Springs. Maylene thought of little Celeste restricted to browns and tans, of little Ashton Wesley being taught to despise his mother as the sinful daughter of Eve and growing up to beat his own wife. She touched the bruises on her neck and her bitten mouth and imagined what Henry would consider proper punishment for erring children. She thought of Wreath Ives crawling toward the altar on hands and knees, publicly humiliated, repenting of trespasses against John Luther's authority. She thought of Genevieve walking out of church and realized for the first time that the expression on her face had been one of concentrated rage and not illness. Maylene touched her swollen lip with the tip of her tongue and recalled the taste of orange slush and French fries. She thought of the sound of her handbag connecting with John Luther's nose.

This is bullshit, she thought.

Taking a deep breath, she got up and hurried down to the niche in the hall wall that contained an old black rotary phone. Quickly, before she lost her nerve, she lifted the handpiece, dialed a familiar number, and listened to the rings on the other end of the line.

"Hello?"

Tears welled up in Maylene's eyes and she reached out to press the button to cut off the call.

"Hello? Is anyone there?"

"Mama?" Maylene whispered, then louder, "Mama, it's Maylene. Can I come home?"

Thirty seconds later, she exited the house with nothing but her handbag, leaving her wedding ring in the toilet and the front door standing wide open behind her. She walked down the road to the gas station where she bought a Nehi grape soda to drink while she waited. Five minutes later, a blue Volkswagen bug drove up. The most beautiful woman she had ever seen jumped out and ran toward her, arms spread wide. Maylene fell into her mother's embrace and abandoned Henry, John Luther Ives, and the Church of His Joyful Sheep forever.

CHAPTER 32
GENEVIEVE

Planning a cold-blooded murder is real different from carrying one out. I sat there in the nandina bushes with my pistol aimed right at the middle of John Luther's sagging chest and I didn't have the guts to pull that damn trigger. It should not be so hard to kill a wife-beating, child-molesting, poor-stupid-Maylene-abusing son of a bitch. I blamed my failure on Bigger.

Lord, if a woman naiver than Maylene MacCallan existed, I hoped to never meet her. When I saw her trot up those cement steps and knock on the door, I almost got up to drag her ass right back to her car. Since I couldn't shoot John Luther, I followed Maylene over to the church, though Lord knows what I thought I was going to do next. She was too beat up by her damn husband and beat down by John Luther to notice me trailing along after her. With each trudging step, she wiped away a tear or touched her hand to her sore throat. Once through the doors, she went straight to the altar and knelt there, fingers intertwined beneath her chin, eyes closed, lips moving in what I assumed was impassioned prayer. While her back was turned, I slipped inside the building and hid in the cloak area at the back where they kept the choir robes. Ugh. Some of them needed a trip through a washing machine, but there was nowhere else to hide, and I wanted to see what happened when John Luther got there. Depending on how he treated Maylene, I still might could overcome my cold feet and shoot him dead despite Bigger's interference.

As soon as he stepped into that church, it was plain as strawberry preserves on white bread that there was something wrong with John Luther. He passed within eight or ten feet of me, putting his feet down like he wasn't sure the ground under them was solid. At first, he just harangued poor Maylene with all the sins of Eve, then right in the middle of a sentence, he stared around the room with his eyes bugging out of his skull and his mouth hanging open like a half-witted hound dog. I thought I heard him bark a laugh as he twisted his fist in the hair of Maylene's head, dragged her up, and I swear to any god that is out there, bit her in the face.

I'd have shot him right then except I was afraid I'd hit Maylene. Having failed to commit justifiable homicide as well as premeditated murder, I ran out the door. A shovel, forgotten by the caretaker, was stabbed into the bare ground between building and lawn. I wrenched it out of the clay and swung the head right into the nearest window. Honestly, I only intended to knock out one window to distract him long enough for her to get away, but when that first waterfall of glass cascaded into the church, my brain flat shut down. Fueled by a tidal wave of adrenaline, I smashed every single window on the south side of the church, one after the other, banged my way back to the entrance along the same wall, slung the shovel at the door, and hightailed it into the trees like a juvenile delinquent playing ding dong ditch. Maylene's screaming stopped me there in the shadows. My hands shook so hard I could barely scrape my hair back out of my face. The pulse in my temple leapt beneath my fingers, auguring the beginning of a bad headache. The single thing I wanted on God's green earth was to run back to my truck and drive straight home, but I couldn't leave her there with him.

The old reprobate came through the door holding that girl in front of him like a shield and staring at the woods as if the Rougarou himself might be hiding behind a tree. I wished I was a

Cajun werewolf so I could rip out John Luther's cowardly throat. He dragged Maylene along so fast that she tripped and fell face-down in the parking lot. Instead of picking her up and taking her straight to the hospital to make sure her baby was okay, he jerked her upright and shook her so hard by the neck that it was a wonder that her head didn't snap off. I started out of the trees at a run then, but before I got a quarter way across the yard, she hauled off and clobbered him with the big old leather purse she always carried. He reeled backward, hands to his face, screeching like a scalded cat. Maylene jumped in her car and took off out of there like a moonshiner with a revenue man in hot pursuit. God bless that girl; many a boxer would give up his left arm for a right hook like the one she laid on John Luther Ives that night. I threw up both arms like she'd scored a touchdown, reversed direction, and ran down the dark forest path to my truck, giggling like a fool the whole way, every one of my voices laughing with me.

The next day, Mercer came home from work with no more to say than usual, but he gave me kind of a funny look as he headed off to the bathroom to clean up for dinner. Being in the middle of breading veal cutlets and struggling some to get the breading to coat the meat, I didn't pay him much mind. I finally got enough of the batter to stick to call it good and set the meat in a pan to cook while I mashed potatoes and warmed up some of Miss Wreath's home-canned purple hull peas. She'd promised to show me how to can vegetables when the harvest started coming in. I checked a new cookbook out of the library to read up in advance on canning so she wouldn't have to start with a complete idiot to teach.

As was our custom during dinner, I propped a book up next to my plate, this time to read about hot water baths, while Mercer fed Boomerang two bites for every one he ate himself. Boomerang loved the veal and potatoes but spat the purple hulls out on the floor, so Mercer ate most of the peas himself. I always made a mental note to myself of table food Boomerang wouldn't eat to increase the chances of getting what I figured was enough food down Mercer. His bones weren't covered with enough meat to tempt a starving turkey buzzard.

After dinner, Mercer piled the dishes into the sink and filled it with hot water and soap. I finished the chapter on jams, jellies, and preserves, then flipped through the dessert section to check out the cake recipes. I was determined to bake a decent cake someday. To the gentle homely clink of plates and silverware, I considered the relative merits of plain sponge cake over Lady Baltimore sponge cake with fruit and nut filling. A moment of silence, then Mercer sat back down across the table from me.

"What do you think of chopping up figs, nuts, cherries, and raisins together?" I asked.

"I don't like raisins," he answered.

I looked up at him, shut my book, and leaned my crossed arms on the table. "Okay, Mercer. Spill it."

He ran his fingers through his shaggy hair. "John Luther called Gil out to the church this morning to look at his car. Said he went to drive home last night and found a bunch of water moccasins laying on the seat. Walked all the way to the farm."

"Nah," I said skeptically. "How would water moccasins get in a closed car? It was closed, right?"

"I guess. Gen, you wouldn't . . . you didn't . . ."

I stared at him in total disbelief. "Me touch a water moccasin? Are you crazy? Those mean sons of bitches can kill a person!"

Mercer laughed. "Genevieve, I watched you carry rattlesnakes like you were transporting kittens."

"That's different, and you know it."

"Not till now I didn't. Well, anyway, Gil didn't find anything, but said John Luther kept insisting there were a dozen snakes in the car just waiting to bite him on the leg or maybe in the neck. Gil figured he was a little bit loopy from breaking his nose, and just imagined he saw something on the car seat."

"He broke his nose?" Aw, good girl, Maylene!

"Yeah. Someone busted out most of the windows in the church

last night and the old bastard ran into a door trying to catch the guy. At any rate, he won't even get in the car anymore." Mercer gave me an apologetic grimace. "Sorry, cousin. I shouldn't have . . ."

I waved the apology aside. He nodded, rose to his feet, and disappeared into his own room. I set my elbows on the table and propped up my chin in my hands. John Luther had been acting about half a bubble off plumb even before I wreaked havoc on the church windows, and it sounded like he didn't get any better after I left. I wondered why. I'd have thought he was too self-absorbed for ghosts to bother with, but he'd sure as hell been looking at something in that church that I couldn't see. His savage attack on Maylene's poor face seemed out of character, too, not because he wasn't capable of viciousness, but because he preferred to inflict damage on buttocks, thighs, and no doubt other private places hidden by clothing. He'd sunk his nasty teeth into Maylene's lower lip with no regard for the visible damage it caused. Lord, he'd looked just like a vampire I saw in a movie, only he went for her mouth instead of her throat.

As for cottonmouth water moccasins being in his car, I reckon he must've been seeing things. I sure hadn't put one there, never mind a dozen. Those things scare the hell out of me.

CHAPTER 33

GENEVIEVE

Sometimes the voices damn near drove me nuts, and I wished I could be anywhere except inside my own head. Lord knows, every one of them had an opinion about what I was doing and wasn't the least bit shy about sharing it. Which ghosts were genuine, and which were my own thoughts barking at me about my failures and shortcomings? A couple of days after I busted up the church windows, I leaned against the kitchen counter, coffee in hand, staring out at the predawn darkness and thinking if there was a pill I could take to give me some peace, I'd swallow it without worrying about side effects, up to and including extreme weight gain and death. Maybe I should've let the doctors dose the ghosts out of me years ago. Maybe I could just ignore them. Maybe while I was at it, I ought to pack up and run away to the circus again. Caring about people led to a bunch of complications I'd never considered back when I was spinning romantic notions of returning to my roots.

I sighed, drank the last of my coffee, and decided to get rid of the evidence of the crime I hadn't managed to commit. Granted, John Luther Ives was not worth the powder it would take to blow him to hell, but it still should not be so dang hard to put an end to him. Halfway to the door, I heard a noise behind me and turned to see Mercer ambling into the kitchen. He picked up my empty cup and filled it for himself from the electric percolator.

"You can use a clean cup," I said.

"Tastes sweeter if I use yours," he answered, "and no extra dishes to wash."

"You are bone lazy."

"Yes, ma'am, I am that." He nodded at the keys in my hand. "Where you going so early on a Saturday?"

"I need to throw a pistol in Red River."

He paused in mid-sip to think about that. "You shoot somebody?"

"Not yet."

"You gonna shoot somebody?"

"Not if I throw the pistol in the river first."

"Good plan, especially if it's me you're after. Mind if I tag along?"

I gestured through the doorway with a welcoming sweep of my hand.

Early morning is my favorite time of day, particularly in hot weather, and Lord knows, spring that year felt more like summer than some summers do. We drove through the gray light of pre-dawn with the windows down and the wind making conversation impractical, if not impossible. Mercer fiddled with the pistol as we drove, clicking its various parts in and out till he like to drove me crazy.

"This is a piece of crap," he said. "You're lucky it didn't blow up in your fist the first time you fired it."

"I never fired it."

He looked sideways at me and raised one eyebrow. He couldn't intimidate me that way. I raised one of mine back at him. Must be a genetic skill.

"You even know how to shoot, Gen?"

"Sure, I do," I said, stung to the core of my pride. What was to know? You poked bullets in the little slots, popped the turny spinny thingy back into place, pointed at what you wanted to blow away, and pulled the trigger.

He sighed and used a built-in rod thing to push the bullets out of the spinny thing. The bullets went into his shirt pocket. He tucked the gun back into the glove compartment. We drove in silence past Crossroads and down the long stretch of road that split the pine forest in half. At Fulton, I wound through the quiet streets and turned west on 67 Highway. In a few seconds, the beautiful arch of the five-span bridge over Red River came into sight.

"You're fuckin' serious, aren't you?" Mercer said when I stopped at the highest point of the center arch. I put the truck into park and leaned over to get the pistol out of the glove compartment.

"Bullets." I held out my hand. He dropped them into my palm. "Thanks."

I climbed out of the cab and walked over to the railing. He joined me. For a couple of minutes, we stared down into the roiling rusty water far below. I extended my left arm and tilted my wrist to let the bullets roll off my palm, one by one. Despite the brightening sky, I couldn't tell when they hit the water. Without hesitation, I dropped the pistol after them and imagined I could see the muddy water swallow it up. That was a relief.

"Who were you planning to shoot?" Mercer asked.

"Your father," I answered.

He stood looking at the river another moment, then said, "Do I want to know why?"

I shook my head. We climbed in the truck. I managed a three-point turn on the narrow road and aimed the truck back the way we'd come. Mercer was quiet, but he didn't seem all that upset by my revelation, just kinda thoughtful.

"Do you know where Cypress Lake is?" I called over the roar of the wind through the windows, as much to break the silence as anything.

"Yeah."

"Can we go there?"

"Belongs to a hunting club that's particular about who gets in."

"Oh." The corners of my mouth drooped. Mercer eyed me suspiciously. Probably wondered if I wanted to scope out the possibilities of drowning John Luther since I didn't manage to shoot him.

"Why you want to go to Cypress?"

"Bigger said he used to duck hunt there. I just want to look at it."

Mercer grinned at me just as the sun came out and lit up his face with a bright beam of gold light. "I can take you in, but you may be sorry by the time we get there."

We left the truck way off a back road next to the remnants of a tin-roofed barn that looked like it hadn't had a horse in it since the Dead Sea felt just a little bit under the weather. Mercer led me up the road a piece, then veered into the pine trees and undergrowth down a trail so thin that I wondered if he only imagined it existed. Moss-covered dead branches and wait-a-minute vines tore at my jeans. Before long I was wishing I'd grabbed my long-sleeved work shirt out of the truck before we set off, and maybe my boots as well. The ground beneath my feet got soggier with every step. Once a serpentine body slithered across the path between me and Mercer. Water moccasin. Ew. I squared my shoulders and kept on going, even though I dearly wished I could fly straight back to the truck.

Being intent on watching where I stepped, I bumped smack into Mercer when he stopped. I raised my head and saw that the pine and hardwood forest had given way to cypress trees big enough that a family of four could shelter cozily in one of the trunks. Fascinated, I took a cautious step toward the nearest tree. Mercer put out a hand to stop me and I realized we stood at the edge of a shallow lake so choked with vegetation that it looked like a meadow.

"Duckweed," Mercer told me when I asked about the cover. "Water crowfoot, featherfoil, bottombrush—hell, I don't know what all. Stuff's so thick in places that the hunting club folks flag channels for the boats to follow so some fellow doesn't stay out a little too late, drink a little too much bourbon, and spend the next week paddling around in circles. Lake's not deep—hell, you could probably wade all the way across it and never get your hair wet—but we're looking at four square miles of water, trees, and bushes to get lost in."

"I have never in my life seen cypress trees as big as these," I whispered, reluctant to stir the quiet with a full-voiced word. "Lord, that one must be thirty feet around the trunk."

"The science teacher at school told us that some of the trees in Cypress Lake are over three hundred and fifty years old."

"How'd he figure that?"

Mercer shrugged. "Beats me. He knew somebody who knew somebody and got to spend a summer out here looking around and measuring stuff. Learned a lot about what lives in and around Cypress and made sure his students learned it, too. See those big, tall clumps of stuff scattered over yonder like little islands? That's rice grass. Gets ten or twelve feet high in places. Sharp edges. It'll cut you good if you brush up against it. When the gators aren't swimming around looking for something to eat or scaring the fishermen out of a year's growth, they hang out in those clumps of rice grass."

"Alligators?" Automatically I checked the area around us for lurking reptiles.

He nodded, proud as if every one of the beasts was his best friend. "One time when Jim and me were still too young to drive legally, we took off with his daddy's car late one night and came out here for a private party. Parked down at the cabins, bold as brass, and took one of the flat boats tied up at the dock since no one was around to tell us not to. Drank some beer and were having us a good time when we heard something in the water. Jim got out the flashlight and shined it in that direction. Lo and behold, we saw a red glowing coal right out in the middle of the lake. Couldn't imagine what it was, so I picked up the pole and started pushing the boat along toward it. We got some closer, and that one coal separated into two. I figured I'd had too much beer. Jim leaned so far out of the boat trying to see that I thought he was going to fall in the water. All of a sudden, he hollered, 'It's a goldang alligator, Mercer, and he's headed our way.' " Mercer chuckled. "You never saw a pole boat move so fast in all your life. That was our last trip out on Cypress in the middle of the night."

Still grinning at the memory, he crooked his finger at me and pushed through the ferns that edged our little clearing. Some of the frilly leafed things were taller than me, and I'm a long drink of water for a girl. After a long damp ramble along the edge of the lake, we came to an ancient oak tree that supported a homemade wooden deer stand that looked almost as old as the tree. Mercer climbed up to the broad seat, testing each rung for strength and stability. Once ensconced on the camouflaged throne, he gestured for me to climb up. I shook my head.

"Too much weight. Might break."

"No, it won't." He bounced up and down on the seat to demonstrate.

"There's not room for us both."

"You can sit on me," he said, then mischievously added, "unless you're *skeered*."

He raised an eyebrow at me to underline the old childish taunt. I sighed and put my foot on the first rung of the ladder. Death before dishonor. After a cautious assent (Lord, the thing creaked like an old lady's knees), I managed to get turned around right and settled on his lap. He wrapped a cousinly arm around my waist to hold me steady and we looked out across the incredible wilderness of the lake.

"We aren't supposed to be here, are we?" I asked.

He grinned at me. "Nope. Worried we'll get caught?"

"Hell, yeah. They probably feed trespassers to the gators. How'd you know where to find that path?"

"My grandfather Hughley started bringing Jim and me here when we were still too small to see over the ferns. Papaw hunted and fished at Cypress his whole life. A hunting club bought the land in the fifties and blocked legal access to everyone but a handful of rich doctors and lawyers and such from Texarkana. Local people had used the lake for a hundred years, so Papaw and his twin brother, your grandfather Hughley, trespassed every time it suited them. Came close to getting caught a time or two, but they were willing to get wet and those tracking 'em weren't, so Papaw and Great-uncle Floyd always got away."

"Suppose Bigger came down that path, too?"

"Naw, my family used a trail that started on m'cousin's place, 'bout a mile from where y'all come in."

I looked over my shoulder to see Bigger perched on a tree branch, comfortable as if he'd been sitting on Boomerang's sofa at home.

"Don't care who holds paper on the place, Cypress Lake belongs to folks that hunt for food and not those out to blast a few ducks between foreclosin' on farms and killin' patients with snake oil. M'whole family used to come out here, includin' my grandmama. She didn't much like gettin' her feet wet, but the idea of puttin' one over on a bunch of rich white boys tickled her."

"Trespassing is a time-honored tradition at Cypress," Mercer agreed.

"Yes, sir, I mean to say." Bigger looked across the lake wistfully. "Man, I missed this. I surely do appreciate y'all comin' today. I ain't been able to get here by myself."

"If I'd known, I'd have come sooner," Mercer said.

"I didn't know my own self until I figured it out just now. Looks like I need one or the other of y'all for transportation. Can't seem to go nowhere on m'own."

"Well, where would you like to go next?" I asked, shifting around on Mercer's lap so I could see Bigger without putting a crick in my neck.

"Home," he said, and disappeared as quickly and unexpectedly as he'd arrived.

CHAPTER 34
WREATH

The oldest resident of Columbus, Miss Sophronia Missouri Price, age 103, died peacefully in her sleep on a beautiful morning in late May. Her long-deceased husband had been a charter member of the Church of the Flock of the Good Shepherd. It was in Mr. Price's honor that John Luther Ives agreed to preach Miss Sophronia's funeral himself, arranging for Jared to preach in his stead at a weekend tent revival in Louisiana. John Luther insisted the rest of the family attend the tent revival as well, saying he knew they'd all looked forward to the treat and he didn't want to deprive them of it.

Just like him, Wreath thought as she looked through the kitchen cupboards for the sweet tea thermos. *Not one of us cares a thing about that revival except Jared and Delilah. I'd rather stay home with the children, but John Luther says go, so off we go. Lord forgive me, hating that man is a black mark against my name, but I cannot help myself.*

Wreath hadn't spoken a word to him since the night she learned about wife lessons. She'd barely spoken a word to anyone except Jezzie and Leah. After some of the shock faded, remorse, shame, and grief moved in, alternating with denial (Delilah was a first-class liar) and a desperate mental search for a way to protect Jezzie just in case Delilah was telling the truth. Despite her few shreds of hard-won courage, now bolstered by Genevieve's presence in her life, Wreath still feared John Luther. She knew in her heart and soul that a battle over Jezzie's future was inevitable, and that she herself had no chance of coming out of it unscathed. The trip to Louisiana offered a brief reprieve from the confrontation, though she wasn't looking forward to a long drive with Delilah and two colicky infants, or to sitting through a series of long-winded exhortations to repent of a laundry list of sins. When told about the "treat" in store for them, Jezzie and Leah drooped like the last roses of summer.

"I bet I know who's gonna get stuck with those cranky babies while Delilah visits and Sweet Jesuses herself all over creation," Jezzie grumbled. Leah nodded glum agreement, resigned to her fate, but not happy about it.

The phone rang, interrupting Wreath's thoughts. She abandoned her search for the thermos and hurried up the hall to answer.

"Wreath? Honey, this is Anita. Listen, Abby brought Leah home for lunch. The poor little thing got a sick headache, so I put her to bed with an aspirin and a cold cloth. If you'll call school, I'll keep her here till she feels better."

"Bless your heart, I surely do appreciate that," Wreath said. "I hate that she inherited those headaches. We're headed down to a revival in Springfield this very afternoon; we can pick her up then."

"Oh, honey, she's feeling so bad that the last thing she's gonna want is a ride in a car. Tell you what, Leah's never a bit of trouble. Just leave her with us and y'all can pick her up on the way home."

As they discussed arrangements, Wreath noticed a faint layer of dust on the phone table. It was Leah's job to dust the hallway pictures and phone niche; she gave it a good effort, but sometimes she missed spots. Wreath stuck a hand in one pocket of her apron in search of a dust cloth and came up with the cloth and an open package of morning glory seeds, of all things. She hadn't planted morning glories in two years. She shook her head, dropped the packet back in her pocket, and dusted the phone niche. With a final word of thanks, she put the handpiece back in its cradle, wondering how on earth someone as unpleasant as John Luther managed to get sweet-natured Anita for a cousin.

After an irritating search, Wreath located the stainless-steel container at the far back corner of a lower cabinet. She pulled it out, muttering to herself, "I know I put that thing behind the Jell-O molds. How on earth did it get all the way back there?" Delilah, of course. In her not-so-subtle campaign to drive Wreath out of her own house, Delilah had taken to rearranging cabinets so no one but her could find anything.

I reckon she's got reason to hate me, she thought disconsolately. *Lord help me, I don't like her much, either.*

She carried the thermos to the sink and twisted open the lid to rinse it out. Half a dozen morning glory seed packets tumbled out. Wreath spread them out face up on the countertop, then pulled the open package from her pocket. She checked the dates on the packages. New seeds, all of them. She poured a few from the open package onto her palm. Whenever she planted morning glory, she nicked the hard seed coats with a fingernail file and soaked them over night, but these seeds were crushed. What on earth? As she tilted them back into the package, a terrible idea came to her. Dreading what she might find, she reached up on the top shelf over the stove and took down a small white mortar and pestle used for grinding herbs. A few grains of coarse brown powder clung to the sides of the small bowl.

"Oh, dear Lord," she whispered. She washed the mortar and pestle in hot soapy water. She started to replace them on the shelf, then changed her mind and hid them at the bottom of the trash can. Better safe than sorry. Taking a deep breath, she went to the bookshelf and took down the herbal that had held such fascination for Delilah a few weeks earlier. She'd said she was looking for new ideas for pickling spice.

Wreath sat down at the table, consulted the index, and opened the book to the page on morning glory. Half a dozen lines were faintly underlined. As she read, the reason became clear for Delilah's sudden interest in baking treats no one but John Luther would eat, as well as the explanation for John Luther's upset stomach, and even for the snakes in his car. Looked like Wreath wasn't the only one Delilah hated. She shut the book, covered her face with her hands, and rocked back and forth, mourning this final loss of the little girl she'd lovingly held in her arms so long ago.

Several hours later, she sat in the backseat of the car with one of the babies on her lap. Delilah sat up front and held the other child in her own arms. There'd been some talk about purchasing car seats, but Jared decided it was a needless expenditure. He'd never had an accident, never intended to, and had survived childhood just fine without being confined by straps and plastic seats. Babies were happier in their mothers' arms and quieter as well. On a car trip, Jared's peace of mind depended on quiet babies.

When they drove by Hope High School without even slowing up, Wreath said, "Jared, we're supposed to pick up Jezzie out by the football practice field."

Jared didn't answer. Delilah kept her face resolutely forward.

"Hey, y'all," Wreath said louder. "We need to stop for Jezzie."

"Change in plans," Delilah said without turning around.

A wisp of panic flickered in Wreath's stomach. "What do you mean, a change in plans?"

"Jezzie's going home like always. Somebody has to cook dinner for my daddy while we're gone."

Wreath gripped the baby in her arms so hard that he whimpered in protest. "You turn this car around right now."

"Now, Miss Wreath," Jared said soothingly, "Jezzie is old enough to cook dinner and wash dishes by herself."

Wreath reached forward and smacked Delilah on the back of the head.

"Hey!" Delilah twisted around in the seat to glare at her.

"Does he know what is going to happen?" Wreath demanded. Delilah's glare smoothed out into a hard, satisfied smirk. *"Does he know?"*

"Don't be silly, Mama. Nothing is going to happen except Jezzie will learn a bit of responsibility."

Wreath reached for the door handle and realized for the first time that it had been removed. Sick and half dizzy with horror, she looked out the window. They'd reached the edge of town and were accelerating to highway speeds. "Jared Fuller, you stop this car and let me out of here."

He kept driving. Stunned, she sat back in the seat and stared at Delilah. "What in Jesus' name is wrong with you?"

"Not a thing, Mama. Not a blessed little ol' thing," she answered and faced forward again.

Wreath watched the countryside flash past the window. Even if she could get the door open to jump out, at this speed she'd kill herself and that wouldn't help Jezzie a bit. She thought of time passing, of Jezzie getting on the bus, going home to—

Slowly and deliberately, Wreath slid a hand into the bag sitting on the seat next to her and wrapped her fingers around the heavy stainless-steel thermos. Then she waited, eyes focused on the road in front of her, watching for her chance to move. It came sooner than she expected but later than she'd hoped. A yellow school bus lumbered onto the road in front of them just north of Lewisville. A mile down the road, the bus's rear lights flashed a warning. Wreath laid the sleeping baby down on the seat and tucked him in tenderly, arranging his blue blanket to keep him from rolling off the seat. Hiding the thermos bottle in the folds of her skirt, she angled her body toward the door.

Jared slowed the car and rolled to a stop as the flashing lights turned red. As soon as the tires stopped turning, Wreath raised the thermos in both hands and smashed it against the window. It bounced off the tempered glass like a ping-pong ball. Jared yelped and Delilah looked over the seat, eyes wide. "What on earth?"

Wreath hauled off and slammed the window again. The thermos barely had time to bounce before she hit the window a third time. A mosaic of fractures bloomed across the window.

"Now, Miss Wreath, don't you take on like that," Jared said in distress, reaching back to grab at her. Wreath brought the thermos down hard on his forearm. "Ow! Get that thing away from her!

Lord, John Luther said she wouldn't take kindly to leavin' Jezzie to do for him, but—ow!" He jerked himself out of range as she swung at him again. "Quit that, you crazy old—Delilah! Move!"

Delilah thrust the baby at Jared and climbed out of the car. She pulled up the back door handle, intending to seize the bottle and slam the door again, secure in the knowledge that she was younger, stronger, and faster than her mother. She no more than got the door ajar when Wreath hit it hard with her shoulder and barreled through the opening like a bucking horse released from a chute. Charging straight at her astonished daughter, she swung the thermos up in a long arc that ended abruptly on the point of Delilah's chin. Arms flailing, Delilah staggered backward, caught her heel in a hole in the pavement, and landed hard on her bottom. Wreath fled down the highway as fast as her legs would carry her, still clutching the silver bottle.

"What did you have to go and hit me for?" Delilah wailed after her mother, cupping her hand around her ballooning chin and lower lip. She leaned forward to keep a trickle of blood from falling onto her third-best dress. Her tongue touched a newly chipped spot on a front tooth. *Oh, Lord, is that going to show when I smile? If it does, I swear I will break every tooth in her serpent-tongued mouth.* "Jared, what are you waiting on? Stop her!"

Jared put the crying baby on the center of the bench seat, curled his fingers around the steering wheel, and watched a small group of school children cross the road in front of him.

"Shut up and get in the car."

"But—"

"Get in, Delilah. This is between her and John Luther. I knew forcin' her to come with us was a real bad idea, and now I'm thinkin' there's a lot someone isn't tellin' me, startin' with who took the inside handles off the back doors. Get. In. Now."

Sobbing with hurt and fury, Delilah got to her feet and checked to make sure the baby in the back seat was still sleeping and secure. Then she crawled into the front seat, scooped the crying child into her arms, and closed the door. The car continued toward the Louisiana border, leaving Wreath to flee, unhindered, toward home.

She ran almost a mile before the adrenaline burned away, leaving her shaky and lightheaded. She staggered to a walk but didn't stop moving as she unscrewed the lid of the thermos, lifted it to her mouth, and took a few deep swallows of tea so heavily laced with sugar that it tasted like syrup. By the time she recapped the bottle, she felt better physically, but mental anguish threatened to overwhelm her. Lewisville was a good forty miles from Columbus. If she walked and ran by turns to save energy, she could manage maybe four miles an hour, but to keep it up for ten hours? Blisters were already forming on her heels and the ache in her left knee suggested she wasn't sixteen years old anymore. Even if she didn't fall facedown on the ground from exhaustion, in ten hours the damage to Jezzie's life would be done.

Far down the highway behind her, a sixteen-wheeler's tires whined on the pavement. Without a second thought, shy, retiring, cautious Wreath Hughley Ives stuck out her thumb and looked at the truck hopefully. A moment later, air brakes sounded. The truck passed her, then slowed to a stop a few yards down the road.

"Oh, my goodness," Wreath gasped and ran to ask for a ride.

The trucker took her clear to Hope and dropped her off on the corner of South Main Street and West Third Street before he headed northeast toward Arkadelphia. Wreath thought about calling Anita to ask for a ride but rejected that thought; she needed Anita to keep Leah safe and unaware. As she walked, she tried to think of who else she could call, but John Luther had kept her isolated for so many years that she couldn't think of a soul in Hope she knew well enough to ask for help. Mercer worked in town when he was able to work, but she didn't even consider the notion of calling him. He'd ask too many questions, and if he found out what John Luther was planning . . . Wreath blanked that thought out. She stopped in the Piggly Wiggly to use the phone, hoping against hope to hear Genevieve's voice on the other end of the line, but all she heard was ring after ring in an empty apartment.

She hung up and pressed her fingers against her eyelids to force back tears. Seventeen miles from home and she might as well be a hundred.

She turned onto Hervey Street and walked almost two miles before a lady in a station wagon stopped and offered her a ride as far as Crossroads. Wreath accepted gratefully.

"I'd take you all the way to Columbus, but I got ice cream in the back," the woman apologized when she stopped at the turnoff to Washington. Wreath thanked her and climbed out of the car right where John Luther had given her that first treacherous kiss so many years before.

"Thank you, ma'am, this here is just fine." Wreath waved to her benefactor and set out at a determined walk toward home. The wind at her back blew harder now than when she left Hope, and clouds blossomed overhead into a garden of ominous black-and-purple aerial flowers. Lightning flashed beyond the trees, followed a few seconds later by a roll of thunder.

One more ride, Lord. I do thank you for what you've already sent me, but one more ride would be real good.

She got the requested one more ride, but soon realized the farmer driving the truck was worse for drink. After he swerved out of his lane and almost hit an oncoming car, she pointed out a stopping place near a farmhouse and jumped out of the vehicle, thankful to still be on her feet and not lying dead on the highway. With that, the Lord apparently thought He'd done enough for one afternoon. The sky collapsed and rain fell in sheets, drenching her as she limped along on battered, blistered feet. Few cars appeared and none of them slowed up. One passed so close to her that she jumped sideways and fell into the flooded ditch just a couple of feet off the shoulder of the road. She didn't know whether to laugh or cry. Picking herself up out of the water, she decided it didn't matter which she did; one was sure to turn into the other at some point. She slogged on. By the time she turned in at her own driveway, she was shivering, aching, and ready to drop. She'd trudged halfway up the hill when Jezzie screamed somewhere inside the house.

CHAPTER 35
JEZZIE

❦

Jezzie shifted her books back and forth between tired arms and finally set them down in the pine needles in Martha Smith's yard across the street from the practice field. She looked down East Sixteenth Street for the hundredth time in an hour and ten minutes and wondered what on earth was keeping Mama and them. Miss Martha had already taken pity on her twice, once to bring her a glass of sweet tea and once to keep watch while Jezzie ran in to use her bathroom.

"If they don't get here soon, we'll call 'em to see what they're thinkin' to leave you standin' here in the heat this long," Miss Martha advised as she headed back to her rose garden. They'd met half an hour earlier when the old lady had abandoned her hoe to see why the girl had been standing in her front yard for so long. Ten minutes of conversation with voluble, gruffly concerned Miss Martha, and Jezzie knew she'd made a friend for life. "If nobody answers, I'll take you home myself."

Jezzie nudged her history book with the toe of her saddle ox-ford, thinking how ironic it was that the ugly shoe style she'd been forced to wear all her life was suddenly in vogue for teenaged girls. Well, at least she could be fashionable for fifteen minutes before everyone went on to something prettier. The shoes looked okay as long as her skirt was rolled up to a couple of inches above her knees, but once she was forced to smooth it out to upper calf length, she looked like a refugee from her mother's high school photos.

She peered down the street for the hundred and first time. A two-toned blue Ford Country Squire station wagon turned the corner on Main Street and rolled inexorably toward her, bearing not her mother, sisters, nephews, and Jared, but the person she least wanted to see in the world.

She scooped up her books and held them like a shield between her and the oncoming menace. The car came closer, and she saw her stone-eyed father at the wheel, thick lips looking pink and damp, his square chin softened with age and overindulgence in the sweets Delilah had been churning out for him several times a week. She thought about fleeing across Martha Smith's yard into the forest beyond where she could hide until someone else came looking for her. Alas, whoever found her would only take her back home to him, and a punishment for running away would be added to whatever he already had planned.

He stopped the car across the road from her and waited, eyes straight ahead, for her to approach the car. She shuffled across the asphalt, shoulders hunched, head down and pulled in close to her chest. As she opened the driver's side back door, Martha Smith's voice hailed her.

"I see your ride got here. You come on back to visit sometime, Jezzie. Roses'll be in full bloom in a couple of weeks."

Jezzie wiggled her fingers at the brusque, good-natured gardener, wishing . . . wishing what? She didn't know. She climbed into the back seat.

As usual during a drive, John Luther rambled on about whatever was on his mind: church matters, the weather, backsliding members of the Flock, Miss Sophronia's funeral service, and what he wanted for his supper later that night. The one thing he didn't mention was why she was riding toward Columbus with him instead of toward Louisiana with everyone else. Mama had told her that very morning where they'd pick her up and what time. Mama'd even helped her pack her overnight bag and reminded her to take her new toothbrush and throw the old one away. Had the revival been cancelled and everyone was waiting at home? Jezzie crossed her fingers, but John Luther's next words dashed her hopes.

"Delilah tells me you show no interest in the culinary arts. That must change, Jezebel. It is a woman's obligation to keep a fine table, and I will not suffer a daughter who cannot cook and serve a meal. Given your shortcomings, I do not expect you to make an elaborate supper for me tonight. Steak, baked potatoes, rolls, buttered corn, and green beans should be within your ability. Surely you can manage to open a couple of cans and bake some potatoes. You must take especial care with the steak, however; I like meat nicely pink on the inside, not too rare, and not too done. An overdone steak is inedible and unsalvageable. I will not see good food wasted in my household, so mind what you are doing. You do not need to bake a dessert tonight. Delilah made a raisin pie before they left for the revival."

"Who went?" Jezzie asked, heart in her throat.

John Luther looked at her in the rearview mirror. "They all went. I am sorry if you are disappointed to be left behind, but someone must cook and clean for me, and you are the logical person, though your domestic skills are sadly lacking. School will adjourn for the summer next Wednesday. I will allow you to finish the year out, but then you will leave the classroom behind."

"What do you mean, leave the classroom behind?"

"You will be fifteen this summer. Mercer and Delilah both left school at fifteen. So shall you."

"No!" Jezzie sat straight up and glared into the rearview mirror. "I don't want to quit school. I've got straight A's now that I've brought up my algebra grade and the school counselor said if I work hard, I can get a college scholarship."

"This is not open to discussion, Jezebel," John Luther said. "You will do as you are told. You will not argue or defy me."

The hell I won't, Jezzie thought, settling down into a sullen lump on the backseat, arms folded tightly across her chest. *Gennie will help me. She said she would get me to college if it took every drop of her blood, and she means it.*

"Your mother has overindulged your academic aspirations and cannot be trusted to prepare you to take up a woman's responsibilities. A woman's duty lies in service to God and man, first her father and then her husband."

Jezzie's stomach twisted into such a knot that it bent her double with pain. *No, no, no, no, no.*

"After due deliberation and discussion, I have contracted you in marriage to John Evert. The ceremony will take place on the Saturday following your birthday in July. That gives Delilah and me less than six weeks to teach you to be a wife and helpmate to John, and a proper mother to his children."

Wife lessons.

Jezzie gagged and threw up on the pristine carpet of John Luther's brand-new car.

He turned off the highway and drove a quarter mile down a dirt road before he jerked her out of the car and slammed her upper body flat across the hood where combined heat from the engine and the afternoon sun burned through her thin blouse. For the first time, Jezzie was grateful for the binding bands wrapped around her chest because they kept the hot metal from searing the tender skin of her breasts even as it blistered her stomach. She pressed her hands against the metal, burning the palms as she fought to push herself upright, but he easily held her down with one big hand while he pulled his belt out of the loops and flipped up her skirt with the other. She kicked back at him, connected with his shin, had the satisfaction of hearing him yelp. The next second, he knocked her feet far apart, putting her off-balance and unable to kick again without falling. The burn of the belt across her upper thighs and buttocks joined the burn of the hot metal on her stomach. Jezzie thought she'd faint from the pain before the sound of a car slowing down to turn off the main road stopped the beating. John Luther shoved her into the back, got his belt buckled, and returned to the driver's seat before the car passed them. He raised a casual hand in greeting that the other driver returned just as casually. Jezzie stayed where she was, facedown on the seat, unwilling to try and sit up on her bruised flesh. The smell of what was on the floor roiled her stomach, but she had nothing else to bring up.

As soon as they got home, he set her to cleaning not only the back floorboard but the entire car while he stood and watched with narrowed, angry eyes. He made her scrub the soiled carpet half a dozen times, then lost his temper when he realized the carpet no longer looked new. He marched her into the kitchen and drove her toward the stove with a hard swat of his bare hand. Pain from her battered backside shot up her spine and down her legs, but she managed to choke back the shriek that would've given him so much satisfaction.

I am going to kill you, she thought. She looked at the drawer where the knives were kept and pondered her chances of grabbing one before he stopped her.

"Steak. Potatoes. Corn. Green beans. Rolls." He pointed at the refrigerator.

She couldn't get anywhere near the knife drawer with him watching her every move. Had he deliberately chosen a meal that could be prepared without cutting a single thing? She wrapped potatoes in aluminum foil and put them in the oven to bake. She boiled water to make fresh tea and dropped half a dozen tea bags in the teapot to let them brew. As she worked, she contemplated slinging the pot of boiling water into his face, then when he was blinded, finishing him off by a blow to the head with the cast-iron griddle that the steaks lay on. It was a thought. When the tea was strong enough, she added cold water, poured the results into the carnival glass pitcher, then filled it to the top with more cold water. Maybe she could hit him with the griddle, shove his face in the pitcher, and drown him instead.

Having worked up an appetite from abusing his daughter, John Luther pulled a knife from the drawer and cut himself a generous slab of raisin pie. She had a moment of hope, but he returned both pie and knife to the pie safe and closed the door. He sat down at the trestle table to eat, his eyes never leaving Jezzie as she took out the potatoes, warmed corn and beans, and broiled the steaks.

Too bad I don't have any rat poison to season these, she thought as she mashed yellow butter into a potato. The green beans simmered along with a piece of fatback. The steaks sizzled. The rolls browned. The red burns on her stomach and hands stung. An open welt on one thigh oozed blood.

He finished his pie and shoved the plate and fork aside. Silently, she picked them up and put them in the sink, then laid the table in front of him with a clean plate, flatware, napkin, and a glass of sweet tea. Her fingers itched to grab the steak knife and drive it into his black heart, but it was too short to penetrate his thick hide deep enough to reach any vital organ. Really, he was getting fat as a tick, and would get even fatter if he kept devouring a quarter of a pie before each meal. She spooned the corn and beans into bowls and placed them on the table along with the steak and rolls.

"Serve it to me," he ordered.

Thunder rolled in like waves on a shore. The air tasted of rain, and she drooped under the pressure of the oncoming storm. He sat in majestic silence while she filled his plate with food, then he fell to his meal with good appetite. She stood to one side of the table as instructed, ready to refill his tea glass or supply him with another piece of meat or helping of vegetables at his command. Seething with resentment, she plopped corn on his plate with such force that a few kernels bounced onto the tablecloth. John Luther frowned.

"You lack grace and humility as well as domestic skills. It is lucky that your face and figure are comely enough to attract a husband, especially one as well-to-do as John Evert."

"How much is he paying you?"

"Excuse me?" John Luther said, turning a hard look on her. Despite her fear, the look Jezzie gave him in return was every bit as hard.

"What did you get for me? A new roof for the church? Access to his prize breeding bull? Or just plain old cash?"

John Luther slammed his hands down on the table, pushed himself to his feet, and made a grab at her. Jezzie danced backward out of his way. The storm broke overhead with a fury that shook the windows. Her conscious mind screamed at her to shut up, to not talk back, to not make things worse than they already were, but her mouth irrepressibly kicked into high gear.

"I don't care how damn rich he is, John Evert is mean as a snake and so ugly he'd stop an eight-day clock. His children are brats, I hate his guts, and nothing in God's creation can make me marry him."

John Luther lunged at her again, lost his balance, and crashed belly down on the table with a ridiculous "ooof" of forcibly expelled air. Half hysterical with fear, fury, and malicious amusement, Jezzie left him lying there in the spilled tea and green beans and made a run for the phone. She had the handpiece in her grasp and her finger in the dial when he seized her from behind by the waist and flung her to the ground.

Bad idea, she thought dazedly as she tried to push herself off the floor. *I should've run for the back door.*

He jerked the phone cord from the wall, flipped her over like a pancake, put his knee in the middle of her back, and tied her wrists together. Grasping her by one elbow, he towed her down the hall, exhorting God to look down on the evil within his household and give him the power to root it out. Jezzie fought him every step of the way, kicking and twisting in his grasp.

"'I suffer not a woman to usurp authority over the man, but to be in silence,'" he bellowed. "'For Adam was first formed, then Eve. And Adam was not deceived, but the woman being deceived was in the transgression.'"

"Eve was framed!" Jezzie shrieked at him. "Adam was a rat fink!"

"'One shall ruleth well his own house, having his children in subjection with all gravity.'" John Luther dropped Jezzie as the hall walls toppled toward him. He put one massive hand against each wall and shoved outward to hold them into place, feeling as powerful as Sampson in the temple, except he kept the walls from caving in instead of tearing them down. "'For if a man knows not how to rule his own house, how shall he take care of the church of God?'"

Jezzie rolled away and clambered to her feet. Her body was awash with pain, but she didn't have time to count the stripes or stem the blood. John Luther blocked her escape into the main part of the house, so she darted into the dining room and kicked the door shut. With complete disregard for the keepsakes inside the whatnot cabinet, she put her shoulder against it and shoved it inch by inch to brace the door while John Luther continued his erratic exhortations in the hall.

"God was manifest in the flesh, justified in the spirit, seen of angels, and I have seen angels! Angels appeared to me, came at my summoning, and I knew my power! I know my power!"

Jezzie brought her bound wrists as low as she could, sliding them over her stinging bottom. She sat on the floor and pulled her wrists along the back of her legs, bending her knees and ankles, straining the bonds until she managed to slip her feet through the loop of her arms, bringing her wrists in front of her.

The door crashed against the whatnot cabinet, knocking a dozen pieces of decorative glass to the floor. Jezzie ran to the window and struggled to turn the latch, but her fingers, numbed by the tight bonds, wouldn't cooperate.

"I shall cast out devils; I shall speak with new tongues; I shall take up serpents; and if I drink any deadly thing, it shall not hurt me; I shall lay hands on the sick, and they shall recover."

Jezzie tugged at the drawers of the credenza to reach the silverware. All she needed was one good strong knife to pry open the latch, but the drawers, as always during wet weather, were stuck into place. An old copy of Michelangelo's *Last Supper* hung on the wall over the credenza. Jezzie seized it and flung it through the window. A peal of thunder deadened the sound of shattering glass. The next thud of door against the whatnot cabinet almost toppled that sturdy piece of furniture. She snatched a piece of broken frame up from the floor and used it to knock the broken glass from the window as wind-driven rain poured in to dampen the carpet.

Escape. Escape.

"I shall lay hands on the dead and they shall recover!"

The cabinet crashed to the floor and John Luther pushed through the door. Jezzie screamed, holding the pitiful piece of wood out in front of her like a weapon. She dodged and bobbed, keeping the dining room table between her and the madman who sought to grab her. He lunged across the table to snatch at her. She stabbed him through the hand with the broken piece of frame. Blood flew everywhere as he pulled back his wounded hand, howling like a child.

Abruptly he stopped yelling, stopped moving, almost stopped breathing as he stared around the room at something Jezzie couldn't see. A fierce smile curved his mouth. He turned back to her and as casually as if he were turning a page in a book, he picked up the heavy table and flipped it into the wall. In one long stride, he crossed the space, grabbed Jezzie's blouse at the neck, and jerked her up to balance on the tips of her toes. She shrieked, bringing her hands up to protect herself. He seized her by the throat, squeezing until her vision turned red and blood pounded in her ears. With a low growl, he bent his face to hers and bared his teeth.

I am going to die, Jezzie thought, and closed her eyes so she wouldn't see it coming.

Something hit John Luther so hard that he staggered forward and released his grip on her neck. Gasping, Jezzie opened her eyes in time to see her mother leap on her father's back, knocking him to his knees. Wreath beat at him with both fists, pummeled him with both feet, and screamed, "Run, Jezzie, run!"

Jezzie reeled with the effort to draw breath through her bruised throat. John Luther caught Wreath's thin wrists and transferred them to one hand as he lumbered to a standing position. She kicked his knees, his shins, and did her best to knee him in the groin, but he was too tall and managed to shift his body away from that blow. Infuriated by the attack, he seized the back of her head with his free hand and slammed her face-first into the wall. She dropped to the floor without a whimper and lay there, unmoving.

Jezzie stared at her mother, willing her to get up, to turn over, to say something, anything. John Luther didn't give his crumpled wife a second glance. He grabbed Jezzie by the hair and dragged her from the room.

"You killed her," Jezzie tried to say, but her lips moved without sound. All the fight drained from her muscles, bones, and mind. She allowed herself to be towed down the hall, through the kitchen, and out into the teeth of the storm.

"I shall raise the dead!" John Luther shouted. He shoved her into the front seat of the car and slammed the door. "I shall raise the dead and you shall be my witness."

Jezzie pressed her face against the rain-streaked window, staring at the house where her mother's body sprawled amidst the debris from the fallen china cabinet, a pool of blood beneath her head. So much blood . . . *Oh, Mama, don't be dead.*

" 'For the Kingdom of God is not in word but in power!' " The words swept into the car with the wind-driven rain as he wedged himself behind the steering wheel. " 'All power is given unto me in heaven and in earth!' "

She turned her back on the raving lunatic and ducked her head to gnaw desperately on the bonds that cut into her wrists. The metallic tang of her own blood flooded into her mouth, but the knots held firm. She tugged harder. *Please, God, don't let her be dead.*

Bellowing Bible verses into the howl of the storm, John Luther barreled down the dirt road, disregarding potholes and a red pickup that steered onto the verge to avoid getting hit head-on. He took the turn into the church parking lot at thirty miles an hour, then stomped on the brakes, sending the car into a skid on the loose gravel and Jezzie smashing into the dashboard. She pushed herself back onto the seat and fumbled for the door handle. She managed to slide her numb, swollen fingers under the latch, but he seized her by the hair, dragged her across the seat, and out through the driver's side door. With one hand still tangled in her hair and the other gripping the back of her neck, he propelled her through the driving rain and into the sanctuary where Sophronia Missouri Price lay in her closed coffin beneath a wreath of red roses.

CHAPTER 36
JOHN LUTHER

Tall male angels sang a paean as John Luther strode into the church, full of power and certainty. Rose-colored light filled the sanctuary, growing brighter with each flash of lightning. He forced Jezzie, pale and trembling, to her knees in the middle of the aisle.

"You are blessed among women for you shall witness a miracle here tonight."

He turned to the plain oak coffin and forgot everything but the task that lay before him. He tossed aside the funeral wreath and pried up the lid to reveal an ancient woman attired in a blue dress, her hair neatly combed into fine, thin waves. Without hesitation, he raised his arms as if in benediction and shouted, "Sophronia Missouri Price, come forth!"

Miss Sophronia didn't move.

Again he shouted, louder and more commanding this time. "Sophronia Missouri Price, come forth!"

To his genuine bemusement, the old lady lay still. He dropped his arms and considered her a moment. He turned to the nearest angel, who he took to be Michael based on the fiery sword the heavenly being had bound to his side, and demanded, "Why is she not getting up?"

"Lazarus was in his tomb four days when the Lord arrived at his grave," Michael replied.

"Of course." John Luther returned his regard to the old lady. "I cannot very well raise her from the grave if she is not in the grave, can I?"

He slid his arms beneath the frail body and lifted it off its bed of white satin. Flopping his delicate burden across one shoulder, he contemptuously shoved the coffin half off the bier. It made a satisfying thud against the wooden floor. By the time he was done with the old lady, this coffin could go back to the undertaker. He chuckled aloud to think that she might take great pleasure in returning it herself. Followed by the angel, he hauled Miss Sophronia up the aisle, barely noticing the girl who slid out of his way and hid between the pews as he passed.

He took no heed of the storm; he could calm it after he got Miss Sophronia back on her feet. The sound and light display in the sky would make an impressive background for the miracle he was about to perform. Maybe he'd call the storm to order just as the old lady rose out of the grave. That would be appropriate, a nice touch of theater to underline his accomplishment for the witness. He hesitated a moment. Where was his witness? She should've been right on his heels, head bowed submissively, bound hands humbly clasped beneath her bound breasts. For a moment, he regretted he was stuck with his headstrong, unappreciative daughter as a witness, then the lightning flashed, illuminating the graveyard, and he forgot all about human witnesses. The archangel Michael could vouch for the miracle. John Luther glanced over his shoulder to make sure the angel was still with him. Michael had paused to readjust the fiery sword at his waist. He looked up from his task and winked at John Luther, who graciously bowed his head in acknowledgment.

The groundskeepers had dug Miss Sophronia's grave earlier that afternoon at the far side of the cemetery, near her husband and a daughter who had died in the 1918 flu epidemic. The hole was covered by a temporary grave building with short wooden walls and a peaked roof meant to keep the grave from flooding. Four men had strained to lower it so that it sat evenly over the open grave. John Luther dumped Miss Sophronia on the wet grass. Standing at one long side of the shelter, he inserted his fingers between wall and ground and, with a grunt of effort, lifted it to knee level. He paused to take a deep breath, then heaved upward, sending the building toppling onto its roof on the far side of the grave. It broke a neighboring tombstone with a loud crack, but an unmistakable buzz at his feet commanded his attention.

He took a hasty step back from a glistening heap of coils surmounted by the wedge-shaped head of the snake that had sought shelter under the grave house. The next flash of lightning revealed the distinctive black-and-white scale pattern that marked a big eastern diamondback rattlesnake, a species native to the Gulf coast, hundreds of miles away.

For a moment, fear weakened him. He took two more quick steps backward and bumped into Michael, who said, "This creature is provided by God as a test of your faith in Him. You have already failed once; the serpents in your car were the first test. Your Heavenly Father is generous, but you will not be granted a third chance. Pick her up and prove yourself to be God's True Son." The angel gave him a prosaic pat on the shoulder and with that touch, John Luther felt the Holy Ghost sweep through his veins like molten gold. He seized the pathetic earthly remains of Sophronia Price and hurled them over the now quiescent rattlesnake into the dark pit beyond. A faint thump and splash echoed out of the earth.

Flinging up his arms, he howled, " 'He that believeth and is baptized shall be saved, but he that believeth not shall be damned!' I believe, Father, and in Thy Name I shall take up this serpent. When I have vanquished Satan, I shall raise this woman from the grave and set her on her knees that she may praise Your Holy Name."

He dashed the rain from his eyes and reached down to seize the big diamondback rattler with both hands. He expected her skin to feel slimy, but it was silk damask to his touch. Her weight and girth astonished him: his big hands didn't quite manage to encircle her body. She was longer than he was tall, and her head was the size of one of his palms. As he raised her, she swiveled her neck to face him. The awareness in the eyes that met his shocked him. In that moment, he saw his own doom. She struck.

CHAPTER 37
JEZZIE

From her place huddled on the floor between the pews, Jezzie watched John Luther bear Miss Sophronia out into the stormy night. As soon as he was out of sight, she climbed to her feet and hurried for the door, head bent again to the bonds around her wrists, tugging with her teeth at the knots in the telephone wire. She peeked through the open doorway to see John Luther carrying poor Miss Sophronia through the rain to the cemetery. Lord, there was going to be an uproar when news of this night's work got out.

Lightning flashed. Automatically, she counted the seconds between the flash and corresponding clap of thunderclaps. The intervals were getting shorter. In a few minutes, the worst of the storm would be right overhead. She abandoned gnawing the knots long enough to run across the lawn to the office. Once inside the dark room, she lifted the phone receiver and laid it on the desk while she dialed home. She put her teeth back to work, anxiously listening to the phone ring.

Answer, Mama. Pick up the phone. Tell me you're okay.

The first knot finally loosened, and she pulled it apart, the taste of plastic thick in her mouth. The second knot was easier, and the third and final knot almost undid itself. She rubbed her wrists and numb hands, crying from the sensation of blood flowing back into the deprived tissue. Stupid bastard. Another half an hour and her hands probably would've fallen off. Reluctantly, she gave up on the phone at home and dialed Genevieve's number.

Flash of light. Crack of thunder. Rain drummed on the roof so hard that she almost couldn't hear the distant sound of the phone ringing.

"Hello?"

"Gennie!" Jezzy almost wept with relief. "John Luther has lost his mind. He hurt Mama and brought me to the church. Now he's out there tossing poor Miss Sophronia into her grave so he can raise her back out."

"Whoa, whoa, slow down, Jezzie. Where are you?"

"Phone in the office."

"Are you hurt?"

"I'm okay, but Mama—"

Flash-Crack. The phone went dead in her hand. With a shriek of frustration, she beat the handset against the desk until the mouthpiece broke off and rolled to the floor. She shoved the pile of papers off the desk after it and would've thrown the paperweight through a window if she could've gotten her burning fingers to hold it.

Fuck this, she thought. She ran out the door into the teeth of the storm and sped toward home as fast as her feet would carry her down the muddy county road. *Please don't be dead, Mama. Please don't be dead.*

She slipped and fell into a puddle, landing on her hands and knees. Pain shot up her arms into her shoulders, so intense that she thought she was going to faint. Her thighs and bottom hurt from the beating that afternoon so she couldn't sit down on the ground. All she could do was kneel in the deepening mud puddle, hold her injured hands and wrists to her chest, and cry. Her scalp ached from being jerked around by her hair. Her knees rested on gravel that didn't do any good to her kneecaps or the skin over them. Everything hurt, but the worst pain was inside her heart.

Don't be dead, Mama. Come and find me. I'm sorry I thought you were a coward. I was so wrong. You fought for Mercer, and you fought for me.

She took a deep, sobbing breath and forced herself to stand, hands still pressed against her body to ease the ache. The first few steps told her she couldn't run without risking another fall, so she put one foot in front of the other and walked.

Flash-Crack.

CHAPTER 38
GENEVIEVE

❧

"What the hell is going on here?" Mercer demanded, his normally pale skin so red it was almost purple. "What are you hiding from me? I got a right to know what's going on with my own sister." He stepped so close to me that we were almost nose to nose. I'd never seen him so angry, and until now, he'd never done anything that even suggested an attempt to physically intimidate me. It surprised me so that for a moment, all I could do was stare at him and wonder how to diffuse his fury, explain things so that he wouldn't be so upset, and apologize for keeping things from him. Shades of trying to keep Lorcan from losing his cool. Irritation prickled behind my eyes.

"Well?" he demanded belligerently.

At that exact moment, I pure-dee reached the end of my patience with Mercer Ives.

"Well, if you ever quit crawling in and out of whiskey bottles long enough to open your goddamn mouth and ask how your mama and the girls were getting on, I might've told you. When's the last time you called Miss Wreath without me dialing the phone for you? When's the last time you took Jezzie fishing or asked Leah to go for a ride? For your information, you son of a bitch, she'd do almost anything to climb on that bike and have an excuse to put her little arms around you. But have you noticed? Nope. Hide things from you?" I stepped forward so aggressively that he took an involuntary step backward. "You keep your eyes closed tighter than a skinflint's fist, cousin, and I'm damned if I'm going to stand here and take the blame for you not seeing what is right at the end of your nose."

I shoved past him, grabbed my keys off the hook next to the door, and stormed down the stairs two at a time. By the time I reached the truck, the flood from the sky had soaked me to the skin. I squished onto the seat and managed to jam the right key in the ignition just as Mercer hauled open the door and plopped into the passenger seat. We didn't speak as I barreled down the narrow lane and out onto the highway where I pushed the old truck harder than was legal or safe. The windshield wipers couldn't keep ahead of the water pouring down the windshield.

"Tell me," he said.

Furious and so anxious about Jezzie and Miss Wreath that I could hardly breathe, I shot him a glance that should've peeled back his hide. His color was still high, but his eyes were clear, and I didn't hear explosions or screams of dying men. I struggled to calm myself down enough to where I could talk without hollering at him or bursting into tears.

"Please," he added.

Olive branch offered and accepted. I gave him the CliffsNotes version of the last couple of months, starting with seeing John Luther take his belt to Wreath and ending with the reason for Jezzie's panicked phone call. We didn't look at each other once during the recital, but I could feel him reel under the onslaught of information. Too much, too fast, murmured the voices in my ears. I thought they were right, but I didn't give a rip. Well, maybe I gave a little rip, because it hurt me to see the agony and guilt spread across his face.

"You busted his head with the rock and broke out the church windows?" he asked when I stopped talking. "Threatened him with pictures you never took?"

"Damn straight."

"He's the one that wrecked our place."

"Probably."

"You were gonna shoot him to keep him away from Jezzie."

I didn't answer.

"Fuck," he said and shut up.

"Fuck," I agreed and shut up, too.

I barely slowed up at the stop sign at Crossroads. I'd heard the expression "taking a turn on two wheels," but I'd never done it before. Any other time, the thump back onto four tires and the sickening lurch of the truck would've scared me to halfway to Christmas, but concern for Jezzie and Wreath drove everything else out of my brain.

"Genevieve, the truck's hydroplaning. You gotta slow down."

"What the hell is hydroplaning?" I demanded, then figured it out as the vehicle floated sideways without me turning the steering wheel. Automatically, I lifted my foot from the accelerator and felt the tires grip the pavement again as the vehicle decelerated. After I caught my breath from that fright, I resumed peering through the rain-streaked windshield, face almost touching the glass in my effort to see. The headlights, never very good, barely penetrated the gloom ahead of the truck. Lightning cast weird shadows and reflections on the wet trees and asphalt. I slowed down a little more. All I needed on God's green earth was to hit another deer and kill Mercer and me both before we could get to Jezzie.

The lights burned in the church, shining through the newly glazed and frosted windows on the south side and through the front door that stood wide open to the wild night. I turned the truck into the parking lot and skidded to a stop on the wet gravel. John Luther's car sat at an odd angle near the church, looking like it had been abandoned rather than parked. Nothing moved anywhere I could see. Mercer tugged the handle on his door and a curtain of rain washed into the truck.

"She called from the office," I said, "but she could be hiding anywhere. I'll check the office; you check the church."

He was out the door and gone without another word. I ran through the rain to the covered porch that guarded the office door. Cautiously, I peeked through the side window into darkness. The knob turned under my hand. I opened the door a crack and whispered, "Jezzie? You in here? It's Genevieve."

Silence.

Throwing caution to the wind, I slid a hand around the door-frame, found the light switch, and flicked it on. A tangle of heavy black wire spilled across the desk. I picked it up and saw teeth marks on it. The floor was littered with pages of lined notebook paper filled with cramped writing. The phone was busted to pieces. What had ended the phone call? I checked under the desk, in the closet, in the tiny bathroom with its toilet and sink. Jezzie wasn't there.

"Where is she?" I demanded of the spirits that trailed me through my life, commenting, criticizing, reminiscing about their time among the living. "Just once, could you tell me what I need to know instead of what you want me to hear?"

They all shut up. Typical.

Dear Lord, if only I'd killed him when I had the chance.

CHAPTER 39

MERCER

Mercer splashed through ankle-deep puddles of rain to the gaping church door, calling Jezzie's name in a voice tight with anxiety. The church didn't offer many places to hide. He checked the restrooms, cloakroom, and the front of the church where a pale oak coffin rested half on and half off the bier that was supposed to support it. A wreath of red roses lay trampled on the floor at the foot of the damaged casket along with the white satin pillow that still held the impression of the head that had lain on it.

The hell . . . ? Mercer looked behind the podium and under the draped bier. "Jezzie? Are you in here?"

No answer. He strode out of the church and checked the nearby garden shed. Nobody. Now what? He jogged toward the office.

Genevieve stood under the scant shelter offered by the roof of the office's porch, looking lost. When she saw Mercer round the corner of the church without his sister, she threw up her hands in despair, and wailed, "Jezzie!" into the storm. He joined her on the porch, and she caught at him, as distressed as he'd ever seen her. "Where else could she hide?"

Mercer draped an arm over her shoulders and led her back into the building. "Sit down a minute and let me look around."

"I don't want to sit down! I want to find her!"

"Sit down," he repeated and pulled the chair out from behind the desk. "Cup your hands over your mouth and nose. You're starting to hyperventilate."

"I never hyperventilate," she gasped, collapsing onto the chair and doing as she was told.

He knelt on the floor to examine the papers that the wind had scattered there when Genevieve opened the door. Pages from John Luther's Sunday sermon, he thought.

"Let's go," said Genevieve, her voice muffled by her hands. "On the phone, she said something about your mama being hurt. I bet she headed home. Maybe we can catch her on the road." She leapt to her feet, hyperventilation forgotten but not quite vanquished. Mercer steadied her with a hand under her elbow.

"Where's John Luther?" he asked, thinking of the empty coffin and trampled flowers. "What in the hell is he doing?"

"Who cares as long as he doesn't have Jezzie!"

Mercer nodded once. "Valid point. Okay. Run start the truck. I'm gonna go make sure he can't drive out of here."

Genevieve nodded and splashed her way to the truck. Shielding his eyes from the downpouring rain with one hand, he sloshed over to John Luther's new car. He pulled a Swiss Army knife out of his jeans pocket and opened the largest blade. It almost wasn't strong enough, but he persisted in jabbing at the sidewalls of the two rear tires until they deflated with long hisses of air. That should keep the old bastard from following them home.

Thunder rolled down from the sky, underlined by a guttural scream that welled out of the graveyard. The cacophony rocked Mercer's unsteady sense of reality off its foundations. He ran toward the scream, ducking beneath the glare of incoming tracers and flares, all senses primed for rescue, triage, and the hope of cheating death for one more soul. A sheet of lightning threw up the silhouette of a man wrestling with an enormous snake at the far side of the graveyard, Laocoön incarnate. Mercer grabbed two spikes that topped the iron fence, and held himself upright, his vision seared with the afterimage of man and serpent, intertwined, embattled, the snake striking again and again. Thunder reverberated in his skull just as a bolt of lightning hit a pine tree in the forest, peeling its bark back like paper on a popsicle. He dropped to his knees, arms over his head. If he cried out, the storm swallowed the sound.

Hard hands under his armpits hauled him to his feet.

"C'mon, c'mon, c'mon!" Genevieve shrieked in his ear. "Get away from that fence! You want to get electrocuted? No, don't go that way, get in the goddamn truck!" She dug both heels in the ground and held onto his elbow as Mercer pulled toward the graveyard gate, moving so determinedly toward the place where he'd seen the soldier battling with a serpent that he pulled Genevieve along with him. Her feet left long streaks in the mud that disappeared under the onslaught of the downpour as quickly as they appeared. The standing water was almost ankle deep.

"Mercer!" she yelled as they reached the gate. "There's nothing in there but ghosts you don't want to talk to."

Still lost in the half reality of battle, he jerked open the gate. The next lightning strike hit the steeple. The golden hand with its pointing index finger erupted in sparks and flame. The force of the strike threw them both backward into a heap on the ground. They lay a moment, stunned and scared, then Mercer got back to his feet, ears ringing like a tympany. No time to waste. Marines were dying.

Bigger rose before him, blocking the way into the graveyard. Lightning lit the world and shone through him. Dark blood glistened on his face like rain glistened on Mercer's.

"Get the one over there!" Mercer yelled at him, gesturing to Genevieve, who was shakily sitting up behind him. "I'll get the other."

Bigger's voice came low, compassionate, and as clear as if a storm wasn't raging about them. "Ain't nothing in there for you, Doc."

Mercer started to push past him. A wall of cold stopped him, a wall so solid that he bumped into it and staggered backward. Confused, still half deafened by rockets and grenades, Mercer looked up into Bigger's face. "I have to help him."

"Nobody there to help," Bigger said.

Mercer peered past him, blinking rain from his eyes. The sound of the storm replaced the cacophony of battle. He realized the smoke still rising from the church steeple resulted from a lightning strike and not a rocket. Rain wet his hands, not the blood of marines. No screams. No movement. Just tombstones lit by decreasingly frequent bursts of lightning as the storm moved north.

"Bigger . . ."

"Go home, li'l brother," his friend said gently. "Ain't nothin' for you to do here, and you mama needs you."

Mercer nodded, still not quite sure where or when he was. Beset by the weird juxtaposition of an Arkansas storm overlaid by a Vietnam monsoon, his eyes flickered to Genevieve, and he wondered for a second if she was just another manifestation of his tortured imagination. Nah, that was Genevieve. He was sure of it . . . almost. He extended a hand to her and grimaced with relief to feel the muscle and bone of the hand she placed in his. Yeah. She was real. No anyone he ever met was more real than his redheaded cousin, however unconventional she might be. He hauled her to her feet, then walked unsteadily toward the truck, watching the ground for tripwires and water moccasins, lost between worlds.

CHAPTER 40
GENEVIEVE

Bigger stood, unmoving, in the gateway, barring my way as surely as he had Mercer's. He didn't need to worry about me trying to get past him, though: I didn't want to know what had happened out there in the cemetery and I sure as hell didn't want to go looking for the leftovers. Unfortunately, the howling began before I could get away. I put both hands over my ears, trying to shut out the horrible sound that overrode the rumble of the diminishing storm.

"Bigger," I whispered. "He's so angry. Can you keep him away from me?"

"He can't follow you, li'l sister. He got other places to go."

Even as Bigger spoke, the insane ranting died to a distant murmur, continued for a long moment, then with an absurd little fizzle was gone. With it went the tension and adrenaline that had been keeping me upright for the last half an hour. I sagged like a broken doll, grabbing the fence to keep from falling on my nose, heedless of the lightning that still flashed. The touch of his hand laid over my own had less weight than a baby's sigh, but the compassion in that touch burned the dross off my soul. More than anything, I wished I could throw my arms around him and hug him tight, but a person can't hold onto light and shadow. I turned and slogged across the wet ground, leaving the ghosts, old and new, behind in the falling rain.

Mercer didn't say a word during the mile drive to the farm, but by the time we came in sight of the boundary fence, his expression was focused and aware. Jezzie had barely beat us to the driveway. My heart leapt to see her. Her clothes streamed water, a mass of wet bedraggled curls crowned her head, and her shoes were so clumped with mud that it was a wonder she could lift her feet. She shoved the gate wide for the truck and ran around the house to the backdoor, calling out for her mother. Mercer jumped out of the truck before I got it stopped good and sprinted after his sister. The screen door banged, leaving me alone in the night. I put my head down on the steering wheel, terrified of what I might hear when I went in the house. Of all the voices I didn't want added to the chorus that followed me through life, Miss Wreath's was at the top of the list.

I've done a lot of hard things in this life but climbing out of the truck and walking into the house that night ranks as the one that took the most resolve. Mercer and Jezzie were kneeling beside her so I couldn't see her head and shoulders, but at the sight of her unmoving slender legs sprawled there on the dining room floor, I knew she was dead. Mechanically I moved forward, breath caught in my throat, a hole gaping where my heart and lungs should've been.

Mercer looked up at me. "Go get an armload of blankets off one of the beds. Jez, find her big sewing scissors."

Alive. Thank you, God. Thank you, Jesus. Thank you, whatever else is out there in the universe. Damn it, why'd y'all let things go this far in the first place? Undependable fuckers.

Jezzie and I raced up the stairs side by side, both of us grateful to be told what to do. By the time we got back with the blankets and shears, Mercer had done a quick assessment of his mother's injuries and eased her into a more comfortable position on her back, with her knees supported by a pillow from the living room couch. He took the scissors Jezzie thrust toward him and began to cut away Wreath's wet, muddy, bloody dress. Jezzie seized a blanket off the stack I'd dumped on the floor and unfurled it, ready to drape it around her semiconscious mother as soon as the dress was gone. I eased off her soaking shoes and stockings and rubbed her cold feet between my hands.

"He grabbed her by the neck and rammed her headfirst into the wall," Jezzie said, voice trembling. "She fell on the floor and he just left her here. Oh, Mercer, there's so much blood!"

"Head wounds bleed like the very devil," Mercer told her. "Don't let it scare you, Jez. She's got a set of pretty good abrasions, but all that blood looks worse than it is."

We got her wrapped in layer upon layer of dry blankets and in a few minutes, the violent shivers that racked her eased off. I filled a big bowl with warm water, found a couple of clean tea towels, and under Mercer's supervision cleaned the blood from her face. At the touch of the wet cloth, she opened her beautiful eyes and looked around at us, like she wasn't quite certain who we were. Her gaze stopped on her daughter, and she reached a shaking hand out to Jezzie.

"Are you okay? I tried to follow you, but first I couldn't see right, then when I could see good enough to get up, my feet kept gettin' tangled together and I fell back down. Oh, Jezzie, honey, I'm so sorry."

Jezzie knelt to next to her, holding her hand. "I'm fine, Mama. He didn't hurt me. I'm fine."

"Where is he?"

"Not here," I said firmly. "Don't you worry about him, Miss Wreath."

She tried to nod, but the effort made her close her eyes. "Room keeps spinnin'."

"Mercer?" Jezzie gasped, panicking as Miss Wreath's voice trailed off. I put a reassuring hand on her arm. I thought I recognized the symptoms from the time the rock hit me in the back of the skull, and Mercer's next words confirmed it.

"Concussion," he said. "She's also been out in the rain and laid here wet for way too long. I think she'll be okay, but she needs to go to the hospital to make sure. Gen, would you run out to the garage and bring the car up as close to the back door as you can get it? Keys are hanging by the back door."

"No hospital," Miss Wreath said clear as a bell. "There's nothin' to be done about a concussion except wait until it gets better. I'm dry, I'm gettin' warm, and I'm not leavin' home."

"Mama, you need a doctor to look at you," Mercer said patiently. "Your skull could be cracked. Might be some internal bleeding."

"No," she said. "I've had worse headaches than this one. Not much worse, but still . . ." Her brave attempt at a smile almost broke my heart.

Between the three of us, we got her up to the room I'd stayed in on my first night back in Arkansas. Her room on the porch was too cramped for us to watch over her there and she didn't want to go to the room filled with John Luther's things. Jezzie got a soft cotton gown from her own room. I helped her slip it over Miss Wreath's head and uplifted arms. She breathed a sigh of relief as she settled into her bed, and soon drifted off to sleep. Mercer sent Jezzie and me to bed, too, saying he wanted to keep an eye on his mother for a while.

It wasn't until Jezzie pulled her wet dress over her head in her bedroom that I realized she was not all right. Bruises bloomed on her fair skin from her throat to the tips of her fingers. I caught sight of her from behind and almost choked.

"Oh, my God, oh my God, oh my God," I gasped, grabbing the dress from her fingers. Frantically, I started unwrapping the long bandage that flattened her breasts. How in the world could she even breathe with it on so tight? "Oh, Jezzie, why didn't you say something? How could I not have seen?"

"Guess I am kind of a mess," Jezzie said wryly, looking at her swollen, abraded wrists. "I don't think I can sit down, but maybe . . ."

"Mercer!" I yelled. "Mercer!"

I was helping her ease facedown onto her bed when Mercer burst into the room and took one look at her.

"Go get me another pot of warm water, those scissors, and some towels out of the bathroom," he ordered. "Check on Mama, too. Make sure she didn't wake up when you yelled at me. If she did, don't tell her—"

"I'm not a goddamn idiot," I snapped, but of course I was. We both were. How could we not have seen how hurt Jezzie was? I checked on Miss Wreath, who continued to sleep unaware of the drama down the hall, then fled the room to collect the things Mercer needed. As soon as the water was warm, I ran back up the stairs, stopping in the bathroom for towels and a pathetic bottle of aspirin.

It took us a long time to get those ugly drawers off Jezzie. The wounds had stuck to the coarse cloth and even soaking them in warm water didn't help much. Jezzie barely twitched as we worked, soaking, and easing, and cutting the fabric, though every muscle in her body was tensed and I found a hole in the pillow-case later where she'd gnawed through it.

At last, the horrible ordeal ended. Mercer dressed the wounds, then went to wait in the hall while I helped her get ready for bed. I got a clean nightgown on her and handed her a couple of aspirins along with a glass of water.

"I don't know why he left," Jezzie said with a faint giggle. "It's not like there's anything left on me he hasn't seen."

"He probably went somewhere to cry," I answered. "That's what I'm going to do as soon as you go to sleep."

I held her hand until she dozed off, then slipped out the door to find Mercer. He was on the porch nailing a sheet of plywood over the broken dining room window. With some effort, I righted the fallen whatnot cabinet, then fetched the broom and dustpan to sweep up the glass on the floor. Between the two of us, we got the table set back into place and the chairs ranged around it. I washed the blood from the wall, the floor, and the table. The stained towels went straight into the garbage; I never wanted to see them again. The clock struck midnight, then one before we finished, but neither of us wanted to leave the damage until daylight.

We checked on Miss Wreath and Jezzie before thinking about bed ourselves. Jezzie was running a little bit of a fever; she woke up long enough to swallow another couple of aspirin and allow Mercer to check for infection before falling back to sleep. Their mother hadn't moved an inch from the position she'd fallen asleep in, but her breathing was deep and regular, her face peaceful. I wished she didn't need to know what had happened to Jezzie, but I suspected it wasn't anything that she hadn't seen before. Somehow, that was the worst thing of all.

"Mercer," I said. "Would you misunderstand if I asked to sleep with you tonight?"

"No, ma'am."

We undressed and lay down together in the narrow bed in his old room, arms wrapped around each other, breathing in the same air, my head on his shoulder, sharing the silent aftermath of the evening's storms.

"Is he dead?" Mercer finally whispered.

"Yes."

"Is he gone?"

"I think so. At first, I was afraid he wasn't going to leave, but Bigger said he had other places to be."

"Do you know what happened?"

"No."

Mercer heaved a deep sigh. He tightened his arms around me, kissed my hair, and after a while, I fell asleep.

Chapter 41
Wreath

For the next fifty years, whenever folks in southwestern Arkansas gathered on twilight-dimmed porches or around summer bonfires to tell stories, someone was bound to relate the tale of John Luther Ives dying of snakebite in an open grave on Midsummer Eve. Never mind that he died three weeks earlier; Midsummer Eve had a gratifyingly eerie ring to it. The story grew, as such tales will, until every child in Hempstead, Miller, and Howard Counties knew that Reverend Ives had been visited on three subsequent nights by a demon who warned him to stay home on the summer solstice lest he witness the dead being dragged from their graves by evil spirits. Each time, Reverend Ives commanded the demon to be gone in the name of Jesus Christ, and each time the demon evaporated with an unearthly howl. Despite the warnings, Reverend Ives arrived at the Church of the Flock of the Good Shepherd on Midsummer Eve to prevent the desecration of the graveyard. A parishioner who'd spoken to him shortly before twilight reported Reverend Ives to be in a high good humor, exulting in the power of Jesus's name to banish threatening spirits. The next morning, Reverend Ives was dead, marked with fangs of at least half a dozen snakes and crumpled at the bottom of an open grave whose occupant lay on the grass nearby.

The storm had dropped seven inches of rain in an hour, flooding half of Hempstead County. With law enforcement and other emergency personnel run ragged rescuing people stranded in the flood waters, Sheriff Ferguson and a deputy made a cursory survey of the bizarre scene at the graveyard, took a few photos, and turned the bodies over to the coroner before getting back in their pickups and heading out to check on families awaiting rescue near McNab. The sheriff felt bad for Miss Sophronia's people. He had to tell them her body had been taken from its coffin, but he forbore to mention it had been crushed into the muddy bottom of the grave by John Luther's bulk. Vandals, he told them, maybe the same vandals who had wrecked the church earlier in the spring and slashed the sidewalls on John Luther's car that night. Miss Sophronia's family nodded sadly and sent her back to the funeral home for repairs.

Wes Ferguson didn't give a brass tack about John Luther Ives's death except to wonder how in the hell the man managed to get bitten in the face by a pit viper. No snakes were found in the grave with him, though a two-inch section of a rattle the size of a man's thumb was found on his body. Big damn snake, maybe even a western diamondback. Wes had heard they lived in Hempstead County, though he'd never seen one himself. Whatever it was, it deserved a nice fat possum as a reward for its part in doing away with the menace that had been John Luther Ives. Maylene refused to say what had happened during her time in the Church of the Flock of the Good Shepherd, but she filed for divorce the day after she got home. The papers were served on Henry MacCallan in the county jail where he languished on charges of aggravated assault and battery.

Coroner Jim Bryant hated the necessity of having a family member identify John Luther's body with its grotesquely swollen features. He opted to call Mercer rather than Wreath, figuring the man had seen enough death in Vietnam to enable him to deal with the sight of his dead father better than his mother. To Bryant's surprise, and somewhat to his dismay, Wreath came instead and insisted on identifying the body herself, having ordered Mercer to stay in the car. White-faced but calm, she looked down on John Luther, lying cold and silent on the metal table. Bryant heard her murmur something as she turned away, but he must've misunderstood her words. "Burn in hell," was not something quiet, well-mannered Wreath Hughley Ives would ever have dreamed of saying to anyone, let alone the man to whom she'd been married for almost three decades.

Miss Sophronia's family refused to lay her to eternal rest in a snake pit in the cemetery where her poor body had lain exposed to the rain and mud for hours, opting instead for a less grizzly site in Rocky Mound Cemetery. They bore no grudge against the preacher, assuming that John Luther had been striving to save Miss Sophronia from the vandals when he ran afoul of the snake. Wreath accepted the family's gift of the abandoned plot. Two days after the coroner's office released the body, John Luther Ives was laid to rest at the scene of his death beneath a plain gray stone with his name and the dates that spanned his life. Wreath declined to have the words "Beloved Husband and Father" inscribed on the stone, leading to raised eyebrows among the Flock. Eyebrows flew higher when Wreath transferred her church membership and those of her two youngest daughters to the First Baptist Church half a mile down the road from the Church of the Flock of the Good Shepherd. Jared Fuller stepped in to fill the pulpit for the Flock; Delilah sat in the front pew in Wreath's former place. Both the new pastor and his wife refused to ever discuss the subject of Wreath's return to the church of her childhood or their decision to move into a house of their own. Jared continued to use the Ives pastures and farm equipment, but he paid Wreath a generous rent for the privilege.

The day after John Luther's burial, Delilah confronted her mother and demanded that Wreath trade the large bedroom at the end of the hall for the smaller one Delilah and Jared shared with the twins. Mouth primly set and a glint of greed in her eyes,

Delilah said, "After all, Jared is the man of the house now, and it's up to me to take over the household."

Wreath shook her head. "This is my house, Delilah, and my farm."

A self-satisfied smile split Delilah's face. "My daddy left the farm to Jared in his will. He told us so. Now, me and Jared are willing to give you and the girls a home, but you're just going to have to realize—"

"John Luther Ives never made a will in his life," Wreath said. "By Arkansas law, everything passes to me. That only seems right since this was my family's farm and not his."

Delilah smirked and went into the living room where she extracted a narrow wooden box from behind the mantle clock. She reached around the picture of Jesus in the Garden of Gethsemane that hung above the clock and pulled out a small key that was taped there. As she worked the key into the box's lock, she said, "My daddy told me and Jared where he put the will. Told us not to tell you because you'd be mad he hadn't willed the place to Mercer. Huh, as if Mercer deserves anything when Jared and me have worked our fingers to the bone on this place."

She removed an official-looking envelope from the box and waved it at her mother triumphantly. "You see? This is my house now, and you better get that straight in your head."

"I raised you to have better manners than you're usin' right now, daughter."

Delilah's mouth thinned to a straight line. She untucked the flap of the envelope, shook out the folded paper inside, and held it up for her mother to read. Wreath peered at the paper.

"Let's see. 'Five cups sour cherries. One tablespoon lemon juice. Quarter cup sugar.' Lord, if you don't use at least a cup of sugar, that pie will be too tart to eat."

Delilah gasped, grabbed the paper in both hands. Instead of "Last Will and Testament," the paper read "Classic Sour Cherry Pie." She put her hand on her heart, not believing what she was seeing, then burst into furious speech. "You stole it! You wicked old woman, you sto—"

"Enough," Wreath said sharply. "As long you and Jared are stayin' here, I expect you to be respectful and keep a civil tongue in your head."

"You owe me! I earned this place. Why, if I was to tell anyone what went on here when I was too young to protect myself—"

"Morning glory seeds."

Delilah went white, but she didn't pretend to misunderstand. "I'll tell everybody you gave them to him. I'll say I saw you do it."

"Poison mushrooms."

"Accident. Joe brought in those mushrooms himself."

"The only person I have to convince is Jared," Wreath said. "Don't know if you've noticed, but he doesn't look at you quite the same way as he did before y'all kidnapped me. Wouldn't take but a word or two, and you'd be out on your ear. No preacher's wife status in the church. No husband. No children. No nothin'."

"You wouldn't dare!"

Wreath smiled at her. "Macelyn Duffy came by here the other day. She said there's a place for rent out toward Crossroads that might suit you and Jared just fine."

CHAPTER 42
MERCER

He had to stop a time or two for directions before he found the place. He parked his bike on the gravel driveway in front of the house and climbed three wooden steps to the screened-in front porch. An old-fashioned knocker hung next to the door. He banged the brass ring against the strike plate and stepped back onto the walkway to wait. For a few moments all was silent, then the door of the house opened to reveal a tall black woman in a flowered housedress and matching slippers. She crossed the porch and stood in front of the screen door, leaving it closed to make a barrier between her home and the stranger. Mercer's heart bumped in recognition; she looked just like the photograph Bigger always carried in his pocket.

"Mrs. Ives?"

"Yes," she said cautiously. A man came up behind her and placed a hand on her shoulder. He was so tall that he could look right over her head. Mercer's throat tightened and he knew this was what Bigger would've looked like had he been granted an extra thirty years of life.

"Leon and I served together," he said.

"Are you Doc?" the big man asked.

"Yes, sir."

Mrs. Ives flipped the latch on the door, pulled it wide, and stood aside to let him in. Mercer nodded to her and accepted the metal chair that Mr. Ives pulled forward for him. The big man sat across from him on a white glider that had been painted so many times that there wasn't a single hard edge anywhere on it. Unconsciously mirroring each other, they both put their hands flat on their knees and looked down at the wooden floor. Mrs. Ives disappeared into the house and came out a few minutes later with three glasses of sweet tea on a small tray. Mercer took the glass she offered him with a word of thanks and wrapped his hands around the cold, sweating glass. She handed a second glass to her husband and sat down next to him on the glider.

"I came because . . . I thought you might want to . . ." Mercer's throat closed up and for a moment, he struggled to draw breath. Mrs. Ives made a soft sound of sympathy that surprised him as much as it touched him. That this woman who had lost her only child could spare someone else's child sympathy . . .

"Leon was my best friend from the moment I set foot in-country," Mercer said. "If it hadn't been for him, I'd have set my face on Vietnamese soil before I got a foot on it. Helicopter pilots, they don't like to put down when they're delivering troops to a firebase. My first trip to the boonies, I sorta fell out of the helicopter and Bigger—Leon grabbed my arm before I went headfirst into the dirt. Told me his nickname was Bigger Than You."

"Bigger'n You?" A smile broke across Mr. Ives's face, and he caught his wife's eye. "We didn't know that."

Mercer nodded. "He was bigger than all of us in a lot of ways. Bigger size, bigger heart, bigger courage. Bigger sense of humor. He loved to laugh, and he could make the rest of us laugh when there wasn't much to laugh about. His favorite joke was our name—my last name's Ives, too. Leon always told folks we were brothers and called me the white sheep of the family."

"White sheep," Mrs. Ives repeated with a soft laugh. She poked her husband with a gentle elbow. "Must be your side of the family."

Mercer dug deep into his memory for happy stories about Bigger. "Leon loved kids. He didn't smoke, but he collected cigarettes to use as a kind of currency. Traded for canned peaches for himself and chocolate for the kids. Lord, the way he could talk jarheads out of their chocolate . . . He always had a good stash of it for me to take on days when we went out into the villages for med calls. Sometimes he got to go with me, and man, those kids swarmed him like a jungle gym once they figured out he wasn't as scary as he looked and that he had chocolate. One kid thought Bigger was chocolate himself—made a fair attempt at taking a bite out of Bigger's arm, then cried when he found out Bigger didn't taste all that good. Bigger just laughed, gave the little guy a chunk of the real thing, and got me to clean up the bite wound later in the day."

Mercer told them all the good things he could think of: the practical jokes Bigger loved, his ghost stories, the tenderness he showed scared children facing stitches or vaccinations, and the kindness he extended to terrified new recruits on their first trip into the boonies.

"I don't think I ever saw him genuinely lose his temper," Mercer said, "But he had a way of letting folks know when they'd gone too far. Once in a while, he'd come up against bigots who didn't have enough sense to keep themselves to themselves and had to open their mouths to prove how sorry and ugly they could be. Bigger just let the comments roll off him like rain. Once I lost my temper and jumped a son of a bitch who—sorry, ma'am, sir . . ."

"That's all right, Doc," Mrs. Ives said gently.

"Anyhow, I got in a fight I shoulda known I was going to lose because the guy was half again my size. I was on my back trying to break his nose with my head before he choked the life out of me when all of a sudden, that marine flew straight up in the air like a helicopter. I wiped the blood out of my eyes and saw Bigger holding the guy about four feet off the ground by the back of his collar and the seat of his pants. He said he was sorry to have to hit another marine, but he felt 'obligated to whup the shit out of anyone who incites Doc to riot.' That was just the way he put it. He let go of the guy's pants, propped him up against a tree trunk, and pulled back his fist. Guy started screaming for help, but we all just stood around and waited to see what happened next. Bigger thought about it, unclenched his fist, said, 'Naw, ain't worth the skin off my knuckles.' He grabbed the guy by the collar and britches again and tossed him across six feet of space into a bomb crater that was half full of water. Don't think that fellow said another word until the VC turned his ass to grass a couple of weeks later."

Mercer took a deep breath, focused his attention on the glass of tea in his hand and spoke of the times when Leon Ives carried wounded marines on his back through knee-deep mud and rain so heavy that it fell like a veil across the world. He told the quiet couple about how Bigger had covered retreat after retreat alone, holding off attackers while his comrades escaped, escaping himself at the last second, then laughing about it afterward like it had been nothing more than a huge game of cowboys and Indians.

"He saved my life twice. First time, we walked into an ambush, and I was one of the first ones hit. Bigger jumped on top of me to keep me from getting hit again. Was all I could do to push him off so I could get on with my job. Second time . . ." Mercer's throat closed and for a long moment, he struggled to draw breath.

Mrs. Ives reached out to her husband. He took her hand in both of his. A bee tapped against the screen door, over and over, looking for a way into the beautiful day beyond the dimly lit porch. Mercer got up and opened the door to set it free, then sat back down on the chair, still clutching the glass of tea.

"We were walking through a jungle, just like we'd done a hundred or a thousand times before. And just like another hundred times before, we were in the wrong place at the wrong time and walked straight into an ambush."

Mercer closed his eyes, half deafened by the sound of battle that exploded around him. He forced himself to talk over the screams of firepower and dying marines. "We got hit hard, and before we could move under cover, there were men down everywhere. I found a sort of hollow in the ground, dragged the closest wounded guys into it. Bigger yelled at me to take care of them and he'd get the rest. He went out of that hollow a dozen times, right into the teeth of battle to bring in men. It was like he was charmed: all those bullets and nothing touched him. His size always made him a target, easy to see, but he never got a scratch.

"I don't know how long I'd been slapping patches on marines, trying to stabilize them enough to get them back to base. Bigger'd disappear for a while, then come back with another man slung over his shoulder or dangling from one arm while he shot back with the other hand. He'd hand the marine over to us corpsmen and take off to the battle again.

"He came back once with two men, one over his shoulder, and his arm around the waist of another guy who managed to limp along with Bigger's help. Another corpsman and I went to help him with the unconscious man. We'd just eased him to the ground, and I was about to triage him, when something came flying into the hollow and landed right at my feet. I just stood and stared at it like a spotlighted deer. Out of nowhere, Bigger comes roaring in, shoves me head over ass and falls right on top of that fucking grenade. Right on top of it. I didn't die that day and neither did a dozen marines. Bigger died instead."

Mrs. Ives sat, head up, face glistening with tears. Her husband placed a gentle arm around her shoulders. Mercer saw them in his peripheral vison, unable to look at them straight on.

"He was still alive when I got to him. He asked me, 'How many?' I said, 'Just you.' He grinned—I swear to God, he grinned at me, said, 'Good.' And he was gone."

Quiet. The guns abruptly quit firing. Men quit yelling and screaming. Somewhere in the yard, a mockingbird settled on a limb and broke into song. Mercer stared at his hands, seeing Bigger's blood covering them, soaking into the cuts and gashes in his own skin. The untouched tea was warm between his palms, the ice long melted.

"Your son was the best person I ever knew," he whispered. "I will miss him all my life."

They sat together, thinking, remembering, grieving. At last, Mrs. Ives whispered, "Thank you, child."

"You're welcome, ma'am." He placed the tea glass on the floor next to his chair, got to his feet, and turned to leave. Bigger stood at the door, his face whole and handsome, his body undamaged, watching his mother and father. Mercer put his hand through his friend's chest, pushed open the screen door, and left the bereaved family alone to mourn.

CHAPTER 43
MERCER

~~❦~~

He guided the motorcycle up the driveway, wheels swerving a bit when he hit the sandy spot halfway up. Genevieve's old truck was already parked at the top of the rise with Boomerang sprawled in its shade. He cut the motor and pushed the kickstand into place. The sound of happy feminine voices floated through the air from somewhere on the other side of the house, ranging from Genevieve's soft alto to Leah's high, excited treble.

"Outnumbered again," he said aloud, reflecting on his family's propensity for producing girls and wondering again about allowing himself to be coaxed into attending. As he got off his bike, a slender figure appeared around the corner of the house, cried out, and raced toward him, arms outstretched. He caught Leah and swung her around in a circle to keep her momentum from bowling them both over.

"You came! You came!" the child cried in delight. "Oh, Mercer, I was so afraid you wouldn't."

"Why wouldn't I come, honey?" he asked, touched by the reception.

"Mama's been cooking since last night," she said, grabbing him by the hand and towing him along behind her. "Jezzie says she's gonna make you your own plate of fried chicken in case she doesn't pass it fast enough to suit you."

Behind the house in the shade of the sassafras tree, the picnic table was laden with every kind of food Mercer had dreamed of while he grimly tucked ham and lima beans into his mouth day after day in Vietnam. Jezzie wandered through the screen door carrying a pitcher of tea and a big handful of forks. With a cry of delight, she plopped them onto the tablecloth and ran to take the arm opposite the one Leah clung to.

"You came!"

Mercer was torn between being touched by the reception and chagrin that he'd been so distant since returning home that his mere presence was a source of surprised pleasure to his sisters.

"Of course I came," he said gently, and let them lead him to a place of honor at the table as Wreath placed a big bowl of potato salad next to the fried okra. He smiled at her as he slid onto the bench. To his astonishment, she put a hand on his shoulder, and kissed his cheek before taking a seat at the table next to him.

The picnic was the welcome home Wreath had so anxiously prepared for him months earlier, a joyous celebration without preaching, oratory, or appetites dampened by the same. Sure enough, a plate laden with several choice pieces of golden fried chicken sat just to his left. He unrolled the slip of paper he found tucked under a leg and laughed out loud to read "the fucking chicken" inscribed in Jezzie's small, careful writing.

After supper, Wreath, Genevieve, and Jezzie insisted Mercer sit in the shade and enjoy the evening while they toted food and dishes back to the kitchen. "Only take a minute with the three of us." He settled into the glider and Leah slid in beside him.

"Mercer, are you gonna marry Gennie?" she asked.

"No, honey, we're just friends."

Leah sighed. "I was afraid of that." She lowered her voice. "Gennie's our cousin. Did you know that?"

"Yes, ma'am, I did."

"Wish I could trade her out for Delilah so she could be our sister since you're not fixing to marry her."

"That would be a good trade, all right," he answered and slipped an arm around his sister's thin shoulders. She snuggled against him, happy to have back the big brother she recalled from before he left for the Navy, the one who'd carved her toys from blocks of wood, took care of skinned knees and elbows as gently as he took care of hurt animals, and told her endless elephant jokes he'd heard when he was in her grade. Mercer had scared her that horrible homecoming day with his dive into the shrubbery, his fury at dinner, and his disappearance.

As evening wore on and light faded from the sky, Mercer shifted the cast-iron washpot off its foundation and built a fire in the uncovered pit. Wreath produced a bag of marshmallows and Jezzie and Genevieve straightened out wire coat hangers for toasting sticks. They gathered around the flames, talking in quiet voices, listening, fascinated, to Genevieve's stories of life in the circus. At some point, Leah turned to Mercer and asked if he knew any ghost stories. The girls at school had had a slumber party and talked the next day about ghost stories. Mercer froze, and for a moment, Leah was frightened, thinking she'd inadvertently said something terrible.

Bigger, handsome as the day he'd kept a newbie corpsman from tumbling into the dirt, lowered himself into a sitting position next to Mercer. "Tell the child a ghost story, Doc. Tell her mine 'bout Perlie. It goes like this: Once upon a time, they was a man named Perlie . . ."

"Once upon a time, there was a man named Perlie," Mercer repeated softly.

"Now, Perlie, he was a good-lookin' man, but he could not find himself a wife."

"Now, Perlie was a good-looking man, but he couldn't find himself a wife . . ."

Genevieve listened to the double story as Mercer repeated it word for word as it was given to him by Bigger, edited for children. At the end, they all clapped their hands, and Leah proclaimed it the best and scariest story she'd ever heard.

"Where did you learn it. Mercer?"

"My best friend told it to me."

Bigger smiled at Mercer. Mercer smiled back. Bigger faded away like the Cheshire cat, the last thing left being the ghost of his smile. Not a bad farewell for a fellow who swore he'd never heard of Alice in Wonderland.

"Where does he live?"

"Just in my heart, honey," Mercer said gently. "He died."

Leah slipped her slim hand into his. "I'm sorry, Mercer."

He squeezed her hand and said, "Thank you, little sister. I am, too."

CHAPTER 44
GENEVIEVE

❧

Two weeks after his belated welcome home party, Mercer was gone. I woke up one Saturday morning to Boomerang's mournful howl and a note on the kitchen table telling me the rent was paid on the apartment through the first of the year. He didn't tell me he'd keep in touch, but I figured he would when he could. His going was a mighty sadness to me, though not a surprise. There'd been signs, after all. He found homes for most of the strays in his animal infirmary and shifted the rest of them into Leah's care. He did a bunch of repairs around the farm, including fixing the broken dining room window, and he argued my employer into replacing the worn-out tires and battery on my truck. I think he'd been to see Bigger's folks, too, because I never again heard from or saw Bigger after Mercer's party. I missed him almost as much as I missed Mercer.

I stood in the door of Mercer's bedroom, looking around at a space that wasn't much emptier than it had been before he left. While I'd collected dishes, curtains, pictures, and other items that filled a home, he'd never kept much more than a few clothes and personal items in the place. No more, I realized now, than he was able to carry on his motorcycle. He'd never planned to stay.

"Just what in the hell am I supposed to do with an extra room?"

I said aloud. I sure didn't want another roommate. Trust Mercer to leave me with such a dilemma. Inconsiderate bastard. Deserter. Nothing like having your best friend run out on you. I drooped against the doorjamb and added to the river of tears I'd shed since coming back to Arkansas a few months earlier.

Truth be told, with Mercer gone, I didn't know if I could stay in Arkansas myself. What was I supposed to do with the long evenings and weekends? Who was I supposed to look after? Talk to? Bake ugly cakes for? It wasn't like anyone else needed me. Wreath, who had asked me to drop the "Miss" from her name, was doing just fine in the aftermath of John Luther's death. When the librarian at the Columbus branch of Hempstead County Library retired to have a baby, Wreath applied for the position. The departing librarian gave her such a shining reference that I'm not sure the county even interviewed anyone else before giving Wreath the job.

Jezzie and Leah were thriving as well. Leah devoted herself heart and soul to her animals and almost drove the good-natured veterinarian crazy with phone calls in her determination to do the best for the creatures in her care. One day he dropped by the farm to look over her infirmary and to help out with a wounded squirrel. Impressed by what he saw, he told her to call him when she turned twelve and he'd give her a job helping in his clinic, just like he'd done for Mercer years before. Leah walked on air after that.

Jezzie passed algebra with flying colors and signed up for geometry and chemistry in the upcoming school year. She rigged up a hammock in the shade of the cedar trees and spent hours swinging and reading, making up for all the bleak years when everything but schoolbooks and the Bible were forbidden. One night at dinner, she announced that she intended to change her name from the hated Jezebel to Jessica. I helped her fill out the paperwork. She barely slept the night before Wreath filed the petition at the courthouse. The day she officially became Jessica, the four of us celebrated with dinner in Texarkana, my treat. I knew how she felt about leaving a name and the bad memories bound to it behind like a shed skin.

Life improved for everyone when Jared and Delilah moved out, accompanied by the shade of Joe Fuller. Joe was still furious about being poisoned but didn't seem to resent his brother for marrying his wife. Probably figured being married to Delilah was its own punishment. It hurt Wreath some to see her twin grandsons move down the road, but they stayed at the farm a lot. Delilah preferred churchwork to full-time motherhood and Jared was too cheap to pay a babysitter when Wreath would take the boys for the love of them.

Yeah, they were all doing great, and there I stood in a doorway feeling sorry for myself. Wreath and the girls included me in everything, just like I'd always been part of the family, so what was wrong with me? It wasn't like I didn't have plenty to do: my job, studying for my GED, meeting with my quilting friends. My first quilt adorned my bed, a flamboyant symphony of green, orange, and white that Mercer said would keep a sensitive person awake at night. I'd started a second quilt in quiet blues for Mercer, even though he slept on the bare floor by choice. Now what in the sam hill was I going to do with a blue quilt?

A knock on the door startled me out of my pity party. I wiped my eyes with the back of my hand and went to find Mercer's pal Jim standing on the porch.

"Mercer's not here," I said, standing back to let him into the kitchen.

"I know," he answered. "He asked me to come by and give you this."

I took the envelope he handed me. To my dismay and absolute fury, it contained enough money to pay for a semester of school, books included. Jim watched my face with amusement. When I thrust the envelope back at him, he held both hands up. "You better take it. Mercer said if you try to give it back, I'm supposed to use it to buy flowers for John Luther's grave once a week until the money runs out."

"Son of a bitch," I said in disgust. This was the very reason I hated to play chess with Mercer: he checkmated me every damn time.

I tossed the envelope and its infuriating contents on the kitchen counter and made coffee. Six months' rent and a semester of school. I could've killed him. Rat bastard. I handed Jim a cup and we went out to sit in the shade on the porch steps.

"Does he think I can't take care of myself?" I demanded.

"Nope."

"Then why did he go spreading money all over my life?"

"Maybe because he's a generous guy," Jim said. "Maybe because he's got a protective streak and didn't want you to pay your way through school by dancing in roadhouses."

I sat up, madder than ever. "He told you!"

"Why wouldn't he? You ashamed of it?"

"No!" I glared at him a second, then sighed. "Well. Maybe a little."

"Shouldn't be. A job's a job." Jim drained his coffee in a couple of gulps and stood up to go. "Speaking of jobs, I gotta get to mine. Listen, I go fishing every Sunday morning. You want to come go with me tomorrow?"

I looked up at him, shading my eyes with my hand.

"You'll have to bait your own hooks," he added. "You know how?"

"Reckon I can figure it out," I answered dryly. I thought a moment, then shrugged. "Yeah, I'll go with you."

He nodded. "Pick you up about dawn. I'll bring the bait and sandwiches if you can get us some cokes."

"Okay. What kind?"

"Dr. Pepper's my favorite, but anything's okay." He clomped down the steps, climbed in his truck, and drove off without another word. I spared a thin smile in his wake. Rent, tuition, and Jim to keep me company through the first pangs of loneliness. Fucking Mercer, looking out for everyone but himself. No, that wasn't right. Looking out for himself, too. That's why he left.

I got up off my butt and went to put my house in order.

Wreath called when I was halfway done with washing the kitchen floor and asked if I'd like to come for lunch. Neither of us mentioned Mercer, but I could tell she knew. I arrived at the farm a couple hours later to find Wreath and the girls subdued but resigned to Mercer's departure.

"He told us he was going," Leah confided while we were admiring the new litter of kittens that the latest stray cat produced less than an hour after Leah found her crouched under the front porch. "Told us yesterday. We all cried, including Mercer, a little, but he'll be back sometime, even if it isn't to stay. He said the trees suffocate him and the humidity gives him nightmares."

"He didn't tell me," I said, cut to the heart. "Just left me a note this morning."

"He couldn't tell you face-to-face, Gennie," Leah said gently. She took my hand and stroked it like it was one of the new kittens.

"Why not?"

She shrugged shyly. "I think because he loves you in a real special way and was afraid if he tried to say goodbye, it would be too hard to leave."

I put my arm around her. "How'd you get to be so smart, Leah?"

"Good genes," she said and grinned up at me. "Mama's side of the family."

Conversation at lunch lagged. No one knew where Mercer was headed, how long he'd be gone, or anything. All we knew was he had to leave. After we cleared away the dishes, Leah took off to the barn and Jessica wandered out toward the cedar trees with *The Hobbit* under her arm, a glass of sweet tea in one hand, and a fistful of cookies in the other.

Wreath dried her hands and hung the dishtowel on the stove handle. "I need to take Macelyn Duffy some fig preserves and rose slips this afternoon. Want to come with me?"

"Macelyn Duffy? Name's kind of familiar."

"I hope to goodness it is. She's Hempstead County's very own Famous Person. Back in the twenties, she ran off to be an actress

328 *India Hayford*

in Hollywood. She showed me an old publicity picture of her wearin' a beaded flapper dress with her hair bobbed and her knees rouged. Said bein' an actress was good fun while it lasted, but she came back home after a couple of years and married her childhood sweetheart. She can still do a mean Charleston." Wreath's eyes twinkled. "When she heard about John Luther, she came to the house with some marijuana to help me celebrate."

"No." I was shocked by how shocked I was. Wreath laughed out loud at the sight of my face.

"I didn't smoke it, honey, but I was right glad to see her. She was my mama's friend and always has the best stories."

Miss Macelyn sounded like my kind of girl. I offered my truck for the trip. Wreath loaded some pint jars of preserves into a basket along with several rooted rose cuttings, then went upstairs after a white parchment envelope that she tucked in one side of the basket. "You got a dollar, Gennie? Can I have it?"

I pulled four quarters out of my jeans pocket and handed them to her. Without explanation, she dropped the quarters into her own pocket and scooped the basket handle over her arm. "Let's go."

It was a nice day for a drive, sunny but not too hot. March, April, and May had been eaten up with summer temperatures, and now in June, it looked like we were going to get at least a few days of spring. Wreath worried a little about how it would affect the heat-loving plants in her vegetable garden, but admitted some cooler weather was worth a delayed harvest. We talked about quilting, roses, new kittens, and why my cakes kept falling in the center. We made plans to carry Jessica and Leah into Texarkana to buy them some new summer clothes, including shorts, sleeveless shirts, and tennis shoes, things neither girl had ever worn.

"When you supposed to sign up for college classes?" she asked.

My mind went blank. I stared ahead at the road spooling out in front of the truck, thinking I might be long gone before classes started in September. I wasn't even sure I was going to take the GED exam the end of the month. I hadn't been in a real school since I was Jessica's age. The study materials for the exam were all familiar to me, thanks to Dema's fine nuthouse tutoring in science and math and my own propensity for reading everything from novels to the backs of cereal boxes. It wasn't the classwork intimidated me; it was the idea of venturing into a world of newly graduated high school girls who'd been pep squad members and prom queens and who'd never danced in a circus sideshow or been given a pistol in return for a hand job. How was I even going to talk to people like that? I knew at that very moment what Mercer meant when he said the trees suffocated him, and I wanted nothing more than to run away, too. From the corner of my eye, I saw Wreath glance at me. I was afraid she'd pursue the subject, but she didn't.

"These here rose slips are from the Glory of the World in my yard," she said. "You know that big bush at the corner of the house that's covered in red roses right now?"

I nodded.

"The original slip came from a rosebush in Aunt Lela's yard," she continued. "Lord, she just loved those roses; said they smelled like angels singin', which doesn't make a bit of sense, except, of course, it does. I got it off her bush after she died. House was gone in the big storm, but it didn't even touch Glory of the World. She planted one on your mama's grave; did you know that?"

"Yes, ma'am. I was with her when she planted it."

"I always intended to plant one for Aunt Lela, too, but somehow just never got around to it. Now, when you get to the highway, just keep goin' straight like you're headed to Aunt Lela's place. Macelyn lives about a mile down the road from the old farm. You know the place with all the blue bottle trees in the front yard? That's her house. She puts those bottles out to catch any bad spirits that might come creepin' around her yard. Guess it must work; she's the least haunted person I believe I ever met."

I smiled. Wreath Ives had gotten downright chatty in the last few weeks, like someone had taken a gag out of her mouth and she had thousands of stored-up thoughts to share. That wasn't too far from true. For a quarter of a century, she'd been scared to speak for fear a wrong word would bring some terrible form of punishment down on her head or those of her children. Some of the things that came out of her head amazed me; I could see where Jessica got her brains. Wreath was the one who ought to be going to college, not me. She'd make a hell of a botanist.

We drove through what had once been Washington's business district before fire, hard times, and moving the county seat to Hope took its toll on the old town. Just past the abandoned red-brick high school, the road turned to dirt and headed downhill.

Wreath pointed at a two-story white frame building. "That was the capital of Arkansas back when the Yankees had control of Little Rock. Did you know this stretch of road was part of the Trail of Tears?"

"No, ma'am, I didn't." I did know, but I wanted to see what she might tell me about it that was news to me.

"Was. Hundreds of Choctaw Indians walked down it on their sad way to Indian land after Andrew Jackson forced them out of their homes back east. My great-grandmother told me that in those days, her grandmother lived where Aunt Lela's house was. Seein' those poor souls footsore and run out of their homes like to broke her heart. She raided her own larder for stores and stood on the side of the road to offer them water and food, but most of 'em wouldn't take it. Guess they thought it might be poisoned or they were too proud. Can't blame them, can you?" Wreath shook her head. "Wonder if they'd felt different had they known she'd had to leave her own home to give her girls a better life."

"Was that the grandmother from New Orleans?"

Wreath nodded. "Madeleine Charbonneau."

I looked at her in astonishment. "I thought no one remembered her name."

"I do," Wreath said. "She's buried somewhere in the Old Pioneer Cemetery, but I'm not sure where."

I thought of Meema showing me Jacques Quatrepomme's lonely stone in the far back of that cemetery and thought I knew about where Madeleine lay. Then I thought of something else: the name on the birth certificate stored in a safe place in my closet.

"My name is Genevieve Madeleine Antoinette Charbonneau," I said.

Wreath smiled. "And isn't that coincidence a wonderful thing? Look, we're almost to Aunt Lela's place. Why don't you pull over and we'll take a peek over the gate."

I parked on the side of the road and turned off the truck. I wasn't sure whether or not I wanted to know, but I had to ask. "Do you know who owns the place now?"

"Oh, yes. No one minds if we stop and look around a little bit."

I got out and walked to the gate. Without hesitation, Wreath climbed over the barrier and led the way down the trail I'd cleared one day under Bigger's supervision. Pretty soon we stood on the lower edge of the spring-fed pond, looking through the clear water to the muddy bottom.

"There were two farms in my family. One passed to my mama and then to me. This one passed to Aunt Lela and would've passed to your mama had she not died so young."

My throat closed up. Lord, was I going to cry again? I needed to move out of this country just to keep from turning into a soggy-eyed mess. "Who got it when Meema died?"

Wreath silently held out the envelope she'd tucked into her basket with the preserves and rose slips. I hesitated a second, then took it. "What is this?"

"Open it."

It was a deed. I read, "For One Dollar and other valuable considerations . . ." My eyes automatically went to the name.

"Oh, dear Lord," I whispered.

"Aunt Lela didn't trust your daddy to do right by you when he disappeared after Mirth died, so she put the place in my name to hold for you. We talked with a lawyer to make sure John Luther couldn't get hold of it if something happened to me. He never even knew this deed existed. I added Mercer on the deed with right of survivorship in case I died before we found you. We went to the courthouse in Hope and deeded the place to you a while back. We were gonna give you the deed to celebrate your first day of school, but I think now is a better time."

I could not take my eyes off the paper in my right hand, even when I felt her fold something into the fingers of my other hand.

"It's a nice day and I'm gonna walk down to Macelyn's place to spend the afternoon. You come on over when you're ready. No hurry."

The sound of her footsteps on the soft pine needle duff faded away long before I could move again. At last, I looked to see what Wreath had put in my left hand.

I drove to Old Washington Cemetery, parked, and took the shovel out of the back of my truck. A mockingbird in the big oak tree at the entrance sang like she was proud I came to visit. I smiled up at her and headed to the edge of the graveyard where Mama and Meema lay. The chorus of voices that accompanied me through life was respectfully silent as I dug a hole in the grass atop Meema's grave, planted the Glory of the World rose slip, and carefully soaked it with water scooped up in a bucket from the pond. On Mama's grave, the old rosebush that Meema and I had planted so many years before was awash in a froth of small, fragrant red blossoms. Eyes closed, I leaned down and kissed the soft petals.

EPILOGUE
LEAH

Leah looked around her small domain with a contented smile. Kittens purred under the rough tongue of Mama Cat. The squirrel scampered back and forth between the trees and the barn where he'd been nursed back to health after being wounded by a predatory bird who'd missed a meal by a fraction of an inch. A puppy, once abandoned, starved, and parasite ridden, sat at Leah's feet, eyes shining with adoration, pink tongue lolling from one side of his mouth. She grinned at him, her very first dog, and tucked her hand into the pocket of her skirt to feel what was hidden there.

"I think it's time, don't you, Spot?"

Spot, who had not a single spot anywhere on his furry brown body, wagged his tail, ready to agree to anything and go anywhere with her. She wooled his ears affectionately and set off down the path to her secret place at the lower part of the farm. No one else knew about this refuge but Mercer. Before he went away to war, he'd helped her clear out a pine bough–roofed hollow next to the creek, then furnished it for her with a gateleg table and thumbprint chairs he'd found in a junk store on the road between Hope and Fulton. She'd dug a little firepit on her own, lined it with broken bricks, and used it to cook pretend meals over pretend fires for pretend friends. She hadn't been able to visit her hiding place since the big storm and was delighted to discover the flooded creek had not washed away the furnishings.

While it was true that eavesdroppers rarely heard any good of themselves, the other things they heard made up for it. One night when she climbed out on the porch roof to look at the stars, she'd overheard Delilah and Jared talking in their bedroom. What she learned that evening came in very, very handy when John Luther died.

Spot watched his mistress clear leaves and pine needles away from the edges of the firepit before she built the first real fire she'd ever lit there. The fire was tiny but sufficient for her purpose. One by one, Leah fed the tattered pieces of John Luther Ives's Last Will and Testament to the flames. She watched, still as the air, until only ashes remained.

AUTHOR'S NOTE

What is a blue bottle tree and why does it sing? For generations, Southerners have decorated small bare trees by placing bottles over the ends of the branches. Tradition favors bottles of cobalt blue, a color Southern folk magic associates with ghosts, and crepe myrtle trees, which offer protection against evil spirits. Night-ranging spirits are attracted to the blue bottles only to find themselves sucked inside by the power of the crepe myrtle. As if that's not bad enough, the captured phantoms are doomed to perish as soon as the morning sun illuminates the tree. When the wind is just right, it passes over the lips of the bottles, producing an eerie keening that is said to be the sound of ghosts mourning their incarceration and imminent destruction.

Washington and Columbus are real places, though they've changed considerably between the book's setting in 1967 and the present day. Old Washington State Park now encompasses the town of Washington, featuring renovated buildings, historical reenactments, and traditional craft workshops scheduled throughout the year. The public buildings in Columbus were razed decades ago; only the post office and scattered residences remain today. The cemeteries mentioned in the book all exist, though I can't vouch for the ghosts.

Some of the minor characters in the book were real people. Sam and Charity Woolsey were my great-grandparents. Martha Smith was a woman of my grandparents' generation with whom I spent many happy hours talking about old houses, roses, and the significance of the blue bottle trees in her yard. Martha would be particularly delighted to be included in this book: bookshelves piled with well-read books lined almost every wall in her house. All other characters are figments of my imagination.

Southwestern Arkansas is at the heart of my family history and mythology. Wreath's farm is based on my family farm during its most productive days. Lela's farm is based on my farm as it is now, with the land gone to trees and only a collapsed brick chimney and a storm cellar left to mark the house's former location. *The Song of the Blue Bottle Tree* is set in a past I am familiar with through personal experience and stories told by my elders, some of whose personal memories stretched a century into the past. A handful of those stories are incorporated into the book, including my father's tale of getting chased by an alligator on the lake I chose to call Cypress in the book.

For most of my adult life, I've lived where the high plains meet the Rocky Mountains. This is home, but every March I leave behind the snowy sagebrush steppe to spend time among the greening pastures and forests of Hempstead County. You can take the girl out of Arkansas, but. . . .

THE SONG OF THE BLUE BOTTLE TREE

ABOUT THIS GUIDE

The suggested questions are included to enhance your group's
reading of India Hayford's *The Song of the Blue Bottle Tree*!

DISCUSSION QUESTIONS

1. What is the significance of the blue bottle tree? How does it relate to Genevieve and Mercer?

2. Southwestern Arkansas is an integral part of the story, as is Vietnam. How would the story be affected if it was set in a different time and place?

3. Why was an eastern diamondback rattlesnake, a species native to neither northern Alabama nor Arkansas, chosen as a character?

4. The Church of the Flock of the Good Shepherd revolves around the teachings of a single controlling man. What entices people to follow narrow, harsh, and/or unbalanced leaders?

5. What holds Bigger to the living world and prevents him from reuniting with friends and family who died before him? Why can he only travel in conjunction with Mercer or Genevieve?

6. Wreath stays with John Luther despite horrific abuse. Why did she marry him in the first place? When does the tide begin to turn in their relationship?

7. How does Genevieve's arrival in Columbus become a catalyst for change that extends from her family to Maylene to the church?

8. The lives of Genevieve and Mercer intersect when she is seeking a home and he is looking to leave home. How does their relationship support their different goals—or does it?

9. Compare the ways the Ives children responded to abuse. What did each do to survive? How did each resist or adapt?

10. Why did panic attacks beset Genevieve when she temporarily returned to a profession that had not bothered her in the past?

11. What's in a name? Why was a name change so important to Genevieve? To Jezzie?

12. At the end of the book, were you surprised by the identity of the Last Will and Testament thief? Why or why not?

Visit our website at
KensingtonBooks.com
to sign up for our newsletters, read
more from your favorite authors, see
books by series, view reading group
guides, and more!

BOOK / CLUB
BETWEEN THE CHAPTERS

Become a Part of Our
Between the Chapters Book Club
Community and Join the Conversation

Betweenthechapters.net

Printed in the USA
CPSIA information can be obtained
at www.ICGtesting.com
CBHW011623270724
12209CB00004B/7